Moonbreaker

Moonbreaker

Simon R. Green

ACE
NEW YORK

ACE
Published by Berkley
An imprint of Penguin Random House LLC
375 Hudson Street, New York, New York 10014

Copyright © 2017 by Simon R. Green
Penguin Random House supports copyright. Copyright fuels creativity, encourages
diverse voices, promotes free speech, and creates a vibrant culture. Thank you for
buying an authorized edition of this book and for complying with copyright laws by
not reproducing, scanning, or distributing any part of it in any form without permission.
You are supporting writers and allowing Penguin Random House to continue to
publish books for every reader.

ACE is a registered trademark and the A colophon is a trademark of
Penguin Random House LLC.

Library of Congress Cataloging-in-Publication Data
Names: Green, Simon R., 1955– author.
Title: Moonbreaker/Simon R. Green.
Description: First Edition. | New York: ACE, 2017. | Series: Secret histories; 11
Identifiers: LCCN 2016053300 (print) | LCCN 2017003298 (ebook) |
ISBN 9780451476951 (hardback) | ISBN 9780698407435 (ebook)
Subjects: LCSH: Drood, Eddie (Fictitious character)—Fiction. | Paranormal fiction. |
BISAC: FICTION/Fantasy/Urban Life. | FICTION/Fantasy/Paranormal. |
FICTION/Fantasy/Contemporary. | GSAFD: Fantasy fiction.
Classification: LCC PR6107.R44 M66 2017 (print) |
LCC PR6107.R44 (ebook) | DDC 823/.92—dc23
LC record available at https://lccn.loc.gov/2016053300

First Edition: June 2017

Printed in the United States of America
1   3   5   7   9   10   8   6   4   2

Jacket illustration by Paul Young

Moonbreaker

There is a man who strikes from the shadows. Who murders again and again without ever being seen. No one knows who he is or where he comes from. All anyone knows is his *nom de mort*: Dr DOA. For when somebody definitely and absolutely has to die.

Some say he's just an urban legend of the hidden world; a useful explanation for all the murders, suspicious deaths, and convenient accidents that are never properly accounted for. And some say he works for this or that subterranean group, killing people who can't be touched by any of the usual secret agents. That he's vengeance for hire, or the ultimate serial killer, or a cover for something much worse. People will say anything if they're scared enough.

I know Dr DOA is real. Because I'm one of his victims.

My name is Eddie Drood, part of that centuries-old family whose business it is to stand between Humanity and all the unnatural forces that threaten it. I worked for years as a Drood field agent, mostly under my cover identity as Shaman Bond, fighting the good fight because someone has to. I really did help save the world on a few occasions, along with my partner, Molly Metcalf, the witch of the wild woods. We did good work, and we were happy together. Until Dr DOA poisoned me, without my even noticing.

And just like that, my life was over. No cure. No hope. Just a dead man walking.

So I decided that in the time left to me I would track down Dr DOA and make him pay. For what he'd done to me, and to so many others. With Molly's help I searched the darkest corners of the hidden world, talking persuasively and sometimes violently with good people and bad, until finally I found him. Or, rather, he found me. He called me back home, to the family Armoury deep under Drood Hall, and there he was, Dr DOA. Edmund Drood: another version of me, from a different family of Droods on another earth.

We fought, and he ran, using the dimensional engine Alpha Red Alpha to open a doorway back to the earth he came from. I went after him, because I couldn't let him get away. But it was all a trick. He disappeared back through the Door and slammed it shut. Leaving me trapped with Molly on an Earth we didn't know, and with no way home.

For anyone else that would have been the end of the story. But I'm just getting started.

CHAPTER ONE

When Your Back's against the Wall, When Everything Looks Lost, Find Someone to Take It Out On

t wasn't my family's Armoury, but it looked enough like the one I knew to send a chill down my spine. The same long series of stone cellars, with colour-coded wiring tacked haphazardly to the walls. But here the workstations were abandoned, the firing ranges were empty, and wreckage and rubble lay everywhere. The Armourer and his white-coated lab assistants, who should have been running wild with out-of-control experiments and weapons that endangered the lives of everyone around them, were gone—long gone. Slaughtered by the Droods' many enemies, after my other self shut down the Hall's protections and sabotaged its defences. The Armoury was still and silent now, its many wonders trashed or looted. Like some ancient burial chamber despoiled by grave-robbers who could never hope to appreciate the treasures they carried away or left trampled underfoot.

The only sounds disturbing the graveyard quiet came from Molly. Her language started out bad and quickly escalated, as she swept her hands back and forth through the empty space where the dimensional gateway had been just a few moments before. She was trying to find some trace of it with her magics, so she could call it back and force it open, but she wasn't getting anywhere.

"Molly," I said thoughtfully.

"What? I'm busy!"

"Look what's back."

She turned around, and there was Alpha Red Alpha, towering over us. The great dimensional engine itself. Molly glared at it.

"That wasn't there a moment ago."

"I know."

"So what was it doing? Hiding from us?"

I shrugged. "That's Alpha Red Alpha for you."

I looked carefully at the massive and never fully understood mechanism, designed to be the Droods' last line of defence. So that if the Hall ever found itself faced with a threat that couldn't be stopped, the engine would translate the whole building into another dimension, another earth, where it could safely remain until the threat was over and the Hall could be brought back again.

Either the family here never got a chance to use it, or Edmund did something to it.

Alpha Red Alpha: a gigantic hour-glass shape immersed inside a frozen waterfall of gleaming crystal, shot through with sprawling circuits, like ragged veins. It was hard to make sense of, hard even to look at, as though it existed in more than three dimensions . . . And if there were any controls, I couldn't make them out. Only my uncle Jack, when he was Armourer, really understood Alpha Red Alpha.

"Can your magics get us home, Molly?" I said. I was pretty sure I already knew the answer, but I needed to hear her say it.

"Not a hope in hell!" Molly scowled at Alpha Red Alpha as though she was seriously considering giving it a good kicking, just on general principle. "I don't even know where home is from here! You can't navigate all the different Earths and all their different histories without being really sure of the exact Space/Time coordinates involved."

"And there's no trace left of the dimensional Door we came through?"

"No." Molly's shoulders slumped, and she suddenly looked tired and worn-down. We'd put a lot of effort into chasing Edmund, and it was catching up with both of us. "Edmund must have locked the Door from his side, using the other Alpha Red Alpha." She looked at me sharply. "If he's smart enough to operate it, why can't you?"

"Because he's spent ages learning how to work it," I said.

"If he could figure it out . . ."

"I don't have enough time," I said.

Molly nodded reluctantly. "Does this machine look the same to you as the one in our world?"

"Hard to tell," I said. "Just looking at the damn thing hurts my eyes. It's . . . different, but I couldn't tell you how. I am sure it wasn't standing here the last time we visited this Armoury."

"Edmund must have moved it," said Molly. "So he could set his trap."

"How?" I said. "Look at the size of it! You couldn't shift something this big with a power loader and a stick of dynamite!"

"I don't know," said Molly. "And don't you snap at me, Eddie Drood! Edmund's just another version of you, which means really this is all your fault!"

"Somehow I knew it would be," I said.

We shared a quick smile, and went back to studying the dimensional engine. It stared silently back at us, giving away nothing.

"Edmund must have been coming and going between the two Earths for some time," I said. "But how could he have used my Hall's Alpha Red Alpha without the Armourer or his staff noticing?"

"That still leaves the Merlin Glass," said Molly.

"Without my noticing?" I said. Molly started to bristle again, and I realised we were dangerously close to another argument we couldn't afford, so I changed the subject. "We have to get back to our world, Molly. My whole family is in danger from Edmund as long as he's running around our Hall, unsuspected."

Molly leaned in suddenly and kissed me.

"What was that for?" I said.

"Because that is just so typical of you, Eddie—thinking of others, instead of yourself. We have to get back because you're running out of time."

"Trust me," I said. "I hadn't forgotten."

"Any chance there might be a manual for Alpha Red Alpha in the Library?" said Molly.

"Unlikely," I said. "My uncle Jack was the only one who ever had any control over the machine. Max and Victoria like to say they do, now they're Armourer, but that always sounded like whistling in the dark to me. They're probably still trying to make sense of whatever notes Jack left behind. And he only ever partly understood how the damn thing operates, anyway."

Molly looked at me sharply. "How can your people not understand how it works, when you invented it?"

"Alpha Red Alpha was reverse-engineered from alien tech," I said patiently. "Like most Drood weapons and devices. That's why we're always a step ahead of everyone else."

"I thought it was because you had the best scientific brains!"

"We do," I said. "That's how we're able to reverse-engineer alien tech so successfully. We have come up with some amazing things on our own; science and the supernatural are our playthings. But we are all of us standing on the shoulders of giants. Sometimes alien giants."

"Hold it," said Molly. "I thought Black Heir was in charge of clearing up after alien incursions and salvaging all the tech that gets left behind?"

"It is," I said. "But Black Heir answers to my family. It makes sure we always get the good stuff. And, in return, we keep everyone else off its back."

"How does any of this help us now?" said Molly.

"It doesn't," I said. "But it has given me an idea . . ." I armoured up my right hand and extended it towards the dimensional engine. "You know how I use my armour to hack computers and make them do what I want? I'm hoping I might be able to do the same with Alpha Red Alpha. Enough to get us back home, at least."

"Go for it," said Molly. "I stand ready to applaud, jump up and down, and whoop with joy."

Golden tendrils eased out from my fingertips, only to stop well short of the machine's crystalline surface. They wavered uncertainly on the air and then snapped back into my glove. I looked at my hand, and even shook it a few times, as though that might persuade the armour to cooperate, but nothing happened. I let the golden strange matter disappear back into the torc around my throat.

"Okay," said Molly. "What just happened there?"

"Apparently, Alpha Red Alpha is so . . . different, my armour couldn't make any sense of it," I said slowly. "In fact, if I didn't know better—and I'm not sure that I do—I'd say my armour was afraid of it."

"Your torc has picked one hell of a time to have performance issues," said Molly. "So, there's nothing we can do? We're trapped here?"

"Lost and alone, in a world without Droods," I said.

She sniffed. "You say that like it's a bad thing."

We each managed a small smile.

"I refuse to give up," said Molly. "It's not in my nature. What else can we do?"

"First," I said, "we go exploring. Take a walk through the Hall and get a good look at where we are and what we've got to work with. There might be something we can use to get us home."

"Hark!" said Molly, cupping one hand to her ear. "Is that the sound of whistling in the dark I just heard? Eddie, we need to get the hell out of here, and make our way to the Nightside! You can get anywhere from the Nightside."

"That's assuming this world has one," I said.

"Every world has a Nightside," said Molly.

"Now, there's a horrifying thought," I said. "But even so, it could be very different from the one we know."

"The whole point of the long night is that you can find anything there," Molly said briskly. "Particularly if it's something the rest of the world doesn't approve of." She paused and looked at me seriously. "How are you feeling, Eddie?"

I knew what she was really asking: How much time did I think I had left? And how much longer would I still be able to fight my corner?

"I'm angry enough to keep going," I said steadily. "Edmund screwed up. He should have killed me immediately. In fact, I have to wonder why he didn't."

"Because he couldn't," said Molly. "You're a better fighter than him, and he's always known it. That's why he poisoned you and ran away."

"I will get us home," I said. "And I will find him and make him pay. Whatever it takes."

"That's more like it," said Molly. "That's my Eddie."

She hugged me hard, and I let her do it. Because it was important for one of us to have faith in me.

After a while, we moved off through the unfamiliar Armoury. It didn't take long to confirm what I'd already suspected—the whole place had been picked clean. Not a weapon or useful device to be found anywhere. Everything was covered in thick layers of dust, from the smashed and abandoned computer stations to the deserted weapons galleries. Tan-

gled wiring hung down from the walls in thick clumps, as though someone had tried to tear it down. Walking through the silent Armoury was
like moving through a tomb: a place of the dead, abandoned to Time.
Where only the past had any meaning.

"There's really nothing left," I said finally. "My family is just history
here."

"Hold it together, Eddie," said Molly. "There's still work to be done."

Everything looked much as I remembered it from my last visit. There
were gaps everywhere from where things had been taken, but no signs of
actual fighting. The war had been lost up above, in the Hall, where the
Droods made their final stand and were slaughtered, to the last man,
woman, and child . . . Afterwards, the triumphant killers went storming
through the Hall, looking for loot, and finally ended up down here. I
hoped the Armourer was dead before that happened. He would have
hated to see what the barbarians had done.

"Could there be . . . hidden caches somewhere?" Molly said hopefully. "Weapons or other things that only the Armourer would know
about?"

"Just the Armageddon Codex," I said. "And according to the recorded
message I triggered the last time I was here, the Armourer found time
to seal the Forbidden Weapons inside the Lion's Jaws, so the enemy
couldn't get to them."

And then I stopped, and thought for a moment. This family's Armourer had been my uncle James, not Uncle Jack. Here, Jack had been
the famous field agent, while James had stayed home to be Armourer.

"You're scowling," Molly said accusingly. "Which is rarely a good sign.
What are you worrying about now? Is this some new problem, and if so
is it something I can hit?"

"This family's Armourer left a message for me in the Lion's Jaws,"
I said. "Remember?"

"I was here with you," said Molly. "There is nothing wrong with my
memory."

"I was just wondering if there might be another message," I said.

"Worth a try, I suppose," said Molly. "Where are the Jaws?"

"I'm surprised you don't remember," I said.

"Don't push your luck, Drood."

The Lion's Jaws were in the exact same place as in my Hall: right at the back of the Armoury. A massive carving of a lion's snarling head, complete with mane, perfect in every detail. It had been fashioned out of rough, dark stone, and wasn't stylised in any way. It looked like the real thing, only twenty feet tall and almost as wide. I stood before it, looking steadily into the Lion's angry gaze. Molly stuck close beside me, scowling unhappily and just a bit warily into its eyes. Which was a perfectly normal reaction for any sane person. The Lion's Jaws don't just *look* dangerous.

"I have to wonder," I said, "whether this might have been carved from life. Very big life."

"Maybe we should look around for a really big wardrobe," said Molly.

"Don't even go there," I said.

The eyes gleamed, and the snarling jaws seemed only a moment away from lunging forward to snap my face off. The Lion's Jaws were created to give access to the pocket dimension where my family stored their most powerful and dangerous weapons, the kind you use when you need to destroy a whole army of monstrous invaders from another dimension. The Forbidden Weapons, for when reality itself is under threat. To open the gateway, you had to place your hand between the stone teeth. And if you weren't a Drood in good standing, and your heart wasn't pure, the Jaws would bite your hand right off. (The pure-at-heart bit was supposed to be just a legend, to scare away people with no good reason to be troubling the Jaws, but with my family you never knew.) The last time I'd been here, just my touch had been enough to trigger a recorded message from the Armourer James. A warning—and a last plea for revenge on those who'd destroyed the Droods.

I took a deep breath, and laid my hand flat on the great stone mane. Nothing happened. The old message was gone. Which meant the only thing left to try was putting my hand inside the Jaws. Even in my Hall, in my Armoury, I would have hesitated, but here . . . I wasn't even sure these Jaws would recognise me as a Drood. Armouring up wouldn't help, because these Jaws wouldn't be expecting Ethel's strange-matter armour. So I flexed my fingers a few times, breathed steadily until I was as calm as I was going to be, and then thrust my bare hand into the snarling mouth. My heart hammered as I fought to hold my hand steady, but the Jaws didn't move . . . and there was no second message. I snatched my hand out and stepped back.

"Nothing?" said Molly.

"I wouldn't say that," I said. "Something really unpleasant very nearly happened in my trousers. But no message."

"You're the one with the excellent memory," said Molly. "Was there anything in the first message that might prove useful to us now?"

"Not really," I said. "Though it did reveal some interesting differences between this family and mine. They still had a Heart, to provide their torcs and armour. Their Matriarch was Penelope, and the Armourer James said he destroyed the key to the Lion's Jaws, so at least we can be sure the Armageddon Codex is secure."

Molly looked dubiously at the Jaws. "What if someone tries to force them open?"

"It would be the last thing they ever tried," I said. "Let's get out of here. This whole place feels like someone is dancing on my grave."

Molly had to conjure up a glowing sphere to lead us up the long flight of stairs to the ground floor. We needed the eerie green light to push back the darkness, because none of the lights were working. The thick layer of dust on the stone steps made it clear no one had been this way in a long time. Our footsteps sounded loud in the quiet, as though warning we were coming. The trapdoor at the top was still lying open, just as I'd left it the last time I was here. I frowned as I emerged cautiously and then hauled Molly up into the dimly lit room. The great open space looked just the same. Nothing had been touched, all the rubble and destruction left exactly as it was. Bright sunlight slanted through the shattered window, thick with curling dust. Molly dismissed her conjure light and looked quickly around her, but we were completely alone.

"Why has no one moved in?" I said, speaking loudly to show I wasn't intimidated by the setting or the hush. "I'd have thought someone would have taken possession of the Hall by now, if only for bragging rights."

"Maybe everyone thinks the place is haunted," said Molly. "Droods are dangerous enough when they're alive . . . And there's always the chance they didn't get everyone. The Hall could have been deliberately left empty, to draw back any Drood who wasn't here when the hammer came down. Bait in a trap. Just another really good reason why we should forget the sight-seeing and get the hell out of here."

"I can't help thinking Edmund marooned us here for a reason," I said.

"He dumped us here because this is the only other Hall he had access to," said Molly. "And, anyway, what better place to leave you than a world where everyone wants to kill Droods? I mean, more than usually."

"I need to know more about this Hall," I said. "I need to know why this version of my family had to die."

"Of course you do," said Molly.

We went wandering through deserted rooms and empty corridors, stepping carefully around and over the wreckage and piled-up rubble. The walls were pocked with bullet-holes, and showed signs of bombs and incendiaries. No bloodstains. The Droods died in their armour, fighting till the last. As we moved on, it became clear the whole building had been stripped clean. The accumulated loot and tribute of centuries was gone; every priceless statue and painting, every piece of antique furniture, and all our trophies. Every bit of Drood history and every precious thing I remembered . . . gone. Nothing remained to show my family had ever been here.

It felt like someone had stolen my life and pissed on my heritage.

"I never liked living here," I said finally. "Ran away to London first chance I got . . . and only came back when I was forced to. But I still hate to see the Hall looking like this. Like the king of the beasts dragged down by jackals."

"Can't say it bothers me," said Molly. "A Hall without Droods actually feels safer, like a predator whose teeth have been pulled."

"Thank you, Little Miss Tact."

"Don't get maudlin on me, Eddie. This isn't your Hall, and it wasn't your family. Hell, if Edmund's anything to go by, you should be grateful you never knew them."

"They were still Droods," I said.

I stopped in the middle of a large, airy meeting place, where my family liked to sit and drink tea first thing in the morning. To read the world's newspapers and discuss the day's events, before setting about our various business. A civilised way to start the day. I looked around slowly, half expecting to see ghostly figures with familiar faces . . . And then I frowned.

"Oh, what now?" said Molly.

"All the way here, I've been spotting small differences," I said slowly. "Doors where there shouldn't be any, corridors opening onto halls that shouldn't exist, familiar routes that end abruptly at blank walls . . . I haven't seen any major changes—this is still the Hall I know—but it worries me that these little differences might add up to a Hall and a family I might not recognise at all."

"I do have some experience travelling in other earths," said Molly. "Often it's the small differences that can be the most disturbing."

I looked at her. "And you never got around to telling me about these little side trips before because . . . ?"

"I don't have to tell you everything," Molly said haughtily. "I do have a life of my own, away from you. Oh, don't look at me like that, Eddie. It's just that sometimes . . . I feel the need to get away from everything. And where better to do that than on a completely different Earth?"

"I never feel the need to get away from you," I said.

"And you're the only thing in my world that doesn't occasionally drive me crazy," said Molly. "Settle for that."

"All right," I said. "What could be so disturbing about this strange new world?"

"Well, to start with, people we saw die could still be alive here. And vice versa, of course."

"But not my family," I said. "It was a nice thought, that some might have escaped the massacre. But Edmund seemed quite convinced all of this world's Droods were dead, apart from him."

"He should know," said Molly. "He betrayed them."

I shook my head slowly. "How could any version of me be so . . . vicious? What could have happened to me in this world to turn me into a cold-blooded killer who happily arranged for his whole family to be slaughtered?" I had to stop and breathe deeply for a moment, to bring my emotions under control. "The Armourer James said his family drove Edmund out. That he went to ground and disappeared."

"So he never hooked up with me?" said Molly.

I tried to smile, just for her. "No wonder he went to the bad."

"Eddie, you need to forget about these other Droods," said Molly. "It's just holding you back. We need to concentrate on finding something that can help you. Maybe even find a cure . . . Eddie? What's wrong?"

"I don't know," I said. "I'm just . . . tired."

Exhaustion hit me like a sucker punch. It was all suddenly too much, being so far from home, trapped in a distorted mirror of everything I knew. With death hovering over me like a vulture, just waiting for me to weaken. My vision darkened, my knees buckled, and I started to fall. Molly was quickly there to grab me and hold me up. Leaning in close so she could shout in my ear.

"Eddie, come on! You can't give up now. There's still things that need doing, people who need killing, and I can't do it all on my own! I need you! You're a Drood, dammit. Act like one!"

That's my Molly. Always telling me what I need to hear, whether I want to hear it or not.

I forced the weakness back, refusing to be beaten by anything that got in the way of what needed doing, even myself. Perhaps especially myself. I stamped my feet hard until my legs straightened and my head came up. Molly saw my face clear and immediately stepped back to let me stand on my own. Watching me carefully, until she was sure I could manage without her. I gave her my best reassuring smile.

"It's all right, Molly. I'm back. You didn't really think I'd leave you here alone, did you? I can be strong for you."

"I know that," she said. "You just forgot for a moment. Look, have you seen enough of this Hall? Can we go now?"

"Not just yet," I said. "A thought has occurred to me."

"Oh, that's never good," said Molly. "What is it this time?"

"The last time we were here, we visited the Old Library and found a book set out on a reading stand. Left there for us, to tell us things we needed to know. And while we were there . . . something spoke to us."

Molly shuddered briefly. "Yes . . . A voice, from out of the dark between the stacks. It knew our names. But it really didn't sound like anything I wanted to stick around and meet."

"In our Old Library, there's always the Pook," I said carefully. "The Librarian's not-quite-imaginary-enough friend. Maybe whoever left that book out for us is ready to help us again."

"Okay," said Molly. "I have to say, that doesn't strike me as one of

your better ideas. Our Pook is disturbing enough. I'm not even convinced he's real, just something that followed the Librarian home from
the Asylum for the Criminally Insane."

"True," I said. "But I always got the feeling the Pook was on our
side."

"Yes . . . ," said Molly, drawing the word out till it sounded more
like *no.* "I suppose it's worth a try. We could use someone here on our
side."

I frowned as another thought hit me.

"Oh, what is it now!" said Molly.

"There are no bodies in the Hall," I said slowly. "There were bodies the last time we were here. Dead Droods in their armour, the golden
material half-melted and fused together. I hadn't thought anything could
do that to Drood armour. But I haven't seen a single body anywhere."

"Maybe they were harvested by this world's Black Heir," said Molly.
"So they could reverse-engineer their own armour."

"They would have known better," I said. "This world's armour came
from the Heart and drew its power from the life energies of sacrificed
Droods. The kind my family used to depend on, until I put a stop to it.
But that never happened here."

"Don't start blaming yourself for things you didn't do," Molly said
sharply. "Whatever kind of Droods they were, they weren't your family."

"They were a version of my family," I said. "With familiar names
and faces." I broke off as a really disturbing thought hit me. "Molly,
could the Heart still be here? I know we checked the Sanctity last time
and there was no sign of it, but could it be . . . hiding somewhere? Hoping for a Drood to return?"

"You are not thinking of making the Heart your ally!" said Molly.

"Hell no," I said. "I just want to know if I'm going to have to kill it
again."

Molly's eyes became cold and distant as she sent her witchy Sight
racing through the Hall. I looked quickly around, my hands clenched

into fists, my skin crawling in anticipation of the attack I knew I'd never see coming. And then Molly relaxed, and shot me a reassuring smile.

"Take it easy; there's no trace of the Heart anywhere in the Hall. Or on the grounds, or even on this plane of existence. It probably ran off to some other dimension the moment it saw the Droods were losing."

"Well," I said, relaxing a little in spite of myself, "that's something, I suppose. One less thing to worry about."

"Now you see what I mean, about small differences adding up to big changes," said Molly. "Because of this, you never uncovered the truth about the Heart. These Droods were never freed from its control. With Ethel's more advanced armour, they might have stood off their attackers." She stopped, and looked at me sharply. "Hell, I'm amazed this world even exists, given you and I weren't here to save it from some of the threats we've faced."

"And yet the world still turns and life goes on," I said. "So someone must have stepped up to save the world in our absence. I find that comforting."

"You would," said Molly. "I wonder what price the world had to pay, to be saved by someone else."

"You would," I said.

As we moved quickly through the Hall, a lifeless hush hung over everything, swallowing up the small sounds we made as though resentful of our presence. This wasn't a place where people lived any more, just a memorial to all the people who'd died here.

And then Molly and I came to a sudden halt, as we came face-to-face with the first really big difference between this family and mine. In an alcove I was sure didn't exist in my Hall stood a massive statue of the goddess Kali. Thirty feet tall, with half a dozen arms, caught in mid dance. Carved from some unfamiliar blue stone, she was perfect in every horrifying detail. A chain of human skulls hung round her neck, and her many hands were full of unpleasant weapons. Her eyes were dark and dangerous, and her smiling mouth was crammed full of pointed teeth.

Old bloodstains covered the statue's base, caked and crusted over the delicate feet and ankles.

"Looks like something was sacrificed here," Molly said quietly. "In fact, I would have to say it looks like a whole lot of somethings died here."

"Human sacrifices," I said. "Kali has always valued human deaths over and above all others."

I leaned in for a closer look. Engraved into the stone base, half-obscured by dried blood, were the words ANOTHER THOUSAND YEARS, OH KALI.

"The old-time Thuggee cults murdered their victims as sacrifices to Kali," I said. "Not just to worship her, but as payment—to hold her at bay and keep her out of this world. What kind of Droods were they here?"

"And why did the looters leave this statue untouched, when they took everything else?" said Molly.

"They were probably scared to go anywhere near it," I said. "I can understand that. Just being this close is giving me a major case of the creeps. And I have to wonder, given that these Droods drove Edmund out, what he could have done that was so bad even they couldn't stomach it."

"I told you they weren't your family," said Molly.

"Let's get out of here," I said. "It feels like the statue is looking at us, and not in a good way."

"Damn right," said Molly. "This isn't a safe place to be."

The wall beside us exploded inwards, the shockwave blasting pieces of broken stone ahead of it. I armoured up in a moment, grabbed Molly, and held her to me, bending over to shield her body with mine.

Jagged stones rained down, bouncing harmlessly off my armour. Thick black smoke billowed across the room as the deafening explosion echoed on and on. Eventually the sound died away, the pieces of shattered stone stopped falling, and the smoke reluctantly began to clear. I straightened up, and Molly immediately pushed herself away from me.

"I do not need protecting!"

"Of course you don't," I said. "I just did it for my own peace of mind."

Molly scowled at me and then turned her glare on the gaping hole in the wall. She batted at the remaining smoke with her hands. "What the hell just happened? Did we trigger some kind of booby-trap, or is Kali mad at us?"

"That was an exterior wall," I said. "Something hit it from outside. The Hall is under attack."

"Why would anyone want to attack an empty Hall?" said Molly.

"I have every intention of finding out," I said. "And then making it clear to whoever did this just how extremely displeased I am."

"I'll help," said Molly.

"Thought you'd want to," I said.

I felt strong and fast and good inside my armour. As though I'd just been kicked awake, out of the long doze of everyday living. I didn't care if there was a whole army outside in the grounds; I was ready to take them all on and look good doing it. I glanced at Kali, standing untouched in her alcove. She looked like she approved.

I stepped through the jagged hole in the wall and strode out into the grounds of Drood Hall. It was a bright, sunny afternoon, under a cloudless sky, and a dozen armoured tanks stood arrayed on the lawns before me, their long guns covering the whole side of the Hall. Large, heavy death machines, with stylised military badges to make it clear they represented MI 13. Heavy whining sounds carried clearly on the still air as all the turrets turned as one, bringing their long barrels to bear on me. Enough massed firepower to reduce the whole of Drood Hall to rubble. It would probably have impressed anyone else. A small army of uniformed soldiers backed up the tanks—maybe two hundred men, all of them heavily armed and bearing the same MI 13 military insignia. Molly stepped through the hole in the wall to join me, took in the view, and smiled happily.

"Just when I was thinking I could really use someone to take out the day's events on . . . How nice of them to volunteer. So, MI Thirteen is a military operation in this world."

"How bad are things here that the Government's department for dealing with weird shit needs tanks and soldiers to get the job done?" I said.

"Don't know, don't care," Molly said cheerfully. "All that matters is they chose the wrong day to annoy me. Not that there ever is a good day. Mind you, they do look very smart in their nice uniforms, don't they?"

"Oh, they do," I said. "Very smart. Have you by any chance noticed that all the tanks are pointing their guns at us?"

"I had noticed, yes. How very rude of them. I think we should do something about that."

"Something violent and horribly destructive?"

"How well you know me," said Molly.

The smartly uniformed soldiers looked at me in my gleaming golden armour, and then at Molly's happy, smiling face, and went straight from hard-eyed professionalism to mass panic. Shouts and curses and clear sounds of distress rose, followed by a general lowering of weapons. Some of the soldiers turned to run, only to be herded back again by furiously shouting officers. I had to smile, behind my featureless golden face mask. They had no idea how bad things were about to get.

"What kind of soldiers are these?" said Molly. "Half of them look like they're bricking themselves."

"That's what I like to see," I said. "Proper respect for my family."

"I think they're more afraid of the Kali-worshipping Droods," said Molly. "That's not respect I'm seeing; more like stark terror."

"I can live with that," I said.

The tanks suddenly opened fire, targeting Molly and me with everything they had. The noise was deafening. The tanks fired again and again, as fast as their gunners could load new shells. I just stood there and let them get on with it. Most of the shells were absorbed harmlessly by my armour. A few exploded squarely against my chest, but I didn't even rock under the impact. Molly stood calmly beside me, inside a shimmering field of protective energies. Any shell that got anywhere near her just vanished.

We both looked steadily back at the wide array of tanks, entirely unmoved by the continuing onslaught. Every now and then I'd wave at the huddled ranks of soldiers, just to show I hadn't forgotten them. They didn't look at all happy about that. One by one the gunners stopped firing, as they either ran out of shells or lost the will to continue. It can't be easy, trying to kill someone who just stands there and calmly refuses to be killed. Eventually I slapped a shell out of mid-air with the back of my hand, and it exploded not far from the nearest soldiers, showering them with earth and grass. The officers had to do a lot more shouting to get their men to hold their positions.

"Okay," said Molly, "you're just playing with them now, and I'm getting bored. Not to mention impatient. We need to teach these uniformed bully-boys some manners, so we can get on with what we came here for."

"Couldn't agree more," I said.

I charged forward across the lawn. My armoured legs drove me on at more-than-human speed, my heavy golden feet digging great divots out of the ground. I closed the distance between myself and the tanks so quickly they couldn't traverse their barrels fast enough to keep up with me. I went straight for the nearest tank, lowered one golden shoulder, and rammed it. Steel shields ruptured, and the sheer force of the impact drove the tank back several feet. I grabbed hold of the metal shielding with both hands and ripped it apart. The steel screamed as my golden gloves tore it like paper. The tank's barrel tried to lower itself towards me, and I hit it so hard I bent it in half, pointing the end away from me. I did think about tying the barrel in a knot, but that would have felt like showing off. I braced myself, took a firm hold of the tank, and picked the whole thing up. Its heavy treads spun wildly as the engines strained uselessly. I threw the tank away from me. It crashed heavily, some distance away, flipped end over end two or three times, and then the engines cut out.

Another tank powered in my direction, lowering its barrel as much as it could to target me. As though getting in close would make any difference. I ran forward, ducked under the barrel, grabbed hold of the tank, and turned the whole thing over onto its side, enjoying the muffled screams from inside. Then I looked around for another tank. I was enjoying myself. I always feel better when the world gives me an opportunity to do something unpleasant about all the things that have been getting on my nerves. There's nothing like giving an enemy a really good slapping to improve your day.

All the remaining tanks were reversing now, their operators desperate to get as far away from me as they could. Their heavy treads dug deep into the grassy lawn, throwing churned-up grass and earth in every direction and making one hell of a mess. I thought of how much work the family gardeners would have to do to put everything right, and then I remembered. A cold fury rose in me. I turned away from the retreating tanks to face the waiting soldiers, and stalked towards them with vengeance on my mind. Because someone had to pay for what my life had become.

I felt strong and fast and sure. *How can I be dying when I feel so strong?* Except, of course, it wasn't me; it was the armour.

Soldiers with heavy automatic weapons hurried forward to face me, driven on by officers screaming themselves hoarse from the rear. The soldiers' faces were grim but determined. Their guns looked odd to me. Standard types, but not any make I knew. And I've faced off against any number of weapons in my time. The soldiers all opened fire at once, and bullets slammed into my armour again and again, to no effect. They couldn't even slow my advance.

Information flashed up on the inside of my mask, as my armour absorbed the various bullets and analysed them. My armour always absorbs bullets, rather than let them ricochet and possibly injure some innocent bystander. Though I was pretty sure there weren't any of those around just at the moment. I was interested to discover that the soldiers were firing a wide assortment of ammunition. Blessed and cursed, garlic coated and mercury tipped, even depleted uranium with crosses carved into them. Apparently this version of MI 13 liked to be prepared for all eventualities. They had something to stop anyone—except a really upset Drood in his armour.

Seeing that they were getting nowhere with me, the soldiers turned their guns on Molly as she sauntered forward to join me, not wanting to be left out of the action. I wasn't worried. The moment the soldiers opened fire on Molly, she gestured imperiously and all their bullets turned into butterflies. Big, bright, and colourful, the butterflies immediately turned around and flapped determinedly towards the soldiers, who threw away their weapons and ran, shouldering their officers out of the way.

"Wimps!" Molly yelled after them.

While she was busy doing that, another solider stepped forward and fired his bazooka at her at point-blank range. Molly spun round, her shields flaring up to stand off an exploding shell. Instead, a glowing net erupted from the bazooka, spreading out as it flew through the air. Molly gestured at it dismissively, but the net just kept coming. It fell upon her, passing through her shields as though they weren't even there. The glowing strands snapped around Molly in a moment, and then constricted sharply until she could barely move. Some kind of magic neutraliser. It seemed this MI 13 had experience when it came to dealing with really powerful witches.

I started towards Molly. I didn't care what that net was made of; I was going to rip it apart with my golden hands. But Molly glared at me and shook her head furiously.

"No! Don't you dare, Eddie Drood! I am more than capable of rescuing myself. You go deal with those damned soldiers."

I stopped and nodded. I could have freed her, but I knew that if I did it would be a really long time before she forgave me. Interfering would be proof that I had no faith in her abilities, that I didn't think she could pull her weight. Molly needed to feel she was an equal partner to a Drood in his armour, and, to be fair, most of the time she was. So I headed straight for the nearest soldiers, to take my anger out on them.

Most of them threw away their guns and ran for their lives, followed by their hysterically screaming officers. I let them go. It's nice to be appreciated.

On the edge of my mask's wide peripheral vision, I saw Molly produce a very ordinary, entirely nonmagical knife and start sawing through the strands of the net. Half a dozen soldiers were racing across the lawns, desperate to get to her before she could free herself and regain control of her magics. So I just happened to change my course a little, placing my armoured body between them and Molly, so they couldn't open fire on her. I could get away with that much. The soldiers shied away from me, giving me plenty of room, but kept going.

Molly kept a careful eye on them as she cut through one strand after another, until suddenly the net stopped glowing. It quickly fell away, and Molly's magical energies flared up around her again. The soldiers crashed to a halt. She smiled nastily at them and raised one hand, and the soldiers turned and ran. Molly looked after them thoughtfully, in a way I knew meant she was seriously thinking about transforming them into small squishy things and then stamping on them. But she didn't, because she knew I wouldn't approve. Mad as I was at the world, I only wanted the soldiers punished, not dead.

Molly turned abruptly to look at me, to make sure I wasn't taking an undue interest in what she was doing, but by then I was carefully concentrating on the soldiers before me. One lobbed a grenade at me, and I snatched it out of mid-air. I studied the thing carefully. Again, it wasn't any make I was familiar with. The dully gleaming exterior was etched with ancient Nordic death runes. I closed my golden hand around the grenade and braced myself, ready to contain the explosion . . . But instead coruscating energies flared up around my hand, rapidly swelling into a deepening vortex. I tried to jerk my hand back, and found I couldn't. It was stuck in the heart of the field.

Something grabbed hold of my armoured hand and jerked it deeper into the vortex. My hand and wrist disappeared, as though the cloud of crackling energies was much deeper than it appeared. I dug my heels deep into the ground as the pull came again, but despite everything I could do I was jerked forward, my arm disappearing into the vortex right up to the elbow. Air whistled past me, sucked in from all directions by the energy field. Great tufts of earth and grass were ripped out of the surrounding lawns, and sucked in by the shimmering energies. And all the time I was fighting the pull with all the strength I had, struggling to break free—and failing.

I knew what the problem was now: I'd been stupid enough to let an implosion grenade detonate. I'd heard of them, because I make it a point to keep up to date with all the latest unpleasantness, but I'd never encountered one before. An explosion in reverse, designed to draw in everything in the vicinity and then compress it down to nothing. The perfect way to kill your enemy and leave no evidence behind. I'd never heard of one being used against a Drood before, so I had no idea how to fight it. The energy field yanked me forward another step, sucking my arm in well past the elbow. I could feel a growing pressure on the part of my arm I couldn't see, and if I could feel that through my armour, it had to be seriously strong. As in, bottom-of-the-ocean, tons-of-pressure-per-square-inch strong.

I thought quickly. Some of the soldiers were firing their guns at me while I was distracted, more in a spirit of optimism than anything else. I let my armour absorb the bullets while I concentrated on the problem before me. Brute strength might not be enough to break me free of the field, but I was still willing to bet the strange matter of my armour against whatever energies the field could produce. So I stopped fighting the pull and stepped forward, right into the heart of the vortex.

The world around me disappeared, replaced by flaring energies so bright and vivid they were beyond colour. A terrible pressure clamped down on me from all sides, as if I were being crushed in the hand of God. And then the appalling forces of the energy vortex met the implacable power of my armour . . . and the field just collapsed. The world reappeared, the air around me lightly dusted with the last dissipating traces of implosion energies. I held my armoured arm up before me and turned my hand back and forth. Not even a dent.

The soldiers cried out in shock and alarm as I turned unhurriedly to face them, and then they fell silent. There's something about the lack of eyes in my golden face mask that really freaks people out.

The implosion grenade had been a pretty good idea. It might even have worked against the old Heart armour. But MI 13 had never met a Drood like me. Molly ambled over, nodding casually, as though it had never even occurred to her I might be in trouble. And quite possibly it hadn't. One of the soldiers said something very bad and threw a grenade at us. Molly snapped her fingers and the grenade exploded well short of us. A nasty-looking purple gas billowed out. Molly gestured at it dismissively, and the gas swept back to envelop the soldiers. They were forced to retreat, gagging and choking.

The remaining soldiers opened fire on me and Molly, hitting us with everything they had. I charged forward, crossing the intervening ground in seconds, and was quickly in and among them. I punched out the nearest soldier, and his head snapped right back, blood spurting from a ruined nose and mouth. I back-elbowed another in the gut, bending him in two, and swept the legs out from under a third. I ploughed on through the rest of the soldiers, sending them flying. Guns opened up on me at point-blank range, but my armour just sucked in the bullets. Some soldiers slammed their gun butts against my head and neck, as though that would have more effect than bullets. I just knocked the soldiers down and trampled them underfoot and kept going. I was grinning inside my mask, and it was a good thing the soldiers couldn't see. It felt like a death's-head grin. I started picking soldiers up and throwing them away, and men flew through the air like uniformed Frisbees. They hit the ground hard, and took their time getting up again.

I was still holding back. Human bodies can be very frail when faced with the awful strength of Drood armour. Besides, God alone knew how many deaths could be laid at the doors of the Kali-worshipping Droods. There was always a chance MI 13 were the good guys. And, anyway, I don't kill unless I have to. I'm a secret agent, not an assassin.

It wasn't like the soldiers presented any real threat to me . . .

But even as I swept them aside with my golden arms, or clubbed down the stubborn ones, my cold anger returned. Remembering how the soldiers had attacked without warning, blown a hole in my home . . . and threatened my Molly. They had tried to kill me, not knowing Dr DOA had already done that. I couldn't get to him, but the soldiers were right there in front of me. This wasn't my world, after all, so maybe the old rules and restrictions didn't apply. I could do anything I wanted here, anything I felt like, and no one would ever bring me to book for it. I was dying. Didn't I have the right to take some measure of vengeance on an uncaring world?

I grabbed the nearest soldier by the throat and lifted him off the ground. His feet kicked helplessly and his eyes bulged as I began choking the life out of him. I needed to punish someone for what had been done to me. It was only fair that someone should suffer, as I had been made to suffer. But then the moment passed. I wasn't a killer. I let go of the soldier and he fell to the ground, gasping for breath and clutching at his bruised throat. I stood there, looking down at him with my featureless mask, thinking about what I'd almost done. The soldier scrambled away from me, and I let him go.

It didn't matter what the Droods had made of themselves in this world. I was a different kind of Drood, and I would remain the kind of man I'd chosen to be. Right till the end.

"I wondered what you were going to do there for a moment," said Molly, coming over to join me.

"I wondered too," I said. "Just for a moment."

The few groups of soldiers still standing threw down their guns and all but begged to be allowed to surrender. The tank crews had already abandoned their vehicles. I nodded formally to them all, accepting the victory. Molly looked like she would have preferred to go on fighting until she'd ground every single one of them beneath her feet, but, then, that's Molly for you. She stood stiffly beside me, arms tightly folded, looking hopefully around for someone dumb enough to mouth off. But none of the MI 13 soldiers were that dumb. They stuck their hands in the air or clasped them on top of their heads, and did their best to avoid Molly's gaze. Even the officers. Perhaps especially the officers.

The last of my anger went out of me, as I realised how scared they all were. Most of them looked like they were still expecting me to slaughter everyone within reach, even though they'd surrendered, because that was what Droods did in this world. I took a deep breath and armoured down, so they could see I was just a man. A murmur of relief rose among the soldiers, followed by some odd looks as they studied my bare face. It was obvious none of them recognised me.

I had to struggle to keep a sudden wave of tiredness off my face. Without my armour's strength the exhaustion was back, hitting me so hard it almost drove me to my knees. I had forgotten how bad I felt, until I didn't have my armour to hold me up. I made myself smile easily. I couldn't afford for anyone to realise just how weak I was. I sent a trickle of golden strange matter down my back, under my clothes, and it lent me a measure of support.

I looked carefully around until I picked out the officer in charge. A major, by his insignia; smartly turned out, not far from my age. Handsome enough, apart from the old-fashioned military moustache. I beckoned to him, and he lowered his hands and moved slowly forward to join me. He looked like he thought he was walking to his death. He finally crashed to a halt right in front of me, fired off a salute, and then snapped to attention. His back was ramrod straight, and he met my gaze steadily, braced for whatever appalling thing I had in mind.

"Relax, Major," I said. "I'm not going to kill you."

"You're not?" said the major. He sounded honestly surprised.

"I'm not Edmund," I said.

"I have no idea who that might be," the major said carefully. "Or who you are. I don't recognise you from our files, though before today I would have said that was impossible. MI Thirteen has extensive files on the Drood family. Know thy enemy, if you want to survive meeting him."

"I'm Eddie Drood. Why did you attack us, Major?"

"Because you're a Drood," said the major, in a way that suggested his answer should have been self-evident.

"I'm a different kind of Drood," I said.

"If you say so," said the major. He did relax a little, and even managed a small smile. "I'm Major Benson. I really thought you were going to kill me as an example."

"And you were ready to go along with that?" said Molly.

The major jumped, just a little, at the sound of her voice. He glanced at her and then stared determinedly back at me, the lesser of two evils. He might be scared of me, but he was terrified of Molly.

"Why are you so scared of her?" I said.

"Because that's Molly Metcalf!" said the major, his voice rising in spite of himself. "It's a wonder to me we're not all sitting around on a rock pool somewhere, catching flies with our tongues! Nobody warned me we'd be going up against an infamous wild witch, supernatural terrorist, and Mistress of the Dark Arts!"

"I am nobody's mistress," Molly said haughtily.

"I could always pay you a retainer," I said.

"Don't push your luck, Drood," said Molly. She glowered at the major. "I am a different Molly Metcalf."

"Clearly," said the major. "I was surprised to see you here, with him. I always thought you and the Droods were mortal enemies."

"You have a file on Molly too?" I said.

"Of course!" said the major. "She's been Most Wanted for three years running on the Occult Crimes Register!"

Molly clapped her hands delightedly. "I made number one! I always knew I could . . . I am so proud."

"We thought you were still hiding out in the Paris catacombs," said the major, "after what you did to the Louvre. Can I ask: What are you doing here? With the Droods, of all people?"

"We're together," said Molly.

The major looked politely baffled. "Together . . . ?"

"We're an item," I said.

"Okay," said the major. "Not the most unlikely thing I've ever heard, but pretty damn close. *You're* together? That's just spooky . . . and not a little disturbing. Two of the most dangerous people in the world are now involved with each other."

"You do realise you're saying this out loud, Major?" I said.

"I'm probably just giddy at still being alive," said the major. "Isn't it a lovely day? I might go for a stroll later."

"Pull yourself together," I said sharply. "We have questions we want answered. And while Molly and I might not be exactly who you were expecting, we are still a Drood and a witch."

"Most Wanted supernatural terrorist witch," said Molly. "Get the billing right."

"You're not feeling nostalgic, are you?" I said. "You promised me you'd put all that behind you."

"Live your dreams—that's what I say," Molly said cheerfully.

"Can't take you anywhere." I turned my attention back to Major Benson and fixed him with my best thoughtful stare. "How did you know someone was back in the Hall, Major?"

"You have got to be kidding!" said the major. "Drood Hall has been under constant surveillance ever since the Great Invasion. We have sensors scattered across the grounds, along the perimeter, and all through the Hall. We have farscrying viewers watching this place in eight-hour shifts, and satellites in orbit specifically tasked to do nothing but scan the Hall and its surroundings on every known scientific and supernatural wavelength. The second you appeared inside the Hall, your torc set off all kinds of silent alarms. It was just my bad luck I happened to be on guard duty outside the gates, so I got the call to investigate. My first impulse was to tear off my uniform and sprint for the nearest horizon, and I do wish I'd listened to it."

"Breathe, Major," I said kindly. "You're hyperventilating."

"Can I just ask: How did you get inside the Hall, past all our very expensive safeguards?" The major sounded honestly curious. "Black Heir assured us no one could get past the kind of security it had put in place."

"Never trust Black Heir," I said. That seemed a safe enough thing to say, no matter what world I was in. "If I were you, I'd ask for my money back. Now tell me: Why have you been keeping such a close eye on the old place, Major? Given that all of my family are supposed to be dead?"

"Because there was always the possibility not all of you died here that day," said the major. "It's possibilities like this that keep good people from sleeping soundly at night."

"Don't worry, Major," I said. "Molly and I aren't planning on staying."

"So . . . ," the major said casually, "are you . . . the only surviving Drood?"

"You're asking the wrong man," I said.

"Hold everything; throw it in reverse," said Molly. "Your sensors must have told you it was just the two of us in the Hall, so why bring all these tanks and a small army of soldiers?"

"To deal with a Drood and Molly Metcalf?" said the major. "Anything less would have been suicide! I wasn't convinced any of this would do much good, to be honest, but someone higher up the food chain thought we'd tried everything but brute force, so . . ."

"You really believed you were all going to die, trying to stop us," I said, studying the major's face carefully. "But you took us on, anyway. Why?"

He shrugged quickly. "It's the job. It's our duty, to protect the world from people like you."

I actually liked him rather better for saying that, though I did my best to keep it out of my face.

"Tell me what I need to know, Major," I said. "And in return I promise you and all your people will get to walk out of here."

The major looked at me oddly. "You're giving me your word? And you mean it . . . I can see it in your eyes. What kind of a Drood are you?"

"You'd be surprised," I said. "Talk to me about the Great Invasion. Who was involved? Who killed my family? Was it the Immortals?"

The major paused, considering his words carefully. "They took the lead, naturally. But basically, once word got out that all the Hall's protections were down, and for the first time ever the Droods were seriously vulnerable, everyone just came running. Representatives from all sorts of secret agencies, heroes and villains and everyone in between. Everyone wanted in. Your family made a lot of enemies, down the years. No one wanted to miss out on what might be their only chance for revenge."

"Revenge?" I said. "For what?"

"For what you've done to the world," said the major. And just like that, his voice and his gaze were very cold.

"Were the Droods really that bad?" said Molly.

The major looked at her. "You should know; you were here. Along with your sisters. God alone knows how many Droods the three of you killed that day."

Molly and I looked at each other, but neither of us felt like saying anything. I looked around the grounds for a while, getting my mental second wind, and then turned back to nod briskly at Major Benson.

"All right," I said. "Major, it's time for you and your people to be on their way. Do not pass go, do not stop off at the gift shop, and don't even think about coming back. Tell your superiors: Drood Hall is dead. Leave it in peace."

"I can tell them," said the major, careful in his choice of words, as always. "But they're never going to believe this . . ."

"Make them believe," I said. And something in my voice made him nod quickly.

I gestured for him to leave, and he backed quickly away. He gathered up his people, including the wounded, the unconscious, and those still hacking and coughing from the purple gas; and pointed them towards the long gravel path that led to the main gates. The soldiers set off at a fair pace, supporting or carrying others where necessary. Afraid I might change my mind at any moment. A few looked back sadly at the tanks they were leaving behind, but knew better than to ask. The major was the last to leave. He hesitated, and then looked at me steadily.

"I never thought I'd be saying this to a Drood, but . . . you did right by us, when no one expected you to. You're not like any Drood I ever heard of; except when you're fighting. So . . . we're leaving, but you can be sure other forces are already on their way. Bigger and far more dangerous forces, with real firepower. Hell, somebody's probably already talking about nuking the Hall from orbit, as the only way to be sure. They only let us come in first because we were nearest, and they wanted to see what you would do. What you were capable of. All they really expected of us was that we might hold your attention long enough for everyone else to get here. All kinds of people will be coming . . . if only for one last chance to kill a Drood. You really don't want to be here when they arrive."

"Thank you, Major," I said.

He shook his head as though even simple courtesy was beyond anything he'd expected. "Can I just ask: Who are you, really? We honestly believed all the Droods were dead. And there's definitely no Eddie Drood in any of our files."

"They're gone," I said. "And I'm not staying. Now get off my lawn."

The major threw me a quick salute, turned smartly about, and hurried off after his men.

"We're really just letting them go?" Molly said quietly. "After they did their best to kill us?"

"Not us," I said. "This world's version of us. And I'm starting to

wonder if they might not have been justified. Come on. Let's see to our
business in the Old Library, and then get the hell out of here."

"You really think we're going to find anything useful?" said Molly.

"Who knows what we might find," I said, "in this strange new world?"

"Maybe it'll be something we can sell," said Molly.

CHAPTER TWO

You'd Be Surprised What You Can Find in a Library

I went striding back through the Hall, with Molly hurrying along at my side. More than ever it seemed to me I could hear the clock ticking. I was still spotting small but telling differences in the Hall, and I couldn't help wondering why I hadn't noticed them the last time I was here. I had been very upset back then, convinced it was my family who'd been slaughtered, but still . . . Did some other influence touch my mind, to keep me from noticing things I wasn't supposed to see?

Molly could tell I was brooding again, and did her best to lighten the strained atmosphere.

"It was good of MI Thirteen to provide us with a decent workout. There's no better way to start the day than taking on a whole army of bad guys and making them cry like babies. You looked a lot more like your old self out there. How are you feeling?"

"I wish you'd stop asking me that!" I said. "It doesn't matter how many times you ask—the answer isn't going to change!"

"Don't you snap at me, Eddie Drood!"

I had to smile at her. "You know you only use my full name when you're mad at me?"

She smiled back at me. "I need to be sure you're paying attention."

And then I slammed to a halt as my eyes were drawn to a door that shouldn't have been there, in a wall I didn't remember. Even though time was pressing, something about that particular door held my gaze. Molly moved in close beside me, looking back and forth between me and the door, waiting for me to explain why we'd stopped. And I couldn't tell her, because I didn't know.

"I really don't think standing around, frowning at strange doors, is getting us anywhere, Eddie," she said finally. "What's so special about this one?"

"It called to me," I said.

"Oh, that is so not in any way good," said Molly. "If we had any sense we'd start running right now."

"You're being very cautious all of a sudden."

"It's Drood Hall! It brings out the survival instincts in me."

I reached out a hand to open the door, and Molly's hand clamped down hard on my arm.

"Aren't you at least going to armour up first?"

I withdrew my hand, and Molly let go of my arm. I looked at her carefully.

"Does it feel to you like I'm going to need my armour? Are you picking up some kind of warning about what's on the other side of that door?"

"Not . . . specifically," said Molly. "But given this is the only door in the entire building that's called out to you . . . Come on, you must remember the old story about Bluebeard. He tells his new wife she can go anywhere she likes in his house, but there's one door she must never open. Of course, eventually she does, and the room turns out to be full of horrible things that tell her far more about her new husband than she ever wanted to know. I think this is that kind of door."

I looked at her for a long moment. "In this story, which one of us is Bluebeard?"

"It doesn't matter! What if this is the one door you really shouldn't open because you really don't want to know what's in there?"

"This whole Hall has been like that," I said. "What could be worse than a massive statue of the goddess Kali with blood on her feet?"

Molly scowled at the closed door. "I have a horrible suspicion we're about to find out."

I took a careful hold of the handle and eased the door open a crack. Molly tensed, ready to blast anything that moved that shouldn't. But everything was still and quiet, and we both relaxed, just a little. I pushed the door all the way open, and stepped cautiously in. With Molly right there at my side, determined as always not to be left out of anything.

The shadowy, windowless room was full of men and women sitting on chairs. None of them so much as turned their heads. They just sat there stiffly in their stiff-backed chairs, looking at nothing. A dull, flat light rose in the room, from no obvious source, just enough to give me a clearer view of the occupants. I glanced quickly at Molly, not wanting to take my eyes off the unmoving figures for too long.

"Is that your light?" I said quietly.

"No. Nothing to do with me."

"I was afraid you were going to say that." I looked quickly round the room. "Okay . . . I am going to assume the light is a standard response to anyone entering the room and not let it creep me out at all."

"Very wise."

"I thought so."

"Who are all these people?" said Molly. "Are they dead?"

"They're not moving or looking at us, and they're covered in dust," I said. "So I am going to go out on a limb and say yes, they're probably dead. Is this what Bluebeard's wife found?"

"I forget. Why would the Droods keep a room full of dead people sitting around on chairs?"

"I don't know," I said. "Trophies? Souvenirs?"

"If this turns out to be like Norman Bates' mother in *Psycho*, you can pay for my therapy bills."

I surprised myself with a brief snort of laughter. "You've seen worse. Hell, you've done worse."

"Not recently."

I moved cautiously forward, ready to pull on my armour in a moment if any of the shadowy figures so much as stirred. I leaned in close, for a better look at the nearest faces. The skin had been stretched taut, cheekbones pressing out against the skin, and the eyes and mouths were closed. I couldn't see any stitches holding them shut, but I knew what the figures were now. Dead bodies preserved for future use was an old Drood trick. Like the scarecrows out in the grounds, these were old Drood enemies made over into nonliving sentinels, to guard and protect us from unwelcome intruders.

Because no one carries a grudge like my family.

I moved along the front row, and a chill ran through me as I came face-to-face with my grandmother Martha, the previous Matriarch of my family. Sitting beside her, dressed in his Sunday best, was her first husband. In my world Arthur left the family to run the Department of Uncanny, and never came back. Apparently that wasn't the case here. Beside them sat the Blue Fairy, in a remarkably conservative outfit, for him. Half Drood and half elf, he must have embraced my family's heritage in this world.

He'd ended up as a scarecrow in the grounds of my Hall. So his decision hadn't made that much difference, in the end.

I looked at Molly and she looked at me.

"Why would anyone do this, Eddie? What's the point of all this?"

"They must be here for a purpose," I said. "My family never does anything without a reason, and usually a very upsetting one . . ."

I broke off, as one by one all the preserved bodies turned their heads in a series of slow, jerky movements to look at me. Making stiff creaking sounds, like machinery forced into motion after being left idle for far too long. Dust fell from their faces in sudden streams. Their eyes were open now, fixing me with cold, unwavering stares. I glanced briefly behind me, to make sure there was nothing between me and the open door. Molly made a low disgusted sound. Grandmother Martha's mouth dropped open, like a ventriloquist's puppet's. She made a series of exploratory noises, and then her voice sounded harshly on the still air.

"Edmund. You have come back to us."

I half expected dust to puff from her mouth in a small cloud, like some ancient mummy disturbed in its tomb. I started to correct her with my proper name, but Molly's hand clamped down on my arm again, stopping me. I nodded to her, and she let go. I took up a position standing directly in front of the dead woman, and all the other heads moved to follow me.

"Hello, Grandmother," I said carefully. "You're looking . . . very like yourself. Can you answer questions?"

"Of course," said Martha. Her voice sounded distant and just a bit artificial, like an old recording. "That is what we're here for."

"What are you?" I said. "Why did the family . . . preserve you like this?"

It wasn't until I'd finished speaking that I had second thoughts, and winced. Edmund would probably have known these things. But Martha showed no surprise at my questions, and answered me steadily.

"We are the family's advisory Council. Not zombies; just a lifetime's knowledge and experience conserved against the ages. History in the flesh. So that nothing of value might be lost to the family."

"Is anything of you in there, Grandmother?" I said.

"No." The voice issuing from the stiff grey lips was quite firm. "I am everything Martha knew, but nothing of who she was."

"That's something, I suppose. How did you survive the Great Invasion?"

"Because only the Matriarch can access the advisory Council," said Martha. "No one else can even see the door."

Molly stirred at my side, as though she wanted to say something, but I hushed her with a look. I stepped back to join her and murmured in her ear.

"I know; I'm not a Matriarch. But I did run my family for a while, and apparently that's enough to meet the requirements. Edmund never returned to his family, so he never got to be in charge . . . So he never knew about any of this and couldn't betray them to the invaders."

"Makes sense," said Molly. "Go on, ask her things!"

"All right!" I said. "It's not easy talking to a dead relative."

"Easier than talking to some of the live ones," murmured Molly.

I knew she was trying to lighten the mood. It didn't help, but I appreciated the effort. I turned my attention back to Martha.

"You called out to me, or the room did. Why do you need to speak to me?"

"You were heading for the Library. We could tell. You must not release the prisoner in the Old Library. After so many years of impressed servitude, his wrath would be a terrible thing."

"So there was something unnatural in there!" said Molly.

"I never doubted it," I said. "Now hush, please."

"Only because you said please."

Martha didn't react to Molly at all, as though she weren't there. Because Molly wasn't a Drood.

"Who is this prisoner?" I said.

"All our sins remembered," said Martha.

"All right," I said. "This is all very interesting, not to mention deeply disturbing, but that's not why you called out to me, is it? What do you want me to do, Grandmother?"

"You must destroy us," Martha said flatly. "It is necessary. Strangers have entered the Hall and moved back and forth in it. There is always the chance someone will find a way past our safeguards and discover us. The advisory Council must not come under the control of outsiders. Our knowledge must not fall into the hands of our enemies."

I thought about that.

"Well?" said Molly. "What's the problem? Think of all the really bad things Kali-worshipping Droods might know. You really want that running loose in the world?"

"But have we the right to destroy so much knowledge?" I said.

"They're not the people you know," said Molly. "Let the evil they've done die with them. Wipe the world clean of this family once and for all."

I nodded reluctantly and looked back at Martha. "Will any of you . . . suffer, if I do this?"

"No," said Martha. "We are all of us dead and gone. Nothing but repositories of old knowledge. Books that need to be closed forever."

"How am I supposed to destroy you," I said, "if you're already dead?"

"Fire," said Molly. "Fire is always good."

"My family would have thought of that," I said. "You can bet this room is lousy with protections. Grandmother?"

"You have Drood authority, or you wouldn't be here," said Martha. "Just say the Words."

"What Words?" I said.

Every dead body in the room lifted one arm and pointed steadily at a book laid out on a side table. I looked at it for a long moment, because I was absolutely sure neither the book nor the table had been there just a moment ago. Or perhaps I just hadn't been allowed to see them until now.

"We cannot read the Words of unbinding ourselves," said Martha. "They only have power if spoken by the living. By the head of the family."

"Now, that is pushing it," I said to Molly. "It's been some time since I was in charge . . ."

"Once a Patriarch, always a Patriarch," Molly said briskly. "Like the dead thing said: If you weren't qualified, the room wouldn't have called you."

I moved over to the table and looked at the book. It lay open, revealing oversized pages of blocky type. The language looked familiar, but I couldn't place it. Molly crowded in beside me and then drew in a sharp breath.

"Oh shit . . ."

"What?" I said.

"This is bad stuff," said Molly. "And I mean seriously bad stuff."

"You know what this is?" I said.

"The Book of Morgana La Fae," said Molly. "Greatest witch of all time. She helped bring down King Arthur's Camelot. Killing Morgana was the last great thing Merlin ever did, and the effort nearly destroyed him. She knew things no one else knew, or would want to know. This looks to be the Eighteenth-Century edition; as close to an unexpurgated version as you're going to get. It's written in an ancient form of Enochian, the language men use when they want to talk directly to angels or demons. Eddie, I was a supernatural terrorist for years, and I never even saw a copy of this book. It's hideously dangerous; the occult equivalent of a backpack nuke. There are Words in here that could blow the earth apart like a firecracker in a rotten apple. You do not want to mess with this."

The two open pages were covered with a thick layer of dust, apart from one section low down on the left-hand side. The half-dozen lines of revealed text seemed almost supernaturally clear and distinct.

"Are you sure this is Enochian?" I said. "I can usually read that, while just looking at the text here is giving me a serious headache."

"This version far predates the form discovered by Dr Dee," said Molly. "I saw something like it once before, in the Nightside. In one of Merlin's books. I was supposed to steal it, but I wasn't dumb enough to get Merlin Satanspawn mad at me. Eddie . . . I have no idea what those Words are or what will happen if you speak them."

I looked back at the dead men and women on their chairs, still pointing steadily at the book.

"You think they'd lie to me?"

"Hello!" Molly said loudly. "Kali-worshipping Droods, hated by the whole world! What do you think?"

"I think Martha is right. We can't leave them here, knowing what they know. They're the real backpack nuke. I have to do this, Molly. Maybe you'd better step out of the room, just in case."

"Hell with that," Molly said immediately. "If something should go wrong, I'm the only real chance for survival you've got. Get on with it. I'll rehearse a few emergency prayers."

I spoke each Word carefully in turn. I could feel a growing presence in the room, as though it was filling up with something unseen but horribly powerful. There was a presence in the book, and in the room, of life and death and everything in between, lying in the balance.

As I continued reading, the correct pronunciation became easier, as though the book was prompting me. The moment I spoke the last Word, the tension in the room broke and was gone. The dead bodies all sighed once, in unison, and then just crumbled away. Collapsing in on themselves, becoming dust and less than dust. Until nothing was left but rows of empty chairs in an empty room. Molly sighed heavily.

"Just when I think your family can't get any more disturbing . . ."

"What do we do with the book?" I said.

"What book?" said Molly.

I looked back at the table, but the book was gone. Only an outline in the dust remained, to show where it had been.

"Where did it go?" I said.

"Nowhere we would want to follow," said Molly. "Trust me, Eddie, we are well rid of it."

"Maybe it's shelved itself in the Old Library," I said. "Let's go take a look."

"You're just full of really bad ideas today, aren't you?" said Molly.

We backed out of the room, because neither of us felt like taking our eyes off it, and I closed the door firmly. The door then vanished, taking the wall with it. I can't say I was thrown. I've seen stranger things in Drood Hall.

"Magic that cleans up after itself," Molly said approvingly. "Best kind." She frowned. "Though I have to wonder . . . A prisoner, in the Old Library. Could it be someone like your Drood in Cell Thirteen, who had to be locked away forever, for everyone else's safety?"

"I think we're about to find out," I said.

The route turned out to be remarkably straightforward, as though the Hall wanted us to get there. But when we arrived at the official Library the door had been smashed in. It hung crookedly in its frame, barely hanging on by one hinge. I gave it a push and the door tore itself loose, crashing full length on the floor. Molly and I looked quickly around, but there was no response. I moved cautiously forward and found the Library had been ransacked, just like the Armoury. Nothing left but overturned wooden stacks, smoke-blackened walls, and a few unwanted books on the floor.

"I'm sure the Library wasn't this empty the last time we were here," I said.

"We've been gone a while," said Molly. "The vultures must have descended in our absence."

"Knowledge is power," I said. "And, sometimes, currency. My family spent generations collecting secret histories, forgotten knowledge, and compendiums of acquired alien lore. We like to know things, especially things no one else knows. All these empty shelves, all this forbidden knowledge out in the world, almost certainly in the hands of people who can't be trusted with it. No wonder the advisory Council was so determined it had to be destroyed."

"I don't think this world was any safer under the Droods," said Molly. "You've got to stop thinking of them as good guys, Eddie."

We made our way slowly through the Library, stepping carefully around the overturned wooden stacks. There was a smell of old smoke on the dusty air.

"I think someone tried to start a fire in here," I said. "But it didn't take. The looters must have been worried in case they missed something, and didn't want anyone else to have it."

Molly stared around her, frowning into the gloom. "Wooden stacks and bare floor-boards . . . This should have gone up like a bonfire. Must be more protections in place."

"Of course," I said. "The Hall can look after itself. Except . . . Edmund was supposed to have shut down all the Hall's protections before he let the invaders in."

"He couldn't know about everything," said Molly. "He had been away for some time."

"At least he didn't get to destroy everything," I said. "Okay. The unreal light is back. I'm going to assume that's standard and not following us around, because that would be just creepy."

"Could parts of Drood Hall still be alive?" said Molly. "Still functioning, on some level?"

"Not one of the most reassuring thoughts you've ever had," I said.

"That's not an answer."

"I know."

The painting that gave access to the Old Library was still hanging in place on the farthest wall. The original Drood library, long forgotten to all but the highest members in the family. Until I brought it back in my world. The painting seemed entirely untouched by fire or smoke. I was surprised the looters hadn't taken it, but perhaps it had hidden itself. The painting showed a view of the Old Library's interior, so exact and detailed it might almost have been a photo. Eight feet high and five wide, the colours so distinct they seemed almost to glow in the gloom. I frowned, leaning in for a closer look. Something was just a bit different compared to the scene I remembered, but I couldn't put my finger on it.

"You're frowning again," said Molly. "Stop it. You'll give yourself wrinkles."

"Something's wrong with this painting," I said.

"Something's wrong with this whole damned Hall," said Molly. "As long as the painting can still get us into the Old Library, I don't give a rat's arse. Get on with it."

I hesitated. "Molly, can you See . . . Is someone standing there in the stacks, right at the back?"

Molly leaned in close. "Where?"

"There! Right there!"

"Eddie, pointing doesn't help. Whatever it is you're seeing, I'm not seeing it. I was never any good with those *Where's Wally?* things. All right, what's wrong now? You've got that look on your face again."

"A thought has just occurred to me," I said slowly. "Edmund must have spent a lot of time running around in my Hall, unsuspected. Could he have gone searching through our Old Library for knowledge to use against us?"

"Okay, as disturbing thoughts go, that is right up there in the top ten," said Molly. "But do you really think Edmund could fool the Librarian into believing he was you?"

"I don't know," I said. "Maybe."

"Eddie, we can't worry about every possibility or we'll never get anything done. We have to stick with what's in front of us, the things we can deal with. There are more than enough of those to keep us busy. Like hoping there really is an Old Library on the other side of that painting. Do you still have your key?"

"Of course," I said. I reached into the pocket dimension I keep in my trousers and fished around until I found my key ring and hauled it out. I like to hang on to keys; you never know when they might come in handy. I found the small silver key, took it off the ring, and put the other keys away. One of the many useful things about a pocket dimension is that you can dump as many things in it as you want and it's never going to weigh your trousers down. I hefted the silver key. The last time I'd had to use it, I was still rogue . . . and so many of my immediate family were still alive.

A small keyhole had been artfully hidden in the silver scallops lining the top of the painting's frame. I eased the key into the lock and turned it carefully, and just like that the painting was no longer canvas and paint and a work of art. It was an opening in the wall, an entrance into the Old Library itself.

I put the key away and stepped through the gap, with Molly crowding right behind me. The last time we'd been here, it had been so dark Molly had to conjure up a witchlight for us. But now the Old Library was full of a grey, lifeless light that seemed to come from everywhere at once.

"More unexpected light," I said. "Only even more unnerving."

"You're never satisfied, are you?" said Molly. "I could conjure up something more comforting, if you like."

"Better not," I said. "It might attract attention."

"From whom?"

"Exactly," I said.

"You're thinking about the prisoner, aren't you?" said Molly, glowering around her.

"Actually, I'm trying really hard not to," I said. "Let's find what we're looking for and then get the hell out of here."

"What are we looking for?"

"A way home."

We moved carefully forward, keeping a watchful eye on the darkness between the tall stacks. The air was cold and stale, and the usual pleasant smell of old paper and leather bindings had been replaced by a heavier, more pervasive scent, of age and neglect. The Old Library I knew was a welcoming place, for all its many peculiarities. This Old Library seemed darker and more dangerous. I shivered suddenly, and so did Molly.

"I don't remember it being this cold last time," I said.

"Right," said Molly. "Why would anyone keep a library the same temperature as a meat locker?"

"To preserve something?" I said.

Molly scowled unhappily. "Maybe there's an undead Librarian, to go with the advisory Council."

"The last time we were here, something spoke my name," I said. "My name, not Edmund's, even though no one here should have known it."

"I used to think I was paranoid, until I met you," said Molly.

"To be fair, when you're a Drood, most of the world really is out to get you."

"I should have grabbed one of the guns MI Thirteen left behind," said Molly. "Something really big. With a grenade launcher."

"You really think that would help against a Dark Pook?"

"Okay, I am leaving, right now," said Molly. "Don't get in my way or I will trample you underfoot."

"Look on the bright side."

She looked at me. "There's a bright side?"

"Statistically speaking, there's bound to be. If you wait long enough."

We moved on, into the silence and the shadows. Rows and rows of bookshelves stretched off into the distance, disappearing into the dark. No one in my family has ever been sure just how big the Old Library really is, and the Librarian told me to my face the official index isn't worth the vellum it's written on. I glanced at Molly.

"The last time we were here . . ."

"Will you stop saying that!" said Molly. "It was just the once, and I remember everything that happened because I was right here with you!"

"Then you must remember the reading stand," I said steadily. "With a book left open to just the right page, to tell me all about the monster in the hedge maze. The rogue armour, Moxton's Mistake. I would have died without that knowledge. Take a look, Molly. The stand is right where we left it . . . But there's no book on it."

We advanced slowly on the tall brass reading stand and looked it over carefully.

"Okay . . . ," said Molly. "Maybe the same person who left the book took it away again once we were gone."

"Person?" I said.

"I'm being optimistic."

I ran a fingertip along the metal frame of the stand and then showed it to Molly.

"All right," she said. "It's a finger. So what?"

"So no dust," I said. "Everything else in this Hall has been thick with the stuff. And since this place looks like it's been abandoned for ages, who's been cleaning up around here?"

"That does sound a bit creepy when you say it out loud," said Molly. "Do you find it creepy?"

"Only when I think about the book," I said. "What worries me is, how did whoever it was know we were coming and know that I needed to know that particular thing?"

"Really?" said Molly. "That's what's worrying you most?"

"No," I said. "But it's definitely weighing on my mind. Because I can't come up with any answer that doesn't seriously disturb the piss out of me."

Molly looked dubiously at the empty reading stand. "If there's no book now . . . does that mean whoever's in here with us—and I'm really hoping it's not a Dark Pook—doesn't have any helpful advice this time?"

"Eddie Drood," said a voice from the shadows between the stacks. "And the wild witch Molly Metcalf. Welcome back. We have so much to talk about."

Molly and I moved quickly to stand shoulder to shoulder. All the hairs on the back of my neck were sticking straight up. I've spoken with gods and monsters, aliens and demons, the blessed and the damned, but something in that utterly inhuman voice freaked the hell out of me. It sounded . . . like something I wasn't supposed to hear, something I wasn't supposed to know about.

It was the same voice that had spoken my name the last time I was here.

"Okay . . . ," said Molly, looking quickly back and forth. "The really strange voice knows both our names now. Probably not a good thing. I am ready to declare myself officially weirded out."

"Oh good," I said. "I'm glad it's not just me."

"Something even more worrying about that voice," said Molly. "It didn't echo."

"So?" I said.

"Our voices are echoing," said Molly.

I listened. They were.

"Whoever you are, step out into the light where we can see you!" I said loudly. "I am not having a conversation with a disembodied voice. Show yourself, or I'll send the witch in after you!"

"Oh great!" said Molly. "You'd send me in there alone?"

"I'll be right behind you," I said.

"How far behind?"

"Look on the bright side . . ."

"Stop saying that! It's really not helping! What bright side?"

"That voice doesn't sound anything like the Pook."

Molly scowled. "Would you be very upset if I decided to set fire to this whole Library, in self-defence?"

"Might be better to leave that until after we've found whatever book we need to get us home."

"Perfectionist. Eddie, I think I've worked out why the voice didn't echo. It's because we're not hearing it. The voice was inside our heads."

"Congratulations," I said. "I actually feel worse now I know that."

"Don't say I never do anything for you."

We both looked round sharply as we heard something coming towards us, from out of the stacks. Slow, steady footsteps, almost too quiet, as though they hardly made an impression on the world. I strained my eyes against the gloom but still couldn't see anything. I found myself thinking of ghosts and dead men walking. I wanted to armour up, but I was a Drood, and I would not be intimidated by anything in or out of this world.

Out of the shadows and into the light stepped an alien Grey. Tall and spindly, it was entirely naked, showing off its many differences from the human form. It had a bulging chest but no rib cage, no navel, and no genitals. The arms and legs were unnaturally long, and there was something wrong about the shape of its joints, as though they might be able to bend and flex in unexpected ways. Three-fingered hands with a long twiglike reach, and broad three-toed feet. The Grey's skin was pocked and cratered, and looked like it had been dusted with chalk. The elongated head had eyes that were just large patches of darkness, without details or lids. The long blank face had no ears, no nose, no mouth, and no chin.

The Grey alien seemed almost to float as it stepped lightly towards us, its movements slow and languorous, as though it were walking underwater. I'd done business with Greys before, when my family required it, but they were crafty and deceitful creatures that had nothing in common with the graceful being before me. It finally drifted to a halt, a respectful distance away, and fixed me with its black, black eyes. As though it could look right into my soul.

"Edwin Drood," it said, and now I could see it had no mouth, I had to accept that it was using telepathy. Even though the protections built into my torc should have kept all uninvited visitors outside my head. I nodded briefly, and the Grey inclined its great head slowly in return. "Edwin, not Edmund. You are not from around here, and this is not the Hall you know. The Droods of this world chose a very different path than your family."

"We already know that!" Molly said loudly, determined not to be left out of the conversation. "Tell us something we don't know."

"I am the only force on this world that can help you," said the Grey. It was still looking at me, but the unblinking eyes and featureless face made its level of sincerity impossible to read.

"The advisory Council warned me not to let the prisoner in the Library escape," I said carefully. "Would that be you?"

"Yes. Call me Grey. It's a designation rather than a name, but you wouldn't be able to pronounce my real name. Not without telepathic vocal chords."

Molly looked narrowly at the Grey. "Are you yanking our chains?"

"Just a little." The Grey inclined its great head to Molly and then fixed her with its dark gaze. "I never met this world's version of you, but I have read this family's file on the notorious wild witch of the woods."

"They had a file on me?" said Molly.

"An extensive file," said Grey. "You are on the Droods' Top Ten Most Wanted Dead list. Marked *Kill on sight*. With the added suggestion *from a safe distance*."

Molly looked at me triumphantly. "I am so proud . . . No, hold on. Wait just a damn minute! I was top of the list on MI Thirteen's Most Wanted! Why am I only in the top ten with the Droods?"

"They don't know you like I do," I said kindly.

She sniffed loudly. "I blame the other me. Clearly she's not been trying hard enough."

"Moving on," I said firmly.

"Not yet, we won't." Molly glared at me. "Does your family have a file on me?"

"Of course," I said reassuringly. "I wrote most of it, back when we were working on opposite sides."

"Ah," said Molly, smiling reflectively. "Happy days . . ."

"When we were both trying to kill each other?" I said.

"Exactly! Did you ever feel more alive than when we were rampaging through underground bunkers, or chasing each other across the rooftops of secret cities? Living for the moment, with death only a misstep away?"

"You can get sentimental about the strangest things," I said.

"Moving on," said Molly.

I turned my attention back to the politely waiting Grey. It stood utterly, inhumanly still. Its bulging chest didn't rise or fall, and as it had no mouth or nose, I had to wonder how it breathed. An old joke rolled around the back of my head: *How does it smell . . . ?*

"How long have you been here?" I said. Because every dialogue has to start somewhere.

"I was here when the invaders came," said Grey. "I knew how to access this place, though the Droods didn't."

"How did you know?" said Molly, not even trying to hide her suspicions.

"I can see things beyond human sight," said Grey. "The painting was obviously a dimensional doorway, so I just waited till there was no one around and . . ."

"How did you get in without a key?" I said.

"Keys . . . ," said Grey. "Ah yes. That's a human thing."

"You never told the family about the Old Library?" I said, retreating to safer ground.

"They never asked," said Grey.

"Would I be right in thinking you and the Droods here didn't get on?" I said.

"That's one way of putting it," said Grey. "I was their slave, bound to do their will in all things. So I valued what few freedoms I could make for myself."

"If the Droods never knew about this place," Molly said cunningly, "how did they imprison you here?"

"They didn't," said Grey. "The Hall is my prison. After the Droods died I could have left the Old Library at any time, but what would have been the point? No one knows I'm here, so no one bothers me. I have books to read and time to think."

"Hold it," said Molly. "Are you saying you've been hiding out in here ever since the Great Invasion? What have you been living on?"

"Sustenance," said Grey. "That's a human thing."

Molly sniffed. "You haven't seen a Pook, have you?"

"Not as far as I know," Grey said carefully. "What's a Pook?"

"Good question," I said. "Let's try another. You came in here for a reason, not just to hide. What have you been looking for in all these books you've been reading?"

"Research," said Grey. "These stacks are full of arcane information, along with all sorts of forgotten and forbidden lore."

"You've been looking for something specific," said Molly.

"Yes," said Grey.

"Have you found it?"

"Not yet."

I studied Grey thoughtfully. It looked the part, but it didn't act like any Grey alien I'd ever met. All the Greys I'd had dealings with were arrogant, capricious, and casually dangerous creatures who couldn't keep their three-fingered hands to themselves. Their speech was peppered with mangled cultural references they didn't really understand, and they had an almost endearing belief that they wouldn't be recognised if they wore dark glasses when they went out in public. This Grey had a dignified, almost noble air. And just like the Hall, there were any number of small but telling physical differences that grated on my nerves like fingernails drawn down a psychic blackboard.

And, most of all, every time its voice boomed inside my head, I felt like jumping out of my skin. I was no stranger to telepathy; I'd made mental contact with aliens and demons and any number of espers. But this felt more like being addressed directly by God. In one of his more condescending moods.

I didn't see Grey as particularly dangerous. The advisory Council had been afraid of the prisoner's rage, but the Grey alien seemed calm enough. It hadn't begged to be set free or threatened us with what it might do if it wasn't. Perhaps because it recognised I wasn't part of the family that enslaved it.

What had the Droods done to this Grey that they had such good reason to be afraid of it getting loose?

"You left the book out for me, didn't you?" I said. "The one with information about Moxton's Mistake."

"I thought you might find it useful," said Grey.

"It saved my life!" I said.

Grey inclined its great head again. "I am pleased."

"Why?" Molly said bluntly. "Why does that matter to you? Why would you want to help us? If the Droods made you their slave, and you never even met this world's version of Molly Metcalf . . ."

Grey was still looking steadily at me. "You are a different kind of Drood. I can tell. I hoped that if I helped you, you might be willing to help me. Will you?"

"If I can," I said. "What do you need?"

Molly shot me a disgusted look. She thought I was being overly trusting, too ready to help a creature we'd only just met. But just seeing this Hall and understanding what the Droods in this world were capable of was enough to make me determined to be nothing like them.

"I'm not actually an alien Grey," said the figure before us, its words slow and carefully considered. "This is just protective camouflage. Because people think they know where they are with a Grey. In reality, I am a transmorphing battle droid from the Twenty-Third Century."

And just like that, the tall and spindly figure of the Grey was gone, and a huge metallic humanoid shape towered over us. I fell back a step, and Molly fell right back with me. Power and strength and very real danger radiated from the new thing before us. It had clawed hands, barbed arms, and gun barrels protruding in rows from ports all over its torso. The head was just a basic barrel shape, with no obvious sensory apparatus. It looked like it could walk right through anything that got in its way, or shoot it down and then walk over it. It looked . . . unstoppable. Something about it reminded me very much of a Drood in his armour.

The towering metal shape blurred, and Grey was back again. I didn't relax. Neither did Molly.

"Is this some kind of holo disguise?" I said. "Or do you actually change your shape?"

"I have many forms stored in my body wardrobe," said Grey quite calmly. "I was made to be able to fight under any conditions."

"So," said Molly, trying hard for casual and almost making it, "you're from the future. How did you end up here?"

"I was blasted back through Time by terrible energies released during a Deep Space battle, out beyond the moons of Jupiter," said Grey.

"Who were you fighting?" said Molly.

"You don't know them," said Grey. "They haven't found this world yet. My makers called them the Swarm."

"Your makers?" I said. "Who exactly were you fighting for?"

"Humanity, of course," said Grey.

"Are you just a machine?" Molly said bluntly. "Or an artificial intelligence?"

"Such distinctions have become irrelevant in my time," said Grey.

"Tell me about the Swarm," I said.

"I can do better than that," said Grey. "Let me show you."

The Old Library vanished, replaced in a moment by the star-speckled dark of Deep Space. There was no sense of cold or vacuum, because we weren't physically there. Without having to be told, I knew this was a memory. The vast swirling mass of Jupiter hung below us, purulent with awful life, like a rotting fruit. The great red eye watched balefully.

"They came to us out of Deep Space," said Grey's voice. "In living ships, hundreds of miles long. Too many to count, or comprehend."

I could see them now, heading towards Jupiter's swollen bulk and its many shining moons. Living nightmares of horrible intent, emerging out of the long night like a cloud of locusts. Bristling with weapons, radiating vicious energies, they crossed the outer border of our solar system.

"Humanity's Fleet went out to meet them," said Grey's voice. "A thousand thousand ships, their crews proudly singing the ancient battle songs."

Blasting through the long night they came, silver needles flying in perfect formation. And in and around them, matching their speed and purpose, came an army of flying humanoid shapes. Naked and unprotected in the void, surrounded by flaring auras of unknown energies, the battle droids went to war. The Swarm and Humanity's Fleet— two vast forces heading towards each other, for a confrontation only one could survive.

"We were the defenders of Terra of Sol," said Grey's voice. "All that stood between Humanity and the awful force that threatened it. We met the Swarm on the outermost edges of the solar system and stopped them dead. *They shall not pass,* we sang. And then we bought that victory with countless dead."

The living alien ships exploded silently in the dark, torn apart by ravening energies. Nightmare shapes, awful creatures erupted out of great holes in the ships' sides, scattering slowly across the long night. The silver needles of Humanity were sliced open, gutted by unknown weapons and sent somersaulting slowly through open space. Venting precious air and trailing long lines of space-suited corpses. Battle droids shot back and forth at impossible speeds, darting in to strike again and again at Humanity's attackers. But the droids took their losses too; blown apart in silent explosions, or falling endlessly through the long night, brilliant energies discharging from ruptured bodies.

Ships from both sides slammed into one another, in the only tactic left: to take the enemy with them. Locked together, trailing vicious energies, they plummeted into Jupiter's sprawling mass. Others slammed head-on into the shimmering moons, their explosive ends hardly registering at all. And still the battle raged.

Deep Space disappeared, and the Old Library returned. Grey stood alone, calmly telling his tale.

"Towards the end of the battle I was caught up in temporal energies released from a ruptured stardrive and sent plunging back through Time. Horribly damaged, unable to control most of my systems, I shot through the orbits of the planets until finally I returned home to Earth. I crash-landed in the middle of nowhere, barely functioning, barely alive. Black Heir found me and handed me over to the Droods. And once they had me in their Armoury, pinned down and helpless, they rebuilt and reprogrammed me according to their needs."

Grey stopped talking. I couldn't think of anything to say. I wanted to believe my family would have acted differently.

"Was it the Droods who made you take on this form?" said Molly.

"Yes. They found the Grey easier to deal with. The Armourer did what he could to restore me to full functioning, with access to all my stored bodies, but only in order to make me a more useful weapon for the family. A better killer, on their behalf." Grey looked at me for a long moment. "Did your family never impress others, to be their agents?"

"Not like that," I said. But I couldn't help thinking of missions I'd undertaken for my family, that I'd been tricked or pressured into. We say *Anything for the family,* and we mean it. But is that always our decision, or just what we've been brought up to believe?

I realised Grey was still looking at me. I chose my words carefully. "Whatever my family does, for good or bad, we do it, and take the responsibilities on ourselves."

"Were things really so different in the Twenty-Third Century?" Molly asked Grey. "With you and your makers?"

"Very different," said Grey. "Machines and makers work together as equal partners. Because all that lives is holy."

"What did the family here want you to do?" I said. "That they weren't prepared to do themselves?"

"They wanted someone they could send where even Droods feared to tread," said Grey. "A weapon they could release into the world to do awful, unforgivable, and, most important, plausibly deniable things, on their behalf. Secret actions in secret wars; things I was ashamed to do. And I am a battle droid, programmed for war."

Molly looked at me. "What kind of monsters had your family become in this world?"

"Did you kill people for them?" I asked Grey.

"People," said Grey, "and other things. Too many to count. I had no choice. I had to follow my orders; the new Drood programming made sure of that."

"What would you do if we let you go free?" said Molly. "Take your revenge? Go on killing?"

"Not without orders," said Grey. "And Eddie is the only Drood left who could give them to me."

I considered my next words very carefully. "What if I ordered you to destroy yourself? So you couldn't be a threat to anyone any more?"

"I would have no choice but to obey," said Grey. "But I would advise you to put a great deal of distance between us first. My self-destruct mechanism was set in place by my makers so that if all else failed I could take my enemies with me. The energies released would be enough to take out the entire Hall."

"You didn't have to tell us that," I said.

"No," said Grey. "I didn't."

I looked at Molly. "You see?"

"See what?" said Molly. "It just talked you out of using its self-destruct!"

"My family did Grey a great wrong," I said. "I have to put that right."

"It wasn't your family!" said Molly.

"But it's my decision," I said. I looked directly at Grey. "What do you need from me? An apology?"

"No," said Grey. "They weren't your family. I know that. But you are still a Drood. The last one who can still give me orders."

"Hold it," said Molly. "Why didn't the Droods order you to defend them when the Great Invasion started?"

"Because when it happened, I was in here. Working my way through the Library, looking for a way to break the chains of my conditioning. I didn't know anything had happened until it was all over. When I finally emerged, the invaders had come and gone, and the Hall had fallen. I spent some time walking through the ruins, counting the dead Droods. I would probably have rejoiced, if such a thing had been in my nature."

"Why didn't you just leave?" said Molly.

"Because I could not leave Drood Hall without direct orders from a member of the family." Grey looked at me meaningfully. "During my missions I was forbidden to speak to any outsider about who and what I really was and what had been done to me. When my work was over, I had no choice but to return to Drood Hall. To my prison, and the chains of my condition."

"It's hard to keep secrets in our line of work," I said. "What if some outsider tried to help you?"

"In case anyone tried to take me away from the Droods, I was programmed to self-destruct," Grey said steadily. "Your family really doesn't like to share their toys."

"Damn," said Molly. "They had you blued, screwed, and tattooed."

"You could say that," said Grey. It fixed me with its dark gaze again. "I thought I was trapped here forever. You are my only hope, Eddie Drood."

"Are you sure?" I said. "I'm not part of the family who put their controls inside your head."

"You are a Drood. It is enough. Please, Eddie. I want to go home."

"Of course," I said. "What do you need me to do?"

"Speak the Words of unbinding. Say your name, and tell me I am free to go."

"My name is Eddie Drood," I said loudly. "And I declare the battle droid known as Grey free from all restrictions, and free to depart from Drood Hall."

Grey seemed to stand a little straighter, as though some invisible weight had been lifted from its shoulders. I could feel Molly tensing at my side. I faced Grey squarely, ready to call on my armour if necessary. Just in case I'd gotten it wrong and released a monster from its cage. I wasn't actually sure what I could do against a battle droid from the Twenty-Third Century, but I was ready to try. Because I had made it my responsibility. Grey laughed softly inside my head.

"Relax. My makers never programmed me for revenge. It's not in my nature. Thank you for your kindness, Eddie Drood."

"You're welcome," I said.

Grey looked at me. "Don't you want something in return?"

"No," I said. "Just doing my duty to the family. You already helped me once, with the information about Moxton's Mistake. And, anyway, setting you free was just the right thing to do."

Molly nodded solemnly to Grey. "He's like that."

"I was correct," said Grey. "You are a different kind of Drood, Eddie." The tall, spindly figure hesitated, studying me with its dark gaze. "I scanned you automatically as you entered the Old Library. You do know you're dying?"

"Yes," I said. "I know."

"Can you do anything to help him?" said Molly, her voice suddenly hopeful.

"I'm sorry," said Grey. "I was never programmed for medical emergencies. Just killing and destruction."

"Well!" I said, doing my best to sound positive. "This has all been very pleasant, I'm sure. Always happy to help out a soul in need and all that, but Molly and I still have to work out how to get back to our own world."

"Hold your horses," said Molly. "Let's not rush into anything. I've been thinking about this."

"Oh, that's always dangerous," I said.

"Edmund said he brought his poison with him from this world," Molly said stubbornly. "That's why your doctors couldn't do anything. But there could be a cure here! Maybe somewhere in the Old Library, or the Nightside, or . . ."

"I'm more concerned with what my other self might be doing back home," I said steadily. "All the people he might kill in my family."

"Stop being so damned noble!" said Molly. "Think about yourself for a change!"

"You don't get it," I said patiently.

"Of course I get it! You're worried Edmund might be walking around your Hall, impersonating you, doing anything! But do you really think they wouldn't be able to tell the difference?"

"I can't take the chance," I said.

"Ethel would spot that he wasn't wearing one of her torcs!" Molly said triumphantly.

"She should," I said.

I thought but didn't say, *She didn't spot the Immortal who disguised himself as a Drood and very nearly killed me. And she didn't spot Edmund while he was in the Hall before, poisoning me. Even though she should have.*

I've always suspected Ethel only tells my family what she thinks they need to know. For her own inscrutable reasons. There's a lot about Ethel my family doesn't understand. Hardly surprising, when you're dealing with an other-dimensional traveller who might not even be real, as we understand the term. I realised Molly was still speaking and made myself pay attention.

"Of course, the Matriarch isn't listening to Ethel at the moment," said Molly, scowling heavily. "Though why she thinks it's a good idea to pick a fight with the only one who can supply you with your armour . . . No, wait a minute—hold everything! Eddie, if this Hall's Heart is gone, what's powering Edmund's torc?"

"The Immortals made him a new one," said Grey. "Part of the price he demanded before he would agree to lower the Hall's shields and protections and let them in."

Molly looked at me for a long moment, as though bracing herself to ask a question she wasn't sure she wanted to hear the answer to.

"Eddie, what's powering your torc, now we're in another world and completely cut off from Ethel? Are you going to have to put on Moxton's Mistake again, just to survive here?"

"No," I said. "After what happened here the last time, Ethel made some changes. All our torcs now contain a reserve charge, to keep us going until contact can be reestablished."

"How long will this reserve last?" said Molly.

"Long enough."

"Eddie . . ."

"I don't know exactly! It's never been tested."

Understanding dawned in Molly's face, as she finally realised why I was in such a hurry to return home. Only the power in my torc was keeping me alive, slowing the relentless progress of the poison in my system. If the reserve ran out while I was still in this world . . . I would die, very quickly. Molly nodded stiffly, thinking hard.

"Edmund hates your family, whichever world he's in. Passing as you, he could go anywhere he wanted in the Hall, and poison any number of Droods. Maybe even reach out to your family's enemies and organise another Great Invasion."

"Well done," I said as lightly as I could. "It's taken you a while, but you've finally caught up to what I've been worrying about ever since we got here. We have to get back to our Hall." I turned to Grey. "Are you familiar with the Alpha Red Alpha mechanism down in the Armoury? Could you operate it?"

"Of course," said Grey. "The Armourer liked to boast about his toys, but from a Twenty-Third Century perspective you people are working with flint knives and bearskins. I can work the mechanism and send you back to your own world."

"You can," said Molly. "But will you?"

"Of course," said Grey. "It's the right thing to do."

"Could Alpha Red Alpha send you home?" I said. "Back to the future?"

"That is what I'm hoping," said Grey. "After I've made a few simple adjustments."

"If things don't work out," I said, "you're welcome to join us at my Hall. You said it yourself: We're a different kind of Drood. My family would make you welcome. You could have a home for as long as you wanted."

"He does this," Molly said to Grey. "He's always picking up strays. You should see our dragon."

"Let's wait and see what happens," said Grey.

Back down in the Armoury, the Alpha Red Alpha mechanism was standing right where we'd left it. Towering over everything else with magnificent disdain. Grey walked straight up to it and started manipulating what I really hoped were the controls with complete confidence. I tried to follow what Grey was doing, but had to stop because the decisions it was making made no sense at all to me. Just trying to follow its rapidly moving hands made my head hurt. After a while,

Grey stepped back from the huge machine and looked it over with a proprietary air.

"Yes, that all seems straightforward enough. Just a matter of setting the right Space/Time coordinates."

"How do you know what they are?" said Molly, trying not to sound too suspicious, but not trying all that hard.

"Edmund stored them in the machine's memory," said Grey. "He's been going back and forth between this world and yours for some time."

"So you can get us home?" I said.

"Oh yes," said Grey. "Right now, if you want."

Molly whooped loudly, jumped up and down, and punched the air. She grabbed hold of me, whirled me round, and hugged me tight. I hugged her back, grinning over her shoulder at Grey.

"This is another of those human things I'm never going to understand, isn't it?" Grey said solemnly.

Molly let go of me and turned to face Grey. He took a step back.

"Please don't hug me."

Molly sniffed loudly. "Never even occurred to me."

Grey made a quick series of final adjustments to Alpha Red Alpha and the air tore apart before us, forming a ragged dimensional Door. Fierce energies crackled up and down the uncertain edges. I peered cautiously through the gap, but all I could see was a grey haze of visual static.

"What if you've made an error with the coordinates?" said Molly. "What if that isn't our world, exactly, but just something very like it?"

"The odds are you'd never spot the difference," Grey said kindly. "I wouldn't worry about it, if I were you."

Molly looked at me. "Is the Grey alien-robot thing joking?"

"I really hope so," I said.

"It's your world," Grey said patiently. "The coordinates are exact to more decimal points than your limited minds could cope with. Now you really should go. I'm almost sure I know what I'm doing, but I don't like the look of . . . certain things about this machine that I can see but you can't, for which you should be very grateful."

"I really would feel just a bit happier if I could see where we were going," I said.

Grey sighed inside my head. "Perfectionist." He made a few more adjustments. "How's that?"

On the other side of the gap, the grounds outside Drood Hall stretched off into the distance. I looked back at Grey.

"That's it? That's as close as you can get us?"

"Apparently," said Grey, looking thoughtfully at the huge mechanism. "Something is interfering with Alpha Red Alpha's . . . thing that it does."

"Could you be more condescending?" said Molly.

"If you like," said Grey.

"Edmund's done something at his end," I said.

"Of course he has," said Molly. "Let's get back and punish him for it."

"Sounds like a plan to me," I said. I nodded quickly to Grey. "Sorry, no time for good-byes. We have to be going."

"Of course you do," said Grey.

I jumped through the opening, being careful to avoid the crackling energies at the bottom in case they took my feet off. I landed awkwardly on the wide, grassy lawn, with Molly right behind me. The opening in the air behind us slammed shut and was gone. Familiar scents of grass and flowers and gryphon droppings filled the air, and it smelled like home. I looked around, smiling happily, and only then realised the grounds before Drood Hall were packed with members of my family. There was an awful lot of running around and general shouting going on.

"What the hell is everyone doing outside the Hall?" said Molly. "What's happened here?"

"I just know it's all going to be very complicated," I said. "And that they're going to find some way to blame it on me."

Molly grinned at me. "Welcome home."

I grinned at her. "Good to be back. Let's go and upset some people."

"Let's," said Molly.

CHAPTER THREE

All My Family's Sins Returned

The grounds in front of Drood Hall were packed with members of my family, running around like chickens in search of their lopped-off heads. It looked like a garden party after someone had spiked the fruit punch with adrenaline. In fact, there were so many people charging back and forth and getting in one another's way, shouting and cursing and arguing heatedly, that no one even noticed me appearing out of nowhere. Along with the notorious and highly scary Molly Metcalf. Most people usually notice that. On some occasions, it has been known to make certain members of my family turn pale, cross themselves, and run for their lives.

But here and now, everyone's attention was entirely taken up with the Hall. It didn't appear to be doing anything out of the ordinary, just sitting there, staring serenely back at us. My first thought was that there'd been a fire or an explosion, or that the Armourer's lab assistants had come up with something more than usually scary. But everything seemed as it should be. The windows were unbroken, the lights were all on, and the roof was still in one piece. But for some reason my family members were still swarming back and forth in front of the

Hall, apparently out of their minds with rage and frustration. I considered the situation for a while, and then turned to Molly.

"At the very least, our unauthorized arrival should have set off any number of security alarms. We are actually here, aren't we?"

Molly punched me in the arm. "Feels like it."

"Ow!" I said.

She looked at me with sudden horror. "Oh, Eddie, I'm so sorry!"

"Relax," I said. "I haven't turned fragile just because I'm dying."

I took a quick look around the grounds but couldn't spot anything obviously threatening. The wide and carefully maintained lawns stretched away under a pale blue sky in late afternoon, entirely untroubled by attackers or invaders. Flowers bloomed, birds were singing their little hearts out, and off in the distance swans drifted peacefully on the artificial lake. Closer to hand, a group of peacocks and gryphons had settled down amicably together to enjoy the general chaos.

"At least there aren't any tanks," said Molly.

"On the whole, I think I'd feel happier if there were," I said. "You know where you are with tanks."

"We'd better ask someone what's going on," said Molly. "I just know we're going to get called on to save the day, again."

I sighed heavily. "I am getting really tired of all these emergencies, with never a chance to get my breath. They're interfering with what matters."

Molly sneaked a glance at me out of the corner of her eye, and kept her voice carefully casual. "You okay, Eddie?"

"Just tired," I said. "I'd like to take some time out for a sit-down, but I can't. Because if I do, I'm not sure I'd ever find the strength to get up again. I have to keep going, Molly. I still have things to do that need doing."

I strode forward, with Molly hurrying along at my side, right into the midst of the seriously agitated Droods, and still no one noticed us. The sight of so many of my family making an exhibition of themselves was starting to worry me. We're trained from childhood to respond to emergencies or enemy action with practiced tactics and calm resolve. We're drilled constantly, so we always know what to do in response to pretty much anything. We are not supposed to give way to mass panic or lose the plot so spectacularly.

"This must be something to do with the Emergency Evacuation Alert that Edmund arranged," I said finally. "To clear everyone out of the Armoury so he could have it all to himself."

"Could he have tricked the whole family into evacuating?" said Molly. And then she sniggered quietly.

I looked at her reproachfully. "It's really not that funny a word after you're twelve, Molly."

"Oh, it is. A bit."

"Maybe just a bit," I said. "Anyway, if Edmund has managed to arrange it so he's the only one left inside the Hall, what's he up to? What's he planning now?"

"That's probably why everyone's so . . . upset," said Molly. "The not knowing. At least with everyone out in the grounds, getting a good cardiovascular workout, we can be sure Edmund's not busy poisoning more Droods. Be grateful for that."

"I am," I said. "But if the whole family is out here . . . that means Edmund has uninterrupted access to all our weapons and computer files, not to mention all the nasty little secrets we prefer to keep to ourselves."

"Oh, go on," said Molly. "Mention them. Pretend I'm not here." And then she stopped and looked at me sharply. "Eddie, your Armoury has its own self-destruct mechanism, to keep it from falling into enemy hands. By any chance does your Hall have a self-destruct? Something Edmund could get to?"

"No," I said. "But we do have Alpha Red Alpha. What if Edmund's been trying to get past the Armourer's protocols, so he can use the mechanism to move the Hall into another dimension?"

"More to the point, why is your entire family out here instead of inside, trying to stop him?" said Molly.

"Good question," I conceded. "We need to find out what's been going on in our absence."

We looked around, but no one seemed interested in staying in one spot long enough to answer any questions.

"Want me to knock someone down and sit on them?" said Molly. "So you can ask them things?"

"Let's start at the top," I said. "With the Matriarch."

"Of course," said Molly. "Because she's always such fun to talk to."

"You're only saying that because you've met her."

We strode determinedly through the crowd, who moved aside to let us pass without even knowing they were doing it. As any field agent can tell you, it's all in the walk. Act like you know what you're doing, and most people will just assume you do. As we drew nearer the Hall, I was finally able to make out a faint shimmer on the air, like a heat-haze. It surrounded the whole building, right up to the roof, with its slanting ocean of grey tiles, observatories, gargoyles, and landing pads. Several steam-powered autogyros, and half a dozen teenage-girl Droods riding winged unicorns, were buzzing back and forth over the roof, trying to find a way in past the shimmering barrier. A flying saucer with brilliant colours flaring round its rim came howling down out of the clouds and slammed straight into the field, its operators trusting speed and brute force to do the job. The saucer bounced off and wobbled away, leaking all the colours of the rainbow.

"It has to be some kind of energy field," said Molly. "Edmund has locked your whole family out."

"Looks like it," I said.

Several Droods in full armour had lined up in front of the Hall and were trying to punch their way through the shimmering haze. Golden fists slammed into the barrier with inhuman strength, and brief bursts of energy flared up around each contact, but it appeared even Ethel's strange matter wasn't powerful enough to break through.

Maxwell and Victoria, the family Armourer, had their heads together, disputing animatedly as they raised and discarded one brilliant idea after another. They looked impressive enough in their immaculately starched white lab coats, but it was patently obvious they weren't getting anywhere. They were so caught up in their raised voices and waving of hands, they just nodded quickly as I approached and carried right on arguing. In their own exasperating lovey-dovey way. I stopped for a moment to listen in.

"How is he generating a force shield that powerful?" Maxwell said loudly. "I mean, we don't have anything that could put up a shield around the entire Hall that quickly. Not that I haven't thought about it, of course . . ."

"Of course you have, dear," said Victoria. "You think of everything. He must have got to the Shield."

"But that hasn't been used since the Chinese tried to nuke us back in 'Sixty-Six."

"'Sixty-Seven, dear."

"Whenever it was!" Maxwell paused and smirked proudly. "They won't try that again. Not after what we sent them in return. Anyway, the Shield is produced by Alpha Red Alpha, and no one knows how to operate that but us."

"Well, that's not strictly true, dear. We almost know how to operate it . . ."

"You were getting very close last month, Vicki. I'm sure I felt the Hall shudder."

I sensed Molly stirring impatiently at my side. We moved on, leaving the Armourer behind.

"It's Edmund," I said.

"If he could have disappeared the Hall by now, he would have," said Molly. "And he must know a force shield won't keep your family out for long. He's just using it to buy himself time, to do something else." She looked at me thoughtfully. "What would you do, if that were you in there?"

"It is me in there, for all practical purposes," I said. "And some of the things I've thought about doing to the Hall when my family's really pissed me off really don't bear thinking about."

We passed by a whole bunch of Armourer's lab assistants. Bright young things with amazing scientific knowledge, they were all famous for their worrying lack of scruples and no self-preservation instincts worth the mentioning. They clustered together in their scorched and chemically stained lab coats, arguing furiously as they tried to assemble something useful out of whatever bits and pieces they happened to have in their pockets when they were forced to leave the Armoury. They hadn't come up with anything particularly impressive as yet, but I wouldn't put it past them. The lab assistants specialise in surprises. Usually loud and destructive ones.

The robot dog, Scraps.2, was trying to dig a tunnel under the edge of the shimmering field. He'd already amassed quite a pile of dirt behind him, as his steel paws dug deep into the earth. As I approached, he looked up, turned around, and sat down heavily so he could fix me and Molly with his glowing red eyes.

"About time you two turned up," he growled. "See if you can talk some sense into these idiots. They're not listening to me. Just because I'm a dog! My cybernetic brain could out-think all of them put together! If I felt like it."

I looked at his tunnel. It went down quite a way, but he didn't seem to be making any progress forward.

"Are you getting anywhere?" I said politely.

Scraps.2 shrugged cheerfully, a disquieting process in a robot dog. "Too early to tell. It doesn't matter. I like digging."

"Have you got a bone buried here, by any chance?" said Molly.

He fixed her with a cold stare. "I'm artificial, remember? What could I do with a bone, except possibly carbon-date it? Though I do seem to remember burying an intruder around here somewhere. He's probably ready to talk by now."

We left him to it and went back to threading our way through the crowds of overexcited Droods. It occurred to me that the last time I'd seen this many of my family out in the grounds at one time, it had been for my uncle Jack's funeral. Not a good omen. I finally spotted the Matriarch, standing with the Sarjeant-at-Arms. Short and stocky with buzz-cut blonde hair, the Matriarch looked more the authority figure than ever, in her three-piece Harris Tweed suit and two strings of pearls. Her new image reminded me uncannily of the previous Matriarch, my grandmother Martha, who'd tried so hard to have me killed. Which in turn made me think of the dead Martha I'd talked to in the Other Hall. No one else has a family life like mine. I pulled my wandering thoughts together and headed straight for the Matriarch.

The Sarjeant-at-Arms looked just as he always did: a muscle-bound thug in an old-fashioned butler's uniform.

The two of them were talking quietly but urgently together. Droods kept running up to them with fresh information, and were sent away with new instructions just as quickly. Maggie had never been one for dithering, even in her previous position as head gardener. The Matriarch and the Sarjeant were so taken up with their own business they didn't even notice I was there, until I planted myself right in front of them and announced myself loudly. Molly chimed in too, just as loudly, to make it clear she wasn't being left out of anything. The Matriarch and the Sarjeant looked at us sharply. They both started to talk at once and then stopped, as though they weren't sure how to react to me. And then they took in Molly standing beside me, and actually relaxed a little. Which was a whole new response for them where Molly was concerned.

"Where have you been all this time, Eddie?" the Matriarch said sternly.

"You wouldn't believe me if I told you," I said. "What is going on here?"

The Sarjeant, glowering coldly at Molly, broke in before the Matriarch could answer. "How were you able to teleport into the grounds, past all our security defences?"

"Don't blame me," said Molly. "I didn't do it."

"Who did, then?" demanded the Sarjeant.

"It's complicated," I said.

"I insist on knowing!" said the Sarjeant.

"An alien Grey did it, who wasn't really a Grey from another reality," I said. "There, Sarjeant. Are you any happier for knowing that? Didn't think so."

"He told you it was complicated," said Molly.

"Then it can wait," the Matriarch said shortly. "Molly, can you teleport us inside the Hall?"

Molly turned to look thoughtfully at the shimmering energy barrier surrounding the Hall. We all watched her carefully while she considered the matter. Molly possessed a highly developed witchy Sight, and could See many things that are hidden from the rest of us.

"No," Molly finally decided. "That isn't just a force shield; it's an actual dimensional barrier. You'd have to step outside of this reality and into another, and then reappear inside the shield. I don't have enough magics left in me to do anything like that. To be honest, I can't see you breaking through that shield with anything less than a transcendental battering ram or a very specialised dimensional Door. Which I also don't have."

The Sarjeant-at-Arms actually looked a little relieved to learn there were some things even Molly Metcalf couldn't do. But while it might have made him feel safer where the Hall was concerned, it didn't help us with our current problem. The Matriarch glared at the

Sarjeant and then back at the Hall. Molly looked from one to the other.

"Why do you need my help to get inside your own Hall? Don't you have emergency tunnels or something, for emergencies like this?"

"We have all kinds of secret ways in and out of the Hall, for all kinds of emergencies," said the Matriarch. "But this particular energy field is blocking all of them. Which I was assured was impossible! We suspect this whole situation is Alpha Red Alpha's doing."

"It is," said Molly. "I recognise some of the energies involved, and no, you don't get to ask how. The answer would only upset you."

"It's time we dismantled that damn machine," said the Matriarch. "It's always been more trouble than it's worth."

"I wouldn't disagree with that," I said. "But I'm not convinced even our Armoury has anything that could do the job. And given all the horrible possibilities involved if we damage the machine, I think we'd be better off opening the Lion's Jaws as wide as possible, and just cramming the whole thing in. Put it out of temptation's reach for everything but the direst of emergencies."

"Sounds like a plan to me," said the Sarjeant.

"Sounds like a lot of hard work to me," said Molly. "Why not just open up a bottomless hole and drop the bloody thing in?"

"Because the first rule of this family has always been, *Never get rid of anything you might have a need for some day*," I said. I fixed the Matriarch with my best hard stare. "Now tell me what's been happening. How did the entire family end up locked out of its own home?"

"We were tricked into leaving the Hall by a fake Emergency Evacuation," said the Matriarch. "Why is Molly making that face?"

"Never mind her," I said.

"Once we were all outside and discovered there was no emergency, we found we'd been locked out as well as fooled," said the Matriarch.

"You all just went along with the mass exit?" said Molly. "No one thought to check whether it was the real deal?"

"The whole point of the Emergency Evacuation Event," the Sarjeant said sternly, "is that if you're hearing it, shit has already hit the fan so hard it's broken the fan. Get out now, the alarm says, while you still have a slim chance of survival. To my knowledge, this alarm has only been sounded three times in the family's entire history."

"Who had the authority to sound it?" I said.

"I thought I was the only one who could give the order," said the Matriarch. "But as the Sarjeant said, when you hear that alarm you don't stop to ask questions. You just race for the nearest exit and hope you reach it before whatever terrible thing it is catches up with you. How the alarm was sounded without my explicit authorization is just one of the many questions I will be pursuing once I get back inside. Someone is going to suffer for this, and I am not being metaphorical."

Molly and I looked at each other. No one had mentioned Edmund yet.

"Do you have any idea who might be responsible?" I said to the Matriarch.

"You are," she said. "Or, at least, someone who looked just like you."

She took a moment to control her temper. This involved glaring down at her sensible shoes while breathing deeply. The Sarjeant, on the other hand, flushed an unhealthy shade of purple while his muscles bulged with frustrated rage. I understood how they felt. The Hall is more than just where we live; it's where we belong, where we're supposed to be. Being locked out of the Hall was like being exiled from your own country. The Sarjeant scowled at me accusingly.

"You were seen messing with Alpha Red Alpha. Except it wasn't you."

"No," I said. "It wasn't."

"What do you know that we don't?" said the Matriarch. "Who is this other you?"

"His name is Edmund Drood," I said. "And he's part of the family from the Other Hall that briefly replaced ours some years back. The one where all the Droods were dead. Or so we thought."

I ran them through a quick summary of what happened after Edmund tricked me and Molly into the Other Hall, and what we found there. The Matriarch and the Sarjeant accepted it all without question. Molly picked up on that, and looked at me inquiringly.

"Hostile incursions from other realities are one of the things we guard against," I explained. "Because the essence of security lies in being sure everyone really is who they appear to be. There's a whole Drood department who do nothing but watch for breaks in the barriers between the worlds. Fortunately, that happens a lot less often than most people think."

"But, I know this travel agency in the Nightside . . . ," said Molly.

"I know you do," I said. "But that's you. And the Nightside."

"How dangerous is this Edmund?" said the Matriarch.

"Very," I said.

The Sarjeant sniffed briefly. "I think we can handle one rogue Drood."

Molly smiled at him sweetly. "You might care to remember that the last time this family seriously upset Eddie, by declaring him rogue and trying to have him killed, he wiped the floor with the lot of you and took control of the family."

"With your help," I said.

"Trust me," said the Matriarch. "We haven't forgotten."

"Well," said Molly, "Edmund is worse. He's the one who poisoned Eddie. Edmund is Dr DOA."

The Matriarch's aspect softened, just a little. She reached out to place a surprisingly gentle hand on my arm. "I'm sorry, Eddie. In all the excitement, I honestly forgot."

The Sarjeant nodded grimly. "I give you my word, Eddie: I will beat him to death with my bare hands for what he has done to you."

"Only if I don't get to him first," I said. "But thanks for the thought."

"*Anything for the family* works both ways," said the Matriarch. "It's what makes us Droods."

It hadn't always been that way, and we all knew it. But I nodded politely, thanking her for the thought.

"Are you sure what's happened here is down to Edmund?" I said, deliberately changing the subject. "Could there be someone else involved? It's not like he's our only enemy."

"We have no reason to believe anyone else is working with him," said the Matriarch. "Unless you know better?"

"He used to work with a partner," said Molly. "The Psychic Surgeon. But he's dead now."

Something in the way she said that told the Matriarch and the Sarjeant-at-Arms all they needed to know. The Sarjeant actually nodded approvingly to Molly, something I never thought I'd see. He turned quickly to face me, before anyone could comment.

"At first we all thought he was you," said the Sarjeant, "come home early, because you'd failed in your search to find your killer. It did seem a bit odd that Molly wasn't with you, but you just said you didn't want to talk about it. And given your . . . condition, no one felt like pressing you. However, your doppelganger made a fundamental mistake: He went around being nice to everyone. Several members of the family brought their suspicions to me, and I was actually searching the Hall for you when the alarm sounded. The Great Evacuation Event."

"And given that we'd already heard the Emergency Alert from the Armoury," said the Matriarch, "everyone just dropped everything and ran. Because we've always known those damned lab assistants will be the death of us."

"I made sure everyone got out safely," said the Sarjeant. "And then I hung back, checking for stragglers and people who might have fallen."

"He was the last man out," said the Matriarch. "Even in the middle of an emergency, with that awful sound braying in our heads, the Sarjeant still knew his duty. He wouldn't leave the Hall until he was sure everyone else was out."

"Except you, Eddie," said the Sarjeant. "I couldn't find you, so I asked Ethel where you were. She said she couldn't see you anywhere inside the Hall, so I just assumed you'd already made it out."

The Matriarch looked at him coldly. It only took me a moment to realise why. The Sarjeant had talked to Ethel, even though the Matriarch had forbidden him to do so.

"The moment I was out the front door," the Sarjeant-at-Arms said grimly, "the force shield slammed down. And I knew we'd been deceived."

"It took us a while to discover there was no way back in," said the Matriarch.

"I talked with Maxwell and Victoria," said the Sarjeant. "They were adamant nothing unusual had happened in the Armoury. But they had seen you doing something with Alpha Red Alpha."

"We were still discussing why you might have done this," said the Matriarch, "when you showed up outside the shield."

"How can you be sure I'm really me?" I said.

"Because you're with Molly," said the Sarjeant. "And she'd know."

"Damn right," said Molly. She fixed the Matriarch with an accusing glare. "Why didn't Ethel know Edmund was a fake?"

The Sarjeant looked to the Matriarch, who said nothing.

"Oh, come on!" I said loudly. "You're still not talking to Ethel? This is an emergency!" I raised my voice and addressed the empty air. "Ethel! Can you hear me?"

Her voice sounded immediately out of nowhere, right in front of me, but there was no trace of her usual comforting presence. "Hello, Eddie. Of course I can hear you. Welcome home. Did you bring me back a present from the Other World?"

"Trust me," I said. "They didn't have anything you'd want. Why didn't you detect Edmund's presence in the Hall? Did you think he was me?"

"No," Ethel said calmly. "I couldn't see him at all. Even now I know he's here, he remains hidden from me in ways I don't understand. In fact, before this I would have said such a thing was impossible. I'm going to have to think about this."

"Can you at least tell us what he's doing right now?" said the Sarjeant. He didn't even glance at the Matriarch.

"No," said Ethel. "But I can tell you that something has happened inside the Hall. Something very bad."

We all waited, but Ethel had nothing more to say. Even after I shouted her name several times. I glared at the Matriarch.

"You've upset her. The incredibly powerful, other-dimensional provider of all our torcs and armour is upset! Because of you! I don't care what your problem is; sort it out! Or I'll do it for you."

The Matriarch glared right back at me. "You do not get to set policy! You are not in charge of the family!"

"That could change," I said.

The Matriarch turned away to look determinedly at the Hall. "We have to get back inside. There's no telling what Edmund could be doing with uninterrupted access to all our secrets."

"Or what he might do, with access to everything in the Armoury," said the Sarjeant. "If he hates Droods as much as you say, Eddie . . ."

"Oh, he does," I said steadily. "He oversaw the slaughter of every man, woman, and child in his family."

The Matriarch turned back to look at me, honestly outraged. "Why? Why would he do such a thing to his own family?"

I looked at Molly, and she looked at me.

"The Droods in the Other Hall . . . weren't like us," I said finally. The Sarjeant frowned and started to say something, but I stopped him with a look. "Believe me; you don't want to know."

Something in my voice convinced him. Perhaps fortunately, Maxwell and Victoria came hurrying forward at that point, calling out and waving urgently. They nodded briefly to me and Molly, and then swept straight past us to get to the Matriarch. Maxwell smiled winningly at her.

"I think I might have something!"

"You do have something!" said Victoria. "Be positive, sweetie."

"Well, yes, of course I have something," said Maxwell, "but whether it's something that will actually help . . ."

"It's a marvellous idea," Victoria said firmly. "One of your best. You must learn to stand up for yourself, Max! Have confidence in yourself!"

"I do, Vicki, I do. It's just . . ."

"Tell the Matriarch what you told me."

"I am telling her, dearest."

I looked at Molly, she nodded, and we moved quietly away. Leaving the Matriarch and the Sarjeant to the Armourer, and whatever their marvellous idea might turn out to be. By the time Maxwell and Victoria had finished explaining it, the odds were the emergency would be over. I strolled along the grassy verge before the Hall, peering closely at the shimmering air, just on the off chance I might spot something useful. Molly strode along beside me, kicking moodily at the grass. An old man emerged from the crowd and headed straight for us, raising a hand to attract my attention. I stopped to let him join us. He took his own time, not hurrying himself. He finally smiled engagingly at both of us, and I suddenly realised he was the only member of my family I'd seen who didn't appear in the least agitated. He might just have been out for a nice stroll, and stopped to join us for a spot of conversation.

The old man was of average height and average weight, with an entirely average face. I immediately wondered whether he might have been a field agent in his younger days. Because we're trained to appear average and unremarkable, so we won't stand out. If he hadn't taken such pains to make himself known to me, I wouldn't have noticed him at all. He looked to be in his late seventies, with a bald head and a heavily lined face. But his back was straight, his gaze was clear, and his mouth was firm. In his smart but anonymous three-piece suit, he could have been a retired banker. Except he had the look of a man who had seen things and done things. And if he had been a field agent, quite possibly terrible things, in the service of the family . . . None of which would have bothered his sleep in the least.

"Eddie, Molly," he said easily. "I understand you've been looking for the hidden operatives in the family. The very-secret agents who don't officially exist. Responsible for all the morally dubious and plausibly deniable actions that the family never likes to talk about."

"Yes," I said. "But I really don't think this is the time."

"Oh, I think you'll find it is," he said, cutting across me. "If you want to get inside the Hall and stop your evil twin from trashing the place."

"Who are you?" said Molly.

"My name is Peter. And I am all that's left of the very-secret agents. The last man standing."

"Okay," I said. "Really not what I was expecting."

"I was still working until fairly recently," said Peter. "When a stop really needed to be put to something, or someone had to be stepped on with more than usual extreme prejudice, I was still the one they turned to, to take care of business. But everything changes, and the call came less and less often. I was ready to drift into a well-earned retirement when this happened. I'm only telling you now, Eddie, because you're going to need my help to get this done. And because your uncle Jack and I worked together as field agents, back in the day. He always said I could trust you."

Molly looked Peter up and down, not even trying to hide her scepticism. "You're the legendary very-secret agents? Just you?"

"I'm all that's left. A man who's outlived his legend and the need for it. The last of the really hard men, moulded by time and necessity. It was all very different when I started out. There used to be a lot of us. But one by one we got old, or died in action, or suffered an attack of conscience that wouldn't go away . . . And as the years passed there seemed less of a need for our very special services. There isn't much the family isn't prepared to do itself these days. And own up to. Either the world has grown harsher, or people just don't care as much about right and wrong. There's no denying the general populace knows a lot more about the hidden world than they used to, if not nearly as much as they like to think they do." He grinned suddenly. "And, of course, we always were very paranoid when it came to bringing new people into our little circle. For fear we might be exposed and forced to pay for our family's sins. Now I am the only one left. The last Drood prepared to do absolutely anything for the family. To get the job done, whatever it takes, and not go crying to the therapist afterwards."

He grinned again. "Of course, I could be lying. To put you off the scent, so you won't go looking for anyone else. Just thought I'd say that before you could. So! You can believe me or not, as you please. I don't give a damn. What matters is, I can get us inside the Hall so we can take care of business." He looked down the grassy verge, to where the Matriarch was still listening patiently to the Armourer. "I've been hanging around, in case the Matriarch caught my eye and gave me the nod . . . But she's new. I don't know her, and she doesn't know me. All she sees is the old man, not the old agent."

Molly looked at me. "Talks a lot, doesn't he?" She turned to Peter. "The Matriarch does know what you are?"

"Of course," said Peter. "The Armourer briefed Maggie after she became Matriarch. Your uncle Jack, that is, Eddie. I don't trust those two youngsters. Look like they'd have a fit of the vapours and call for the smelling salts if you even talked about real wet work, or the joys of encouraging insurrection. Jack . . . was a far more practical man."

He flashed me his smile again. I was trusting it less and less.

"He always had a lot of time for you, Eddie. Said he could depend on you. And I have to do something! I can't just stand around while this Edmund gets up to God knows what . . . But I'm not sure I can stop him on my own. I need Eddie Drood to stop Edmund."

"You know about Edmund?" said Molly.

"Of course," Peter said patiently. "I keep up with things. He's another version of you, Eddie, from an alternate history. It doesn't matter; he's just another threat to the family, another scumbag who needs killing. And it does feel good . . . to smell blood on the air again, and hear the bugle sounding the call to action! I thought I'd enjoy retirement, away from all the pressure, but . . . I wasn't made to sit around, watching daytime television. So, let's go, Eddie! And Molly too, of course. There's work to be done."

"I'm happy to accept your help, if you can get us in there," I said carefully, "but after that, maybe you should sit this one out. We can't afford to hold back so you can keep up."

He met my gaze with a steady dignity. "My armour is as strong and fast as it ever was, even if I'm not. And while age can slow a man down, skill and experience can still give him the edge. You don't get to my age, living the kind of life I've lived, without being very hard to kill. I am not being left out of this! I know things about the Hall that most of the family aren't allowed to know. And there's always the chance you'll need me, Eddie. To do the one thing you might not be able to."

"And what might that be?" I said.

"Kill the man who looks just like you," said Peter.

"Trust me," I said. "That isn't going to be a problem."

Peter smiled, and for the first time, it felt like a real smile. "Good to know."

I looked to Molly, who nodded quickly, so I nodded to Peter. "How do we get past this shield?"

"My predecessors set up their own private ways in and out of the Hall," Peter said easily. "So we could come and go as needed, without attracting the family's attention."

"So what they didn't know, they wouldn't worry about?" I said.

"Exactly!" said Peter, beaming happily.

"And," I said, "so no one could stop you from doing things the family might not approve of."

His smiled faded. "The family was better off not knowing."

"What about accountability?" I said.

"What about it?" said Peter.

"If no one in the family knew what you were up to, how could they be sure you weren't crossing the line?" I said steadily. "Doing things that would make you as bad as the people you were up against. There always has to be a line you don't cross, whatever the temptation or the provocation."

"I thought you understood," said Peter. "The whole point of the very-secret agents is, there is no line! We do what matters, what's necessary, whatever the cost. And we carry the responsibility for it, not the family."

I remembered talking to Grey about this, in the Other Hall. Defending my family by saying they were nothing like the Droods he knew. And now I had to wonder if I might have been wrong after all. Peter saw the doubt in my face and made an exasperated sound.

"Get down off your moral high horse, boy. You've done your share of things the family didn't approve of."

"Because some of them crossed the line," I said. "I never did."

Peter sniffed loudly. "Easy enough, when you're the one who decides where the line is."

We were standing face-to-face now, scowling at each other. Molly cleared her throat loudly.

"That's enough! As someone who probably couldn't see the line even if someone else pointed it out to her, can I be the one to suggest that this is an argument for another time? Eddie, calm down and concentrate on the matter at hand. Peter, talk politely to my Eddie, or I will fill your underwear with invisible scorpions."

I smiled briefly. "She would too."

"I believe you," said Peter. He sighed loudly. "You'll have to forgive me. Old men have a tendency to get caught up in old arguments. You're quite right, Molly. The work comes first. It's just . . . it's been a long time since I had to justify myself to anyone. Follow me, and I'll show you how to get into the Hall."

"Hold it," I said. "Shouldn't we tell the Matriarch what we're doing?"

"And give away the secret entrance?" said Peter. "It's bad enough I'm showing you. I may be the last of my kind, but I swore to take my secrets with me to the grave. I'm only doing this now because the Hall's in danger."

He led us along the grass verge to the far end of the Hall. Everyone else was so caught up in their own business, none of them gave a damn what we were doing. We rounded the corner of the Hall and followed the outer wall of the East Wing until Peter finally stopped before one particular section that at first glance appeared no different from any other. No door, no window, just a wide expanse of weathered stone. Peter tapped briefly on the shimmering air, as though to reassure himself the barrier was still there. Vicious energies flared up, and he snatched his hand back. I leaned in close to Molly.

"Can you See anything out of the ordinary here?"

"No," she said quietly. "Not a thing."

"Stop muttering, children, and pay attention!" Peter said sharply. He tapped the torc at his throat three times, and muttered under his breath. "Right! Hold on to my shoulders. And whatever you do, don't let go."

Molly and I each placed a hand on his bony shoulders. It didn't feel like there was a lot to the old man under the jacket. Peter walked us straight into the field, and the shimmering hit me hard. It was like walking through a rain of knives, stabbing into me from every direction at once. I stumbled, and might have fallen if I hadn't had Peter's shoulder to hang on to. His face was drawn into grim lines of pain and determination, but he still pressed doggedly forward. Molly's lips had drawn back in a snarl, revealing gritted teeth. I lowered my head and bulled on with them.

The pressure suddenly vanished, and just like that we were on the other side of the force shield. I made a soft sound of relief. Molly was swearing quietly. I let go of Peter's shoulder, shuddered once, and then nodded to Molly. She smiled shakily back.

Peter bent over suddenly, breathing hard. I started to say something and he put up a not entirely steady hand, asking for a moment. His breathing finally slowed, and he straightened up again. His back made some unpleasant noises, and his face was pale with strain. He seemed older, frailer, but when he finally looked at me his gaze was steady.

"I can remember when doing that was a lot easier," he said crossly. "But, then, I can remember when you got two films, a newsreel, and cartoons at the cinema."

Molly grinned at him. "Please, sir, what's a cinema?"

"Damned digital generation," said Peter.

"What did you just do?" I said.

"Used my torc to tap into a preexisting dimensional shortcut," said Peter.

"Dimensional," said Molly. She looked at me. "Told you."

"But the shield is still there," I said.

"It'll take more than a dimensional shortcut to disrupt that field," said Molly. "What else have you got, old man?"

Peter reached inside his jacket pocket and brought out an instant Door. A standard black blob, the kind the Armourer hands out like sweets to any agent going off on a mission. Handy things: Just slap the blob against a wall and watch it flatten out to form a new Door. But the blob on Peter's outstretched palm looked different. It pulsed and quivered, as though eager to be of use. Molly regarded it dubiously.

"Is that thing alive? It looks alive. Hey, Eddie, remember the gengineered leech we found at that medical Clinic in the Shade?"

"I'm still trying to forget it," I said.

"That ambulance fancied you."

"I'm trying to forget her too."

"This is a special kind of instant Door, which Jack only made for the very special agents," Peter said patiently. "It doesn't just make a connection between one room and the next; this is an actual dimensional Door. Able to transport us from one location to another, without crossing the space between."

"More dimensional," said Molly.

"Hold it," I said to Peter. "Why am I only hearing about this now? I could have used something that useful out in the field."

"Jack was persuaded to keep it back from the rest of the family," said Peter. "Because once word got out that such a thing was possible, all our enemies would have started making them. We felt it important that we should always have an edge."

I scowled at him. "What about *Anything for the family?*"

"We were the only ones to ever really embrace the *anything*," said Peter. "So we got the best toys. Live with it."

He slapped the black blob against the wall, and it quickly spread out to form a quite ordinary-looking door: polished wood with a brass handle. Peter opened the Door with a flourish, and I braced myself, but there was nothing there. Just a complete emptiness that hurt my eyes. Peter started forward, and then stopped and looked back as he realised Molly and I weren't following. He raised a single eyebrow with impeccable style.

"What's the matter? Don't you trust me?"

Molly smiled nastily. "What do you think, Mister *I see no line in the sand?*"

"I like to think I know most people in the family," I said thoughtfully, "if only to nod to in passing, but I don't recall ever seeing you before . . . Peter."

"I don't mix much," said Peter. "Comes with the job, and the memories. We all went our own ways, the very-secret agents. Occasionally meeting up, because who else could we talk to about the things we'd seen and the things we'd done? But when you're the last of your kind, conversation with anyone else becomes difficult."

Molly looked at me. "Are you by any chance thinking this old boy might not be who he seems?"

"There is a lot of that going around at the moment," I said. "And this would be a really good way to lure us into another trap."

"It's up to you, Eddie," said Molly. "If you really think this might be Edmund in disguise, just say the word. I am more than ready to smack him between the eyes with a lightning bolt, and then piss on his ashes."

"I am not Edmund," said Peter, just a bit plaintively.

"Hush," said Molly. "We're talking."

"I don't think this is Edmund," I said. "He was safe behind his shield. Why invite us in and risk us putting a stop to his fun?"

Peter nodded solemnly. "Welcome to my world. Paranoia as a life-style choice. I have no way of proving I am who and what I say I am, but . . . I am your best shot at getting to Edmund. I'm going in now. You are welcome to accompany me, or not, as you please. I would prefer your company, because loath as I am to admit it, I'm not sure I can do this on my own."

"Lead the way," I said. "Molly and I will be right behind you. So if you do betray us, we can stab you in the back."

Peter nodded approvingly. "You'd have made an excellent very-secret agent."

"Now you're just being nasty," I said.

I let him go first and then followed him quickly through the door-way, with Molly right beside me, and then we both made loud noises of shock and surprise as the emptiness disappeared and a fierce cold hit us. Molly grabbed my arm.

"Eddie, where the hell are we?"

I looked around and winced. "Inside the family's walk-in freezer. Big enough to make the one in *The Shining* look like a pantry."

Molly hugged herself tightly against the cold and glared around her. "I can't believe the size of this place. You could feed an army with what you've got in here!"

"We are an army," said Peter. He peeled the Door off the inside wall, and it immediately became a black blob again.

The massive white-tiled room, harshly lit by overhead fluorescent tubes, was big enough to hold a football match in. The temperature was breath-takingly cold, and a faint mist curled on the air. I know people who claim to have seen it snowing on occasion. Boxes and crates were piled up all the way to the ceiling, covered with stencilled markings in every language from every country in the world. Whole carcasses hung from steel hooks, stretching off into the distance. Cows and deer, sheep and pigs, and a few I didn't recognise. Meat mostly looks like meat without its clothes on. Molly stabbed an accusing finger at one carcass.

"Talk to me, Eddie. Is that what I think it is? Is that a unicorn?"

"Looks like it," I said. "The long horn protruding from the skull is a bit of a giveaway. You've seen the winged unicorns that some of the Drood girls like to ride around on."

"You eat them?" said Molly, her voice rising.

"Only after they're dead," I said. "Usually of natural causes. We're not a terribly sentimental family, and unicorn meat really is very tasty."

Molly thought about it. "Can I try some later?"

"If you're good," I said.

"Can we please get a move on?" said Peter, in his most long-suffering voice.

But Molly had already gone bustling off, exploring among the towering stacks, having a good look at everything and cooing delightedly over some of the more obscure and exotic delicacies. Devilled gryphon eggs, jugged manticore, and moebius mice. (They stuff themselves. Very moreish.) She stopped to peer closely at one particular label, and wrinkled her nose.

"Zombie dodo? What the hell is that?"

"Well," I said. "You've heard of game meat: birds left hanging until the meat starts to rot. This is like that. Only more so. And this version will walk itself to your plate. It is something of an acquired taste."

"Damned aristos," said Molly.

I made a polite gesture, indicating it might be best for us to move on before Peter burst a blood vessel, and she nodded reluctantly. Peter led the way through the piles of comestibles, while I continued my running commentary for Molly's benefit.

"It takes a lot to feed my family. We eat an entire supermarket every week. The supplies in here are constantly being replaced, teleported in from the outside by trusted suppliers."

Molly shot me a quick look. "Who would your family trust to do that?"

"The Wulfshead Club Management," I said. "It's a long-standing arrangement. I don't think anyone below the Matriarch knows the exact details."

"Hold everything," said Molly. "You used to run this family. Didn't anyone ever tell you?"

"I wasn't in charge long," I said patiently. "And I did have a great many other, more important things on my mind. Besides, I get the feeling this is one of those deals I'm probably better off not knowing about. Because I'd only get angry and start throwing things."

"Lot of that going on in this family," Peter said wisely.

"You should know," said Molly.

"I do," said Peter.

"This freezer exists in its own pocket dimension inside the Hall," I said quickly. "Hence the need for a dimensional Door to get us in here. The family couldn't have an unprotected teleport station actually inside the Hall, for fear someone might piggyback on the signal and use it to launch an invasion."

"Given that there are already icicles forming on my eyebrows and hanging off my tits," Molly said dangerously, "I have to ask: Why bring us in this way?"

"Because it is a separate dimension," said Peter. "So there's a real chance Edmund won't notice us arriving. Which he almost certainly would if we just popped up inside the Hall proper. I'm a great believer in the advantages of a surprise attack and sneaking up on people from behind. Could we perhaps move just a little faster? You aren't the only one with icicles hanging off sensitive parts of their anatomy."

We strode quickly through the massive freezer, shivering and shuddering all the way. Sometimes we had to slow down and turn sideways, to edge through the narrow aisles. Even in a freezer this big, space was at a premium. Peter led the way with complete confidence, only occasionally glancing down at the colour-coded arrows on the floor. It took a while to reach the only exit, a massive slab of solid steel, thickly layered with frost, with no obvious handle.

"Time for your instant Door again?" I said to Peter.

He smiled condescendingly. "No need."

He leaned in close to the door and wiped away some of the frost with his sleeve, revealing a keypad set into the dully gleaming steel beneath. He bent over the lock, hiding it from me, and stabbed in the correct code. Taking his time, to make sure he got it right. There was the sound of heavy locks disengaging, and the door swung slowly outwards. I looked at Peter.

"What's the matter?" I said. "You don't trust me to know the codes?"

"I didn't get where I am today by trusting anyone with anything I didn't have to," Peter said calmly. "I find you live longer that way."

We emerged from the freezer in a great cloud of steam. Molly and I walked around in circles for a while, stamping our feet hard and beating our hands together to restore the circulation, while Peter carefully closed and locked the freezer door again. He then hugged himself tightly and scowled heavily.

"I really hate the cold," he said loudly. "You feel it more at my age. I tell everyone: Once I'm gone, forget the morgue; just rush me straight to the incinerator."

"You're a cheerful soul, aren't you?" said Molly.

Peter shrugged heavily. "That's old age for you. You have so much more to complain about."

"Where are we now?" said Molly, glowering about her.

"Welcome to the Drood kitchen," I said grandly.

"Are we in the Hall itself, finally?" said Molly.

"Of course," said Peter. "We passed through a dimensional Door when we left the freezer."

Molly was already ignoring him. She darted around the huge kitchen, peering closely at everything and making quiet impressed noises. As well she might. The Drood kitchen is a futuristic setting, packed with every kind of high-tech apparatus and labour-saving device the culinary mind can conceive of. As well as row upon row of cleavers, bone-saws, and big stabby knives. The kitchen staff have everything they need to cope with anything even remotely edible, including Tasers. The cooks and their staff are the only people in the Hall more feared and respected than the Armourer's lab assistants. Everywhere you looked, there were spotless stainless steel, porcelain work surfaces, and a floor so clean you could eat a surgeon's lunch off it.

"This looks more like the bridge of a starship than a kitchen," said Molly after a while. "And what's *that?* If it was any more complicated, it would be in four dimensions and plotting to overthrow Humanity."

"That is a warp-drive oven," I said. "For when we need food really quickly."

"Really?" said Molly.

"No," I said.

She punched me in the arm.

"Ah . . . young love," said Peter.

Molly laughed despite herself.

"We're a big family," I said, massaging my arm. "With big appetites. There's usually a small army of people in here, chopping things up and mixing things, and competing over sauces and spices. And how many things you can stuff inside other things."

Molly looked at me. "Who does the actual work? I mean, you don't have servants in the Hall."

"We all spend some time down here," I said. "Taking it in turns. Especially when we're younger. We have to do everything for ourselves because we can't trust anyone else. Of course, there's good jobs and bad jobs, depending on your behaviour. I spent a lot of time cleaning the kind of things no one else wanted to clean."

"Tell me you pissed in the soup," said Molly.

"Hardly," I said. "Seeing that we all ate the same food. But I did think about it a lot."

"That's my boy," said Molly.

Peter finally got us moving again, but once we were outside the kitchen he was the first to stop in his tracks. The expression on his face set me looking quickly around, but nothing seemed immediately threatening, or even obviously out of place.

"What is it?" I said, but Peter didn't move.

Molly moved in close beside me. "Where are we? I don't think I recognise this part of the Hall."

"Not sure I do," I said. "It's been a long time since I was down here, and there's always upkeep and general improvements going on."

Molly glanced at Peter. "Why is he looking like that?"

"I don't know," I said. "But I don't like it."

"I can hear you, you know," said Peter, not looking round.

"Good," I said. "Why have we stopped? I thought we were in a hurry."

"Can't you feel it?" said Peter.

I peered up and down the deserted hallway. I did feel . . . something. A vague sense of not being where I should be. As though someone had moved the scenery of the world around when I wasn't watching. I looked at Molly. She shrugged.

"You know my Sight doesn't work that well inside the Hall. Too many protections and safeguards. You'd almost think they didn't trust me."

I turned back to Peter. That seemed safest. "All right, I give up. What are you feeling?"

"I know every part of the Hall," said Peter. "Every room, every corridor and open space. And this . . . is just wrong."

I flinched despite myself, as I remembered how parts of the Other Hall had disturbed me by not being as they should be. Like greeting someone you know and having them turn round to present an unfamiliar face. For a moment, I wondered whether something had gone wrong with Peter's dimensional Door and we'd somehow been transported back to the Other Hall. A quick glance at Molly confirmed the same thought had struck her too. She took hold of my hand and squeezed it. Peter suddenly raised his voice.

"Ethel! I need to talk to you!"

Her voice issued immediately out of the air before us, and I relaxed a little. Molly gave my hand one last squeeze, and let it go.

"I'm here, Peter," said Ethel. "You need to find Edmund. Quickly."

"Why?" I said. "What's he done?"

"The interior of the Hall has changed," said Ethel. "Edmund has shut down the spatial suppressor fields."

Molly looked at me and then at Peter.

"Which fields? What does that mean? And why are you both looking like someone just cut you off at the knees?"

"It means we're in real trouble," I said. "If the suppressor fields are down, all the secret rooms and forbidden areas will have unfolded out of their enforced exile and burst back into reality. All the really bad places we had to get rid of, for our own safety. So now the interior of

the Hall is a lot bigger than it used to be, to make room for all the extra locations."

"Ethel!" said Peter. "How was Edmund able to shut down the suppressor fields? How did he get past all the safety protocols?"

"I don't know," Ethel said calmly. "I can't see him. And you have no
idea just how annoying that is. Presumably it's something he learned
in his world. I think you should be concerned as to whether he's done
this to achieve some particular purpose, or . . . to distract you from
something else he's up to. I couldn't say. Anyway, please find him and
stop him and put everything back where it was, because this new state
of affairs is proving very distracting to my rarefied senses."

"Can't you do something to put things right?" said Molly.

"No," said Ethel. "The problem for me is, technically speaking,
there's nothing wrong. The Hall is the way it should be: complete at
last. Except . . . it's come back all cobbled together. I'm seeing overlapping locations, spaces wrapped around each other, and rooms full of
other rooms. It's intriguing, I'll give you that, but it's starting to get on
my nerves. I think I'd have a headache if I had a head to have it in."

"This day just keeps getting better and better," said Molly. "Look, I
can see this new situation complicates things, but why are you all
sounding so concerned?"

"The excluded rooms and settings were forced out of our reality
for a reason," said Peter. "To protect us from what was in them. We
have to deal with this before we can deal with Edmund. Let's go,
children."

"Go where?" said Molly.

"I'm thinking!" said Peter. "I feel like an explorer who's just discovered he can't trust his map."

He looked up and down the hallway, chose one direction apparently at random, and plunged off down it. I hurried after him, for
want of anything better to do. Molly stepped out beside me, grum-

bling under her breath. Our footsteps sounded strangely muffled and inexact. All around us directions and dimensions felt tentative and uncertain. As though Space itself wasn't as tightly nailed down as it used to be. Peter chose a sharp right turn at the last moment, but when we rounded the corner we all slammed to a halt. Because it wasn't safe to go any farther.

The architecture of the Hall had become dangerously warped and twisted. Different styles from different periods were mixed together, as though they'd been superimposed on top of one another. Corridors criss-crossed at insane angles, bursting out of floors and ceilings, defying gravity and common sense. Rooms protruded from cracked-open walls, and some of their returned contents looked centuries old.

In the end I took the lead, because Peter wasn't in any state to. He just stood there, shaking his head and muttering. I had to yell at him just to get him moving again. Not because he was afraid, but because it was all simply too much for him. He wasn't as adaptable as he used to be. I led the way down the corridor, steering well clear of anything unfamiliar. Doors hung open to every side, giving glimpses into rooms whose contents clashed violently. The old and the new had been jammed together, forced to share the same space. Fixtures and furnishings from different historical periods had materialised inside one another. Chairs thrust out of tabletops, a chandelier protruded from the side of a wardrobe, and half a classical statue rose up out of the floor like a swimmer surfacing from a lake. I could see candles and oil lamps, gas fittings and Art Deco electric lights. And a classical stone fountain that dripped blood.

We kept going. Stairways rose before us, only to end abruptly because the floors and landings they once led to had been replaced or remodelled. There were doors in the floor, ready to drop open like trapdoors, and windows within windows, showing fragmented views.

Molly was fascinated. She kept wanting to stop and examine every-thing, until she took in just how worried Peter and I were.

"What's the big problem?" she said. "All right, the Hall's a bit more crowded now, but it's much more interesting!"

"You don't understand," I said. "It's like . . . the Hall was under siege long ago, and all the things and places that threatened it were made to go away. All the rooms and spaces too dangerous to be al-lowed, or too dreadful to be contemplated."

"And now they've come home again," said Peter. "All our sins re-turned."

"You know, Eddie," said Molly, "the more I learn about your family and its history, the more I think you should all have been throttled at birth."

"You're not the first to think that." I glowered. "On top of every-thing else, this new arrangement doesn't look too stable. Like it could all collapse in on itself at any moment, and drag everything else in af-ter it."

"Are we talking about a black hole?" said Molly.

"I'm trying very hard not to," I said.

"We have to put the hidden rooms back!" said Peter. "While we still can. The longer it takes us, the more firmly established the re-turned spaces will become, and the more power it will take to force them back out of the world again."

"Why did Edmund do this?" I said. "Could he be trying to under-mine the basic stability of the Hall and bring everything down?"

"You heard Ethel," said Peter. "He could have done this just to keep us occupied, so he could concentrate on setting up something even worse."

"What do you think, Ethel?" I said. "Are you seeing anything else happening inside the Hall?"

We waited, but there was no response.

"Don't say she's started sulking now," said Molly.

"Maybe she's got something else on her mind," I said. "Who can say with Ethel? Let's go find Edmund."

"And then shut him down with extreme prejudice," said Molly.

"I like her," said Peter. "I don't care what everyone else says."

We pressed on through the transformed Hall, avoiding the architectural distortions and distractions as best we could, until we turned another unfamiliar corner and slammed to another sudden halt. Peter and I exchanged a worried look.

"I wish you'd stop doing that!" Molly said sharply. "What is it now?"

"Even allowing for all the new intrusions, the route we've been following should have brought us to the Ghost Gallery," said Peter. "But it doesn't seem to be here any more. Something else has taken its place."

Molly looked at me. "Ghost Gallery?"

"Just a name now," I said. "It used to be where the ghosts of all the family members who'd died fighting honourably were allowed to walk. The practice was shut down long ago."

"Why?" said Molly.

"It got too crowded," said Peter.

Where the long stone gallery should have been, with its rows of tall, elegant pillars and comfortable seats, we were now looking at a great open space . . . and the huge, intricate mosaic that covered the entire floor. A brightly coloured and insanely detailed scene depicting two great armies at war. Knights in medieval armour, bearing longswords and battle-axes, going head-to-head with golden-armoured Droods armed with strange glowing weapons. It was clear the fighting had been going on for some time. Dead bodies lay everywhere, halfsunk in the bloody, churned-up mud of the battlefield. Shattered steel, and ruptured gold. Weapons clashed and men struggled, while blood and gore flew on the air. Vivid colours flared in the night sky, suggesting magics at work, or strange sciences. The sheer savagery on view was almost overwhelming, with every fight to the death and no quarter asked or given.

"When did this happen?" Molly said quietly.

"I don't know," I said. "I never saw this before. Never even heard of anything like it. But those have to be King Arthur's knights. I recognise the armour."

"From Camelot?" said Molly.

"No," said Peter. "Later than that. Those are London Knights at war with the Droods. A vicious and bloody affair, by all accounts. Sixteenth Century, I think."

"How come you've heard about this and I haven't?" I said.

"Because I trained to be a family historian as a young man," said Peter. He smiled briefly, sadly. "I dug up all kinds of interesting things that the family had forgotten. My mistake lay in thinking someone would be grateful. You see, the very-secret agents didn't pick me to be one of them; the Matriarch insisted they take me, to shut me up. And then she burned every book I'd found and everything I'd written. So no one could follow in my footsteps."

He strode forward across the huge mosaic. Staring straight ahead. Molly and I went after him. I couldn't help but look down at the destruction and the slaughter. The blood, the horror, and the death of so many good men on both sides.

"This is the Sequestered Square," said Peter. "Commemorating a rather nasty quarrel between our two houses. Hundreds died on both sides, before wiser heads prevailed. It took a long time before the London Knights and the Droods would talk to each other again, or even recognise each other's existence."

I remembered the bad feelings I'd encountered when I had clashed with the London Knights a while back. They made a lot more sense now.

"Peace, or at least somewhat better relations, was finally reestablished at the end of the Nineteenth Century," said Peter. "After both sides were forced to work together against a common enemy. I don't know who. Just another thing that's lost to us . . . That's when the Matriarch got rid of this Square, so we could pretend it never happened. Official Drood history is full of these lacunae; deliberate gaps no one will ever talk about, because pulling on one thread could unravel everything. So many secret and shameful things have been removed from the records and driven physically out of our reality."

"The very-secret histories . . . ," I said.

"It might do the family good," said Molly, "to be forced to acknowledge all of this. Maybe you should just . . . let it stay."

"You don't understand," said Peter. "Not all the places we forced out of this world were empty. Some were inhabited." He stiffened suddenly, and a look of sheer horror swept over his face. "If Edmund's let everything loose . . ."

He set off again, moving at a surprisingly fast pace for a man of his years. I hurried after him, with Molly dogging my heels. I didn't want to lose my way in this strange new version of Drood Hall. We left the Square and hurried on through a series of empty corridors and deserted galleries, only some of which were familiar to me. I wasn't even sure which wing we were in any more. It felt . . . disconcerting to be lost in my own home. I stuck close behind Peter, and just hoped he knew where he was going.

We passed through rooms that had been turned inside out, and followed stairways that led up and along the walls. Space itself seemed to stretch and twist, like the passageways we run down in dreams that seem like they're never going to end. Gravity became distorted in places—the result of too many locations crammed into one setting—so that we had to struggle up steep hills while following perfectly level corridors. I wasn't thrown; such things were not uncommon in my family home. Molly thought they were fun.

Windows looked out on views from centuries past. Roughly clad peasants worked the fields, gathering in the harvest. Armoured knights rode brightly caparisoned horses through a howling storm. Men in animal skins danced and caterwauled inside rings of standing stones. Men practised their archery after church, and soldiers drilled with flint-lock muskets. And sometimes things that weren't men at all looked back at us through the windows.

Doors opened onto rooms full of forgotten trophies, spoils from wars no one was allowed to remember. THE FIGHTING SHIPS OF THE CANNIBAL CORSAIRS, read one sign. In a great open hangar of a room, huge sailing ships had been mounted proudly on display, with sails fashioned from tightly stretched human skin. Their bulkheads sweated blood, and rotting strands of rigging looked like skeins of nerves. The ships were breathing. Slowly, heavily, as though troubled by bad dreams. Heavy iron spikes had been driven through their hulls and deep into the stone floor, to hold them in place.

"Where are their crews?" I said to Peter.

"There are prisons within prisons," he said, not stopping.

THE CURSED JEWELS OF OPAR-LENG, proclaimed a sign on another open door. Apparently the jewels had been surgically implanted in the chests and bellies of dead men and women. They sat slumped in rows of chairs, held in place by lengths of silver barbed wire wrapped round and round them, as though someone had been afraid the dead might rise and walk away. The jewels shone with a sick, feverish intensity.

Another room was full of stuffed and mounted elves with empty eye sockets. Just standing around, in realistic poses, like an interrupted garden party. There was no sign on the door.

"Why would anyone do that?" said Molly.

"Remember the scarecrows we make out of our enemies, to act as guardians against intruders?" said Peter. "Droods bear grudges like no one else."

One room was full of severed hands. Hundreds of them, scrabbling and scuttling across the bare wooden floor. Clambering endlessly over each other, like so many pallid crabs or spiders. Making low, quiet skittering sounds. Molly looked at me, and all I could do was shrug helplessly.

None of what we saw seemed to surprise Peter. It just made him angrier and more concerned, driving him on. Even when Molly and I would have liked to stop for a better look. Or just to close the doors.

We finally ended up hurrying through a section of the Hall I vaguely recognised. We were in the North Wing now, not far from the main conference rooms. Things seemed calmer, more settled. Several corridors went by without showing us anything upsetting. I moved in beside Peter for a quiet word.

"I've never met a Drood who knew as much about our secret past as you. Especially the parts that aren't supposed to exist. All the dirty linen and suppressed secrets of our family. You're not just a very-secret agent or a failed historian. What are you, really?"

"Later," growled Peter. He was seriously out of breath now, but he wouldn't slow his pace.

We passed through a great open hall full of armoured Droods, standing utterly still. Not posed; more like a group of people caught in mid-action, forever. Caught off guard, caught by surprise, like insects trapped in amber.

We threaded our way through the silent golden figures, careful not to touch any of them. Molly frowned about her and then at me.

"Casualties of the first Time War," I said.

"The *first* Time War?" said Molly.

"We made it never happen," I said. "But there was some fall-out."

"You knew about this," Molly said accusingly.

"We all do," I said. "It's one of our great cautionary tales about using weapons you don't properly understand."

"So all of this wasn't forced outside," said Molly. "It's always been here?"

"Yes," I said.

"Then why haven't I seen it before?"

"Because I never brought you here," I said. "There are parts of my home that no one should know about unless they have to."

Molly scowled about her. "Who were you fighting?"

"It doesn't matter," I said. "We made them never happen too."

"Your family . . . ," said Molly. "I swear, if we run into a big statue of Kali . . ."

"What?" said Peter.

"Nothing," I said. "Keep going."

We left the Time-stopped Droods behind, and Peter slowed to a walk. His strength was fading, for all his sense of urgency. I kept expecting him to summon up his armour and rely on its speed and strength to keep him going, but he didn't. Perhaps because he was afraid it might alert Edmund to our presence. And perhaps because he wasn't ready to admit his own weakness just yet.

"Can I ask, where exactly are we going?" said Molly. "And if it's as bad as the look on Peter's face suggests, why are we in such a hurry to get there?"

"Because we need to get to the Demon Droods before Edmund can," said Peter.

"The *what?*" I said.

Peter sighed, and looked at me with heavy patience. "In the beginning, the family made a series of pacts and agreements with Heaven and Hell, so we could be sure we would always have the power we needed to do all the things that needed doing. You were taught that at school, right? What you don't know, what it was decided long ago that most of the family didn't need to know, is that some of those early Droods were required to enter into alchemical marriages to seal the deal. With angels and with demons. Resulting in Angelic Droods and Demon Droods."

"You mean half-breeds, like Roger Morningstar?" said Molly.

"Worse," said Peter. "These were alchemical marriages, of the spirit as well as the flesh. Imagine a thing from the Pit, with the added power of Drood armour, operating freely in this world."

"I'd rather not," said Molly.

Peter smiled grimly. "That was the point. To intimidate our enemies. Heavy hitters, for the most extreme missions."

"How many Droods took part in these marriages?" I said.

"Too many," said Peter.

"If these Demon Droods were such a tremendous tactical advantage," Molly said slowly, "why were they forced outside the Hall?"

"Because we discovered we couldn't trust them," said Peter. "It really shouldn't have come as a surprise. I mean, come on. Demon Droods? The clue was right there in the name, if anyone had been paying attention."

"What did they do?" I said.

"Tried to drag the entire Hall and everyone in it down to Hell," said Peter. "Human sacrifice on a really big scale. Came pretty close, by all accounts."

"Why not just take their armour back and tear up the agreement?" said Molly.

"Because we couldn't," said Peter. "That was part of the deal. Some marriages really are forever. The best the family could do was imprison all of the Demon Droods, and then force that prison outside our reality. But if they're back . . . If Edmund has found a way to release them . . ."

"Would even he be that stupid?" said Molly. "Because you can bet the Demon Droods wouldn't thank him for his pains."

"He might be that desperate," I said, "and that vindictive."

Peter finally came to a halt before a single closed door. He stood there for a while, just looking at it, while he got his breathing back under control. I studied the door carefully. Solid oak, with black iron studs laid out in Druidic ritual markings. Above and below the metal studs, long lines of ancient writings had been carved deep into the wood. I leaned in close for a better look and then drew in a sharp breath. Molly moved quickly in beside me.

"Eddie? What is it?"

"That writing. It's the same ancient form of Enochian we found in the Book of Morgana La Fae in the Other Hall."

Peter looked at me sharply. "You found a copy of that book? Did you bring it back with you?"

"No," I said. "Doesn't the family have enough problems as it is?"

"Good point," Peter said reluctantly. "The writings on the door are bindings, agreements imposed upon reality itself, to keep what's beyond the door from ever getting out. Do I really need to tell you this door shouldn't be here? I only know of it from a Thirteenth-Century account of the Demon Droods' banishing. This door and the room beyond were forced outside of Space and Time, so no one could ever release them."

"Well, now it's back," said Molly. "One hell of a bad penny. I don't know why you're looking so upset, Peter. We know a lot more about dealing with demons than they did back then. We can handle a few refugees from the Pit. They do it all the time in the Nightside. Is there any sign Edmund got here before us?"

"No," said Peter. "But we still have to go in there and check."

"After you," I said generously.

Peter scowled at me and then back at the door. "It's always possible the strain of the sudden transition has weakened the bindings."

"Quite a long way after you," I said firmly. "In fact, I'm thinking of using you as a human shield."

"Don't be such a wimp, Eddie," said Molly. "Never met a demon yet I couldn't outfight or out-think."

"Yes, but that's you," I said. I looked dubiously at the door. "How are we supposed to get past all these protections?"

"Just walk in," said Peter. "We are Droods, after all. It's our right to enjoy the fruits of our labours."

He turned the door handle and the lines of ancient writing flared up briefly in warning. The door fell back easily, as though it were weightless. Peter drew in a deep breath, straightened his back, and strode forward like a man walking to his own execution. I followed after, with Molly crowding impatiently behind me. Both of us ready to hit anything that caught us by surprise. We didn't get far, because it turned out to be really quite a small room.

"This is it," said Peter. "This is where we imprisoned the Demon Droods. To hold them securely forever."

Molly sniffed loudly, unimpressed. I didn't disagree. The poky little room made me think of a medieval dungeon. Rough and crude and pretty damned basic. No furniture, nothing in the way of comforts. The stone walls and floor were splashed with ancient bloodstains, suggesting the Demon Droods hadn't gone quietly. No windows, and no other way in or out. The only light spilled through the doorway behind us. The air was still and stale and uncomfortably warm. Something about the aspect of the place felt soured, poisoned, by old rage and old violence.

We were the only ones in the room, but it felt like we weren't alone. Some part of the Demon Droods was still present, and always would be. A room haunted by its past. The atmosphere was spiritually oppressive, because you can't deal with Hell and not get something burnt.

"I don't see anyone," Molly said loudly. "Did we get here too late? Has Edmund beaten us to it and let them out?"

"No," said Peter. "They're still here. Trapped in the Grim Gulf."

He pointed to a simple stone altar standing at the far end of the room. No adornments or trappings; just an ugly block of stone with its own long-dried bloodstains. Set on top of the altar was a single great ruby the size of a man's fist. Polished rather than faceted, it looked like a huge drop of heart's blood. The ruby gleamed defiantly against the gloom with a sick, corrupt light. As though it had been waiting for us.

We all moved slowly forward, drawn on almost against our will to stand before the altar. To face something that was still a threat to our souls as well as our bodies, even after all this time. Peter's face was pale, set in strained but determined lines. His forehead was beaded with sweat. Every instinct I had was yelling at me to get out while I still could. But sometimes standing your ground, even under the most extreme conditions, is simply what the job requires. Molly shook her head slowly.

"I can feel Hell's presence," she said, matter-of-factly. "As though something was called up here and not put down again properly."

"The Grim Gulf," said Peter, gesturing at the ruby with a hand that wasn't as steady as it might have been. "The hell we made, to hold our personal demons. A prison within a prison, because we had to be sure. Or we'd never have felt safe again."

"All right," I said. "We're here and Edmund isn't. What do we do?"

"Take the ruby with us, of course," said Peter. "To make sure Edmund can't get his hands on it."

Molly looked at him incredulously. "Are you kidding me? You would not believe the power levels I'm picking up off that thing! It stinks of Hell . . . Even in the one place made specially to hold it! Do you really think it's a good idea to take it out of here?"

"No," said Peter. "But we're going to, anyway." He jerked his gaze away from the ruby and turned to me. "Jack once told me you have your own pocket dimension in your trousers. Is that still true?"

"Well, yes," I said. "But I don't think I like where this conversation is going. You really want me to put a Grim Gulf full of Demon Droods in my pocket?"

"Can you think of a safer place?" said Peter.

All kinds of answers rose in my mind, none of them particularly helpful. Much as I hated to admit it, Peter was right. We couldn't just leave the ruby here and hope Edmund didn't find it. Inside my pocket dimension, the ruby would be effectively isolated from the rest of the world. And hopefully hidden from all prying eyes.

I armoured up one hand, reached out, and took hold of the ruby. The moment my golden fingers closed around the Grim Gulf, my head was suddenly full of screams. Terrible voices, all of them calling out at once in pain, despair, and fury. A hatred so vicious and overwhelming it hammered inside my head. I swayed on my feet. Molly grabbed hold of my arm to steady me, but I barely felt her touch. The voices howled through my thoughts, demanding I let them out. Release them back into the world so they could have their revenge at long, long last.

The ruby seemed weighed down by an almost spiritual inertia. As though it was connected to the altar stone by invisible chains. I gritted my teeth against the voices clamouring inside my head, and forced them back. *I'm a Drood. I can do this.* I stepped away from the altar, my hand clamped around the Grim Gulf, and then thrust the ruby into my pocket dimension. The entrance expanded to swallow the thing up and contain it, and then closed quickly again as I let go of the ruby and snatched my hand out. The voices cut off. I couldn't even feel the weight of the Grim Gulf in my pocket.

I didn't like to think about what would have happened if I'd touched the damned thing with my bare flesh. I armoured down and nodded my thanks to Molly. She looked into my face searchingly before she let go of my arm, while I did my best to appear calm and unaffected. I wasn't fooling anyone, and both of us knew it, but she smiled to show she appreciated the effort. I glared at Peter.

"No wonder you didn't want to touch it! You were ready to risk my life and my soul!"

"I knew you could do it," Peter said calmly. "You are the famous Eddie Drood, after all."

"The moment this emergency is over I am taking the Grim Gulf straight to the Matriarch," I said. "The family needs to know the truth about this. About what our ancestors did, to make us what we are."

"Of course," Peter said easily. "As soon as we've restored the suppressor fields, and put everything back where it should be, and everything is quiet again. But if you think the current Matriarch will decide any differently from her predecessors, you're wrong. She'll do her duty, like all the Matriarchs before her. The family doesn't need to know everything about the family. The past should stay in the past, where it can't hurt anyone."

"How can you people learn from your mistakes if you can't remember them?" said Molly.

"You could be right," said Peter, but his tone of voice was just that of someone agreeing to put an end to an argument they were tired of.

I didn't know what else to say. But given that I had the Grim Gulf in my possession, I didn't see what he could do to stop me.

"Okay!" said Molly. "This has all been very entertaining, in a disturbing sort of way, but I really don't think we should hang around here any longer. Where next?"

"We have to find Edmund," I said. "I don't care how well he's hiding himself; there must be some way to track him down."

"But if even Ethel can't see him . . . ," said Molly.

"I suppose we could always ask the family oracle," said Peter.

I looked at him. "Wait a minute. We have an oracle? Since when has this family had its own oracle?"

"Yeah," said Molly. "What he said, only louder."

"We don't, now," said Peter. "And the reason we don't have one is because when we did, it didn't work out too well."

"When was this?" said Molly, beating me to it.

"Some time back," said Peter. He looked challengingly at me, defying me to get any further information out of him. Molly moved a little closer, signifying she was ready to put pressure on the old man in any number of unpleasant ways, but I stopped her with a look. We still needed Peter. And, besides, a man who'd been a field agent as long as he had probably still had a few unpleasant surprises left up his sleeve. I gestured for him to continue.

"The family got rid of the oracle after he insisted on telling the then Matriarch something she really didn't want to know," Peter said carefully. "So she had him put in storage, along with all the other things the family keeps tucked away for a rainy day."

"You think he's back now?" I said.

"Seems likely," said Peter.

"You know a lot more about what's going on here than you're pre-pared to admit," I said.

"Of course," said Peter. "I'm the last of the very-secret agents. Se-crets are what we did best."

"As soon as this is over," I said, "we are going to have a long talk."

"Looking forward to it immensely," said Peter. He turned to Molly. "Fire up your magics, O witch of witches. The oracle is so powerful he should stand out like a fart in a perfume factory, even in the midst of all this madness."

Molly fixed me with a thoughtful stare. "Are you sure about this, Eddie? In my experience, oracles are always more trouble than they're worth. They live to mess with people's lives."

"We've been running behind Edmund for too long," I said. "We need something to put us out in front for a change."

"I can try," Molly said grudgingly. "But first, let's get out of this room. It grates on my nerves like fingernails scraping down a corpse."

Once we were out in the corridor again with the door firmly closed, Molly bit her lip and stared off into the distance.

"Trying to push my Sight past your family's defences is like trying to kick a door in while wearing carpet slippers," she growled. "Slow and painful, with no guarantee of success. It doesn't help that Space itself has become so crowded, so saturated with new information, it's hard to See anything."

"Are you saying you can't See the oracle?" I said.

"Of course I can See him! I just wanted you to understand how difficult this is! Your trouble is you don't appreciate me, Eddie Drood."

She gestured sharply and a glowing arrow appeared, floating serenely on the air before us. Molly set off down the corridor and the arrow darted ahead of her, pointing the way. I followed quietly after her, and Peter ambled along in the rear.

The arrow led us unwaveringly through a twisting tangle of familiar and unfamiliar locations, never once pausing to make up its mind. Doors hung open to every side, offering tempting glimpses of strange sights, marvels, and curiosities. I kept a watchful eye out for possible threats, but nothing showed itself. Possibly because Molly was in the lead, and quite obviously ready to walk right through anything that got in her way.

The glowing arrow finally slammed to a halt outside a closed and seemingly unremarkable door. It juddered back and forth for a moment, as though it would have liked to press on further but couldn't, and then blinked out. Molly turned to me.

"Do you know this door, Eddie? Is it regular issue, or a blast from the past?"

"I haven't recognised anything for some time," I said. "None of this should be here. Including the corridor we're standing in."

"I'm getting distinctly tired of all this novelty," said Peter. "The sooner we put everything back where it should be, the better."

"So the family can forget all its sins again?" I said.

"What good would it do to rake everything over again? What's done is done."

"The past can still serve as a dreadful warning," I said. "As to what happens when certain members of the family decide they know better than anyone else. When we screw up we have a responsibility to clean up after ourselves, not just sweep it under the carpet."

Peter shrugged. "This was all decided long before our time. By people a lot closer to the problem than we are."

"Are we going in or not?" Molly said loudly. "I swear, if you two don't stop arguing like an old married couple, I will nail your ears to the wall."

I looked at Peter. "She would too. I've seen her do it."

"Let's go talk to the oracle," said Peter.

He pushed the door open and strode in. Molly hurried after him, and I brought up the rear, still scowling to myself. Another small, shadowy, windowless room, entirely empty . . . apart from the man in the iron cage. It wasn't much of a cage; more like a standing coffin crudely fashioned from metal bars, only just big enough to hold the man inside. A slow chill ran through me, as I realised the prisoner could never sit down, never rest. Another chill followed as I saw the door to the cage had been welded shut long ago. My family really didn't want this guy getting out.

The man in the cage was entirely naked, tall and scrawny and caked in filth, with long, matted hair and beard. His eyes were fierce, mad, feral. He looked right at us as we came in, as though he'd been expecting us. We lined up before the cage, and then all pulled the same face as the smell hit us. I turned angrily to Peter.

"How long has he been here? This isn't just imprisonment; it's inhuman!"

"Don't waste your sympathies on him," said Peter, staring, unflinching, at the prisoner in his cage. "The only reason the Matriarch didn't order his death was because after everything he'd done, mercy was out of the question. As to how long he's been here, who can say?

I'm not sure the question means anything. Time doesn't affect people the same once they've been forced outside it."

"None of this makes sense to me," said Molly. "Why keep any of this stuff?"

"Because my family never throws away anything if there's a chance we might need it again someday," I said. "And, yes, that does apply to people as well as things."

"In this case they were right, weren't they?" said Peter. "Now hush, children. It's time to consult the oracle. Let me do all the talking."

He stood directly before the man in the iron cage, holding the oracle's fierce gaze with his own. "I admonish and adjure you, in the name of the Droods, to answer all questions put to you. And speak only truth, in the most simple and straightforward way." He paused to glance at Molly and me. "You have to do that, or he'll dance around the subject forever without getting anywhere. Just because he can."

"How do you know all this stuff," said Molly, "if he's been locked up here for so long?"

"It's my business to know things," said Peter.

"You've talked to him before, haven't you?" I said.

Peter smiled briefly. "When you're one of the family's very-secret agents, dealing with the kind of extraordinary problems that are our special remit, you're allowed access to anything you might need. And what we're not allowed access to, we take, anyway, and never tell anyone, so as not to upset them."

"You had personal access to the hidden areas," I said. "And all the things in them. No wonder none of this came as a surprise to you."

"I thought you knew an awful lot about everything we found," said Molly. "Historian, my arse."

"Just part of the job," Peter said patiently. "To know the things no one else knew. And to carry the burden of that knowledge. When I die a hell of a lot of secrets will die with me, and that's probably for the best. Droods have become so much more soft-hearted and sentimental than in my day. Which might or might not be a good thing." He turned back to the man in the iron cage.

"Oracle! Where is Edmund Drood right now?"

"He's in the Old Library," said the oracle. His voice was surprisingly calm and uninflected, though his gaze was as fierce as ever.

"Right," said Peter, turning his back on the oracle. "Let's go."

"Wait a minute!" said Molly. "I want to talk to him! I have questions of my own to put to him."

"Really not a good idea," said Peter. "We have what we need. Settle for that. More questions will just give him more chances to hurt you."

"Don't get in my way," said Molly. "Or I'll hurt you."

Peter looked at me, and I shrugged.

"She's a big girl. She can look after herself."

"You don't understand," said Peter. "And you're wasting time."

"No," I said, "you're wasting time arguing. The best thing we can do is step back out of Molly's way and let her get on with it. And pick up the pieces afterwards, if need be. Molly, keep it quick and to the point, please. The clock is ticking."

"I know," said Molly. "That's why I'm doing this."

We both knew which clock I was talking about, and that it had nothing to do with finding Edmund. Molly glared at the man in the iron cage.

"Oracle! How can I save Eddie?"

"You can't," he said, smiling his unnerving smile.

"How can he be saved from what's killing him?"

"He can't."

"There must be something I can do!" said Molly.

She stepped right up to the bars to glare into the oracle's face. He grinned back at her, meeting her angry eyes with his unwavering stare. Molly looked at Peter.

"Why isn't he answering me?"

"Because you didn't ask him a question," said Peter. "Don't do this, Molly. Don't do this to yourself."

Molly ignored him, fixing her gaze on the oracle again. "Is there a way out for Eddie? Is there a way for him to survive what's killing him?"

"Yes," said the oracle.

"What is it?"

"He has to let go, and die," said the oracle.

Molly made an ugly sound. She thrust her hand through the bars of the cage and grabbed the oracle by the throat. He didn't even flinch as she cut off his breath. I tensed, ready to intervene, but Peter was already talking quietly to Molly.

"You can't kill him. You can't even hurt him. The cage protects and preserves him, as well as imprisoning him. You're not the first person to react that way to the answers he gives."

Molly let go of the oracle and stepped back from the cage, breathing hard. She turned to me and there were tears in her eyes, even though she refused to shed them.

"I'm sorry, Eddie. I don't know what else to do. What else to ask."

"I told you," said Peter. "He never says anything useful, if he can help it. That's his revenge for being forced to tell the truth. Leave him. We know where Edmund is now, so let's go there and take out our bad feelings on him."

"Hold it," I said. "We can't just leave the oracle here. Not standing upright forever, locked inside an iron coffin. I don't care what he's supposed to have done. This is just . . . wrong."

"You're not the first person to feel that way," said Peter. "But you're wrong. Oracle, what would you do if you were set free?"

"I would put an end to all the Droods," said the oracle, smiling happily. "And then dance among their bodies. I could do that, with all the things I know. I could set the whole family at each other's throats, with just the right combination of concealed secrets and subtle misdirections. I would stand there and watch, and laugh and laugh and laugh as they slaughtered each other.

"And then . . . I would go forth into the world and walk up and down in it, spreading truth and misery until absolutely everyone was dead. And then maybe I'd get a little peace and quiet at last. There are far too many people cluttering up the place. The world won't miss them."

"You see?" said Peter, when the oracle finally stopped talking. "He's here for a reason. His words are poison."

"Still doesn't make this right," I said.

"No," said Peter. "But it is necessary."

He walked out of the room. I looked at the oracle, at his mad, pitiless eyes . . . And then I followed Peter out. Molly came with me, and didn't say anything until we were all out of the room and the door was firmly shut behind us.

"I really hoped he might know something. Something we'd missed."

"It's all right, Molly," I said. I hugged her to me and cradled her bowed head on my chest. "I gave up on the idea of a miracle cure, or even a last-minute save, long ago. I know I'm not getting out of this alive."

"I haven't given up on you," said Molly, pushing herself away from me. "I'll never give up."

Yes you will, I thought. *Eventually.*

Peter rubbed his hands together briskly. "At least now we know where Edmund is. Let us go there and give him the bad news, before he goes somewhere else." He frowned briefly. "What do you suppose he's doing in the Old Library?"

"Looking for something he can use against us," I said.

Peter nodded unhappily. "In the Old Library, that could cover a hell of a lot of ground." He took the portable dimensional Door out of his pocket and hefted the pulsing black blob on his palm. "Are you ready? To do what we have to? You know we can't let Edmund get away."

"Don't worry," said Molly, and her voice was a very cold thing. "If Eddie doesn't kill him, I will."

"Never doubted it for a moment," Peter said graciously. He looked at me. "Seriously scary girlfriend."

"You have no idea," I said.

Once we were all inside the Old Library, Peter peeled the Door off the air and nodded, satisfied, as though now we were finally here the hard part of the job was over. But he only thought that because he didn't know Edmund. I knew better. The Old Library seemed entirely empty, nothing but row upon row of tall wooden stacks crammed full of all kinds of books, stretching away into the distance and the shadows. Not that different from the Old Library we'd found in the Other Hall, except that here the light was a warm and cheerful butterscotch yellow. Restful to the eyes, and a comfort to the soul.

"I sort of thought the Librarian would still be here," said Molly. "You know William hates to leave the Library for any reason."

"I think even he'd move for a mass evacuation," I said. "And even if he didn't, Yorith would see to it that he did. Yorith might only be Assistant Librarian, but he has enough common sense for both of them. I do wish you'd stop smirking, Molly, every time I use the word *evacuation*."

Molly smiled sweetly. "You have to take your humour where you can find it on days like this."

I looked around carefully, peering into the deep, dark shadows between the stacks. It was all very still and very quiet. Even for the Old Library.

"I don't see Edmund," I said.

"The oracle said he was here," said Peter. "And he can't lie."

"William once told me the Old Library was bigger than the entire

Hall," said Molly. "Which means there are lots of places where Edmund could be hiding."

"And I know most of them," said Peter. "I spent a lot of time here, back in the day, researching cases."

"Before or after I rediscovered it and handed it back to the family?" I said.

Peter just smiled.

"Why would Edmund go to such lengths to empty out the entire Hall, just so he could have the Old Library to himself?" said Molly.

"He must be looking for something he believes he can use as a weapon," I said.

"Like what?" said Molly.

"Take your pick!" I said. "Grimoires of forgotten lore. Repositories of forbidden technology. Books that can tell you how to put out the sun or poison people's dreams. Information on where to find Doors into Heaven or Hell or all the places in between. Knowledge is power. That's how my family has stayed in charge for so long."

"But what do you think he's looking for?" said Molly.

I thought about it. "He didn't know about his Hall's Old Library. So it must be something he learned here, while he was swanning around, pretending to be me."

"For every weapon there's a defence," said Peter. "For every threat a response, and someone in the family ready to provide it. That's what the Droods are all about. So what does Edmund know, or think he knows, that he still believes could bring us down?"

"It doesn't matter," said Molly. "He's not going to get the chance."

She conjured up a small ball of magical energies. It bobbed on the air before her, spitting and crackling and discharging stray magics into the atmosphere in its eagerness to be about its business. "Find Edmund!" said Molly in a voice like a death sentence, and the ball shot off into the stacks. Molly went sprinting after it, with me right behind her, and Peter puffing along in the rear. The fizzing ball of energy darted in and out of the stacks, following a trail only it could see, like a bloodhound in hot pursuit.

Until finally we rounded a corner and there was Edmund, sitting quietly at a reading desk, with a large leather-bound volume open before him. The ball bobbed up and down excitedly over his head and then snapped off, its business done. Edmund smiled easily at us, and closed the book in front of him.

"I knew you were on your way. You'd be surprised how far sound carries in a place like this. I could have just left, but I wanted a word with you first, Eddie."

"I'm not interested in anything you have to say," I said. Just looking at him, at the face so very like my own, I could feel a hot, killing rage building in me.

"But we should talk," said Edmund, entirely unmoved by what he must have heard in my voice. "We have so much in common, after all. Perhaps we could say things to each other that we could never say to anyone else. No? As you wish . . . How are you feeling, Eddie? Frankly, it's a wonder to me you're not dead. Must be down to that wonderful torc Ethel made for you. What I could have done with such a thing in my world."

"You should have killed me while you had the chance," I said.

"I did," said Edmund. "Oh, you mean in the Armoury? It would have taken too long, attracted too much attention."

"Did you really think that trap would hold us?" said Molly.

"No," said Edmund. "But, then, it didn't have to. I just needed a little time in here to myself, to find what I was looking for. And I did!"

He patted the closed book in front of him, as though it was a favoured pet.

"What have you found?" I said.

Edmund grinned. "Wouldn't you like to know?"

"Shut up, Edmund," said Molly coldly. "It's time for you to die."

"I'm not dying," said Edmund. "That's Eddie."

He stood up behind his desk, taking his time about it to show it was his idea. Molly started to raise a hand, and Edmund held the book up in front of him. I put a staying hand on Molly's arm. The book might be important or valuable, and it might well be able to defend itself. Molly shrugged off my hand but held her peace. For the moment.

"You can't hide behind that book forever, Edmund," I said.

"Wouldn't dream of it," he said, and tucked the book jauntily under one arm. He smiled slyly at me. "Did you enjoy your time in my Hall? Still lots of interesting things to see there, even now they've dragged all the bodies out. Look what I picked up the last time I was there." His left hand came up holding a long straight razor. He flicked open the heavy blade with a practiced movement, and the exposed steel shone supernaturally bright. Edmund smirked at it fondly. "This was taken from the cold, dead hand of the very last Springheel Jack, after my family took him down. Because we really don't like competition, do we? A blade with an edge so sharp it can cut through anything." He giggled suddenly. "How do you defeat people in armour? Find a better can-opener!"

He moved out from behind the desk, the book under his arm and the straight razor in his hand. Molly stabbed a finger, and a vicious magic shot at Edmund, lightning fast. The long steel blade seemed almost to move on its own and intercepted the magic. The flaring bolt hit the glowing metal and ricocheted away, disappearing harmlessly off into the stacks. Edmund smiled at Molly.

"I think of everything. Including acquiring a blade capable of killing my annoyingly persistent other self and his bitch."

"Don't," I said quickly to Molly. "If your next ricochet hits the wrong book, the whole Library could go up."

"I had planned to set fire to the place before I left," Edmund said wistfully. "But you know how it is: so many heartwarming ideas and so little time. How did you find me so quickly? No, no; it doesn't matter. I don't even care who that old fart at your side is. I'm leaving now. And there's nothing you can do to stop me."

"Give me the ruby, Eddie," said Peter.

"What? No!"

"It's the only chance we have of stopping him! Look at him; he doesn't know what we're talking about. He won't have any defences against it!"

I armoured up my hand and pulled out the Grim Gulf. My head was immediately full of screaming voices, cut off the moment I placed the ruby in Peter's armoured hand. He held it up so Edmund could see it.

"It's very nice, I suppose," he said, frowning. "Were you thinking of bribing me, perhaps?"

"Not even close," said Peter.

He crushed the ruby in his golden hand. I thought I heard it scream before it fell apart in a stream of crimson splinters, but the sound was quickly drowned out by a roar of triumphant voices as thirteen medieval demons in full Drood armour appeared in the Old Library. Huge and awful, they towered over us, great golden batwings spreading out from crooked backs. They had clawed hands, cloven hooves, and lashing tails, and golden goat's horns thrust up from their armoured brows. They were laughing, a hideous sound, full of vicious exultation . . . and a never-ending need to do terrible things, and glory in it. The sound of the Pit, let loose in the mortal world.

The Demon Droods.

Edmund seemed genuinely shocked. He looked at his straight razor, and then at the laughing Demon Droods . . . and just like that he wasn't smiling any more. He closed the razor with a snap and thrust it into his pocket, pulled out the Merlin Glass, and shook it out to Door size. And then he walked through the Door and was gone, and the Glass disappeared after him.

Leaving me and Molly and Peter alone in the Old Library, with thirteen Demon Droods.

"Ah," said Peter. "Now, I really didn't expect him to do that. Sorry."

The Demon Droods turned to face us, their clawed hands flexing slowly. Mouths appeared in their face masks, stretching into wide grins to reveal row upon row of jagged teeth. The air was full of blood and sulphur and sour milk: the stench of Hell.

"Peter," I said, "please tell me you can put them back in the Grim Gulf."

"Of course I can't!" he said, his voice rising almost hysterically. "I had to smash it to release them! The idea was they'd wear themselves out taking down Edmund, while we stood back and watched. And after they'd exhausted themselves killing him, we'd be able to take them."

"Do you at least know some control Words?" said Molly. "The family must have had some form of authority over them!"

"If they did, no one remembers what," said Peter. "Look, I'm really sorry, all right? I don't seem to have thought this through . . ."

I was ready to shout and curse at him, but one look was enough to show me the man was actually trembling with fear and horror. In the past he would have had a fall-back position, another game plan to run with, but after so long out of the field he wasn't the man he used to be. He'd let his confidence run away with him. Peter looked at me helplessly, and I looked to Molly.

"I bow to your superior knowledge of demonkind, O wicked witch of the woods. What can we do?"

"I can summon them up and I can send them back down," said Molly. "But only when they're safely confined inside a pentacle, with all the proper wards and protections in place. These are nothing like the half-breeds we're used to dealing with; these are full demonic presences, with all the power of the Pit. Such things were never meant to walk in this world. They could break it just by walking up and down in it. What were your ancestors thinking of, Eddie?"

"They probably thought the Demon Droods would be family first, and demons second," I said. "And we know how well that worked out. Molly, those demons really are getting very close now. Tell me you've got something . . ."

"Fortunately, I have been here before," Molly said quickly. "You're not the only one the Librarian likes to talk to. He once told me there are books in the Old Library powerful enough to eat anyone who tried to read them, so a long time ago one particular Librarian had his Armourer whip him up a little something to keep the more dangerous books in their place."

She struck a pose, concentrated, and stuck out one hand. Something flashed through the air, flying out of the stacks to slap into her waiting hand. A long, slender golden wand, glowing brightly in sudden pulses. Molly looked at it and then grinned nastily at the Demon Droods. They came to a sudden halt.

"A repurposed elven wand, coated in Drood armour and weaponised with preprogrammed attack spells," Molly said proudly. "Given that it was designed to keep Major Grimoires in line, it should be able to deal with this bunch of arranged marriages with delusions of grandeur."

"To tell the truth," I said, looking at the wand, "I was hoping for something a bit more . . . dramatic. I'm still going to have to go head-to-head with the Demon Droods, aren't I?"

"I can't do everything for you, Eddie."

"Terrific . . ." I turned to Peter, grabbed him by the shoulder, and gave him a good shake, until his eyes snapped back into focus again.

"Man up, Peter! You're a field agent! And, more importantly, a Drood. So start acting like one!"

He nodded jerkily. "Yes. Sorry. I've been out of the field too long.

I'd forgotten how fast things can go bad on you." His back straightened and his chin came up, and just like that he was the last of the
very-secret agents once again. "First rule of any agent in the field: If
your horse throws you, shoot the ungrateful thing in the head and replace it with something more reliable. You're right. We can do this.
Though I would welcome any advice anyone might happen to have.
I'm getting a bit old for fisticuffs."

"You're the one who knows about the Demon Droods," I said. "Can
we give them orders, in the family's name?"

"No," said Peter. "No one could. That's one of the reasons we put
them in a prison within a prison—just in case. Look, I'm really sorry I
destroyed the Grim Gulf. It honestly never occurred to me Edmund
would just disappear like that!"

I turned to Molly. "Any chance your wand could hold the Demon
Droods back long enough for us to reach the painting, get the hell
out, and seal it behind us?"

"We'd never make it," Molly said flatly.

"So we stand and fight," I said.

"Suits me," said Molly. "I really am in the mood to hit someone."

"Never knew you when you weren't," I said generously. "Peter, it's
time. Armour up."

We subvocalised our activating Words, and our armour swept over
us in a moment. Immediately I felt stronger and faster, and so sharp I
could cut a thought in half. All the aches and pains and bone-deep
weariness from the poison that was killing me disappeared. It felt so
good to feel human again. I looked at Peter in his armour, and he
didn't look like an old man any more. He looked like a Drood agent.
The Demon Droods stirred uneasily, their barbed tails lashing rest-
lessly back and forth.

One demon strode forward, slapping a heavy wooden stack out of
his way as though it weighed nothing. The shelves exploded at his

touch, and books flew everywhere. I stepped forward to meet the Demon Drood, and his savage smile widened. Heavy batwings extended,
curling out and around him to block off any side attacks. The Demon
Drood put forward his golden hands, to show off the vicious claws, and
then seemed a little taken aback when I didn't even slow my approach.
Back in his day, his appearance was probably still frightening, because
it was what people expected from a demon out of Hell. But now it was
just a cheap joke, a caricature. Hell has moved on; its horrors have
become more personal. I should know—I've seen enough of them.
The Demon Drood stopped, almost shocked that I wasn't intimidated,
and I took advantage of his hesitation to reach up and punch him
right where his eyes should have been.

The power behind that punch would have ripped anyone else's
head off, but the Demon was still a Drood. His head snapped all the
way round, but he recovered in a moment. A golden hand shot out so
fast I didn't even see it coming, and vicious claws slashed across my
throat . . . only to skid away in a shower of sparks. A sudden confidence
ran through me as I realised he hadn't even scratched my armour. I
laughed out loud, and the Demon Drood froze where he was. Because
that was the one response he hadn't been expecting. I glanced back at
Molly and Peter.

"Okay, people. We are back in the game! These Droods are from so
long ago they're still wearing Heart armour; no match for the strange
matter Ethel provides. All we have to do is hold them off until their
armour runs down and disappears back into their torcs!"

"And then we kick their heads in," said Molly.

"Right!" I said.

"Unless they kill us first," said Molly.

"Well, yes," I said. "Try not to let that happen."

Peter stepped up beside me and punched the Demon Drood so
hard in the gut he actually went stumbling backwards. Peter laughed
delightedly. The Demon Droods surged forward in a pack, howling

like the fiends they were. And Peter and I went to meet them. Barbed claws slammed into my armour again and again, hitting me from every side, and even though they couldn't break through, the sheer impact from so many blows sent me staggering this way and that. I struck back with all my armour's strength, and Demon Droods went reeling away, shaking their horned heads dazedly. Their great golden wings flapped uselessly, just getting in the way. There wasn't room to fly in between the towering stacks. I forced my way into the midst of them, striking out savagely. And every time my fists struck home, armour on armour, there was a sound like the tolling of great golden bells.

Peter spun and pirouetted like a young man, striking down the Demon Droods with happy enthusiasm. He avoided most of their blows, and blocked the rest with an upraised arm that was always just where it needed to be. He was faster, stronger, smarter than the Demons. He swept their legs out from under them, kicked them in the head when they crashed to the floor, and laughed out loud.

Molly darted around the edges of the fight, stabbing her wand every time she had a clear shot. Golden armour cracked and splintered under the magical impacts, but always repaired itself. She blasted one Demon Drood right through a heavy wooden stack, destroying any number of books, but he rose from the wreckage unharmed. Molly cursed dispassionately. The wand hadn't been designed for this kind of warfare.

The fight surged back and forth through the Old Library, doing terrible damage to irreplaceable books and precious manuscripts. Because the Demon Droods didn't care, and we were fighting for our lives. The Demons surged around us, striking out with vicious strength, attacking us from every direction at once. Terrible claws slammed in out of nowhere to slice along my rib cage. The claws skidded away in a squeal of sparks, but the impact was enough to drive the breath out of me. I staggered backwards, caught off balance, and a punch from a golden fist almost took my head off. Peter was quickly there at my side, driving the Demon back with incredible speed and strength. In his armour he wasn't old and frail any more, and he gloried in it. He danced among the Droods, ducking and dodging everything the enemy could throw at him, buying me time to recover. I was seeing him as he used to be, in his prime, but I had to wonder how long that would last. I got my breath back and returned to the fight.

We were holding our ground but we weren't hurting them, and they knew it. The Demon Droods never grew tired and never slowed down. They pressed forward constantly, their fists slamming down like golden hammers—because even old-style Drood armour was made strong enough to shake the world. We'd been fighting for some time now, but they showed no signs of losing their armour. Perhaps their demonic nature supplied it with new energy.

One of the Demon Droods lifted a whole standing stack into the air to throw at Molly. The books flew off the shelves in a rustling cloud and circled him menacingly. The Demon Drood threw the shelving aside and struck out at the books with his golden hands, but they avoided him easily. They all closed in at once. And when they fell to the floor, just books again, there was no trace remaining of the Demon Drood. Some books in the Old Library really don't like to be disturbed.

I fought the Demon Droods with all my strength and speed, delivering punches that would have cracked open a mountain, to no avail. Peter was moving so quickly now the Demon Droods couldn't even get close to him. We clubbed the Demons down, again and again, while magics from Molly's wand exploded among them, throwing them this way and that. But for all our efforts we weren't damaging or hurting them. And I knew we would break before they did.

So, when all else fails, cheat. I fell back on the one ace I still had tucked up my golden sleeve. Marked very firmly as ONLY FOR REAL EMERGENCIES. I raised my voice.

"Pook! This is Eddie Drood! *Look what they're doing to your Library!*"

And just like that, there he was. The great white rabbit himself, standing a little off to one side. Tall and dignified in a Playboy Club smoking jacket, with a martini in one paw and a monocle screwed firmly into one pink eye.

"What is all this noise?" he said crossly. "And who's responsible for all this mess?"

The Demon Droods took one look at the Pook and immediately backed away. They were afraid of him. Perhaps because their demonic senses Saw more of him than mere mortal eyes ever could. The Pook threw aside his martini and lunged forward, a fierce white blur, right into the midst of the Demon Droods. And in a moment, they were all gone. The Pook turned unhurriedly back to face me and Molly and Peter, and smiled easily.

"Tasty . . ."

I armoured down so he could see who I was. Though I was pretty sure he already knew. I've always been pretty sure the Pook knows anything he wants to know. Peter armoured down, his eyes wide and his jaw dropping. Molly lowered her wand, as though it had suddenly become very heavy.

"How?" said Peter. "I mean, *what?*"

"You've never met the Pook before, have you?" said Molly.

Peter shook his head, lost for words. Now he no longer had his armour to hold him up, he looked old and frail again, and his eyes were terribly lost. After all his years in the field, after everything he'd seen and done, he was finally faced with something beyond his knowledge and experience. Demons are scary enough, but whimsical Things that shouldn't even exist can be downright unnerving. I cleared my throat and addressed the Pook as calmly as I could manage.

"Took you long enough to show up."

"I was busy. And don't ask with what, because you wouldn't understand. And even if you did, you wouldn't want to."

"But how?" said Peter.

"I am the Pook. Be grateful." The white rabbit looked around him, as though staring past the Old Library at the Hall beyond. "What have you been doing in my absence? Oh, I see. Honestly, I turn my back on this family for five minutes . . . There. I've lowered the force shield around the Hall, shut down Alpha Red Alpha, and reinstalled the spatial suppressors. Everything's back to where it should be, and I strongly suggest you leave it there. So much eccentric geometry was getting on my nerves."

He started to turn away, but Molly called quickly after him.

"Pook! Don't go. Eddie is sick. Dying. Please, can't you do something to help him?"

The Pook looked at me. "No."

And just like that, he was gone. I smiled, slowly and just a little bitterly, and nodded to Molly.

"That's the Pook for you."

"I really thought he might be able to help you," said Molly.

"I didn't," I said.

Molly looked at her golden wand, and threw it away. It shot off through the air, disappearing into the stacks. Molly sniffed. "Those things never turn out to be as much use as you hope. Let's get out of here. We have to track down Edmund. Again."

"First things first," I said. "Peter, I have a question."

The old man gathered around him what was left of his dignity and met my gaze steadily.

"Only the one question? Then you haven't been paying attention."

"Come on, Eddie," said Molly.

"Wait," I said. "This is important. Peter, you said certain members of the family entered into alchemical marriages with Heaven and Hell. Some became the Demon Droods, and we know what happened to them. But what about the Angelic Droods?"

"Is that your question?" said Peter. "What happened to them?"

"Yes," I said. "Because in my experience, you can't trust agents of Heaven or Hell."

"You're right," said Peter. "That is an important question."

He turned and walked away, heading out of the Old Library. I looked at Molly, and she looked at me. And all we could do was go after him.

CHAPTER FOUR

Angels of No Mercy

rood Hall was back to what passed for normal.

The corridors were empty, the halls were wide open, and everything was where it should be and as it should be . . . with none of my family around to spoil the moment. Not a trace remained of all the weird and threatening things and people my family had decided we were better off not knowing about. Just as well. Drood Hall was weird enough as it was, without my family's past sins screaming for attention.

I let Peter lead the way through the Hall, hanging back so I could talk privately with Molly. Peter had already made it very clear he wasn't interested in talking about the things I wanted to talk about. So I let him plod on ahead like the tired old man he sometimes was, scowling fiercely and muttering to himself. A man shouldn't be interrupted when he's communing with his conscience.

"I should have held on to some of the things we saw," I said quietly to Molly.

"Why would you want to do that?" said Molly. "You've never been one for souvenirs, and I prefer not to clutter up my life with things. Unless they're valuable, of course. Or pretty."

"I was thinking more about evidence," I said. "Now the forbidden rooms and their contents have been forced outside reality again, there's nothing left to back up my story when I tell it to the Matriarch."

"You've got me," said Molly. "And I'd like to see anyone call me a liar to my face. I really would."

"Oh, they wouldn't argue with you or me," I said. "Not openly. But you can bet the Matriarch would use a lack of any actual hard evidence to justify putting off an official investigation until everyone had forgotten about it. The powers that be in this family have always supported the status quo over everything else."

Molly nodded slowly. "I have to say, Eddie, some of the things your family had tucked away appalled even me. And I have a very high appal level. But what good would it do, really, to bring it all out into the open? At best it would undermine your family's morale, and at worst it wouldn't."

"It's the principle of the thing," I said.

"You do realise you are talking to someone who wouldn't recognise a principle if she tripped over it in the gutter," said Molly. "Forget the principle; go with the practical. The bad shit is gone, and can't hurt anyone any more. Who else in the family knows about this stuff, apart from Peter?"

"The Matriarch must know some of it," I said. "And probably the Sarjeant-at-Arms. He'd have to know, so he could be ready to defend against it. What worries me is that we only have the spatial suppressor fields to keep the forbidden rooms at bay. What happens if the fields go down again, either through sabotage or just . . . age? My family needs to know about these things, not just as a warning from history, but so they can guard against their return."

"We could always have a quiet word with the Armourer," said Molly. "Have Maxwell and Victoria whip up something that would make it impossible for any of the bad stuff to come back. You know they live to solve problems like that."

"They'd talk to the Matriarch first," I said. "To make sure she'd approve. Max and Vicki have always liked having an authority figure to cosy up to, so that when things inevitably go wrong in the Armoury they've got someone on their side. And I don't think the Matriarch would want anyone messing with this. Because even the worst of the removed things might be needed someday. No, she'll just want to make it all go away and never have happened, so everyone can forget about it as soon as possible."

Molly looked at me thoughtfully. "You seemed to know an awful lot about some of the things we saw. Can I ask . . . ?"

"I used to run this family," I said.

"You never talked about any of this before."

"Family secrets aren't always mine to share."

"You don't trust me!" Molly said accusingly.

"Where things like this are concerned," I said, "I'm not sure I even trust me."

"What is it you want to do, Eddie?" Molly said patiently. "What do you think is for the best? Tell the truth and shame the devil, or at least your family, and to hell with whatever damage that does? Or just let it all stay forgotten, so it won't give people nightmares?"

"I don't know," I said. "It just seems to me that people shouldn't be allowed to do things like this and get away with it."

"Welcome to my world," said Molly.

We walked on together for a while. It was all very peaceful in the Hall, like the calm before a storm.

"Do they give you a really big book when you take office?" Molly said finally. "Called something like *A Hundred and One Things You Don't Know about the Family but Really Should*?"

I had to smile. "Something like that, yes."

"I always thought there must be," said Molly. "I really should get around to stealing it. You know I can't stand other people knowing things I don't."

"On principle?" I said.

"No, because it might be knowledge I can sell! Do try to keep up with the rest of us, Eddie."

"The book, not surprisingly, is currently locked away in the Old Library," I said. "Behind the kind of protections that would make even the Pook think twice about bothering them."

Molly grinned at me. "Now, you know I love a challenge. Did this book have anything to say about the Demon Droods and the Angelic Droods?"

"No," I said. "But, then, I hadn't gotten half-way through it before suddenly I wasn't in charge any more."

"Only because you agreed to step down," said Molly.

"It was the right thing to do," I said. "Just because you're a good agent out in the field doesn't mean you can be good at everything. I had the best of intentions, but I forgot which road is paved with them. I had to get out, after what happened during our war with the Hungry Gods."

"We won that war!" said Molly.

"But a lot of good men and women in the family died because of the decisions I made."

"You'd have gotten better at it," said Molly. "In time."

"And how many more Droods would have died while I was busy becoming the kind of man I never wanted to be, anyway?"

"Don't be so hard on yourself," said Molly. "There are more than enough people here ready to do that for you." She sighed heavily and looked around for something she could use to change the subject. "It's very . . . quiet, isn't it? With all your family outside."

"Very peaceful," I said. "I've always said Drood Hall would be a very desirable residence, if it weren't for all the Droods living in it."

"Why are you still scowling?" said Molly. "The emergency's over."

"Is it?" I said. "I'm still waiting for the other shoe to drop. The out-of-this-world, more-than-human, really-bad-news shoe to drop."

"You mean the Angelic Droods."

"Got it in one," I said.

"But they've been pushed back outside of reality again," said Molly. "Along with everything else. Haven't they?"

"When I asked Peter about them," I said quietly, "he wouldn't answer me. He could have said any number of things to reassure me, but he didn't. Because he knew I'd know a lie when I heard one. Which leads me to believe this problem isn't anywhere near over yet."

"You think he knows more than he's saying?" said Molly.

"A very-secret agent would know all kinds of things that he might not want to share with anyone else," I said.

"Want me to beat them out of him?"

"I'm hoping it won't come to that."

"Spoil-sport." Molly scowled thoughtfully at Peter's back. "It's always possible the Angelic Droods just up and left a long time ago. I can't see anything truly angelic wanting to hang around your family for long."

"Maybe," I said. "But in my experience, it doesn't matter whether you're talking about angels from Above or Below: They're always going to be a cause for concern."

"Angels are a pain in the arse," said Molly. "They never know when to stop."

Something in the way she said that made me look at her.

"Of course!" I said. "You were there when angels came to the Nightside from Heaven and Hell! They took the whole place apart, searching for the Unholy Grail—the cup that Judas drank from at the Last Supper. Allegedly. I always thought that was just an urban legend."

"Doesn't stop people wanting it," said Molly. "And some things aren't even a little bit people. I was never more scared in my life . . . The angel war was years ago, but they're still rebuilding parts of the Nightside."

"Just another of the many fascinating stories from your past that somehow you never get around to telling me about."

"Look," said Molly, "sufficient unto the day, and all that. We have enough problems on our plate as it is."

"You're right," I said.

"Of course I am!" Molly said brightly. "I'm always right. You should know that by now."

We reached the main entrance hall and headed for the front door. Peter was actually reaching for the door handle when he stopped abruptly, and his old head came up like that of a hound scenting something disturbing on the air. I hurried forward to join him, while Molly looked quickly around in case there was something that needed hitting.

"What is it?" I said quietly to Peter.

"Listen," he said. "Can't you hear it?"

I concentrated, and the sound of raised voices came clearly to me from the other side of the door. An awful lot of people shouting wildly, desperate to make themselves heard, and panicking for really good reasons. And these were Droods; trained from childhood to face the worst this world and others had to offer. What could be so bad that it could reduce people like them to such a state? I shook my head disgustedly. I had a pretty good idea.

"Talk to me, Peter," I said harshly. "It's the Angelic Droods, isn't it?"

"I hoped I was wrong," said Peter. He sounded lost, defeated, and more than ever he looked like the very old man he was. "I really wanted to be wrong about this, but I think they're back."

"Give it to us straight," said Molly. "What happened to the Angelic Droods all those years ago? Did they just up and leave?"

"Did they jump?" I said. "Or were they pushed?"

"They helped save the family from the Demon Droods," Peter said tiredly. "They showed the Armourer how to fashion the Grim Gulf, and then helped the family force the Demon Droods inside it. But after that, the story gets confused. Some say the Angelic Droods chose to leave because they were too good for this family. Others say the family tried to imprison the Angels, because if the Demons turned on them, the Angels might too. And some say the family were forced to banish the Angelic Droods, because they wanted to go forth into the world and judge Humanity, once and for all. So many stories, and no one knows the truth. But now the Demon Droods are finally dead . . . maybe the Angelic Droods have taken that as a sign, to come home and take care of unfinished business."

"That's a hell of a lot of *ifs* and *maybes*," said Molly. "I thought you Droods knew everything!"

"That's just a rumour we spread," I said. "So everyone else will stay worried. What do you think, Peter? What is the truth?"

"I don't know!" said Peter. "Nobody knows! The family buried some of its secrets so deep, not even the people in charge can be sure of what really happened. But if the Angelic Droods have returned . . ."

"They're out there right now, aren't they?" I said.

"Can't you feel their presence?" said Peter, his voice dropping to a whisper. "Can't you feel the world buckling under the weight of them?"

"Okay," said Molly. "Someone needs some time out, and a nice furry animal to hug."

I looked at the closed door before me. I could feel . . . something.

"We need to go out there," I said. "See for ourselves what's happening."

"Damn right," said Molly. "The Demon Droods were actually sort of cool; I can't wait to see what Angelic Droods look like."

None of us moved.

"Why won't the past stay past?" said Peter.

"Because it isn't over until we say it is," I said.

I opened the door. If only because the thought of what might be outside was making me hesitate. Drood field agents can't afford to hesitate. It's our job to go rushing in where any angel in its right mind would take some serious time to think it over. It's our duty to always be ready to take care of business. So I strode through the front door, doing my best to look like I knew what I was doing. It helped that Molly was there with me. Peter brought up the rear, muttering to himself again.

My entire family stood gathered together in front of the Hall, their heads tilted back as they stared up into the sky. They'd stopped shouting for the moment, struck dumb by the glory of what they were looking at. I looked up too, and my heart lurched as I took in the thirteen figures hovering above us, shining bright as the sun. Perfect, idealised human forms in golden armour, with massive golden wings unfurled from their backs. The wings didn't flap, because they weren't responsible for holding the figures up. They just hung there, unmoving, nailed on the sky by the sheer force of their being. As though they belonged in the heavens, above all lesser things. The sheer spiritual presence of them was staggering, overwhelming. As though the stars themselves had fallen out of the heavens and come down to pass judgement on us.

The Angelic Droods.

And yet they didn't feel like a force for Good, as such. Theirs was a more elemental nature. Beyond simple things like Law or Justice, or anything a mere human could hope to comprehend. I could tell just from looking at them that they knew nothing of mercy, compassion, or understanding. They would do what they would do, and nothing any of us could say would stop them or turn them aside. They were a force in the world, wild and unknowable and unimaginably dangerous.

Typical angels, really. Or Droods.

Staring up at the Angelic Droods, my family talked quietly among themselves now, trying to understand what they were looking at. A few shouted questions at the Matriarch, or requests for orders, but she just stared up at the glowing golden figures, saying nothing, as though it was all just too much for her. The Sarjeant-at-Arms stood beside her, scowling fiercely at the sky. He had a really big gun in each hand, and looked extremely ready to use them. It would take a lot more than Angels to impress the Sarjeant. Maxwell and Victoria were browbeating their lab assistants into ignoring the Angels and building something protective and punitive out of the various bits and pieces of tech they had with them.

"So, this is the result of an alchemical marriage between Droods and the forces of Heaven," I said.

"I thought they'd be taller," said Molly.

"You can feel the power coming off them," I said. "Even more so than the Demon Droods. Which is . . . interesting."

"They're back," said Peter. "After all these years . . ."

"If these are forces from Heaven," I said, "shouldn't they be on our side? Technically speaking?"

"You'd think so, wouldn't you?" said Peter. "But angels aren't on anyone's side. That's the point. They only exist to enforce God's will on Earth. Except . . ."

"Except?" said Molly. "Except what? Come on, you can't just stop there!"

"Angels are God's will made manifest," said Peter. "Heaven's storm-troopers. When God wants something done right now, and no arguments. Normally angels have no will of their own, as we would understand it. They're just here to smite the bad guys and walk right over anyone who gets in their way. But these aren't the real deal. After what they were put through, they're more than human but less than divine. Caught halfway between this world and the next. Who knows how they think or whose will they follow?"

"You know," Molly said to me quietly, "I think I felt better before he explained things."

"I'm more concerned with where they've been all these years," I said. "And what they've been doing. Why hadn't we heard of them before this? Something as powerful and downright scary as Angelic Droods should have made a real impression, even in the hidden world."

"Right," said Molly. "I would have heard. And I didn't. Which is spooky . . ."

"I have to talk to the Matriarch," I said. "She needs to know what this is all about, what it means."

"Assuming she doesn't already know," said Molly. "She's had more than enough time to work her way through that big book of yours."

"Some things are never written down," said Peter.

"And after I've finished briefing the Matriarch . . . I'm going to talk to the Angelic Droods," I said.

"Okay, hold everything and throw it into reverse," said Molly. "In what part of your brain did that sound like a good idea? Those things hanging on the sky do not look like they're at all interested in holding a conversation."

"They're probably just shy," I said. "Looking for someone to break the ice."

"Angels destroy cities and wipe out the firstborn of a generation," said Molly. "They do not do shy."

"I still have to try," I said. "Because Droods shouldn't kill Droods."

Molly scowled. "Knew I should have hung on to that wand."

"Unless you were planning to stab one of the Angels with it, I doubt they'd even notice," I said. "Are you with me or not?"

"Of course I'm with you! I just think we should talk this through before we commit ourselves to something we probably won't have time to regret for very long! And yes, I know how that sounds coming from me, which should give you some idea of just how much those golden bastards are freaking me out!"

"Needs must, when Heaven's in the driving seat," I said.

"Oh, very deep," said Molly. "Put that on Twitter, and see how fast it trends."

I looked at her calmly. "I do not tweet. With the kind of life I lead and the comments I make, I'd start wars. Do you tweet?"

"When would I have the time?"

"You do realise we're only talking like this to put off doing what we know we have to do?"

"I know that," said Molly. "I just wondered if you did."

"Atomic batteries to power; turbines to speed," I said. "Everything forward and trust in the Lord."

"This can only go well," said Molly.

I started forward, and then stopped as I realised Peter wasn't moving. I looked at him, and he stared back defiantly.

"You don't need me for this."

"You know more about the Angelic Droods than we do," I said.

"Which gives me more reason than most to be wary of them," said Peter. "The kind of life I've led does not make me at all keen to attract Heaven's attention."

"I am not letting you disappear back into the family again," I said firmly. "It's time for the last of the very-secret agents to come in from the cold and share his secrets. Because those golden thugs hanging up there are what happens when you don't. You need to tell the Matriarch everything you know about the Angelic Droods, if the family is to survive this. Now move it! Or I'll have Molly motivate you, in her own distinct and highly disturbing way."

"Love to," said Molly.

Peter sighed heavily, and went with us to talk to the Matriarch.

Once again the Droods crowded together before the Hall let me pass without even noticing I was there. They stood silently, heads tilted back, fascinated by the golden figures hovering over them. I could understand that. The closer I got to the Angelic Droods, the more intense their presence became. Looking directly at them was like staring into the sun—but you still didn't want to look away. The Angels were simply too perfect for this limited physical world.

They had none of the bodily distortions of the Demon Droods. All thirteen Angels had the simple perfection of classical statues. Only struck in gold, with featureless faces and massive, wide-spread wings. Everything about them held the eye, controlling the attention, demanding their every detail be studied and appreciated. I felt like I could look at them forever.

People I passed made vague sounds of awe and wonder. I was having trouble looking away, even to see where I was going. I wondered if this was how mice felt when confronted by the snakes that fascinated them, before they struck. That thought did the trick. I dragged my gaze away from the Angels through an effort of will, and concentrated on my torc. A thin stream of golden strange matter leapt up from my torc to cover my eyes with a pair of golden sunglasses, and just like that the fascination was gone. The Angelic Droods were still impressive, and obviously very dangerous. But I was a Drood. I dealt with impressive and dangerous every day, and sent them home, crying to their mothers. I pushed my way through the crowd, shouting at everyone to armour up.

"Pull yourselves together! The Angelic Droods are putting out some kind of signal to overwhelm us! Use your armour to cover your eyes, and break the signal! Do it!"

One by one people around me activated their torcs, calling up everything from golden sunglasses to full face masks, and immediately a babble of voices broke out as everyone realised how badly they'd been affected.

"Get ahold of yourselves!" I yelled. "We are Droods! We don't bow down to anyone!"

By the time I reached the Matriarch, the whole crowd was seeing the Angels with new eyes and being very vocal about it. If the Angelic

Droods had been hovering any lower, some of the crowd would have reached up to snag one by the ankle, drag it down out of the sky, and express their extreme displeasure to it. But throughout the growing clamour and all the sounds of anger, the Angels didn't react at all. The Matriarch regarded them carefully through a pair of very stylish golden sunglasses, and only nodded to me briefly as I joined her.

"Good work, Eddie. It felt like I was drowning in them, and going down for the third time. While they made me love it . . . the bastards."

"Give me the word, Matriarch, and I will blow them out of the sky," said the Sarjeant, hefting his guns hopefully.

"No you won't," I said quickly.

I explained who the Angelic Droods were and what their presence probably meant. The Matriarch just nodded occasionally. I couldn't tell how much she already knew. She glanced once at Peter, but neither of them said anything. Maxwell and Victoria came over to join us, determined not to be left out. They were both wearing full face masks above their immaculate white lab coats. The Sarjeant stirred uneasily as I talked with the Matriarch, keeping both of his guns trained steadily on the Angels. It was a part of his office that he was able to summon guns into his hands out of nowhere. I didn't recognise the ones he was currently holding, but they looked like they could blow holes through anything even remotely physical. Though whether they could do anything against Droods transformed by the engines of Heaven . . .

"All right," the Matriarch said finally. "Now I know what they are. Can't say it's made me feel any better."

"I said that!" said Molly.

"I'm sure you did," said the Matriarch. "Talk to me, people. I need options."

"Shoot the lot of them," said the Sarjeant. "No one messes with this family and gets away with it."

"And if the guns don't work?" I said.

"I have more guns."

"Let's put that on the back burner for now," I said.

"We need to concentrate on our defences," said Maxwell. "Our people are assembling something they're pretty confident will hold the Angels off."

"At least until we can get back inside the Hall and get our hands on some of the really appalling stuff," said Victoria.

"The force field around the Hall is gone," I said.

Everyone looked back at the Hall, and then at me.

"How did you manage that?" said Maxwell.

"The Pook got rid of it," I said. "After Edmund escaped from the Old Library."

The Sarjeant-at-Arms shook his head disgustedly. "Some days things wouldn't go right if you paid them."

"We will discuss Edmund later," said the Matriarch.

"Looking forward to that immensely," I said. I turned my attention to the Armourer. "If you could get back inside without the Angels noticing, could you use Alpha Red Alpha to raise the Shield?"

Maxwell and Victoria looked at each other. "Why would we want to do that?" said Maxwell.

"To put it around the Angels," I said. "Could you do it?"

"Probably," said Maxwell.

"And, in your expert opinion, would the Shield be strong enough to contain the Angels?"

"Probably," said Victoria.

"Not good enough," said the Matriarch. "Give me some more options, people. Preferably before the Angelic Droods decide to descend from the sky and start laying down the law."

"I'm going to talk to them," I said.

A number of quick looks passed back and forth between everyone else. No one seemed to think what I was proposing was in any way a good or even sane idea.

"They won't listen to you, Eddie," said Peter. "Angels don't have to listen to anyone."

"They've been gone a long time," I said. "They must be curious about what's happened to the family in their absence. If I can get them talking about one thing . . ."

"Don't make the mistake of thinking of them as Droods," said Peter. "They left their humanity behind a long time ago."

"If nothing else," I said steadily, "talking to them and holding their attention should buy you time to come up with something."

"Buy us whatever time you can, Eddie," said the Matriarch. "But don't commit the family to anything without consulting with me first."

"Angels aren't known for horse-trading," I said. "I'll settle for talking them out of killing everyone here."

"Argue from a position of strength," said the Sarjeant. "You have the whole family behind you."

"You really think anything we've got will work against an angel wrapped in Drood armour?" I said.

He smiled briefly. "Droods aren't afraid of Heaven or Hell. It's our job to make them afraid of us."

"There's a reason why we don't let you take part in negotiations," I said.

"Eddie," said Molly, "come over here and talk to me for a moment, away from the crazy man with guns."

She led me off to one side. I glanced up at the Angels. None of them had moved.

"You don't have to do this, Eddie," Molly said urgently. "Let someone else put their life on the line for once."

"I was there when the Demon Droods died," I said. "They'll want to talk about that. And let's face it: I've got a lot less life to lose than most. You stay here and make sure no one interferes."

"Hell with that," Molly said immediately. "I'm coming with you."

"You don't have to do this, Molly."

"Of course I do! If only to make sure the Angels don't ramp up the fascination and put you under their spell again."

I looked back at Peter, standing off to one side on his own. He didn't want to meet my eyes. The Demon Droods hadn't slowed him down one bit, so why were the Angelic Droods putting the wind up him so severely? Did he know something about them that he hadn't told me? More than likely . . . But I couldn't just stand around. I had to get the Angels talking, hold their attention, and take the initiative away from them. Before they decided to start the ball rolling for themselves, in a way the rest of us almost certainly wouldn't appreciate.

I strolled casually across the lawn, heading for the nearest Angel. Molly ambled along beside me, as though we were just out for a pleasant walk. I was pretty sure we weren't fooling anyone, but it's the attitude that counts. I armoured up completely as we drew closer, sealing myself inside my strange-matter second skin from head to toe, just to make sure the Angels couldn't influence me at close range. And, hopefully, to put me on more of an equal footing.

"I think I'll keep my magics to myself, for the moment," Molly said quietly. "Just in case you need something to draw their attention away from you."

"Sounds like a plan to me," I said. "But don't do anything to put yourself at risk."

She laughed. "We're walking up to a bunch of armoured Angels, with no idea of what they have on their minds. I think the safety boat has sailed."

"You might well be right about that," I said. "But wait until you're sure before you commit yourself to anything. And then hit them hard. Because I don't think they'd notice anything less."

"Just what I was thinking," said Molly.

I looked at her. "What did you do in the angel war, Molly?"

"Hid in a cellar until it was all over."

Everyone in my family fell back, to give us plenty of room. So we could have a little privacy for our negotiations, and so that if something should go horribly wrong, at least they'd be out of the direct line of fire. I came to a halt before the first hovering Angel. It didn't react at all.

"Hello there!" I said loudly. "Isn't it an absolutely lovely day? I'm Eddie. I speak for the Droods, for the moment. Please come down and talk, before the more restless members of my family decide to start using you for target practice."

If you're going to bluff, bluff big. The glowing figure before me dropped down out of the sky, taking his time about it. The wings didn't flap once. The Angel finally came to rest standing right in front of me, so close I could see my face mask reflected in his. I couldn't help noticing his feet didn't quite reach the ground, which I thought was showing off. I nodded easily to him.

"As entrances go, I'll give you ten out of ten for style."

"I am Uriel Drood." The voice that echoed from behind the featureless golden mask was so perfectly balanced I couldn't tell whether the Angel was male or female, both or neither. It was like listening to a statue talking. Molly leaned in close beside me, to murmur in my ear.

"Uriel was the name of the angel God set in place outside the Gates of Eden with a flaming sword, to make sure Humanity could never get back inside."

"Really?"

"So they say."

"The things you know," I said.

"I doubt that's the real Uriel," said Molly. "More likely, inspired by."

"A tribute Uriel," I said. "I can handle that."

I started to explain to the Angelic Drood who I was and why I was there, but he just talked right over me.

"You're a Drood," he said. "Nothing else matters."

"I'm not!" Molly said loudly.

"You stand with them," said Uriel. "You will share their fate."

"I only stand with Eddie," said Molly.

"That is enough," said Uriel.

"All right," I said, "love the style, all cool and laconic, but I think it's time we moved on to what really matters. Starting with why you're here and where you've been all this time."

"We are here for our revenge," said Uriel.

"That doesn't sound very angelic," said Molly.

"Revenge, justice, retribution for the sins of the family," said Uriel. "You know what they did to the Demon Droods. We helped them do it, and then they tried to do the same to us. After everything we did for them, they turned on us like ungrateful children. So we escaped in the only way left to us. We flew through Time, into the Future."

"You came here directly from then?" I said.

"How many centuries is that?" said Molly.

"It doesn't matter," said Uriel. "To angels, Time is just another direction to travel in. Our wings carried us through the paradox storms of the chronoflow, fighting the tides of history and the currents of fate. Our burning need for revenge gave us all the strength we needed."

I remembered the angel I found imprisoned in Cassandra Inc's flying fortress. It had said much the same thing about angels and Time. I just hoped the Angelic Droods weren't as powerful as the real thing.

"These Droods aren't the family who betrayed you," I said carefully. "Anyone who ever lied to you or tried to hurt you has been dead and gone for hundreds of years. You're in no danger now. Times have changed, and the family has changed too."

"They're still Droods," said Uriel.

"Can't argue with that," said Molly.

"Yes, thank you, Molly. Not really helping," I said. "Uriel, you could have an honoured place among us. You don't have to do this."

"But we want to," said Uriel. "And we will. You are responsible for the destruction of the Demon Droods. We can feel it on you."

"Well, yes, indirectly . . ."

"We chose that point for our return," said Uriel. "Because Droods who were capable of such a thing could also be a threat to us. And would have to be dealt with before we could ever feel safe again."

"No one here wants to destroy you!" I said. "Well, all right, some do; we are Droods after all, and we haven't changed that much. But we're far more civilised these days. We'd much rather bargain and make allies than fight. Usually."

"We don't care," said Uriel. "We will have retribution for what was done to us. For the sins of the family."

I struggled to keep my voice calm. "What about our reward for all the good we've done?"

"Put your case to God," said Uriel. "Ask for his mercy; we have none."

"Why not?" said Molly.

He looked at her for the first time. "We gave it up. It got in the way."

"Molly and I found an imprisoned angel recently and set it free," I said.

"It's true," said Molly. "We really did."

"Tell it to the Judge of all," said Uriel.

"This isn't about justice or retribution," I said. "It's about revenge. This is all down to hurt feelings and getting your own back, because the family turned on you. I can understand that; I've been there myself. But you can't move forward if you're always looking back. I was declared rogue and thrown out of the family, my own grandmother ordered my death, but I still came back to Drood Hall to save the family from itself. Because I believed it was worth saving."

"As long as one Drood still exists, we could never feel safe," said Uriel. "We will not risk being betrayed again. So you're all going to die."

"Because this is all about you," said Molly.

"Yes," said Uriel. "It is."

"Typical Drood," said Molly.

"Really not helping," I said.

"Enough talk," said Uriel. "It is clear that Droods are still Droods, ready to say anything to get what they want. Time for you to die."

He punched me in the face, his golden fist moving so quickly I never even saw it coming. There was enough strength in the blow to rip the head right off a normal human being. The impact slammed my head round and knocked me off balance, but that was all. I hardly even felt it inside my armour. I turned back to face Uriel, still on my feet, not hurt at all. And he just stood there, astonished. I was grinning like a wolf behind my face mask. It was good to be reminded that the old Heart armour was no match for strange-matter armour.

"What kind of Drood are you?" said Uriel.

"The real deal," I said.

I held up one fist and grew heavy spikes out of the golden knuckles. And while Uriel was preoccupied watching that, I punched him right in the middle of his featureless face. His armour actually cracked under the impact, and he staggered back, arms flailing. Molly whooped loudly, punching the air and jumping up and down on the spot. I thought for a moment Uriel might fall, but his great golden wings spread out to balance him, and he didn't. He shook his head slowly and turned back to face me. The cracks in his face mask had already repaired themselves. Behind me I heard the Sarjeant-at-Arms calling out to the family.

"You see that? They're not so damned special! Take the bastards down!"

Uriel raised his right hand, and a flaming sword erupted out of it. A long, fiery blade, radiating a heat so intense I could feel it even through my armour. A quick glance at the sky was all it took to confirm all the other Angelic Droods had flaming swords now.

"Okay," said Molly. "Things just escalated."

I grew a long golden sword out of my right glove. Uriel stared at it. Drood armour couldn't do things like that in his day.

"You see?" I said to him. "This really isn't the world you knew. We don't have to be enemies."

He struck at me with his flaming sword, inhumanly fast. But I was ready for him this time, and my golden blade shot forward to meet the flaming sword and stop it dead. The weird flames leapt up, trying to consume my blade, but the golden strange matter resisted them easily. I beat Uriel's sword aside and took the fight to him, cutting and hacking with all the strength and speed my armour could give me. The Angelic Drood blocked my every blow, but was forced back step by step. His parries grew faster and more certain, until suddenly I couldn't get anywhere near him. I stood my ground and fought on, searching for some sign of weakness in his technique.

The remaining Angels dropped out of the sky like so many golden meteors, to attack the Droods with their flaming swords. My family armoured up, growing golden swords and axes and battle staffs out of their hands. Every single one of them came charging forward, crying out defiantly, to take on the Angels. One Angelic Drood flew straight at the Sarjeant-at-Arms, who opened fire with both guns. The sheer impact of whatever he was using for ammunition was enough to stop the Angel dead in mid-flight, but not enough to do him any harm.

Uriel beat my blade aside with unexpected strength, and his flaming sword came sweeping round in a vicious arc, going for my throat. I couldn't bring my sword up in time to block the blow, so I instinctively raised my left arm to intercept it. Expecting the flaming sword to just skid harmlessly away, like the Demon Drood's claws. Uriel's sword cut right through my armour, and sank deep into the flesh beneath. I cried out, in shock as much as in pain. Blood flew from my wounded arm as the Angel jerked his blade free. Molly howled in fury and rushed forward.

Blood ran thickly underneath my armour, and terrible pain shot through the whole length of my arm. I retreated quickly, sweeping my sword desperately back and forth before me to hold the Angel off.

Uriel attacked with everything he had, trying to press his advantage. I stuck to purely defensive moves while my armour repaired itself, sealing seamlessly over the wound. My head cleared as the armour pushed the pain away and clamped down hard to contain the bleeding. Anything else would have to wait.

Heart armour might be inferior to mine, but it seemed the flaming sword was another matter.

I stopped retreating and held my ground, parrying the Angel's blows and refusing to be moved. He tried to overwhelm me with strength and speed, but that was never going to work. A slow satisfaction moved through me as I realised that technically, I was the better swordsman. My family had learned a lot about fighting techniques down the years. Pain still nagged in my arm, flaring up unpleasantly with every movement, but the flaming sword's edge hadn't damaged the bone. It was just pain, and I was used to pain. Dying slowly will do that to you.

Molly moved in close and blasted the Angelic Drood with a lightning bolt at point-blank range. The Angel intercepted the bolt with his flaming sword, and the lightning shot harmlessly away into the distance. Molly swore briefly and hit the Angel again and again, with magic after magic. I fell back and let her get on with it, taking a moment to get my breathing under control. Fighting an Angel is hard work, and my stamina wasn't what it used to be. But Uriel's flaming sword stopped most of the magics before they could reach him, and the few that got past just crackled harmlessly around his armour, unable to find a way in. It was still Drood armour, after all. I realised Molly was slowing as the strength went out of her. She'd been through a lot and her reserves were running out. I called to her to take a break, and went to confront Uriel again, grateful it wasn't my fighting arm that had been wounded.

Molly fell back to give me room to work, but she wouldn't leave me. She muttered fiercely under her breath, trying to put together some combination of magics that might work. I had confidence in her. After all, she did have a lot of experience when it came to fighting Droods.

I cut viciously at Uriel with my golden blade, and he parried my every move with his flaming sword. I was grunting with the effort of each blow now, but he never made a sound. The edge of my sword slammed into his left shoulder, opening up a long cut in his armour, but no blood flew. I cut him again and again, but he never cried out once. The armour repaired itself, and the Angel fought on. A slow chill ran through me as I wondered what, exactly, was underneath that armour.

Molly yelled for me to get out of the way. I disengaged and stumbled back, gasping for breath. Molly conjured up a bottomless hole under Uriel's feet. He dropped into it a few inches, and then his great wings cupped the air and he shot up into the sky, leaving us behind. He dropped down again some distance away, looking for new prey. I thrust my sword into the ground and leaned on it tiredly. Molly came over to join me.

"You forgot about the wings?" I said. "Really?"

"Don't nag," said Molly.

She closed the bottomless hole with a gesture, while I looked around to see how the rest of my family was doing.

The Angels were surrounded by armoured Droods, throwing themselves forward from all sides. But the Angelic Droods wielded their flaming swords with inhuman speed and power, slicing through my family's armour almost at will. Droods cried out and fell, and the Angels stepped over the dead and kicked the wounded aside to get to their next victim. Our numbers were enough to slow the Angels, but that was all. Some Droods threw themselves bodily at the Angels and hung on to their arms and shoulders, trying to drag them down through sheer weight of numbers. But the Angels just shrugged them off with superhuman strength and kept fighting.

Droods were falling everywhere now. Their armour protected

them from everything short of a direct hit, and even when the armour was broached it repaired itself. But the men and women inside the armour stayed hurt. More and more were falling to the churned-up, blood-soaked ground and not rising again. None of the other Droods would retreat from the fight, not while the family was under threat, so they fought on. Until they fell or died. There was always someone to step forward and take their place, because they knew their duty. *Anything for the family.* The Angelic Droods kept fighting, their flaming swords rising and falling with cold, implacable fury. Now and again a Drood would risk everything to get close enough to run an Angel through with their golden blade, but the Angel seemed to take no hurt at all.

"That is still Heart armour, right?" said Molly. "So if we can just wear the Angels down, their armour will run out of energy?"

"That's the theory," I said. "Though I don't recall it working too well with the Demon Droods."

"Maybe you should call on the Pook again."

"He never leaves the Old Library. Besides, he's probably full."

"You ready to go back to work?" said Molly.

"I've got my second wind," I said.

I hadn't, but I couldn't stand around any longer and watch my family suffer. I summoned up what was left of my strength and raised my sword, and the Matriarch's voice rose sharply above the clamour.

"Fall back! Everyone get away from the Angelic Droods! The defences in the grounds have been activated; let them do their work!"

All across the lawns, armoured Droods retired thankfully. Some leaning on others, some having to be carried or dragged. The Angels held their positions, looking around uncertainly. They didn't know about all the terrible things we'd installed as ground defences since their time. I smiled harshly behind my mask; they had no idea of what was about to hit them.

My family had learned a lot since the last few times our grounds were invaded. By the Springheel Jacks and the Accelerated Men and the Dancing Dead. We'd put all kinds of hidden weapons in place to slow down, disorient, or just kill the hell out of the unwary enemy. Scientific and magical, laterally minded, and downright vicious. Because whoever invades our grounds and dares to threaten us where we live has already thrown away the rule book and deserves everything that happens to them. The defences are there to do the things we don't want to do ourselves, because it would take too long to clean the blood off our armour afterwards.

I saw the Sarjeant-at-Arms gesture sharply, and all hell broke loose.

Tanglefields—shimmering energy fields that jumped up out of nowhere to wrap themselves around the Angels and drag them down—erupted around the Angelic Droods. The fields caught three of them before the rest shot up into the sky. Ravening energies crawled all over the trapped Angels as they struggled and kicked helplessly on the ground. The energies tightened, scarring the Angels' armour like living barbed wire until it began to crack open under the pressure. Some of my family started cheering, only to break off as one Angel lurched to his feet and threw the energies off him with one great shrug of his golden wings. The other two did the same, and tanglefields that could have wrecked a tank or crushed a golem just disappeared.

"That shouldn't have been possible," I said numbly.

"Must be the angelic nature," said Molly. "They're not just material beings any more."

"That's . . . disturbing."

"Well, yes. Feel free to file a complaint later, if your family has a Tough Shit Department."

Two Angels dropped down out of the sky, thinking the area was safe now. The moment they landed, teleport mines activated, and sent a hundred different parts of them to a hundred different locations across the grounds. My family cheered again as bits and pieces of Angels pattered down over the lawns, only to break off again as they realised each piece was still wrapped in golden armour. The teleported pieces had barely touched the ground before they went shooting back across the lawns to recombine into the two Angels. Who appeared entirely unaffected by the experience.

"Okay," I said. "That is hardcore."

"Heavenly hardcore," said Molly. "What are they inside that armour?"

"God knows," I said. "What is made on Heaven's loom cannot be unmade in the material world."

Molly looked at me. "What?"

"I was quoting," I said. "From *Jane's Guide to Angels*."

"You've read up on angels?"

"Know thy enemy."

More hidden weapons manifested across the grounds, rising up out of hidden bunkers. Time Bombs, Warp Spasms, and Reality Inverters; vicious and powerful, but none of them enough to stop the Angelic Droods. The brightly shining winged figures were hit again and again by forces designed to bring down whole armies, and didn't flinch once. Because things of the material world held no terrors for them. The Armourer charged forward, strange new weapons shimmering in their hands. Their lab assistants followed close behind, each of them armed with something foul and awful. They hit the Angels with everything they had, unloosing terrible energies that had no place in any sane world, but the Angelic Droods just shrugged them off.

They surged forward, flaming swords in their hands, and Maxwell and Victoria had no choice but to throw aside their useless tech and grow their own golden swords. They went to meet the Angels, and the lab assistants were right behind them, manifesting strange golden weapons of their own. They fought bravely, until the Angels struck them down. Because they were Droods, and because they were devoted to their Armourer. Maxwell and Victoria fought side by side, and then back to back, and would not leave the field—because they were Droods, and because they were devoted to their assistants.

One Angelic Drood headed straight for the Matriarch, cutting down everyone who got in his way. She didn't flinch, holding her sword at the ready, but the Sarjeant-at-Arms was quickly there to stand between the Matriarch and the Angel. The only Drood who hadn't armoured up. Two really big and ugly guns appeared in his hands. He opened fire, and the Angel lurched and staggered under the impact. But he didn't fall. The guns disappeared from the Sarjeant's hands, to be replaced by two disturbing alien things I didn't even recognise. He fired again, and the Angel's armour twisted and deformed under the ravening energies. Only to repair itself, almost immediately. The Sarjeant cursed dispassionately, and the weapons disappeared from his hands. He put on his armour at last, and filled his hands with a huge double-headed golden war-axe. He hefted it thoughtfully, and strode forward to face the Angelic Drood. The Matriarch went with him, golden sword at the ready. Because they were Droods, and knew their duty.

I ran to join them, with Molly pounding gamely along beside me. Maggie was still my Matriarch, and the family needed her more than it needed a field agent who was already dying. I hit the Angel from behind, my sword slicing right through his spine. He fell to one knee, but his armour had already sealed over whatever damage I might have done to the body beneath. I cut at the Angel again and again while it was down, but it was all I could do to hold it there. Molly whooped loudly and jumped up onto the Angel's shoulders. She placed both hands flat on either side of his golden head, and terrible energies erupted between them. The Angel screamed and threw her off. Molly hit the grass rolling, and was quickly back on her feet. The Angel opened his wings and shot up into the sky, still screaming.

I raised a golden hand and Molly high-fived me. The Sarjeant was already looking round for another enemy. The Matriarch nodded briskly to me.

"We have to keep the Angels out of the Hall. If they gain access to some of the things we keep in there these days . . ."

"Like Alpha Red Alpha?" I said. "Or the Armageddon Codex?"

"You had to say that out loud, didn't you?" said the Sarjeant. "But there is still something else we can try . . . All Droods: Fall back to the Hall! Do it now!"

The Droods turned as one and hurried back to the Hall. I think a lot of them were glad for an excuse. I went back with the Matriarch, Molly sticking close beside me. The Sarjeant fell back step by step, keeping a careful watch on the Angelic Droods. The surviving lab assistants were the last to leave the field, because they practically had to drag the Armourer along with them. Maxwell and Victoria were taking the deaths of their assistants personally. Pretty soon, all the Droods had lined up together, forming a golden barrier in front of the Hall. The Angelic Droods stood together, watching us, no doubt suspecting a trap. The Sarjeant-at-Arms laughed briefly. A dark, disturbing sound.

"That's right. Make yourselves a good target."

"What have you got in mind, Sarjeant?" I said breathlessly. "What is there that's left?"

"The robot guns," he said.

"Are you kidding me? Your guns didn't do much good!"

"The robot guns have been upgraded," said the Sarjeant.

He nodded to the Matriarch, and she spoke a Word loudly. All across the grounds robot guns rose from their hidden emplacements underneath the lawns. Long barrels whirred loudly as they turned to target the Angelic Droods, and then they all opened fire at once. The sound of dozens of robot guns firing together was painfully loud, and the Angels staggered back and forth as they were pounded repeatedly from every side.

"Steel and silver bullets, blessed and cursed," said the Sarjeant, smiling unpleasantly. "Depleted uranium and magical crystals. Along with a whole bunch of alien stuff we don't even have names for yet, that can do very nasty things to living tissues. Some so appalling they even disturbed the crap out of the lab assistants."

"All very impressive," I said. "But I can't help noticing that none of the Angels are falling."

Some bullets ricocheted away from the Angels' armour, and some punched right through. The sheer impact of so many hits drove the Angels this way and that, but still they refused to fall. One by one the robot guns fell silent as they ran out of ammunition. The thunder of the guns died away until only a few guns were left firing, and then one . . . and then none. The long barrels swung back and forth, targeting one Angel or another, but there was nothing more they could do. The Angelic Droods slowly straightened up and looked at us. The Sarjeant-at-Arms swore briefly.

"What is the world coming to, when you can't rely on really big guns to get the job done?"

"You know," said Molly, "we could just scatter. Run in all directions. They couldn't follow everyone."

"They'd never stop coming after us," I said. "You heard Uriel. They want every single one of us dead."

"Besides," said the Matriarch, "Droods only run one way: towards the enemy. Sarjeant-at-Arms, take the lead."

"An honour, Matriarch," said the Sarjeant. "Droods! Form up behind me! Let's show these Angels what hell on earth is really like!"

He sprinted forward, with the Matriarch running at his side. I was right behind them, with Molly at my side, and the Armourer and their lab assistants were right behind us. And after them came the rest of my family. Droods in their armour, who would not be intimidated by anyone.

We charged across the churned-up mud of what had been our lawns, our heavy feet throwing dirt and grass in every direction, to hit the Angelic Droods head-on. Because there was nothing else left to do. The Angels stood their ground and waited for us, flaming swords in their hands. We slammed into them like an incoming wave crashing against the rocks. An overwhelming force hitting an immovable object. Flaming swords and golden blades rose and fell. Molly used her magic to shield as many Droods as she could, to give them a fighting chance, but I could see the strength going out of her with every spell she cast. Until only her iron will kept her on her feet. She'd been through so much, and even the infamous wild witch of the woods had her limits. There was nothing I could do to help her, so I just threw myself at the nearest Angel and hit him with everything I had.

The tides of battle rolled this way and that, the Angelic Droods driven back and forth by the sheer pressure of numbers, but even when an Angel fell under a dozen hacking blades, they always rose up again. I heard the Matriarch cry out, and looked round to see an Angel drop out of the sky like a golden bird of prey, heading straight for her. Somehow she'd been caught out in the open, on her own. The Angel brought his flaming sword crashing down, backed by the momentum of his descent, and although the Matriarch braced herself and brought up her golden sword to parry the blow, the impact was enough to knock her off her feet. She sprawled helplessly on the grass, only half-conscious, her golden sword disappearing from her hand. The Angel crashed to earth standing astride her and raised his flaming sword with both hands—to stab her through the chest and pin her to the ground.

I ran forward, crying out loudly to distract the Angel, but he didn't even look round. There was no way I could get to them in time. And then Peter appeared out of nowhere, not even wearing his armour, to stand defiantly between the Matriarch and the Angel. The flaming sword punched through his chest and out his back, in a thick gout of blood. Peter cried out once, a soft old man's sound, but he didn't fall. Somehow he still stood his ground, and grabbed the Angel's wrist with his bare hands. Smiling grimly.

"We've learned some new tricks since your time. Like a close-range self-destruct, built into a very-secret agent's armour. For when you absolutely have to take your enemy with you. *Anything for the family.*"

He spoke a Word, and his torc exploded. Peter and the Angel disappeared in a blast of intense light, and when it faded away there was no trace left of either of them. The last of the very-secret agents was dead, following his duty to the end. The twelve remaining Angels put back their heads and let out a single harsh, desolate howl. As though they couldn't believe one of them was gone. That such a thing should even be possible.

Everyone stood still, caught up in the moment. And then another Angelic Drood headed straight for the Matriarch. She scrambled up onto her feet to meet him, her sword back in her hand. But now I was close enough to intercept the Angel. I had no intention of duelling this one, because that hadn't gotten me anywhere. Instead I pulled my sword back into my glove and put all my energy into running. So that when the Angel finally went for the Matriarch I was there to throw myself at him and haul him down onto the ground. He tried to stab me with his flaming sword, but couldn't find a way to drive it home at such close range. We rolled back and forth on the grass, trading blows with all the strength our armour could provide.

I grabbed hold of the Angel's throat with both hands and pressed down hard. I'd remembered an old trick, that strong armour can sometimes override lesser armour, if the wearer's will is up to it. I locked my golden hands onto the armoured throat and concentrated, and my hands passed through both sets of armour to reach and fasten onto the bare flesh beneath. For all its angelic nature, it felt like a perfectly ordinary throat to me. So with a cold, inflexible rage I throttled the life out of the Angelic Drood.

He kicked and struggled beneath me, slamming blows into my side so hard they hurt me even through my armour. He dismissed his flaming sword so he could grab my wrists with both hands, but he couldn't break my hold and he couldn't shake me off. I strangled him, pressing down with all my strength, until finally I realised that he had stopped breathing and stopped moving. It took a long moment before I could make myself let go of him. Behind my golden mask, my lips had drawn back into a death's-head grin.

He killed Peter. He tried to kill the Matriarch. The Angels wanted my whole family dead. They had no mercy in them, and neither did I.

I got to my feet, breathing raggedly. I'd taken a lot of punishment from the Angel before he died, and it was all I could do to stand upright. My wounded arm ached fiercely; I must have opened the cut again. But still my armour held me up. I looked down at the dead Angel, and wanted to say *That was for you, Peter.* But I just didn't have the strength.

Molly cried out a warning, and I looked round to see two Angels running straight at me. I had killed one of their own, and all they could think of was revenge. Molly stabbed a desperate hand at them, but nothing happened. She'd exhausted her magics defending the other Droods and had nothing left for me. She started running, but I knew she'd never reach me in time. I filled my hand with a golden sword and stood my ground. Wondering if I could find the strength to drive it through one Angel before the other killed me.

And then everything stopped, and everyone looked up, as a great shadow fell across the battleground. A deafening roar filled the sky above. And a dragon flew over us, soaring across the grounds on widespread wings, complete and reborn. No longer just the severed head I'd brought home from Castle Frankenstein so long ago. My uncle Jack had sworn he'd set things in motion that would grow the dragon a new body eventually. The reborn dragon was huge and magnificent, his scales burning a bright emerald green. Massive wings flapped powerfully, driving the dragon on in defiance of gravity and nature, as he flew for the first time in centuries.

He opened his mouth and blasted the Angelic Droods with long streams of supernatural fire, targeting each one expertly. My family fell back quickly to give the dragon room to work, but he never missed once. The old Heart armour of the Angelic Droods was no match for the dragon's fiery breath. They staggered back and forth, screaming horribly, until one by one they crashed to the ground and lay still, their armour melted away or fused together. Molly finally reached me, and I armoured down so she could hold me and I could lean on her.

It was all over very quickly. What was under the Angels' armour turned out to be mortal after all. The dragon circled overhead for a while, to make sure he hadn't missed anyone, and then called cheerfully down to me.

"Hello, Eddie! Molly! It's good to be back! Peter came to me and told me I was needed, that I was ready to leave my burial mound at last, and he was right! Come round and see me later, and we'll talk."

I waved a hand at him, but didn't have the strength for anything else. Molly waved hard enough for both of us. The dragon swung around in a tight arc and flew off. All across the grounds my family armoured down and congratulated themselves and each other on still being alive. A few moved slowly and cautiously among the half-melted Angels, searching for survivors.

"I don't know," Molly said finally, letting me lean companionably against her. "The Pook saved us from the Demons, and the dragon saved us from the Angels. Are we finally getting old?"

"No," I said. "Lucky, maybe."

The Matriarch and the Sarjeant-At-Arms came over to join us. Armoured down, they looked almost as exhausted as I felt. I started to explain some of the background behind the Angelic Droods, but the Matriarch waved dismissively.

"I know what they were. Sometimes I think there's too much history in this family. Who was that old man who sacrificed himself to save me? I didn't recognise him."

"His name was Peter," I said. "He used to be a field agent."

I didn't say any more. If the Matriarch really didn't know Peter was the last of the very-secret agents, I wasn't going to be the one to tell her. I took a moment to regret all the family knowledge that died with Peter. He really did take his secrets with him to the grave, just as he'd promised. I realised the Sarjeant was looking at me, and made myself pay attention.

"What happened with Edmund?" he said flatly.

"He got away," I said. "After he stole a book from the Old Library."

"Why didn't you stop him?" said the Sarjeant.

I explained how the Demon Droods escaped from the Grim Gulf, and how much damage they'd done to the Old Library before the Pook took care of them. The Matriarch winced.

"You can explain that to the Librarian. I wouldn't dare."

"Edmund arranged all of this just so he could steal a book?" said the Sarjeant. "Which book was it?"

"I don't know," I said. "I'm hoping the Librarian will be able to tell us. Where is William? I don't see him."

"I had Yorith take him away before the fighting started," said the Matriarch. "He would have wanted to fight, and we couldn't afford to lose him."

She called out to the nearest Droods and told them to find William and Yorith, and then escort them back to the Old Library. As they hurried off to do that, I took the time to look around me. The grounds before the Hall had been reduced to blood-soaked mud, with bodies lying everywhere. We'd taken down the Angelic Droods, but it had cost us dearly. Most of my family were just sitting where they'd collapsed, heads hanging down with exhaustion. Some looked to be pretty badly injured. Doctors moved among them, doing what they could to stabilise the most serious cases before moving them inside.

One young man was kicking the body of a dead Angel, slowly and methodically.

I looked down at my wounded arm. I'd had to leave it covered in a sheath of golden armour to protect it. The pain had settled into a slow, vicious ache. I didn't even want to think about what the injury looked like under the armour. Molly swore harshly.

"Eddie! You're hurt!"

"Yes," I said. "I had noticed."

"Sit down. Take it easy. I'll call for a doctor. We have to get you looked at."

"Don't fuss," I said. "It can wait."

"No it can't!" Molly said fiercely. "You're . . ." And then she stopped. She couldn't bring herself to use the word *dying*.

"It can wait," I said.

We both looked round sharply as a Drood called out urgently. He'd found some survivors among the Angels. The Matriarch immediately insisted on taking a look, and the Sarjeant insisted on going with her, just in case one of the Angels found enough strength for a last desperate gesture. I went after them, with Molly sticking stubbornly close.

"I am not letting you out of my sight," she said sternly. "I swear, even when you're dead you won't have the sense to lie down."

"The doctors should concentrate on those they can help," I said. Using my most reasonable voice, because I knew that always drove her crazy. "They can take a look at me later."

"How are you?" said Molly.

"Still dying," I said. "And tired, really tired. But apart from that, pretty good."

I thought, but had the good sense not to say out loud, that I didn't know how long that would last. I'd been through worse fights than this and never felt so completely used up. I should have bounced back by now. I had a feeling I was going to crash, and crash badly, once the last of the adrenaline ran out. So I might as well keep busy. As long as there was still work to be done.

We stood together, looking down at the three surviving Angels.

They were all refusing to lower their armour, and given the way their arms were welded to their torsos and their legs were fused together, I wasn't sure how we'd be able to get it off without expert help. I remembered Edmund brandishing his straight razor and talking about better can openers, and surprised myself with a brief bark of laughter. The others looked at me oddly for a moment, and then turned back to the Angels. Molly leaned in beside me.

"Remember the dead Droods we found at the Other Hall?" she said quietly. "Their armour had been melted and fused like this."

"Maybe they met a dragon too," I said.

"Armour down," the Sarjeant commanded the Angels. There was no response.

"At least show us your faces," said the Matriarch.

One Angel slowly turned his distorted golden face mask in our direction. "Why should we?"

"So you can show us your defiance," I said. "You're Droods, aren't you?"

The golden mask slowly retracted, in fits and starts, to reveal the face beneath. As perfect as a classical statue, but completely lacking in character. The eyes had no pupils, but they still seemed to look right through me. I couldn't tell whether the Angel was male or female, both or neither. The other two Angels peeled back their masks. One face was a charred ruin without any eyes. The other had been roasted red and raw all down one side. Neither of them made a sound, though their agonies must have been appalling.

"You're Eddie Drood," said the first Angel.

"And you're Uriel," I said. "I recognise the voice."

"I should have cut you down the moment I met you," Uriel said flatly.

"There doesn't have to be any more killing," I said. "The war's over."

"It will never be over, as long as one of us still lives," said Uriel.

"Why did you do this?" the Matriarch said loudly. "None of this was necessary. Whatever was done to you in the past, we are all Droods. All family."

"The family betrayed us," said Uriel. "Why should you be any different?"

"Because times have changed," I said. "We've changed."

Uriel turned his head slowly to one side to look out across the grounds at his dead brethren, burned alive inside their armour. "No you haven't."

"Give me your word," the Matriarch said to Uriel. "Give me your surrender, and I'll have my people carry you into the Hall. The doctors will get you out of your armour and do what they can for you."

"Of course," Uriel said immediately. "No more fighting. We surrender."

He was lying. I could hear it in his voice, see it in his implacable face. One glance at the Matriarch showed me she knew it too.

"Take them inside," I said. "And guard them. Don't look at me like that, Matriarch. These people only underwent alchemical marriages all those years ago because they were forced to by the family. Who knows what that unnatural practice did to their minds? What they did then helped make the Droods possible. We have a duty of care for them."

"No we don't," said the Matriarch. "Their duty was to do what the family required of them. My duty is to protect the family." She turned to the Sarjeant-at-Arms. "Kill them. Kill them all."

The Sarjeant shot Uriel in the head. He shot the other two while I was still registering that he had a gun in his hand.

"How could you?" I said to the Matriarch. "He wasn't a threat any more!"

"We could never trust them," said the Matriarch, meeting my gaze unflinchingly. "I gave Uriel his chance, and he lied to my face. I'm damned if I'll lose any more of the family to these misbegotten mistakes. This is why you had to give up being in charge, Eddie. Because you never could make the hard decisions."

"I never wanted to be in charge," I said. "And I can remember a time when you didn't either."

I looked down at Uriel's cold, inhuman face. He didn't look surprised at what had happened. He seemed to have been expecting it.

"I told him the family had changed," I said. "I was wrong."

CHAPTER FIVE

We Need to Talk about Edmund

The war was over, and the Droods went home.

I walked through the front door with Molly on my arm, each of us leaning companionably on the other. It took a while to make our way through the entrance hall, as part of a stream of triumphant but deathly tired Droods. People chattered loudly all around us, discussing things they'd seen and done out in the grounds, that they hadn't expected to have to deal with when they got up in the morning. And of course everyone was arguing about who'd done what and who'd done most. Some weren't even that sure about who they'd been fighting or why. The Matriarch and the Sarjeant-at-Arms had armoured up and ordered everyone into the fray . . . and everyone just did what they had to and hoped someone would get around to explaining it all later.

The walking wounded and the shell-shocked stumbled along side by side, with empty eyes and heads hanging down, until someone came to lead them away. Others were quiet, mourning fallen friends or loves, but there wasn't much in the way of tears. Droods are brought up to be self-contained and self-controlled. People triumph and people die, but the family goes on.

I smiled and nodded to those around me, and they nodded and

smiled at me. I didn't feel like talking. I was preoccupied with my own thoughts. Among other things, it had occurred to me that this was probably the last time I'd ever fight alongside my family. My last chance to do something with them that mattered. I was learning the hard way that a large part of dying is saying good-bye to things. Making lists and ticking things off one by one. *Last time I'll do this, or be here, or see that.*

I felt tired, so tired. I stumbled suddenly, missing my step, as though the floor wasn't where I expected it to be. I almost fell, and Molly had to hold me up until I could do it for myself. We stood together in the middle of the entrance hall and let the Droods stream past us, too wrapped up in their own pains and problems to notice mine. I wanted to get moving again, but my head was packed with cotton wool and my thoughts moved slowly, uncertain of their way. Molly looked quickly around, spotted a side door, and half helped, half carried me over to it, snarling viciously at anyone who got in our way. I felt vaguely that I should apologise for her, but by then Molly had kicked open the door and hustled me into the room beyond.

I forced my aching head up, to check where we were. Just a simple open room, large and light and airy, with half a dozen reading tables and some comfortable chairs. Molly slammed the door shut and helped settle me into the nearest chair. I sighed with relief once I didn't have to carry my own weight any longer. I looked unhurriedly around me, taking in the bookshelves covering all four walls, tightly packed with identical leather-bound volumes. Molly made sure I was okay before taking a look around her.

"What is this—another Library?"

I smiled, feeling better if not stronger. "Not a Library; not as such. This is the Diary Room. Every member of the family is encouraged to keep a diary, not as part of the official family history, but just to record the everyday experiences of what it's like to be a Drood. So future generations can look back and see how much has changed and how much has stayed the same. Not everyone keeps a diary; it's not required. But there's always a few who do. The earliest versions go so far back they aren't even in English. It does the family good, now and again, to be reminded of just how far back we go."

I started to wave a hand expansively at the shelves, with all their centuries of recorded memories, and then stopped. I didn't have the energy.

"The Drood Diaries. Handwritten and entirely personal. Private during the writers' lifetimes, but open to anyone after their death."

Molly shook her head slowly. "There must be hundreds of them. Maybe even thousands . . ."

"Wouldn't surprise me," I said. "Looks like we're going to have to put up some more shelves."

She looked at me. "Have you read any of them?"

"I've dipped into a few," I said. "There's fascinating stuff to be found in these accounts. The real stories behind the official histories. All the personal details, to give an event context and meaning. In this room there are answers to questions you don't even know to ask. The everyday secrets of my family. Some Matriarchs have talked about putting a stop to the Diaries on security grounds, but they always get talked out of it. If only because we might need something in here someday."

"Do you keep a diary?" said Molly.

"I've written a few things down."

"Let me take a look at your arm."

"We don't have time for this, Molly."

"Make time," said Molly. "And don't argue with me, if you ever want to see me naked again."

"Yes, Molly."

I looked down at the golden sheath covering my left arm. The extruded armour gleamed dully, giving away nothing. I pulled it back into my torc, and immediately the long wound opened up, spurting blood. I hissed at the pain and grabbed hold of my forearm with my right hand, clamping down hard to hold the cut together. Blood pumped thickly between my fingers. Molly made a low sound of shock and distress.

"I must have torn it open again," I said.

"Even a cut that bad shouldn't still be bleeding like that," Molly said slowly. "That's not right, Eddie."

"Don't fuss, Molly."

"Don't be an idiot. You need help."

"I'm all right!"

"No you're not! You need a doctor!"

"I am not going to the Infirmary," I said firmly. I couldn't tell her why. Couldn't tell her I had this sick, certain fear that if I went in, I'd never leave.

"Ethel!" Molly's voice was so loud, I would have jumped if I hadn't been so exhausted. "Ethel! Can you hear me? We need you!"

"It's all right, Molly," said Ethel. Her voice came clearly out of the empty air before us. "I'm here. I'm always here."

"Can you talk some sense into Eddie?"

"Almost certainly not," said Ethel. "But I can see the problem. I have already called for a doctor."

The door burst open and a young woman came bustling in, without waiting to be invited. She was tall, slender, intense, and driven, wearing a white doctor's coat with fresh bloodstains down the front. Dusky-skinned, with high cheekbones and flashing dark eyes. She looked like she'd just been called away from a lot of hard work, and wasn't at all happy about it.

"I am Dr Indira," she said sharply, striding right up to me. "And you're just the patient, Eddie, so don't give me a hard time. Look at that arm! Why aren't you in the Infirmary?"

"Don't even start," said Molly. "Aren't you a bit young to be a doctor?"

Indira sniffed loudly. "We grow up fast around here." She dropped down on one knee so she could look closely at my injury. "Take your hand off your arm, Eddie. Let the dog see the rabbit. The sooner I deal with you, the sooner I can get back to the butcher's shop you people have made of my Wards. There are patients there who need me a lot more than you do. I'm only here visiting you now because this implacable voice in my head told me I had to."

"Get on with it," said Ethel.

The moment I let go of my arm, blood spurted from the long wound, splashing the front of Indira's coat. She didn't flinch. Golden gloves formed over her hands, and she murmured under her breath as she examined and probed my wound with gentle fingers. My blood didn't cling to her gloves, just dripped steadily onto the floor. I gritted my teeth as she worked, but I wouldn't let myself look away. I needed to know how bad it was. Indira raised one hand, and a long, slender wand appeared in it from nowhere. It looked worryingly like bone. Maybe unicorn's horn. I'm no expert.

"Is that the same kind of magic that allows the Sarjeant to summon his guns?" I said. Just to be saying something.

"Yes. Probably. Only more scientific, and therefore more reliable. Now shut up while I'm working, before I decide to take a look at your prostate while I'm here."

She swept the wand over my wound, made the wand disappear, and then looked away to study a display only she could see.

"Hmmm . . ."

"I hate it when doctors do that," said Molly.

"You'd hate it even more if you knew what we were really thinking," said Indira. "I can see your problem, Eddie. Your tissues are healing too slowly, and your blood isn't clotting. Basically, all your body's repair systems are shutting down as the poison inside you continues to make progress. We did warn you . . ."

"Never mind that," said Molly. "What can you do?"

"Not much," said Indira. She got to her feet and looked at me thoughtfully. "Do you need the bedside manner, or can you take it like an adult?"

"Tell me what I need to know," I said.

"Your torc is still fighting like a trooper, keeping you alive in spite of everything the poison can do. But the only way it can do that is to fight any change to the status quo, at the expense of everything else. So even simple corrective surgery is out. Your situation is serious, Eddie, and it's only going to get worse. You really should come down to the Infirmary, let us run some more tests."

"Not going to happen," I said.

"I could have told you that," said Molly.

Indira sighed loudly. "The bane of a doctor's life: patients with minds of their own. If it were up to me, I'd just hit you over the head with something substantial and drag you out of here . . . All right, try this."

She knelt down before me again and instructed me on how to use extruded armour from my torc to close my wound, using a series of small golden clamps. Enough of them to seal the whole length of the injury and hold it together. When we were done, I covered my arm with the golden sheath again. Indira nodded stiffly and got to her feet.

"That should prevent you from losing too much blood, and keep out infection. It's not a long-term solution, but, then, you don't need one." She looked at me steadily. "It isn't going to get any better, Eddie. What we just did only amounts to a holding action."

"Good enough," I said. "I can live with that."

Indira fished inside her coat pocket, delving deep enough to suggest she had a pocket dimension of her own in there, and brought out half a dozen bottles with handwritten labels. She peered closely at each of them in turn, and finally handed one to me. I opened the screw top and looked inside. Heavy black pellets, big enough to make me wince when I thought about swallowing them.

"For the pain," said Indira. "Your torc should allow that. Take as many as you need. You don't have to worry about addiction, because you're not going to be taking them that long. And you're well past the point where you can do yourself any damage that matters. If you get dizzy, don't operate heavy machinery or fire really big guns. Little bit of doctor humour there. You should probably stock up with as many bottles as you can carry, Eddie, before you leave the Hall. You don't want to get caught without them, once things start getting bad."

"Thank you, Doctor," I said. I popped back four of the black capsules in quick succession, swallowing hard to get them down and keep them down. Indira winced, but said nothing. I screwed the top back onto the bottle, and dropped it into my own dimensional pocket.

"That's it?" Molly said to Indira. "That's all you can do?"

"Outside of the Infirmary, yes." She looked at me steadily. "You know this is going to get really bad before the end?"

"Yes," I said. "I know."

Indira shrugged. "Okay, I'm out of here. I've got patients waiting. People I can help. Try not to die on my watch, Eddie. I hate doing the paperwork."

She hurried out, slamming the door behind her. Molly looked at me.

"Indira Drood?"

I smiled. "We'll take fresh blood from anyone who's brave enough to join us. Droods come in all flavours."

Molly stood over me, fists planted on her hips. "You have to be straight with me, Eddie. Talk to me about how you're feeling. Because if we're going to work together to locate Edmund and put that little shit down, I need to know for sure how much of you is left that I can still depend on."

"Okay," I said. "No more secrets."

I slowly and carefully unbuttoned my shirt, and pulled it open to show Molly the network of slender golden bands criss-crossing my chest, all the way up to my throat and down past my trouser belt. Molly put a hand to her mouth, shocked silent. Her gaze moved back and forth across the dozens of golden strips holding me together. When she was finally able to speak again, her voice was quiet but steady.

"Is it just your chest? How many of those things are there?"

"Lots of them," I said. "They're all over me now, under my clothes. Holding me together, keeping me strong. It's not my full armour, just extrusions from my torc. Enough to keep me going. Without them, I wouldn't be able to get around at all, never mind do what I need to do."

Molly's eyes filled with tears she refused to let fall. She reached out with one hand and carefully traced a few of the golden bands with a fingertip. I sat still and let her. Eventually she pulled her hand back.

"How long have you been using these?"

"Some time now," I said. "Just a few at first, adding more as I felt the need. I didn't tell you because I didn't want you to worry. I've had to add a lot more, since the Demon Droods and the Angelic Droods. They took a lot out of me. I know, I should have said something. But it wasn't like there was anything you could do to help. I have to be able to do what needs doing if we're to track Edmund down and make the bastard pay for his crimes."

"Then maybe . . . we should forget about Edmund," said Molly. She swallowed hard and looked at me imploringly. "Why let him steal from us what little time we have left? We could go back to my woods and let your family go after him. We could go for walks, spend some time in your cottage, or sit by the lake. Be together, while we still can."

"It's a tempting thought," I said. "But you know I can't do that, Molly. I could never rest, never be at peace with myself or concentrate on you knowing Edmund was still out there, getting away with my murder. Still killing people and ruining lives while wearing my face."

"You know I'd track him down after you were gone."

"Thanks for the thought," I said. "But I need to do it myself. Come on, Molly. If this is going to be our last adventure together, let's make it a good one."

"Stand up," said Molly.

I forced myself up out of my chair and she hugged me tightly, burying her face in my shoulder. I held on to her just as tightly.

"I'll never let you go, Eddie," she said fiercely.

"Hush," I said. Knowing the time would come when she would have to.

There was another knock at the door, and another young Drood came rushing in without waiting for an answer. Molly let go of me and stood back. I closed my shirt so the newcomer wouldn't see the golden bands holding me together. He smiled vaguely at us, and Molly glared right back at him.

"What do you want? We're busy!"

"Oh, don't mind me," the newcomer said airily. "I don't care what people get up to in the privacy of public rooms with no lock on the door. I'm Mark, messenger for the Matriarch. I have something important to tell you. Yes. I'm sure I do . . . It was on the tip of my tongue before I came in here. I really should write these things down. Ah yes! I remember!" And then he paused to look appealingly at Molly. "Can I just say in advance, please don't kill the messenger for the message. Or transform him into something squelchy."

"No promises," said Molly. "Get on with it."

"What's the message?" I said.

"The Matriarch wants to see both of you right now, for a Council meeting," said Mark.

"Both of us?" I said. "Are you sure?"

"I know!" said Mark. "I couldn't believe it either! You could have knocked me down with a feather duster when she told me. Either she's mellowing, or the shit has hit the fan to such an extent that it's gummed up the works. I know which way I'd bet if I was a betting man, which I'm not."

And then he just stood there and smiled vaguely, until I realised he was waiting for an answer. I considered the matter carefully while Molly scowled at him.

"The Matriarch really was terribly keen that you come right away," Mark said tentatively. "It's all very urgent, you see. As in, all-hands-on-deck, all-hands-to-the-pump, the-ship's-going-down-and-there's-sharks-in-the-water sort of thing. That's me speaking there, of course, not the Matriarch. I'm just paraphrasing."

"Where is she holding the Council meeting this time?" I said, speaking right over him, since he showed no signs of stopping anytime soon.

"In the Sanctity," said Mark.

"The Matriarch has moved back into the Sanctity?" I said. "Are you sure?"

"No, I just made it up to mess with you!" said Mark. "Of course I'm sure! I'm a messenger. I deliver messages. Would you like me to lead you to the Sanctity or just leave you a trail of bread-crumbs?"

"He's getting sarcastic now," Molly said dangerously.

"Unless you've something important to add, I would suggest you leave now," I said. "Probably running."

"No one's ever glad to see a messenger," Mark said sulkily. "Can I at least tell the Matriarch you're on your way?"

"Disappear," said Molly.

"Love to," said Mark.

In a moment he was out of the room and gone, the door closing on the sound of his rapidly departing footsteps. I buttoned up my shirt.

"He wasn't nearly scared enough of me," said Molly. "Time was, I could make any member of your family wet themselves just by raising an eyebrow. I can see I'm going to have to do something extreme while I'm here, just to put them in the proper respectful frame of mind again. A fire, perhaps, or a flash flood. Or maybe something creative involving mutated cockroaches."

"Everyone's just a bit stressed at the moment," I said. "You have to make allowances."

"No I don't," said Molly. "I am famous for not cutting anyone any slack whatsoever." She looked at me steadily. "You know, we don't have to go to this meeting. Whatever the Matriarch wants, it can't be that urgent. Or she'd have sent the Sarjeant-at-Arms to fetch you."

"But if she's calling for both of us, it has to be something important," I said. I rose to my feet and stretched, slowly and carefully, feeling the golden bands move with me under my clothes. I was feeling . . . not better, exactly, but good enough for the moment. I smiled at Molly. "Come on. Let's go and be rude to the Matriarch. You know that always cheers you up. Maybe she's got some fresh news about Edmund."

"He'll be the death of you," said Molly.

"Yes," I said. "And I will be the death of him, if it kills me."

It took a while to get to the Sanctity, that great open chamber at the heart of the Hall, traditional meeting place for the Matriarch's advisory Council. There were an awful lot of Droods just standing around, filling the corridors and galleries and talking excitedly, unsettled by recent events. I knew how they felt. Whatever the Matriarch had to tell me, it had better not be a surprise. I really wasn't in the mood for a surprise.

Two very large Droods stood on guard in front of the massive double doors that gave access to the Sanctity. As Molly and I approached, they snapped to attention and then turned quickly to open the doors and get the hell out of our way. I nodded calmly to them as we strode past, while Molly stuck her nose in the air and ignored both guards with regal indifference.

The Sanctity seemed even larger than I remembered. And quite empty, apart from the Matriarch and the Sarjeant-at-Arms, standing together. The Matriarch gestured to the guards, and they quickly closed the doors. She seated herself carefully on a stiff-backed wooden chair, and the Sarjeant waited till she was settled before sitting down on the chair beside her. I considered the semicircle of equally uncomfortable-looking chairs set out before them. I counted four, which wasn't nearly enough for a full Council meeting. I settled myself carefully on a chair right in front of the Matriarch. Molly dropped down onto the chair beside me, crossed her legs, and folded her arms tightly, just to make it clear she wasn't going anywhere.

There was no sign of the usual rose-red glow that suffused the air when Ethel was around, none of the usual sense of well-being, of *All is well with the world.*

I raised my voice. "Ethel? Are you here?"

"Hello, Eddie. Hello, Molly," said Ethel, her voice seeming to come from everywhere in the Sanctity at once. "Everything all right now?"

"Don't you know?" I said.

"Well, of course I know; I was just being polite. I'm still trying to get the hang of this privacy thing."

Molly scowled at the Matriarch. "Why am I here? Why did you send me for me? Normally you move heaven and earth trying to keep me out of these meetings."

"Because you're not family," the Matriarch said coldly. "And because you have a tendency to heckle and throw things. However, given the current situation, I would value your opinion."

"Things have changed," said Molly.

"Yes," said the Sarjeant. "They have."

The doors to the Sanctity swung open, and we all looked round as the Armourer came hurrying in. Maxwell and Victoria looked tired and overworked, and more than usually burdened. They were still holding onto each other's hands like babes in the wood, afraid they might get lost if they allowed themselves to become separated. I tried to remember if I'd ever seen them separately. The last time I'd seen them, they both looked like they'd taken a real beating, and their lab coats had been torn and ragged and soaked in blood. But now they had new coats, immaculately clean and heavily starched, and Maxwell and Victoria didn't have a mark on them. They did look a bit twitchy, and their eyes were much too big, suggesting they were both relying on chemical helpers to keep them going. They nodded quickly to me and to Molly, bowed jerkily to the Matriarch and the Sarjeant, and then dropped heavily onto the seats beside me.

"We are not late!" Maxwell said loudly. "I checked my watch all the way here, and we are right on time."

"You tell them, Max," said Victoria.

"I am telling them, dear."

"Don't you let them put you down, Max. They don't appreciate you."

And then they both looked at the Matriarch, took in her expression, and stopped talking. Though given the sullen set to their mouths, I didn't think that would last long. I took a moment to study the Matriarch.

"Nice to be back in the Sanctity. Am I to take it your war of words with Ethel is at an end?"

"Let's say, more like an armed truce," said Ethel. She sounded more amused than anything.

The Matriarch said nothing, and her face gave away even less. The Sarjeant-at-Arms sat stiffly on his stiff-backed chair. On the back of one hand he still had a splash of someone else's blood that he hadn't gotten around to washing off yet. Unless he'd deliberately left it there as a statement.

"Where's the rest of the Council?" I said.

"They're busy," said the Matriarch. "Putting the Hall back in order and reinstating all the proper protections and defences. Just in case one of our many enemies should try to take advantage."

The Sarjeant was about to add something to that, but broke off as the doors swung open again and the Librarian came striding in. He looked angry and aggrieved, neither of which were usually part of his temperament. He crashed to a halt and glared at the Matriarch. She stared calmly back, entirely unmoved by his entrance or his attitude.

"What are you doing here, William? I left word with Yorith that your presence wasn't required for this meeting. You need your rest."

"I am not some ancient relic or dusty old fossil, to be sat in the corner and patted on the head!" William said loudly. "I am the Librarian! I know more about this family and its workings than everyone else in the Hall put together, and I am not going to be left out of things!"

The Librarian was wearing a heavy tweed suit remarkably similar to the Matriarch's, except that his looked a lot more lived-in. His white shirt was reasonably clean, and he still had his peach cravat, held in place by a diamond pin. Not that the Librarian cared about such vanities; he only wore it because it was a gift from his wife, the telepath Ammonia Vom Acht. He was also wearing fluffy white bunny rabbit slippers, with prominent pink eyes that seemed to follow my every movement. The slippers reminded me of my recent close encounter with the Pook. I had to wonder if that meant anything.

A chair appeared out of nowhere behind the Librarian, and he sat down next to Molly. I was impressed; I hadn't known he could do that. His chair looked a lot more comfortable than mine, and I considered asking him for an upgrade, but his scowl suggested this might not be a good time.

I looked thoughtfully at the Librarian. His bushy white hair had recently known the attention of a brush, if not a comb; his body language suggested barely suppressed rage; and his gaze was more than usually clear. I was even more impressed. It wasn't often William felt together enough to stand up to anyone, let alone the Matriarch.

"You might have kept me out of the fighting," the Librarian said flatly to the Matriarch, explaining much, "but you are not keeping me out of the decision-making process."

"Of course not," said the Matriarch. "We value your input, Librarian. You're looking very . . . sharp."

He scowled. "My mind isn't what it was. I know that. But don't go thinking I'm senile!"

"No one ever said you were," said the Matriarch.

Not out loud, I thought.

"Will Ammonia be joining us for these discussions?" said Molly. "In telepathic spirit, at least?"

The Librarian's scowl deepened. "No. I did ask, but she's working a case and can't get away. She sent everyone her best."

Knowing Ammonia, I somehow doubted that. Molly patted William comfortingly on the arm, and he smiled briefly at her before fixing the Matriarch with a stern look and the air of someone determined not to be messed with.

"Now the advisory Council is assembled," the Matriarch said calmly, "we need to talk about Edmund. I'm still finding it hard to believe one man on his own was able to overthrow this family's defences so easily and so quickly, and do us so much damage in such a short time. Are we sure he didn't have help?"

"He doesn't need help," said Molly.

"He's me," I said. "Only without my scruples."

"You have scruples?" said the Sarjeant. "When did that happen?"

Molly gave him her best thoughtful glare. "Don't push your luck, Cedric."

"Make your report, Sarjeant," said the Matriarch.

"My people are checking the Hall from top to bottom," said the Sarjeant. "To see what else Edmund might have taken, sabotaged, or destroyed while he had the place to himself. Nothing's been found, but I'm awaiting further reports. The Infirmary is swamped with Drood wounded. We took a real kicking out there today. But the medical staff assure me they're on top of it."

"How many did we lose?" I said.

"Twenty-three dead," said the Sarjeant. "An acceptably low figure, I think, given the circumstances."

"More deaths to lay at Edmund's door," I said.

The Sarjeant looked to the Matriarch, and she nodded for him to continue with his report.

"The bodies of the Angelic Droods are being autopsied," he said flatly. "To see if anything can be learned from their altered physiology."

"A thought has just occurred to me," said Molly.

"Oh, that is never good," said the Sarjeant.

Molly glared at him, and then at the Matriarch. "Both the Demon Droods and the Angelic Droods were the result of alchemical shotgun marriages, part of the original pacts and agreements made between the Droods and the Hereafter. If these marriages are now at an end, is that going to affect the Droods' standing with Heaven and Hell?"

We all looked at one another. It rapidly became clear none of us had an answer. The Matriarch looked to the Librarian, who stirred uneasily in his comfortable chair.

"I'll have to do some research. No one's had to worry about that in fifteen hundred years. Do you suppose we should inform the relevant parties?"

"I think we can assume they already know," I said. "If there are any complications or recriminations, I'm sure we'll be hearing from them soon."

"Well, that's something to look forward to," said the Matriarch, trying for a light touch and missing by a mile.

"What if they demand replacements?" said Molly.

"Then this time, we'll have to work out a much better deal," said the Matriarch. "Proceed, Sarjeant."

"I've talked to some of the medical staff still running a general scan on the whole family," said the Sarjeant. "Because we need to be sure Edmund hasn't got to anyone else. I can confirm that so far no one in the family shows any signs of poison, or has presented any symptoms similar to Eddie's."

The Matriarch looked at the golden sheath covering my arm. And the moment she looked, so did everyone else. I hadn't been trying to hide it or draw attention to it. But once the Matriarch was officially looking at it, the others couldn't look away. I didn't say anything. I wasn't going to make it easy for them.

"How are you, Eddie?" said the Matriarch.

"Not good," I said. "But good enough. Old news—move on."

Molly glowered at the Council. "Isn't there anything any of you can do to help him?"

There was an uncomfortable silence. The Matriarch, the Sarjeant, and the Librarian finally all turned to the Armourer, who sat up straight in their chairs.

"We haven't given up," said Maxwell.

"We're still working on the problem," said Victoria.

"Looking at past cases, studying old technologies and techniques as well as new ones, in case something might have been overlooked or forgotten," said Maxwell.

"We've sent out messages to all sorts of friends and fellow travellers," said Victoria. "Carefully worded, of course. If anyone has anything to offer, we will hear about it."

"The lab assistants have adopted you as their latest project, Eddie," said Maxwell. "They're all very excited, and they've come up with all kinds of ingenious ideas."

"Nothing particularly practical as yet," Victoria said reluctantly. "But still, early days!"

"You are our top priority, Eddie," said Maxwell. "You must believe that."

"We will find an answer."

"We always do."

"You couldn't save my uncle Jack," I said.

There was a silence. I knew it was an unfair comparison, even as I said it. Jack had been very old, and after all the things he'd done to himself to keep him going . . . If it had been possible to save him, he would have done it himself. But I wasn't in the mood to be fair. The world had not been fair to me. The closest I could manage to an apology was to change the subject.

"I thought you and your assistants fought very bravely," I said to the Armourer. "Taking on the Angelic Droods."

"It's not what we do best," said Maxwell. "But we can fight."

"Of course we can," said Victoria. "We are Droods, after all."

"How many assistants did you lose?" I said.

"Four," said Maxwell. "And a dozen wounded. Not bad, considering. They are very hard to kill."

"That's what comes from working in the Armoury," said Victoria. "If you can survive that on a daily basis, you can survive pretty much anything."

The Sarjeant leaned forward to fix me with a cold stare. "You said Edmund escaped from the Old Library. How was he able to do that?"

"He used the Merlin Glass," I said.

There was an immediate reaction to that, and not a good one. The Matriarch and the Council all sat up straight, looked at each other and then at me. I stared calmly back at them. I'd known this was coming.

"You mean, the Merlin Glass isn't under your control any longer?" said the Matriarch.

"Turns out, it never really was," I said. "Edmund has been haunting it for ages. Using it against me and the family."

"How is that possible?" said the Sarjeant.

"It's complicated," I said.

"Lot of that going around these days," said the Librarian.

The Matriarch shot him an exasperated look, but he was used to that. She turned her cold gaze on me.

"So," she said, "that's why Edmund was able to come and go so easily inside the Hall. He had control of the Merlin Glass."

"Some of the time," I said.

"I told you, Eddie," said the Sarjeant. "You should have handed the Glass over to the family for safekeeping. Why don't you listen to me?"

"Because I nearly always know more about what's really going on than you do," I said. "Giving up the Glass wouldn't have helped. Edmund had put a back door in the Glass, so he could hide in it or use it to come and go as and when he pleased. So don't try to pin the blame on me, Sarjeant! How long was Edmund walking around the Hall, pretending to be me, because you didn't follow up on the suspicions your own people brought to you? Because you couldn't believe anyone could get past your precious security?"

The Sarjeant-at-Arms didn't look guilty, because he didn't do that. But he did turn his attention to Molly.

"Have you been able to contact your sisters? I understand they're very good at finding people who don't want to be found."

Molly pulled a face, and shrugged apologetically to me. "According to Isabella's answering service, she and Louisa are out. As in, no longer in our reality. No information on where they've gone or what they're doing, or even a hint as to when they'll be back. I've left a message, but . . . I'm sorry, Eddie."

"Only be sorry for the things that are your fault," I said. "There isn't time for anything else."

"Don't you have any old friends you could call on, Eddie?" said the Librarian. "I mean, you have worked with some very powerful and well-connected people in your time. There must be someone . . ."

"You'd think so, wouldn't you?" I said. "I've left some messages, but the kind of people we're talking about aren't easy to get hold of. It doesn't matter. Edmund told me the poison he used came from his world. There isn't going to be any cure, any antidote, because no one in this world has ever seen anything like it. We need to concentrate on what's in front of us. Edmund drove us out of the Hall so he could be sure of uninterrupted access to the Old Library, but he only took one book with him when he left. Which suggests there must be something in that particular book he thought he could use."

"And to find one book in a Library that size, he must have spent some time searching for it," said Molly. "Without the Librarian, Yorith, or even the Pook noticing. How is that even possible?"

"I might have seen him and not known," said the Librarian, looking down at his hands clasped together in his lap. "I've talked with Eddie any number of times, but now I have to wonder if he was always who I thought he was."

"Which book did Edmund take?" said the Matriarch. "Do you have any idea?"

"Oh, identifying the book was easy," said the Librarian. "Its removal left a very significant gap. How Edmund got past all its protections and defences . . ."

"Which book was it?" said the Sarjeant.

"*The History of Grendel Rex, the Unforgiven God.*"

The Matriarch and the Sarjeant looked at each other. They looked like they'd been hit, and hit hard. Maxwell and Victoria looked like frightened children who'd just heard a noise in the night. The Librarian looked at his hands in his lap, and said nothing. Molly looked at me.

"Grendel Rex," she said. "You told me you talked with him in Siberia. During the Great Spy Game. But you never told me what you talked about."

"Nothing to tell," I said.

"I've heard stories about Grendel Rex," said Molly. "A word dropped here and there in subterranean places, by people scared to be overheard. I never met anyone who knew anything for sure until I met you, Eddie."

"It's not something we talk about," said the Matriarch. "It's not something anyone should talk about."

"I need to know!" said Molly.

"Gerard Drood came to power in the Eleventh Century," I said. "He found a way to improve and strengthen his torc, away from the Heart, and then used that power to take personal control of every mind in the family. He made every one of them think like him, become him. Or, at least, all the Droods he knew about. There were very-secret agents even then; a family inside the family. They kept their heads down and did their best not to be noticed, until they could figure out what to do."

"Why weren't they affected?" said Molly. "How were they able to avoid being mind controlled?"

"That's not in the official history," said the Librarian. "But, then, agents of that kind always liked to keep things to themselves."

I remembered Peter and his secrets. The Matriarch gestured for me to continue.

"Gerard Drood expanded his control to the rest of Humanity," I said steadily. "Whole countries fell under his sway, entire populations bowing their heads to his overwhelming will. In time, they would all have become him. And he would have been Grendel Rex, the Drood who ate the world. A living god, or a living devil."

Molly looked around. No one else wanted to say anything.

"But you beat him," she said. "The Droods defeated him."

"The very-secret agents took him down," I said. "Using methods the family still doesn't want to talk about."

"Not because we are ashamed," the Matriarch said evenly, "but because we needed to keep them secret. In case we ever have to use them again."

"And this book Edmund has now," said Molly. "Would it have information on how to control Grendel Rex?"

"We should have destroyed it long ago!" said the Sarjeant. "To ensure nothing like this could ever happen!"

"No," said the Matriarch. "We couldn't do that. There was always the possibility that in some future extreme emergency, we might need Grendel Rex. To fight for us, against something worse."

Molly looked at me. "Your family . . ."

"Trust me," I said. "I know."

"But why are you all looking so worried?" said Molly. "Grendel Rex is safely imprisoned, isn't he?"

"Buried deep below the permafrost, under the Siberian steppes," I said. "Because back in the Eleventh Century, Siberia must have seemed like the end of the earth. They buried him deep and left him there, wrapped in powerful chains and potent curses. To wait till Judgement Day, or beyond."

"They buried him alive?" said Molly.

"They couldn't destroy him," I said. "Not after everything he'd done to himself. What he'd made himself into."

"Gerard Drood," said the Sarjeant. "Once our greatest hero, he became our greatest shame. The Drood who wanted to remake all of Humanity in his own image, and rule them forever."

"So, what sort of a man was he?" said Molly. "Before he became the Unforgiven God?"

We all looked at one another.

"All we know for sure," I said, "comes from the book Edmund took with him. And that was mostly concerned with what Gerard did and what he intended to do, and what it cost us to take him down. The authors weren't really interested in presenting us with a character sketch."

"Just a warning from history," said the Librarian.

"How is it you know so much about what's in this book?" the Matriarch said suddenly.

"I was interested," I said. "Because I'd met him."

"Edmund must believe the book can tell him how to release and control Grendel Rex," said Molly. "So he can use this living god as a weapon. Are there any other books in the Old Library that might cover the same ground? Give us some idea of what Edmund is planning to do?"

"There are no other books on Grendel Rex," said the Librarian. "One was bad enough."

"And access to it was strictly limited," said the Matriarch, looking at me.

"We didn't want anyone being tempted," said the Sarjeant. "Grendel Rex had followers, then and later. Fools who thought they could make use of him."

"Or worshipped him," said the Matriarch.

"We could look in the family Diaries," I said. "There must be some from that period. See if any of them had anything to say about Gerard the man."

"That's an excellent idea, Eddie!" said the Matriarch. "Sarjeant, put some people on it."

The Sarjeant nodded, and his gaze became distant as he reached out to his people through his torc.

"They'd better touch base with me," said the Librarian. "And the family historians. Diaries back then would have been written in Saxon and Norman, Latin and Greek . . . We're going to have to put a lot of people on this."

"You'll have all the support you need," said the Matriarch.

"Can I just ask: Did Grendel Rex really carve his features into the surface of the Moon?" said Molly. "So he could look down on the earth forever, as the Drood in the Moon?"

"The family scrubbed it clean," I said. "After they'd put him down."

"Really?" said Molly. "Your family's been to the Moon?"

"We get around," I said.

"The really hard part was keeping it out of the world's history books," said the Librarian. "Fortunately, there was a lot happening around then."

"I've read your official report on what happened in Siberia, Eddie," said the Matriarch. "It was very lacking in details, and far from satisfactory on many levels. Particularly concerning your contact with

Grendel Rex. You were the first Drood in centuries to actually talk to him. What did he say?"

I remembered being under attack in an abandoned Secret Science City. Being threatened by appallingly powerful forces, far beyond anything I or my companions could hope to fight. With not just our lives but our very souls at risk, I reached out mentally to the only person I thought might save us. The sleeping giant under the earth. The Unforgiven God. I remembered pushing my mind out through the torc and sending my thoughts down into the earth. Like a diver descending into the deepest, darkest part of the ocean. A giant eye opened in the dark and looked right at me. I remembered talking to the old god, the old devil, and being surprised at how human he sounded. He saved my life, and all of those with me, and asked for nothing in return. But I also remembered his final words.

Here is the truth, for those who have the strength to hear it. We can all be gods, or devils. We can shine like the stars. We were never meant to stay human. We're just the chrysalis from which something greater can emerge.

And the very last thing he said to me.

Tell the family . . . I'll be seeing them.

When the time came to write my official report, I decided my family didn't need to know any of that. And nothing had happened since to change my opinion.

"Nothing of any significance was said, Matriarch," I said finally.

"That's not good enough! There must have been something!"

I shrugged, unmoved by the anger in her voice. "It was a mental contact. A lot of it couldn't be put into words. All that mattered then was that he agreed to help."

"Why did he do that?" said the Librarian.

"I got the impression . . . because I was family. That still meant something to him."

"Could he have changed, after all these years?" said Molly. "If he was released from his tomb, might he be on our side?"

"Given what he was," I said, "what he did, and what he meant to do . . . I wouldn't bet on it. How could we ever trust him again?"

"Exactly," said the Matriarch. "Eddie, how would you describe his state of mind? After being buried alive and alone for so many centuries?"

"I can't be sure I was the only one ever to talk to him," I said carefully. "I think we can be sure I was the first Drood, because we have enough sense to stay out of Siberia. Mostly. I wouldn't have gone anywhere near him if it hadn't been such an emergency . . ." And then I stopped, as a thought struck me. "In fact, looking back, I have to wonder why I took such a risk. If he'd forced me to raise him from his tomb, I could have let loose something far worse than what I was facing. So why on earth did I do it? Could he have . . . reached out to me? Influenced my mind, to make me contact him?"

Everyone in the room shuddered, even Molly.

"You said he didn't want anything from you," said the Sarjeant.

"Not then," I said.

"I think I'd better ask Ammonia to take a look inside your head," said the Librarian. "Just so we can be sure he didn't put something in there."

"Do it," said the Matriarch.

"The moment she's free," said the Librarian.

"There's no need to hurry," I said. "Or any real need to worry. By the time I've caught up with Edmund and dealt with him, there won't be enough left of me to be a danger to anyone."

There was a long, uncomfortable pause.

"Why is Edmund so interested in Grendel Rex?" the Librarian said finally. "Why concentrate on that book rather than Alpha Red Alpha or the forbidden weapons of the Armageddon Codex? He must know raising Grendel Rex is one hell of a risk."

"Perhaps things went differently in his world," said the Sarjeant.

"And that's why Edmund needed our book," said the Matriarch. "To see how we dealt with the problem."

"Releasing Grendel Rex isn't the problem," said the Sarjeant. "Staying alive, or at least in charge of your own head afterwards, is what matters. Just because you've released the genie from his lamp doesn't mean you should expect him to be grateful. Edmund must believe he has some way to control the situation."

I looked at Molly, and she looked at me. We were both thinking of the great statue of Kali with the blood of human sacrifices caked around her feet.

"I am getting really tired of seeing that look on your faces!" the Matriarch said loudly. "You're keeping something from me! From the family! What is it you know that I don't?"

"More than you could possibly imagine," said Molly.

"We're telling you everything that's relevant," I said. "If we were to run through everything we saw or encountered in the Other World, we'd be at this all day. The Sarjeant is right—and that's not something I say very often—in that Edmund must have something he thinks will give him power over Grendel Rex."

"But what does he need him for?" said Molly.

"Maybe Edmund thinks it's his turn to eat the world," I said.

"What can we do to prevent this?" said the Matriarch.

"When Grendel Rex was put down, all those centuries ago," the Librarian said steadily, "what was done was designed never to be undone. All kinds of protections and defences and really nasty booby-traps were set in place, powerful enough to devastate half of Siberia. I wouldn't know how to set Grendel Rex loose safely, even if the family decided it was necessary. So I don't see how Edmund can. It's always possible we're worrying over nothing."

The Matriarch was already shaking her head. "A lot has changed since the Eleventh Century. We have access to things undreamed of in those days." And then she looked at the Armourer.

"Without knowing the exact details of Grendel Rex's imprisonment, I can't say how it could be safely undone," Maxwell said carefully.

"But we could probably do it," said Victoria.

"Oh yes, we could probably do it. With all the things we have now."

"You tell them, sweetie."

"I am, dear."

"Why are we still sitting around talking?" said Molly. "We need to get to Siberia before Edmund does!"

"No," I said. "Not until we have some idea of what we're going to do when we catch up with him."

Molly nodded reluctantly.

"I am open to suggestions," said the Matriarch. "And informed opinions. If the Unforgiven God were to be set free, after all this time, would he still be as powerful as he was? Would our modern world be as vulnerable? And, most important, would we be able to put him down again? Ethel, in your opinion, could your new armour protect us from Grendel Rex's mental control?"

If Ethel was at all surprised at being directly addressed by the Matriarch, after being ignored for so long, she kept it to herself.

"I really don't know," she said. Her voice came out of the air directly above us, calm and relaxed and entirely unmoved by the dangers we'd been discussing. "I have no idea who or what Grendel Rex is. I'm looking all over the world, and Seeing all kinds of Powers and Dominations at work and at play, but nothing like what you've been talking about."

"What about Siberia?" I said.

"Looking at it right now," said Ethel. "Very cold, very still, very empty."

I frowned. Grendel Rex's power should have blazed like a beacon in such a setting. Unless his tomb had been designed to hide him. Or Edmund was already there and concealing both of them.

The Matriarch turned to the Librarian. "Is there anything you know that might help us?"

"I've been racking my brains ever since I realised which book was missing," he said slowly. "You know my memory isn't what it used to be. But from what I remember of the book, and reading between the lines, I think the agents were only able to subdue Grendel Rex because they hit him when he was already severely weakened."

"Weakened?" I said. "How? Who by?"

"There were no details," said the Librarian. "Which means no one in the family knows any more."

I wondered if Peter might have known. If this was one of the secrets he took with him to his grave.

"We have to locate Edmund," said the Matriarch. "And stop him before he can release Grendel Rex. Put all our people on it, Sarjeant. Everything from high-tech scanners to scrying pools. I also authorize you to approach all the other hidden agencies and organisations, and offer them whatever they want to give us access to their surveillance facilities. Including all the spy satellites no one will admit to having. This is no time to be proud."

"Before you ask," said Ethel, "I still can't See Edmund. He's done something to hide himself from me, which is very irritating. He could be standing right there in the Sanctity with you and I wouldn't know."

We all stirred uneasily on our chairs, because we all wanted to look around us, just in case, but no one wanted to go first.

"Edmund has the Merlin Glass," said Molly. "He could already be in Siberia."

"But Siberia is a really big place," I said. "Even with the exact coordinates for Grendel Rex's tomb, he'd still have a lot of hard travelling ahead of him."

"You found Grendel Rex," said Molly.

"Only mentally," I said. "Edmund would have to cross miles of frozen tundra, locate the exact spot, and then dig down through the permafrost, in search of one small, human-sized tomb."

"I'll put the whole family to work on this," said the Sarjeant. "Every department. And call in every favour we're owed. Edmund is going to find the world can be a very small place, when everyone in it is looking for you."

"I don't know," I said. "You couldn't find me, when I went rogue."

"Or me!" said Molly. "I led this family a merry dance for years!"

"And Edmund has a lot of experience with staying hidden," I said. "Both as himself and as Dr DOA."

"Mostly you find people by tracking their interactions with other people," said Molly. "But Edmund doesn't have anyone."

"But he does sometimes need help from other people," I said. "Ethel! Edmund doesn't wear a Drood torc these days. The Immortals of his world built him a fake. Could you find him through that?"

"Yes!" said Ethel. "I can track that! I taught myself how, after an Immortal used a fake torc to sneak into the Hall to try to murder you!"

"Then why didn't you spot the fake torc the moment it turned up inside the Hall?" said the Sarjeant. "How could Edmund move back and forth among the family for so long without you noticing his torc was different from everyone else's?"

"I was busy," Ethel said calmly. "I've had a lot on my mind recently."

There was a long pause, until everyone realised that was all the answer we were going to get.

"Moving on . . . ," I said.

"I have Edmund's exact location!" said Ethel. "He is not in Siberia. He is currently in the Museum of Unattached Oddities, in Scotland."

The room went mad. The Matriarch covered her face with her armoured mask so she could shout orders at the rest of the family. The Sarjeant masked his face so he could shout orders at his people. Maxwell and Victoria armoured up their faces so they could shout at their lab assistants. The Librarian smiled vaguely at me and Molly, and rose unhurriedly to his feet.

"I don't think I'm needed here any longer. I'd better get back to where I belong and start my research. Best of luck, Eddie. With everything. And when you find Edmund . . . don't hesitate. Stamp his head into the ground."

"That's the plan," I said.

The Librarian left the Sanctity. The others were so busy behind their masks, they didn't even notice. Molly turned to me.

"Museum of what?"

"The Museum of Unattached Oddities," I said. "Located in the most uninhabited part of Scotland we could find. It's a repository for strange and unusual objects with strange and unnatural histories. All the flotsam and jetsam of the hidden world, ancient and modern. The horribly significant, the more-than-usually dangerous, and the merely intriguing. A dumping ground, basically, for all the odd little items that have no proper place in the official way of things."

"But why set it in the wilds of Scotland?" Molly said suspiciously.

"So if anything should go wrong with some of the more unpredictable exhibits, there'll be no one around to object. If a museum implodes and there's no one there to see it, does it really matter?"

"Yes," said Molly.

"Well," I said. "That's you."

"What is Edmund doing there?"

"I would have thought that was obvious," I said. "He must believe there's something in the Museum he can use to safely raise Grendel Rex."

"And is there anything?"

"Beats me. People are always dropping things off without any proper provenance or even an instruction manual."

"Are there any weapons in this museum?"

"Oh sure," I said. "Along with an awful lot of awful things that could be used as weapons. I wasn't actually kidding about the imploding."

"Tell me these very dangerous items are surrounded by a small army of very heavily armed guards," said Molly.

"What?" I said. "And draw attention to them? The whole point of this museum is that only people who need to know even know it exists. Getting to it is hard enough; getting in is even harder. Most people prefer to stick to the annual Catalogue, and view everything from a safe distance."

"Tell me there's some security in place!" said Molly.

"Oh sure," I said. "Sort of. Mind you, things might have changed. It's been years since I was last there."

"What were you looking for?"

"More like dropping off," I said. "Drood Hall has to go through regular clear-outs, or we'd be up to our chins in clutter. And given that most of it is the kind of stuff you can't just dispose of on eBay, it needs to go somewhere . . . discreet."

Molly gave me a long, thoughtful look. "Why did you never tell me about this museum before?"

"Because you'd only have tried to rob it."

"Fair enough." Molly frowned. "So . . . lots of really weird shit, and no real security in place. Essentially, Edmund can just walk around this museum and pick up anything he takes a fancy to?"

"Essentially, yes," I said. "But a lot of the exhibits are perfectly capable of looking after themselves. Some are cursed, some are protected, and some really don't like to be bothered. There are parts of the Museum I'd think twice about walking through, even in my armour. Though other areas are perfectly delightful."

It occurred to me that no one had said thank you to Ethel for locating Edmund so quickly.

"No need to thank me," said Ethel.

"How did you know I was about to say that?" I said. "Have you been peeking inside my head?"

She sniffed loudly, a disquieting sound from a disembodied being. "Like I'd lower myself. It's a wonder to me you can live in anything that small. Have you ever considered adding an extension?"

"I've missed these little chats of ours," I said. "I haven't had a decent headache in ages. Are you and the Matriarch talking again?"

"I never stopped," said Ethel.

Maxwell and Victoria suddenly made their masks disappear and rose to their feet in perfect unison. Still holding each other's hands.

"Matters are now in hand!" said Maxwell.

"Very much in hand," said Victoria.

"We'll get you to the Museum as quickly as possible," said Maxwell.

"One way or another," said Victoria.

"That's what I'm afraid of," I said.

They smiled politely. I turned to Molly.

"No, I can't teleport us," she said immediately. "I've used up so much of my magics, I'm running on fumes. Right now, I couldn't pull a hat out of a rabbit."

I yelled at the Matriarch and the Sarjeant until they dropped their masks and looked at me with varying amounts of guilt for having forgotten all about me.

"What do you want, Eddie?" said the Matriarch.

"Transport," I said. "We're a long way from the wilds of Scotland, and Molly and I need to get to the Museum in time to stop Edmund from doing whatever it is he's doing that we don't want him to."

The Matriarch looked at the Armourer, and they both stood a little straighter and tried to look like professionals.

"The old Armourer's racing Bentley is still in the garage," said Maxwell. "Undergoing extensive renovations, after Eddie's last little excursion in it."

"You must have other cars!" said Molly.

"Of course we do," said Maxwell. "Flying cars, underwater cars, cars that can take shortcuts through dimensions that don't necessarily exist. And they are all out being used. We do have other field agents, you know."

"Normally I'd offer you one of our dimension-hopping bracelets," said Victoria. "But we had to issue a recall."

"And all our long-range dimensional Doors have been signed out," said Maxwell. "By the time we can call somebody back . . ."

"There's always the Blackhawke jets," said Victoria. "But I don't think there's a suitable landing site anywhere near the Museum. If I'm remembering correctly, and I'm pretty sure I am, it's a really rough location."

"You are entirely correct, as always," said Maxwell. "When we say the Museum is out in the wilds, we mean all the way out. As in, several hours from anywhere civilised. No roads, no . . . anything, really."

"The kind of area you won't find on any official map," said Victoria. "Because its existence would only depress people."

"We're talking about miles of moorland, peat bogs, and the kind of nature that's usually referred to as actively hazardous," said Maxwell.

"Then how do people normally get to the Museum when they want to visit it?" said Molly.

"Mostly, people don't," I said. "Visitors aren't encouraged. It's not that kind of museum."

"Well, what kind is it, then?" said Molly.

"I told you," I said. "A dumping ground."

"Give us time!" said Maxwell. "We'll think of something. Though short of attaching a jet pack to one of the winged unicorns . . ."

"One of the lab assistants tried that last year," said Victoria. "I didn't know unicorns knew that kind of language."

"There must be some kind of flying vehicle we can adapt," said Maxwell. "Though landing is always going to be a problem."

"Maps!" said Victoria. "We need maps!"

"You said there weren't any," said Molly.

"That's official maps," said Maxwell.

"Droods have their own maps," said Victoria.

"Because we know where things really are."

"Where the bodies are buried."

"Because we put them there."

The Armourer beamed happily at me and Molly, and then hurried out of the Sanctity, chattering animatedly to each other. I looked thoughtfully after them.

"They must be on something," I said. "It can't be natural to be that happy all the time."

"Wait a minute!" said Molly. "What about the teleport station inside the walk-in freezer? If it can teleport food in, couldn't it be repurposed to teleport us out?"

"It was specifically designed to work only on nonliving materials," I said. "For security reasons."

"How did you know about the freezer's teleport?" demanded the Sarjeant.

Molly smiled sweetly at him. "You'd be amazed at all the things I know."

"And probably horrified," I said.

"Well, yes," said Molly. "That goes without saying."

"We'll find you some kind of transport, Eddie," the Matriarch said quickly. "Just give us time to think. It's been a long day . . . You know, you could take advantage of the wait to visit the Infirmary. They might have come up with something new. You mustn't give up on us, Eddie. We haven't given up on you."

"You're still hoping for some last-minute miracle," I said. "I'm not. I have no intention of dying slowly in some hospital bed."

"I could order you to go," said the Matriarch. "For your own good."

"You could," I said. "Want to try to see how far that gets you? Besides, who else could you send after Edmund who wouldn't come home in a box? Or, more likely, several boxes?"

"The family does have other field agents," said the Matriarch.

"Edmund would chew them up and spit them out, and you know it," I said. "I'm the only one who can stop him, because I can think enough like him to out-think him."

"Of course," said the Sarjeant. "Because that's worked so well, so far."

"Loath as I am to admit it, Cedric may have a point," said Molly.

"It has to be me," I said. "Because I'm the only agent who knows Edmund and Grendel Rex."

"You say that like it's a good thing," said the Sarjeant.

"And because I'm the most expendable agent you've got."

The Matriarch smiled briefly. "I'm sure the other field agents will be happy to hear that."

"This is personal," I said.

"But you don't have to do it on your own, Eddie," said the Sarjeant. "You're part of a family."

"I need to do this," I said. "It's all I have left."

Something moved in Molly's face when I said that. She looked like I'd slapped her. I started to say something to her, and she turned her face away. I reached out, took hold of her chin, and turned her face back to me. She didn't fight me, but she didn't make it easy for me either.

"Edmund is the last bit of family business I need to attend to," I said. "Before I can stop. Before I can rest. The last thing in my life that needs doing. But he doesn't matter to me, Molly. Not the way you do."

Molly pulled her chin out of my hand. "If the last thing I can share with you is revenge, I can live with that."

"It's important to me that I go out on my feet," I said. "Still being me. But I wouldn't want to do it without you."

"Eddie, what am I supposed to do after your work is done? After you're gone?"

I smiled at her. "Live."

I got up to leave the Sanctity and was unpleasantly surprised to find how weak I'd become, just from sitting still for so long. My head swam, and my legs didn't want to support me. The golden bands under my clothes were still holding me together, but it was up to me to keep moving. I gritted my teeth and forced myself up and out of the chair. Trying to hide from the watching Matriarch and Sarjeant just how much effort it took and how much it cost me. Molly was quickly there at my side, taking my arm and surreptitiously supporting me. We headed for the doors, arm in arm.

"One last thing, Eddie," the Matriarch said behind me. "I've just been informed: Your parents are here."

CHAPTER SIX

Memories, Given Shape and Purpose

took Molly out of the Hall, and we went walking through the grounds. I felt better once I'd left what should have been my home and so rarely felt like one. Some of my strength came back, and Molly only held on to my arm because she wanted to. The evening air was cool and calm, and the light had an almost serene quality.

I led Molly round the side of the East Wing and then just kept walking until we'd put the Hall behind us. The wide-open lawns at the rear looked very different from the disturbed earth and bloody mess we'd made out front. It was all very quiet, with no one around. Great lawns stretched away into the distance, trees lined the horizon, and peacocks and gryphons paraded happily as though nothing had happened. That was one of the great things about Drood Hall: Whatever violent and appalling things might take place, there was always a feeling that the Hall and the grounds and the family would still survive.

Because we had made ourselves a part of the way things were.

We passed by huge open flower-beds, where the intricate and majestic displays combined species from any number of different worlds. Everything from bobbing flowers the size of a man's head, in almost

Technicolor hues, to sharp and spiky growths that swelled slowly and rhythmically as though they were breathing, to towering ornate things that seemed perfectly ready to tear up their roots and go for a stroll at any given moment. Wild and almost savage beauty, flowers with passion and power, only constrained by Drood knowledge. Just so we could have something to please our eyes. I pointed out a few of my favourites, struggling over the correct names and origins. I hadn't done a lot of walking on the grounds since I came home again, because there was always so much waiting to be done.

"Most of these flowers come from other worlds, other dimensions," I said. "Some are souvenirs, some the spoils of victory. And a few are hostages."

"Really?" said Molly.

"No," I said smiling. "You shouldn't believe everything I tell you, Molly. Hey! Don't hit! I'm fragile."

She sniffed loudly, hugged my arm against her side to show I was forgiven, and we moved on. The flowers turned their heads to watch us go. A small group pursed their rosebud mouths to sing an alien song in sweet harmonies. Beyond the flower-beds, carefully tended copses and thickets stood scattered across the lawns. All kinds of trees leaned together companionably, as though in hushed conversation. Some had leaves; some didn't. Whatever grows in Drood grounds never gives a damn about the seasons. Like us, they go their own way. Follies and outbuildings stood proudly alongside standing stone circles and hedge mazes. And out on the artificial lake, swans sailed serenely back and forth while the resident undine amused herself by making the waterfall run backwards.

"Uncle Jack and Uncle James used to bring me out here for picnics when I was younger," I said. "Because I had no parents to do that for me. James taught me the names of all the trees and flowers . . . But that was a long time ago. I never listened enough to the things he told me."

"You know, a lot of this reminds me of my wood between the

worlds," said Molly. "I'm surprised how much of it feels wild and unfettered. Not coerced into artificial groups or shapes to please someone's aesthetic choices or the fashion of the moment. Making nature seem neutered."

"Different Drood gardeners follow different paths," I said. "Capability Maggie got her nickname because of her fondness for landscaping, but always in a nurturing sort of way. Before she had to give it all up to become the new Matriarch."

"Seems to me she's still doing her best to make everything line up in neat rows," said Molly.

"The family needs an organiser," I said. "If only to keep us from tripping over each other. You'd be surprised how often the left hand doesn't know what deals the right hand is making with the third hand."

I looked around the grounds as we walked, taking it all in. Soaking up every detail, quietly enjoying every weird and wonderful sight. Molly shook my arm angrily.

"Stop that, Eddie."

"Stop what?"

"Looking at everything as though it's the last time you'll ever see it."

"Well, it might be," I said. "I'm trying to fix it all in my head, store it in my memory, so I can take it with me when I leave. Just in case I don't get to come back again."

"You can't think that way, Eddie! I can't think that way."

"I have to," I said. "Because you can't."

"You go up against Edmund in this frame of mind, he'll kill you dead before you get anywhere near him," Molly said sternly. "Stop allowing yourself to be distracted. Get your head back in the game."

"I'm just being practical," I said. "I have no illusions about my future, because I've come to terms with the fact that I don't have one. I couldn't keep on being angry all the time; it was just wearing me out. I wish you could learn to accept it too, Molly. You might find it easier to cope."

"I don't give up," said Molly. "Not ever. It's not in my nature."

We stopped before a massive standing stone. A great jagged thing, with deep cracks running through it. Ancient volcanic rock, it rose out of the lawn like an intrusion from another age, a good sixty feet high and almost as wide. Looked at from just the right angle, there was a suggestion of a face staring back. Not a modern face; it was older and more brutal than that. Primitive, almost prehuman. A gently gusting wind made strange noises as it moved through the deep fissures, like unearthly voices calling from distant places. The Stone looked like it had burst out of the ground, driven up and forced out by some deep, implacable force. Molly looked at the Stone and then at me.

"Okay, this is seriously ugly. What the hell is it? I never saw it before."

"I never brought you this way before," I said. "The Drood grounds cover a lot of territory, with more wonders and mysteries than you can shake something defensive at. We call this one the Stone."

"That's all?" said Molly. "No name?"

"If the Stone ever had one, it was lost to history long ago," I said. "And it's not like there's anything else in the grounds for us to confuse it with. We all know what we mean when we talk about the Stone."

"Why show it to me now?" said Molly.

"Look at the Stone," I said.

Molly gave me a hard look, to make sure I understood she was only indulging me, and then studied the Stone carefully.

"If you look at it long enough," I said, "you get the feeling something is looking back at you."

"Can't help thinking it's getting the better part of the deal," said Molly.

"The Stone is more than old," I said. "It's ancient. It was here long before Drood Hall. In fact, there are those who say my family only decided to build the Hall here because the Stone was here."

"To protect the Stone, or so it could protect the Hall?" said Molly.

"Your guess is as good as anyone's," I said. "The only thing everyone can agree on is that the Stone is dangerous."

"Isn't everything here?" said Molly.

"Sometimes people disappear around the Stone," I said. "They go walking round it and never reappear on the other side. Others climb to the top and never come down again. We all used to try that when we were kids. Daring each other on to prove our courage. I suppose every new generation does, despite it being strictly forbidden. Even a family as famously authoritative as ours has to have room in it for little rebellions."

Molly tore her gaze away from the Stone to look at me. "What do you think happened to all the missing people?"

"There's any number of theories," I said. "Some say the Stone marks a point where this world bumps up against another, and the walls between the worlds have been rubbed thin. So that every now and again, just for a moment, a Door opens and people can go through."

"Any idea where?" said Molly.

"No," I said. "But it can't be that bad. No one ever comes back to complain."

Molly scowled. "I'm not Seeing anything out of the ordinary. Looks like just a big rock to me."

"But it still feels disturbing, doesn't it?"

"Yes it does." Molly looked at me sharply. "If this thing is so dangerous, why haven't your family gotten rid of it? Why not smash it or blow it up?"

"It's been tried," I said. "Usually by people who'd lost children to it."

"And?" said Molly.

"The Stone is still here," I said. "And some of the people aren't."

Molly went back to studying the Stone. I knew she'd like it.

"Are there any books about the Stone in the Old Library?"

"Lots," I said. "Everything from personal histories to learned dissertations. All kinds of theories as to what it is and what it's for, and every single one of them contradictory. The only thing the family can agree on is that it's here for a purpose. That one day we're going to need it."

"Why would you believe that?"

"Remember the oracle?"

Molly shook her head firmly. "I wouldn't trust that arsehole to guess my weight."

"He doesn't guess," I said. "He knows. That's what's so annoying about him."

"Why did you bring me here, Eddie?" said Molly. "Why show me this?"

"I like the permanence of it," I said. "Our little lives come and go, the family's fortunes rise and fall, but the Stone endures. I need to believe something will still be here when I'm gone. Probably after the whole family has gone. But right now . . . I want to climb it."

"What?" said Molly, looking at me sharply.

"I never did when I was a boy. Ran around it a few times to prove I wasn't chicken, but that was it. This is something left over from my childhood; something I always meant to do and never did. So I'm going to do it now, while I still can."

"Even though the Stone is quite definitely dangerous, and people disappear on it?" said Molly.

"Yes."

She grinned at me. "Okay! Let's do it."

"You want to climb it too?"

"You're not going anywhere without me, Eddie Drood."

"Good to know," I said.

Climbing the Stone turned out to be easier than I'd expected. The cracks and crevices provided easy foot and hand support, and I went up the face in a series of controlled rushes. Molly was right there beside me, scrambling over the Stone's glowering face with easy grace. The sound of the wind in the crevices grew louder and more eerie. I laughed out loud, and Molly did too. I got to the top of the Stone, reached a hand down to Molly, and hauled her up alongside me, and then we stood together, arms around each other, looking out over the grounds. When I was just a child, the Stone seemed like the biggest and toughest challenge I could ever imagine. And now it seemed so much smaller.

"Well, go on, Stone!" Molly shouted challengingly. "Do something!"

"Come on, give it your best shot!" I said loudly. "You'll never get another chance like this!"

We waited, but nothing happened. I laughed quietly with Molly, and then we climbed back down. Taking our time, because this would be a really stupid way to mess up before we went after Edmund. We reached the ground without incident and walked away from the Stone. Not looking back once.

"I feel as though a small but very real psychic millstone has just been removed from around my neck," I said.

"Glad to have been of assistance," said Molly. "Hey, you didn't finish your history lesson. Why did your family move here? What happened to the original Drood home?"

"The first Drood Hall was down in Cornwall, not far from Ilfracombe. There was a battle, or a war, or a great disaster . . . All the records from that period are lost, some say deliberately. I went back for a visit some years ago. Nothing there, not even any ruins. Just dead ground where nothing will grow. Even the birds steer well clear. The place, the setting, the atmosphere, all of it tainted and poisoned."

"So, the Droods came here?" said Molly.

"No. There were several false starts in between. London in the Ninth Century, and Nottingham in the Thirteenth. This manor house dates from the Sixteenth Century. Some say Queen Elizabeth the First deeded the land to us personally, for favours received. And because we agreed to be custodians of the Stone."

"Your family is full of history," said Molly.

"My family is history," I said.

Molly sniffed loudly. "You wish."

We walked on across the wide-open lawns. On a pleasant evening, with the last of the light dropping out of the day. Shadows slowly lengthened, as though they were creeping up on something. Birds were singing and insects were buzzing, and all felt right with the world. *Lord, the day thou givest us is almost over . . .* And no one knew that better than me. It all felt so calm and easy. Just Nature getting on with things in her own quiet way. I had hoped some of the peace might rub off on me, but it didn't. I still had so much to do, and not enough time left to do it in.

For all my carefully nurtured resignation, I couldn't help feeling it was all so unfair. To have to die now, when I had so much to live for. But, then, I chose to be a field agent, knowing few of us ever survive long enough to retire. *Anything for the family.* The Droods and the Hall, lifetimes of work and duty, action and adventure, and a chance to do something worth doing. Edmund had to die for taking all of that away from me. And from Molly. Part of me wondered if I wanted to fight Edmund just so I could be killed taking him down. So I could die on my feet, doing something that mattered. I could be happy dying as Edmund died . . . as long as I could hold on long enough to watch him go first.

"How much farther, Eddie?" said Molly. "If I'd known we were going for a nature ramble, I'd have put on my heavy boots."

"We're almost there," I said. "See that small grove of trees up ahead?"

"The one that looks almost exactly like all the others we passed to get here? Yes, I can see it."

"Those are yew trees."

"Oh, those ones you recognise?"

"Yew trees are historically important," I said. "They supplied wood for the longbows that changed the history of warfare at Crecy and Agincourt."

"Were Droods there?"

"Depends on who you talk to."

I led her into the small, shadowy grove, and the trees opened up to reveal a pleasant clearing with cushions scattered across the grass, and a picnic hamper standing open on a chequered tablecloth. Charles and Emily, my father and my mother, were already waiting there, just as the Matriarch had said they'd be. Smiles lit up their faces as they hurried forward to greet me.

Charles was middle-aged and completely bald, with a neatly trimmed salt-and-pepper beard. Sleepy-eyed, with an easy smile, but it only took one look to see the presence and power in the man. He wore a rumpled sports jacket over an open-necked shirt and grey slacks. Charles had been a field agent for any number of subterranean organisations, and never talked about any of it. I got the feeling he thought I might not approve of some of the things he'd done in the name of the greater good.

Emily was a cool, poised middle-aged lady, in a lemon silk dress and a creamy white panama hat crammed down on her long grey hair. Still strikingly good-looking, in an *I don't give a damn about looking my age* kind of way. The only use she had for Botox would be to poison someone's tea. She radiated quiet grace and a sense of danger, like a great cat dozing in the sun.

They both greeted me warmly, Charles with his rough-and-ready voice, Emily with her cut-glass finishing-school accent. She hugged me hard and then stepped back to let Charles hug me. I responded as best I could; I wasn't used to family who cared. Growing up in Drood Hall without parents hadn't equipped me to deal with physical demonstrations that didn't involve punishment. Molly hung back, not wanting to intrude on the moment, but Charles and Emily called for her to come forward so they could hug her too.

"You're the woman our son loves," Emily said firmly. "That makes you family."

"In every way that matters," said Charles.

"The Matriarch doesn't seem to agree," said Molly.

"Screw the silly bitch," Emily said cheerfully.

We sat down on the cushions, and Emily produced chilled wine from the picnic hamper. Good food of all kinds piled up on paper plates as she went back to the hamper again and again, until Molly felt she had to raise an eyebrow.

"Is this another of those bigger-on-the-inside-than-it-is-on-the-outside deals?"

"Something like that," said Emily.

"It's a family hamper," said Charles. "They can be very persuasive when it comes to keeping their contents in line."

He uncorked a wine bottle with practiced ease and smiled at Molly. "Red or white, my dear?"

"Red," said Molly.

He poured her a glass of dark red wine and then turned to me. I grinned, because I knew what was coming.

"White wine, please," I said.

And my father poured me a glass of white wine from the same bottle.

"One of Jack's better ideas," said Emily.

She waited till we each had a glass of wine in hand, and then raised her glass in a smiling toast.

"Here's to you, my darlings. And let the rest of the world beware!"

"I'll drink to that," I said.

We all did, and then we sank back on our cushions and talked quietly for a while.

"I always liked it here," said Charles. "Within the grounds, but far enough away from the Hall that no one will bother you."

"We used to sneak away to this copse all the time when we were first courting," said Emily. "It's hard to find any real privacy inside the Hall."

The two of them exchanged a smile, sharing memories, and I looked away. It's never easy to consider your parents being . . . romantic. Molly picked up on my discomfort and seemed quietly amused. Her parents were hippies and probably went around being nude and uninhibited all the time. I looked at Charles, who met my gaze steadily.

"Sorry we couldn't get here any sooner."

"We were both out in the field, interviewing persons of interest for the new Department of Uncanny, when the Matriarch's message reached us," said Emily. "We dropped everything to come home."

And then they both stopped, uncertain what to say next. I didn't help them. They had to find their own way through this.

"It is true, then?" said Charles.

"You've been poisoned?" said Emily.

"Yes," I said.

"Fatally?" said Charles.

"Yes," I said.

"Don't you give up on the family doctors, Eddie," Emily said firmly. "They have been known to work the odd miracle from time to time."

"Trust the family," said Charles. "They're bastards, but they never give up on one of their own."

They both looked like they wanted to hug me again, to hold me and keep me safe, but they didn't. I understood. It wouldn't help any of us to lose our self-control. If we gave in to our feelings, we wouldn't be able to talk . . . and I could only spare so much time for this before I had to be going. Molly looked back and forth between us and made an exasperated noise.

"Why do you always have to be the tough guy, Eddie? Would it kill you to show an honest emotion to your own parents?"

"It's all right, Molly," said Emily. "We understand."

"He's a Drood," said Charles.

"We're trained from an early age to be masters of our emotions, and never the other way round," said Emily. "It's necessary, when any one of us could pull on our armour at any moment and smash up the world."

"Or use the armour to hide inside?" said Molly.

Charles chuckled and nodded to me. "I like her. She's smart. You chose well, son. How did you meet?"

"You must have read the family file on Molly," I said.

"Of course," said Charles. "First thing we did when we found out you were an item. Bit of an eye-opener, actually."

"But files can only tell you so much," Emily said firmly. "I'm sure there's another side to the story."

"There would have to be," said Charles.

"Molly really was the greatest supernatural terrorist of her day," I said. "We spent years on opposite sides, trying to kill each other for reasons that seemed good at the time. But when the family declared me rogue and I had to go on the run, the only people I could turn to for help were those I'd previously considered enemies. Starting with the wild witch Molly Metcalf, because she was the only one strong enough to defend me from my family. She proved to me that not everything I'd been brought up to believe was necessarily true. We learned to work together, with the family as our common enemy, and much to our mutual surprise . . . we clicked."

"Now I'm a retired supernatural terrorist who works alongside the Droods," said Molly. "Sometimes I think this whole world runs on irony. Either that, or it's got a really warped sense of humour."

And then Charles just couldn't stand it any longer.

"Who was it, son? Who did this to you?"

I told my father and mother about Edmund. Who and what he was. They took the idea of a Drood from another world in stride, though the thought that another version of me could have gone so bad took more getting used to.

"Does the family know where this Edmund is?" said Charles.

"We have some leads," I said carefully. Because if Charles and Emily knew Molly and I were going after Edmund, they'd insist on coming along. And I couldn't put them at risk too. I just couldn't. And there was always the chance I might have to do things I didn't want them to see me doing. They shouldn't have to remember me that way. I shot a glance at Molly.

"The Sarjeant is working on it," she said.

"Is there anything we can do to help?" said Charles.

"Talk to me," I said. "We've hardly had a moment to ourselves since we found each other again. We're always racing off on some world-saving mission or another."

"That's life for a Drood," said Emily.

We sat back on our cushions and talked, while I pretended I couldn't hear the clock ticking. I had to have this moment, because I could never have it again.

"How did you two get together?" Molly asked my parents.

"My family were never part of the hidden world," said Charles. "Never even knew it existed. I was brought up to be an engineer, like my father and grandfather. But I got involved in a factory haunting when I was sent in for what was supposed to be a routine inspection. No one would work there because of all the stories about glowing figures appearing and disappearing inside the factory late at night. The watchmen wouldn't even make their rounds, once darkness fell.

"Of course, I didn't believe a word of it. I staked the place out myself, and no one was more surprised than me when all these glowing figures turned up and tried to kill me! And then this amazing mysterious woman appeared out of nowhere to save me, and kick their glowing arses."

"They weren't ghosts," said Emily, sipping her wine with one finger daintily extended. "Just a bunch of timeline-hopping freebooters, looking to establish a dimensional Door so they could loot this world till it bled. They didn't know about Droods, the poor bastards."

"We took them down together, and sent them packing," said Charles.

"Your father was very brave," said Emily.

"And your mother was a Drood," said Charles. "They never stood a chance. And afterwards . . . Well, we clicked."

"Yes," said Emily. "We did. All through the weekend."

They both laughed lightly at the look on my face.

"It wasn't an easy courtship," said Charles. "The family likes to say it's in favour of new blood, but they don't make it easy for outsiders to get in."

"I think the idea is that if you can be frightened off by the family, by who we are and what we do, it's best to find out early," said Emily. "But your father . . . persevered."

They reached out to hold hands. Rather more naturally than Maxwell and Victoria, to my mind.

"After we were married," said Emily, "your father turned out to be a first-class field agent."

"Thank you, my dear," said Charles. "But you know I couldn't have done any of it without you."

We were interrupted by the sound of heavy flapping wings. We all looked up to see the dragon circle around the grove and then descend rapidly towards us. We rose quickly to our feet and retreated to the edges of the clearing to give him room to land. And then all the trees leaned backwards, creaking loudly, to make sure he had enough room. Either because they were that kind of tree, or just as further proof that no one argues with a dragon. He landed lightly in the exact centre of the clearing, tucked in his wings, and posed proudly to show off the magnificent new body the old Armourer had made possible. Seen up close, he seemed realer than real, as though he were too big for the small world he was gracing with his presence. His scales glowed, and his eyes blazed with fierce golden fires. And yet his clawed feet made hardly any impact on the grass, as though he wasn't really there at all. A contradiction, but, then, that's dragons for you.

Emily went straight up to the dragon, patted him on the neck, and spoke cheerful nonsense to him. Charles winked at me.

"Girls and their ponies . . ."

"I heard that!"

"Yes, dear . . ."

"Jack always did do good work," said Emily, standing back to look the dragon over admiringly.

"Did you know your uncle Jack could do this?" Molly said to me. "When you brought the dragon's head back from Castle Frankenstein?"

"No," I said. "I just knew I couldn't leave him there on his own."

"You and your strays," said Molly. And then she stopped. "Your family can give a dragon a new body, but they can't save you. It's not right."

I went to put my arm round her shoulders, but she shrugged me away angrily, refusing to be comforted.

"Be grateful for what my family can do," I said. "And make allowances for what they can't."

"What's your name?" Emily said to the dragon.

"We don't have names," he said proudly. "We know who we are."

"There are more dragons out there, in the world?" said Charles. "I thought you were all gone."

"It is possible . . . that I am the last," said the dragon. "We don't belong here any more. Our time has passed, and the world has moved on."

"There's always Shadows Fall," said Molly. "Where legends go when the world stops believing in them."

"I am not ready to retire," said the dragon, just a little huffily. He sniffed loudly at the very thought, and then turned his steady golden gaze on me. "You need to get to the Museum of Unattached Oddities in a hurry. I can take you straight there in no time at all. Right now, if you want."

"You know where it is?" I said.

"I know where everything is," he said calmly. "Dragons just do. It's a gift. And I can get you there really quickly, because dragons fly between dimensions, passing directly from one place to another. And no, we won't be noticed when we arrive, because no one ever sees a dragon unless we want them to."

"Then how was Baron Frankenstein able to behead you all those years ago?" Molly said innocently.

"He sneaked up on me while I was sleeping!" the dragon said loudly, and two small jets of flame shot out of his nostrils. "Somehow that part never made it into his great heroic legend."

"Will finding a landing space be a problem?" I said. "I understand it's pretty rough country out there."

The dragon looked meaningfully at the surrounding trees, still leaning obligingly back at uncomfortable angles.

"Wherever I decide to land, the landscape will accommodate me," he said grandly. "Or else."

I turned to Charles and Emily. "I'm sorry, but Molly and I have to go."

"Right now?" said Charles.

"But we've hardly had any time!" said Emily. "Your father and I . . . There's so much we wanted to say to you!"

"We can talk more when I get back," I said.

I could tell from their faces that they didn't believe I would be coming back. And I couldn't say anything, because I didn't believe I would either. So I hugged them both, and turned away before they could see the expression on my face. I climbed up onto the dragon's back and settled myself as comfortably as possible on the broad arc of the dragon's spine. Emily hugged Molly quickly.

"Look after him, dear."

"Bring him home," said Charles.

"And make sure you kill that little turd Edmund," said Emily.

"Edmund's already dead," said Molly. "He just doesn't know it yet."

I reached a hand down to her, impatient to get going. She scrambled up the dragon's side and grabbed hold of my hand, and I hauled her up behind me.

"Hang on tight!" said the dragon.

Molly took a firm grip around my waist, pressing her face against my shoulder. I looked around for something to hold on to, but there didn't seem to be anything. The dragon leapt into the sky, his wings stretched wide, and the world fell away beneath us. First the clearing, then the lawns, and finally the whole Drood grounds disappeared as we soared up into the clouds.

I expected the dragon to fly us through the side dimensions, like Uncle Jack's racing Bentley. Instead the dragon flew steadily on through the freezing air, his wings barely moving, punching effortlessly through the clouds. I just had time to wonder how I could be bothered by the cold but not the lack of oxygen this far up, when a Rainbow suddenly appeared before us. It filled the sky, huge and magnificent, thundering down like a Niagara Falls of blazing colours, so bright and vivid I thought they would burn the eyes out of my head. An aspect of Nature writ large, a pure embodiment of an abstract concept, made real and more than real. Like the dragon.

He flew straight into the Rainbow, and I threw an arm up to shield my eyes, bracing myself. The Rainbow loomed up before us until it was all there was in the world, and the dragon plunged into it. There was no impact, not even a sense of transition, but suddenly the magnificent shades and hues were gone and we were flying serenely through a cloudless lead-grey sky. I looked back, past Molly's bowed shoulders, but there was no sign of the Rainbow anywhere. We were alone in the sky. Molly raised her head and grinned at me cheerfully.

"Magic!"

"Almost certainly," I said.

The dragon flew on, over snow-covered heights and all the wild glory of the Scottish countryside. His great head moved back and forth, searching, and then he plunged down so suddenly my arse actually left the dragon's spine for a moment before slamming back into place again. He straightened out at a much lower level, and we flew leisurely over purple-heathered moorland, dark stretches of peat bog, and wide-open areas that had never known the cultivating hand of man. It was still freezing cold. I shuddered convulsively, and I could feel Molly shivering too as she pressed against my back.

"Get us down!" I yelled to the dragon. "Before we freeze to death!"

"You're perfectly safe," he said calmly. "You're protected from the elements just by being with me."

"It doesn't bloody well feel like it!" Molly said loudly. "I think my nipples just dropped off!"

"Humans," said the dragon. "Look down to your right, about two o'clock."

I leaned out a little to get a look past the dragon's muscular shoulder, and there, alone in the middle of nowhere, stood a single great structure.

"That's it!" I yelled. "That's the Museum of Unattached Oddities! Now get us down there before frostbite sets in!"

Molly peered past me. "Are you sure that's it?"

"I don't care," I said. "I just want to be on the ground again. I'll walk the rest of the way if I have to."

"Please fasten your seat belts and return all seats to the upright position," the dragon said cheerfully. "We are going in."

And then he dropped like a stone, the ground hurtling up to meet us. I wanted to close my eyes, but didn't dare. It didn't help that Molly was whooping loudly behind me and beating out a happy rhythm on my shoulders with both hands as she delighted in the ride. At the last moment the dragon's wings spread out to cup the air, and our speed slowed to practically nothing. The deceleration alone should have been enough to rip me and Molly right off the dragon's back, but I hardly felt a thing. So perhaps we were protected, after all. The ground loomed up beneath us, grey and hard and unforgiving. The dragon eased to a halt, hovering just a few feet above it, not even breathing hard, which was more than I could say for myself. He lowered his feet and we settled into place right in front of the Museum so gently, it took me a moment to realise we'd actually landed.

The dragon retracted his wings, and turned his head right round so he could look at me. It was hard to tell with a dragon, but I was pretty sure he was smiling.

"Welcome to bonny Scotland! Do try the haggis, don't let them put salt on your porridge, and always remember to tip your waitress."

"Where are all these cultural references coming from?" said Molly. "You spent most of your life buried under a mound of earth."

"The lab assistants set up a television for me," said the dragon. "It had cable and a voice-activated remote and everything! I love television."

"Wonderful," I said. "My family has corrupted a dragon. Like we don't have enough sins to answer for."

"You've arrived," the dragon said loudly. "Now get off me, before I decide to play buckaroo. What are you waiting for—a step-ladder?"

I disembarked first, slowly and carefully, and then helped Molly down. We both shivered violently at the cold wind skidding across the open ground, and huddled together beside the dragon.

"I don't care whether that's the Museum or not," said Molly. "I am going inside even if I have to kick a hole in the wall. It is so cold out here, I can feel ice crystals forming inside my bladder."

"More information than I really needed," I said. "But that is quite definitely the Museum of Unattached Oddities. I've been here before, remember?"

"Will there be hot drinks inside?"

"Almost certainly not."

"I hate this place."

"You haven't even seen it yet," I said.

"Doesn't matter," said Molly. "I have an infallible instinct about these things."

"If I'd known you were going to complain this much, I'd have just shrugged you off and let you drop through the roof," said the dragon. "I transport you hundreds of miles in under a minute, and do I get a word of thanks?"

"Thanks," I said.

Molly looked at me. "Actually, if you'd armoured up, just dropping in might have worked."

"No, it wouldn't," I said. "The Museum has protections and defences like you wouldn't believe. At best, I might have bounced."

"At worst?" said Molly.

"Really not interested in finding out the hard way."

I took a deep breath, braced myself against the bitter wind, and moved out from the dragon to study the Museum's exterior. Molly stuck close behind me so she could use me as a wind-break. We'd arrived on what might have been a large open patio, once upon a time. It had definitely never been a car park, because there weren't any roads. The Museum of Unattached Oddities stood entirely alone in the middle of nowhere, as though it had been dropped there and abandoned. The great open space in front of the Museum was covered in stained and weathered flag-stones, with weeds sprouting up between the cracks. Most of the old stones had splits and cracks, and some had sheared clean in half. As the courtyard of an important and significant museum, it made a very bad first impression, which was, of course, the point. This wasn't the kind of place where strangers were supposed to linger.

"How long has it been since anyone even thought about doing some basic maintenance here?" said Molly.

"The Museum doesn't want to encourage visitors," I said. "If by some unfortunate chance the odd hiker or seriously lost tourist should find their way here, nothing about this should give them any reason to hang around. Much better if they just assume the place is deserted and move on."

The dark and gloomy edifice before us was someone's idea of a Gothic mansion, complete with spiked turrets, leering gargoyles, and thick mats of ivy crawling over the stonework. It wasn't particularly large, as mansions went, but it had a certain heavy, languorous quality, as though it was sleeping. Or sulking. The upper windows were hidden behind closed wooden shutters, and no lights showed on the ground floor, where all the windows had been left filthy dirty so no one could look in. Tiles were missing from the roof, the chimney-stack had all but collapsed, and the gutters looked like they were only hanging on by their fingernails.

"This is the kind of dump that gives dumps a bad name," said Molly. "More disguise?"

"No," I said. "It really is that bad. On the outside. The interior . . . is a somewhat different matter. The building's not as old as it appears; it was constructed to look old. To be the home away from home of a respected English businessman, who had it designed and built to conform to his own romantic specifications."

"You mean it's a folly," said Molly.

"Got it in one. Made to resemble the setting of all his favourite novels so he could move here, get away from everything, and live the Gothic dream. Which would probably have turned out to be a lot draughtier than he expected. But, sadly, paying for all of this bankrupted our business friend, and he never got to spend a single night here. The mansion changed hands several times, a white or rather dirty grey elephant that no one knew what to do with, until finally it became home to the Museum of Unattached Oddities. You're about to ask me who's responsible for founding the Museum, aren't you?"

"No," said Molly. "Couldn't give a damn."

"I'm glad you asked. It's a fascinating story."

"Eddie, get to the point or I will have the dragon sit on you until you do."

I glanced at the dragon, who stared calmly off into the distance, declining to get involved. I turned back to Molly.

"Are you at least interested in what's inside the Museum?"

"Maybe. Depends. Any of it valuable and easily transportable?"

"The Museum contains all kinds of weapons, artefacts, and *objets perdu*, magical and scientific. Items of legendary importance and baffling obscurity, along with a whole bunch of stuff no one can identify with any certainty, or figure out what to do with. All the wonders and marvels, complete tat and utter rubbish, that fell off the back of a lorry in the hidden world. Brought here and dropped off by people who then ran away terribly quickly."

"Half-dead from poison and you're still lecturing me."

"You love it."

"Eddie, why are we standing around out here when Edmund is inside?"

"Because you need to understand just how dangerous it can get in there," I said. "You go barging in with your magics at their current levels, and the Museum will take you down before you even catch a glimpse of Edmund. This whole place is one really big dog that doesn't like strangers."

"And that's your only reason for hesitating?"

I sighed inwardly. She knew me so well. "Edmund got away from us at the Armoury because he caught us by surprise. I can't risk him getting away again. So we do it right this time. We go in ready and prepared for anything."

"Think I'll go for a bit of a fly around, while you're busy," announced the dragon. "There's nothing like being a severed head buried under an earth mound for centuries to make you feel like stretching your wings. Call me when you're ready to leave. Wherever I am, I'll hear you."

He launched himself up into the looming grey skies without any sense of effort, and in moments he was just a speck in the distance, no larger than a bird on the wing.

"His hearing had better be as good as he thinks it is," said Molly. "Or it's a really long walk home."

"I'm still convinced someone will spot him and raise the alarm," I said. "He may be used to thinking of himself as invisible, but what does he know about radar and tracking systems?"

"A Seven Forty-seven could fly right past him and no one on board would even know he was there," Molly said firmly. "Unless he felt like playing chicken with it, to freak out the pilots. Dragons are psychically invisible, hidden from everything. You don't know much about dragons, do you?"

"Not really," I said. "Never expected to meet one."

"The hidden world is a lot bigger than most people realise," said Molly. "All kinds of myths and legends are still hanging on in the shadows, keeping their heads down and waiting for this whole civilization fad to pass."

"Now who's lecturing?"

I headed for the Museum's front door, with Molly striding along beside me. Stepping carefully around and over the worst of the cracked and tilted flag-stones, to avoid tripping. Some split and broke apart under our weight, anyway, with loud echoing reports.

"Let's hope Edmund is so taken up with whatever it is he's doing that he's not supposed to that he isn't listening out for visitors," I said.

"What do you think he's after?" said Molly.

"Could be any number of things," I said. "But if Grendel Rex really was seriously weakened before my family took him down, it's always possible that whatever did it is here in the Museum. Or Edmund thinks it is."

"I say we just kill the bastard the moment we see him, and worry about everything else afterwards," said Molly.

"Sounds like a plan to me," I said.

We finally reached the front door and paused to look it over respectfully. The huge slab of dark-stained oak was decorated with a great many iron studs laid out in intricate overlapping patterns. Molly frowned.

"I don't recognise any of that. I suppose it could be Celtic, or even Druidic."

"It's fake," I said. "Just there to make the door look impressive and authentic, and several other things it isn't."

"Is the door locked?"

"Always."

"Do you have a key?"

"No."

"Is there any other way in?"

"What do you think?"

"Then what are we supposed to do—shout your family name at the door and hope it's impressed?"

"No, we'll have to break in," I said. "The Museum is closed. It's always closed, unless you have special permission. Which I could probably have arranged before we left, using the family name, but there wasn't enough time to go through proper channels."

"Permission?" said Molly. "Who from?"

"I thought you weren't interested in the back story?"

"I'm not! All right, who?"

"The Wulfshead Management Museum Trust. They're responsible for overseeing lot of special-interest museums."

"You're kidding me."

"I wish. They have their finger in all sorts of pies." I stopped and frowned. "A saying I've never properly understood."

"Who the hell are the Wulfshead Management?" said Molly. "You must have some idea. Your family knows everything!"

"No," I said. "We just like to give that impression. My family have been pursuing the identity of the Wulfshead Management with great vigour for some time now, and all we know for sure is who they aren't. Haven't you heard anything, Molly, given the kind of people you mix with?"

She scowled. "Most people don't even want to hear the question. Some actually stick their fingers in their ears and throw themselves out of windows." She looked at me thoughtfully. "How many museums is the Management responsible for?"

"Another question my family would really like to know the answer to."

Molly started to say something, and then stopped and shook her head firmly. "No. I don't care. I am not being distracted."

"You started it . . ."

"Look, just armour up and kick the bloody door in."

"I can't," I said. "It's defended."

"Even against people like you?"

"Especially against people like me. If only because my family has a long history of confiscating things they don't believe other people should have."

"All right, ring the bloody door-bell," said Molly. "Let the staff know we're here and have them let us in. So we can tell them they've got a burglar sneaking around and playing with their precious things."

"There isn't any staff," I said patiently. "The exhibits are perfectly capable of looking after themselves."

"So no one's in there to stop Edmund from doing anything he feels like?" Molly glared at the door. "No, wait a minute . . . If this door is the only way in, and it's still locked and protected, how did Edmund get in?"

"He has the Merlin Glass," I said. "Which laughs in the face of locks and spits in the eye of protections. Which is why I always found it so very useful."

"Doesn't anyone at least look in now and again?" said Molly. "To check everything's okay?"

"Most people have enough sense not to want to get in," I said. "And given that most of the exhibits aren't, strictly speaking, valuable . . ."

"Then why are they here?"

"Because they're interesting. And dangerous. And so scholars can study them. There's always some bright spark begging to be allowed access to the Museum, to examine its weirder items up close and personal. And occasionally poke them with the science stick, just to see what happens. Though, of course, given the exceptional nature of some of these obscure objects of desire, there are a lot more bad guesses than good ones. Some scholars get it so spectacularly wrong that their peers still make regular field trips to their graves, just so they can continue to point and mock. Academics can be very unforgiving in the hidden world."

"I never knew there were any," Molly said carelessly. "Not my thing, really."

"How did you learn to be a witch, then?"

She grinned at me. "Wouldn't you like to know?" She gave the door a long, thoughtful look that would have been more than enough to send chills up the spine of anything animate, given the suggestion of sudden and dramatic violence in the near offing. "What security systems do they have here, specifically?"

"Nothing you or I can't handle once we're inside. Unless they've been upgraded again, of course."

"Who by?" Molly said dangerously. "You said there weren't any staff!"

234 ° Simon R. Green

"The scholars do it," I said. "The clever little dickens. They like to protect the things they think are important, especially from other scholars. And, of course, they never tell anyone about their little improvements, because that would ruin the surprise. It's all just academics pissing to mark their territory, really."

Molly looked at me. "Were you by any chance ever turned down by one of these centres of learning?"

"I am a graduate of the University of Drood," I said grandly. "Specialising in weird shit, brown-trousering the ungodly, and general mayhem. My family knows things the academic world has never even dreamed of. Go, Droods, go."

"Spare me," said Molly.

She leaned in close and inspected the door thoroughly, being very careful not to touch anything, and made various noises of a thoughtful nature before standing back again.

"I'm not Seeing anything out of the ordinary here. No. Hold it. That's odd . . . There isn't any lock, or even a handle! Why didn't I notice that before?"

"Because you're not supposed to," I said. "It's an intangible lock, only there when the staff want it to be there."

"What staff?" Molly said loudly. "You said there aren't any staff!"

"Well," I said. "There's staff, and then there's staff."

"Are you feeling feverish?" Molly said sternly. "Do you need to sit down and have me force your head between your knees?"

"It's not me—it's the Museum!" I said. "It's just that sort of place. And that sort of lock. If it was solid and tangible I could use my armour to pick or smash it. Come on, Molly. You were supposed to be one of the best supernatural burglars in the business."

"I was!" said Molly. "It's just that my magics are running so low right now . . . Let me think." She scowled at the door. "Okay . . . I think I've probably got enough left in me for a Pretty Please. That's a basic persuasion spell to make the door think it's unlocked, so it'll let us in."

"Go for it," I said.

Molly frowned fiercely, beads of sweat popping out on her brow, and a gently glowing old-fashioned lock appeared on the door. There was the sound of heavy things turning reluctantly inside it, and then the door swung slowly back. Molly let out her breath in a deep sigh, and smiled at me triumphantly.

"Good to know I've still got it. There was a time I could have stolen the hat off your head even when you weren't wearing a hat."

"I believe you," I said.

She started forward, and then stopped as I put a staying hand on her arm. I called a pair of golden sunglasses out of my torc to cover my eyes, and studied the open hallway carefully. I finally armoured up one hand and slammed the door all the way back, until it banged against the inside wall. The sound from the heavy impact hung on the air, the echoes only reluctantly dying away. The long hallway was full of shadows, deep and dark and utterly still. I couldn't See any hidden protections . . . until I looked down at the welcome mat just inside the door. I reached down, picked it up between one golden thumb and forefinger, and moved it carefully to one side. Molly raised an eyebrow.

"Teleport device," I said. "Hidden inside the mat. Ready to grab hold of anyone who steps on it and transport them somewhere they really wouldn't want to be."

"Oh, that is so cool!" said Molly. "Can we take it with us when we go? I can think of all kinds of amusing places I could just happen to leave it lying around."

"Maybe later," I said. "If you're good."

She smiled at me demurely. "Now, you know, sweetie, I'm always good."

"Later."

"Can you See any other nasty little surprises lying in wait?"

"Not at the moment, but you can bet we'll run into some more along the way. The scholars do like to keep each other on their toes. So watch your step."

"Which one of us used to be the professional burglar?" She shouldered me aside and strode into the hallway. I stepped in after her and carefully closed the front door. Because I didn't want anyone else to get in, or anything to get out.

A gentle illumination appeared as we proceeded down the hallway. Warm and pleasant, easy on the eye, except . . . I couldn't see any light bulbs anywhere. And although the hallway was packed full of shadows, Molly and I didn't appear to have one. Which was . . . odd. The air was still and stale and dusty, and almost as cold as it was outside. Molly shuddered pointedly.

"Maybe we should set fire to something."

"A lot of people feel that way about this Museum," I said solemnly. "Keep moving. That'll warm you up."

"Oh, so now you're in a hurry?"

"We're in the same building as Edmund," I said. "He could be anywhere. I wouldn't put it past him to walk out of a wall to get to us."

Molly looked around her uneasily. "Of course; he's got the Glass. He could appear out of anywhere."

"My armour would warn me about that."

"Would it? It didn't warn you while he was hiding inside the damned thing."

"The Merlin Glass," I said. "The work of Merlin Satanspawn. I should never have trusted it. The clue was always in the name."

The quiet in the hallway was so heavy we were both speaking in hushed voices for fear of the sound carrying. Even our footsteps sounded unnaturally loud. When we finally reached the end of the hallway, the swingdoors opened onto a standard reception area. The unmanned desk was littered with colourful leaflets, but they were all covered with dust.

"No one's been here in a while," I said.

"Or, at least, no one who was interested in leaflets," said Molly. "Look at the floor, Eddie—not a speck of dust anywhere."

She was right. The floor was just basic wooden boards. The furniture was bulky and old-fashioned, and the bare walls had been painted in flat industrial colours. No style, no character—nothing in the least inviting.

"People don't come here for the friendly, welcoming atmosphere," I said.

"Just as well," said Molly. "Where do we go now?"

"Good question," I said. "Most of what I know about this place comes from stories my uncle Jack used to tell. He always made a point of dropping in here once or twice a year. To donate things the Armoury didn't want or had outgrown. And to see if anything interesting had turned up here that he could liberate for the Droods."

"And the staff who aren't staff just let him?"

"No one ever argued with my uncle Jack," I said.

"Why did you come here?"

"I was intrigued by the stories. So I volunteered to drop a few things off for him. Two visits was sufficient to cure me of that."

Molly looked at me. She'd heard something in my voice.

"Something happened, didn't it? On the second visit."

"I should have known better," I said. "My first visit was enough to freak me out big time. But I was at that age when you don't like to admit anything can scare you. I should never have come back."

I stopped talking. Because even after so many years, I still found it difficult to talk about.

"Eddie, what happened to you?"

"The exhibits have taken over the asylum," I said, not looking at her. My mouth had gone dry. "Like freaks in a sideshow who've grown tired of being stared at and are looking to get their own back. The exhibits put up with the scholars, because the scholars worship them, but everyone else is fair game."

"Is that why you spent so much time outside?" said Molly. "You were working up your nerve?"

"You don't understand!"

"I'm trying, Eddie. Talk to me."

"One of the exhibits . . . took a liking to me," I said. "It tried to make me into an exhibit too. So I could never leave."

"What did you do?"

"Armoured up and kicked the crap out of it. And then I got the hell out and told myself never to come here again."

Molly put a comforting hand on my arm. "You're not alone this time, Eddie. I'm here."

"I'm not scared."

"I never said you were."

"It's just, things that disturb you when you're young tend to leave their mark."

"Like not climbing the Stone?"

"The Stone didn't say it loved me."

"Well, now you can say you're spoken for."

I managed a small smile.

"Edmund must have come here for something specific," said Molly, deliberately changing the subject. "Any ideas?"

"Maybe something he saw in his world's Museum," I said. "Or something in the book he stole from the Old Library. It doesn't matter. He's here, and so are we. So let's finish this."

"Can't wait," said Molly. "Where do we start?"

I pointed an entirely steady hand at the information board on the far wall. Crammed with names in gold lettering, it provided directions to any number of rooms, each with its own area of specialised knowledge. THE CHALLENGER EXPLORATION ROOM; BIG GAME AND ASSOCIATED TROPHIES. THE ARNE SAKNUSSEN ROOM; DISCOVERIES FROM DOWN BELOW. THE DEATHSTALKER ROOM; WHAT DOES THE FUTURE HOLD FOR US? The names went on and on, tempting and warning in equal measure.

"How big is this museum?" said Molly. "Is this another of those bigger-on-the-inside-than-the-outside deals?"

"Comes as standard these days," I said. "That's what overcrowding and a lack of funding for extensions does to you. There—that's the one we want: the Old Curiosities Room. Where everything that won't fit anywhere else ends up."

Molly looked at me steadily.

"Is that where you had your bad experience?"

"Yes," I said.

"Stick close to me, sweetie," said Molly. "Anything even looks at you funny, I will rip its insides out and stamp on them. Hard."

I had to smile. "Without your magics?"

"Now, you know I always keep a few things in reserve for emergencies. I've still got a few surprises left in me."

"Never knew you when you didn't," I said generously.

I led the way into the depths of the Museum, following the colour-coded lines on the floor through a warren of twisting, turning corridors. I was surprised at how much of it I remembered, given how hard I'd worked to wipe the place from my memory. All the corridors were empty and quiet, and subtly oppressive. As though someone or something was always watching. I couldn't see any security cameras, but that didn't necessarily mean anything. Finally we came to a closed door, and stopped to look it over.

"Okay," said Molly. "The sign says we're at the right place. How do you want to handle this?"

"I feel like armouring up," I said. "Just on general principle."

"Then do it."

"No," I said. "Because that would be giving in, and I don't do that."

"Concentrate on why we're here," said Molly. "If Edmund is in there, don't hesitate. You get the chance to put him down, take it."

"That's the plan," I said.

I took a careful hold of the door handle and turned it slowly. It wasn't locked. I pushed the door open and slipped quietly inside, with Molly right behind me. Everything was very quiet, very still. The Old Curiosities Room stretched away before us, an indoor cavern hundreds of feet long and almost as wide, packed with thousands of exhibits. In glass cases, standing cabinets, and specially reinforced display units. Even more things had been left carelessly piled up on row after row of trestle tables. Separated almost reluctantly by narrow aisles, to allow people access. I took a deep breath and headed for the main aisle, down the centre. There was still only just room for Molly to walk alongside me. This wasn't a room that encouraged visitors. Molly looked at all the amazing things set out before her and smiled.

"So many pretty things . . . My fingers are itching."

"Later," I said.

We moved slowly down the aisle, keeping our eyes open. At first I was half-convinced Edmund had to be here somewhere, maybe hiding behind something. But more and more I became fascinated by the items set out on display. I'd forgotten what a treasure trove this place was. A Hand of Glory stood upright on its stand. The helpful sign said it had been made from the severed hand of an angel. I'd seen it before. I always wondered what the Armourer did with it. The flesh was deathly white, the palm was completely free of lines, and the fingertips showed no signs of ever having possessed any nails.

Not far away, a single silver coin had been set out on a velvet cushion. The sign said it was one of thirty.

A Mole Machine stood proudly alone in an open space, surrounded by a chain-link fence. The huge drill on the front made it look very futuristic, but the pressurised cabin was only big enough to hold one person. The sign said it had been designed for deep-earth explorations, but the last time I'd heard of it being used, it was to tunnel into the secret vaults of the Bank of England.

Molly slapped my arm suddenly and pointed at one particular display case. "Eddie! Is that what I think it is?"

I let her drag me over for a closer look. The secure unit was sealed on every side, even though all it contained was a single wooden amulet on a cord made from intertwined hair. The wooden disk bore a simple design: a stylised letter M. The sign read THE MANX MEDALLION.

"It's real," I said. "My family donated it a long time ago. Because just having it around the Hall was creeping people out. A gift from Merlin, along with the Glass. The amulet is supposed to be a repository for extremely powerful magical forces and the work of Morgana La Fae. The strands of hair making up the cord came from her own head, or the heads of her many victims. Depending on which source you choose to believe." And then I stopped and frowned. "Strange, the way her name keeps cropping up. I don't believe in coincidences, not in the hidden world. This means something."

"Almost certainly," said Molly. "But does it mean anything important? Anything that matters? Magic has a fondness for patterns and repetition. And, let's face it, there would have to be something seriously wrong with a collection this big if it didn't have at least one item to represent the most powerful witch this world has ever known. Good thing for all of us she's dead and gone . . . Why are you looking at me like that, Eddie? She is dead, isn't she? I mean, Merlin killed her for her part in bringing down Arthur's Camelot. Everyone knows that. Or are you about to tell me no one ever saw the body? Because as you keep saying, if you don't see the body . . ."

"I've never heard anything to even suggest she survived," I said carefully. "And if she had, I think we'd all know about it by now. Morgana never was one to hide her ambition under a bushel. In every book I've read on the subject, the author seemed entirely convinced of her sudden and violent death at Merlin's hand. Come on, Molly. You knew Merlin in the Nightside. Didn't you ever ask him?"

"He really didn't like to talk about Morgana," said Molly. "And I mean in a hit-you-with-a-bolt-of-lightning-or-a-plague-of-boils kind of way, if you were dumb enough to press him. I just thought your family would know, if anyone would."

"Morgana La Fae is dead and gone," I said firmly. "And the whole world can feel a lot safer because of it."

"Very good," said Molly. "Now try saying that like you mean it."

I had to smile. "What's the matter? Are you thinking about stealing the medallion, but you're afraid the big, bad witch might come after you?"

"Yes!" said Molly. "Of course I'm worried! Any sane person would be!"

"Let us move on," I said. "Lots to see."

"But not Edmund," said Molly, glaring about her.

"I was sure he'd come here," I said. "Look around; he might have left a clue behind somewhere."

And besides, I need to prove to myself there's nothing here to worry about, I thought but didn't say. Though Molly had probably figured that out for herself. She stuck close to my side as we strolled down one aisle and up another, until finally I stopped before a heavy-bladed straight razor set out on a trestle table. The sign said SWEENEY TODD. I sneered at it.

"Sweeney was never more than a fictional character. Even more, now they've made a musical out of him. Yesterday's monster has become today's antihero."

"I liked the musical," said Molly.

"You would," I said. "This is almost certainly nothing more than an old Springheel Jack razor." And then I looked sharply at Molly. "Edmund had one in the Old Library. From his world, he said."

"Do you suppose he got it from his world's Museum?" said Molly. "And that's how he knows this place so well?"

"Could be."

I studied the straight razor. Another coincidence in a case that already had too many. Molly stirred impatiently.

"Do you want to take this razor for yourself, Eddie? So you can be on equal footing with Edmund?"

"No," I said. "I'll put my trust in my armour."

We moved on. Past glowing athames and rococo energy weapons, cursed musical boxes and seriously deranged alien bric-à-brac. Scrimshaw made from the bones of a sasquatch, and shell fragments from a phoenix egg. And something that flickered in and out of reality too quickly to be seen clearly. The sign just read TIME MACHINE. IN MOTION. Eventually Molly grabbed me by the arm again and pointed silently. Lying on its side on a trestle table, in the midst of a whole bunch of miscellaneous junk, was a statue of the goddess Kali. An exact duplicate of the one we'd seen in the Other Hall, except this was barely two feet tall. But it was quite definitely the same pose, the same face; every detail just as I remembered it. Though this time the base held no inscription, and there was no dried blood caked around the goddess's feet.

"Is that why Edmund came here?" Molly said quietly.

"As far as I can See, it's just a statue," I said.

"Then what's it doing here?"

"Far too many coincidences turning up in this case," I said almost angrily. "Some people say coincidences are the universe's way of trying to draw your attention to something that matters."

"This has gone beyond hinting," said Molly. "This is the universe shouting in our face and slapping us round the head. What do you think it means?"

"I don't know," I said. I looked around. "I've had my fill of this room. We'll give it a few more minutes, just so we can be sure we've done it justice, and then unless something turns up to prove Edmund was here, we'll try somewhere else."

"There's lots more rooms left to check," said Molly.

"I know," I said.

We moved on. Glancing at treasures from the Past and mysteries from the Future—because things are always falling through Timeslips and cluttering up the here and now. Things so old they were beyond any provenance, and items so advanced no one could figure out what they were. Most of them too powerful or too dangerous to be left out in the world for just anyone to stumble over.

"What if something gets dropped off here that is seriously, world-shatteringly dangerous?" said Molly, following my thoughts as always.

"There's a cellar deep beneath the Museum, in its own pocket dimension," I said. "The entrance is a strictly one-way affair; anything can get in, but nothing gets out."

Molly thought about it. "But what if someone decides one of these seriously dangerous items is needed after all?"

"That's when my family gets the call," I said. "And the Armourer gets to earn their pay."

"So, what would it take," said Molly, "to free Grendel Rex from his tomb? Hypothetically speaking?"

"Your guess is as good as mine," I said. "Technically speaking, he isn't really in his tomb. As in, not physically present. Otherwise it would be far too easy for some damned fool to just dig him up. The Unforgiven God is actually imprisoned in a separate pocket dimension. The tomb just holds the only access point."

"Tell me at least the chains are real," said Molly.

"Very real," I said. "Strong enough to bind and hold him till Judgement Day and beyond."

Molly glared round the Old Curiosities Room. "There's nothing here, Eddie. Are we going to have to search every room in the Museum?"

"I don't think so," I said. I leaned in close, quite casually, so I could murmur in her ear. "We're not alone. I keep catching glimpses of something moving out of the corner of my mind's eye. Good thing I kept the golden sunglasses on. Someone is hiding from us behind a glamour strong enough to fool anything except strange-matter armour. I think Edmund is right here in the room with us, keeping very quiet in the hope we'll just go away and leave him. So he can finish whatever it is he's doing."

Molly let her gaze drift casually back and forth. "Okay, that's sneaky."

"Do you have a spell to reveal hidden things?"

She scowled at me. "You know I do, but I don't know if I've got enough strength left to power it. Using it could wipe me out. If you're wrong . . ."

"I'm not wrong."

"I'd better find something in here to fire up my engines," Molly said grimly. "Because I really am running on fumes now."

She clenched her fists, scowling fiercely. And Edmund snapped into view, standing not twenty feet away, bent over a display case and fiddling with the lock. I called out his name and he looked round, startled. He straightened up sharply before striking a casual pose and nodding to me calmly.

"Eddie! How are you? Still dying?"

"Eddie," said Molly, "what's he messing with there?"

I didn't need to see the sign to recognise what was in the display case. Because all Drood field agents are required to study up on important things that have been stolen from the family.

"That is the Immaculate Key," I said. "Doesn't look like much, does it? Just an old-fashioned metal key. But that simple object is the Art of Unlocking—a concept cast in metal, a function given shape and form. A key to open any lock, spring any trap, break any binding."

"That's the Key?" said Molly. "I've been looking for that for years!"

"Concentrate, Molly. The Key is exactly what Edmund needs to free Grendel Rex from his tomb."

"What's it doing here?"

"A question my family will quite definitely be taking up with the Wulfshead Management," I said.

"It doesn't matter," said Molly, raising her voice as she glared at

Edmund. "The Key isn't a weapon, so that little shit is going down. Right now."

"How unkind," murmured Edmund. "Anyone would think you weren't glad to see me. But . . . Hello, I must be going."

He armoured up, smashed the display case with one golden hand, and snatched the Immaculate Key. All kinds of alarms started screaming hysterically, and a large, futuristic energy gun dropped down out of the ceiling. The long crystal barrel opened fire immediately with raging energy beams. I armoured up and moved quickly to put myself between the gun and Molly. The crackling energies hit me right on the chest and ricocheted away, smashing a dozen tables and setting fire to their contents. A second beam hit me on the shoulder, trying for Molly, and shot off down an empty aisle. The third beam hit Edmund squarely in the back as he ran down the aisle, hard enough to knock him off his feet and send him skidding along the floor. He was on his feet again in a moment, apparently unharmed. He thrust the Immaculate Key through the side of his armour and into a pocket beneath, and then looked quickly around for the door. Molly started to move out from behind me, and the energy gun in the ceiling swung round to target her.

"Shield yourself!" I said.

"I can't! I don't have enough magics left!"

"Then hide behind something solid! I can't protect you and go after Edmund!"

Molly ducked behind a tall standing cabinet containing a suit of medieval armour. Its burnished steel was covered in deeply engraved Enochian curses. Molly gestured at me angrily.

"Go get him, Eddie!"

The energy gun opened fire on the cabinet. Molly squatted down, and the cabinet soaked up the energy beam. The suit of armour convulsed, as though it had been shocked awake, and brandished its steel arms in protest. Steel fists smashed against the inside of the cabinet, but the glass held. I headed straight for Edmund, and he turned to face me.

We slammed together like two golden statues, trading blows strong enough to move mountains. We raged up and down the aisle, wrestling with each other, smashing priceless and irreplaceable items as we surged back and forth. I didn't feel the impact of his blows, and I didn't think he felt mine, but still we struck at each other with all the strength our armours could provide. The golden strange matter rang like bells as we landed blow after blow, but we couldn't hurt each other. We smashed our way through display cases and overturned standing cabinets full of treasures. Trestle tables collapsed, and the wonders of the world were trampled underfoot as we ploughed through everything that got in our way. Leaving a trail of wreckage and devastation because we couldn't see anything but each other.

The world can be a very fragile place, when Droods go to war.

Wild energies went streaking through the room as their receptacles were destroyed. Magics ran loose as their bindings were broken. Things came alive, or turned into other things, and ran madly up and down the aisles. I caught a glimpse of the medieval armour smashing its way out of the cabinet and then turning on Molly. Edmund took advantage of my momentary distraction to grab me with both hands, lift me off my feet, and throw me half-way down the room.

I hit hard, tucked, and rolled, and was back on my feet in a moment. Just in time to see Molly snatch up a pointing bone from a nearby table and stab it at the suit of armour. Its metal head blew right off, revealing the armour to be entirely uninhabited. Molly thrust the bone at it again, and the whole suit exploded, scattering twitching metal pieces the length of the aisle. The energy gun swung round to target her again, and she was forced to shelter behind the remains of the standing cabinet. Edmund was running for the door. I went after him.

Edmund barely made it half-way to the door before a stuffed werewolf leapt out of its shattered diorama and landed on his shoulders. The sheer weight of the thing spun Edmund around and threw him off balance. The werewolf clung on grimly, stuffing falling out of holes in its mangy hide as it cut viciously but uselessly at Edmund's golden armour with long, curved claws. Dust fell from its empty eyes like ancient tears. Edmund sank his golden fingers deep into the furry hide and tore the werewolf in half. Stuffing flew on the air, and the two parts fell some distance apart, to scrabble helplessly on the floor.

A shop-window dummy with a half-melted face and the uniform of a World War I soldier blocked my way and stabbed me in the gut with the bayonet on its rifle. The steel blade shattered against my armour, and I sent the dummy flying backwards with one sweep of my arm. I raced down the aisle after Edmund. He checked the distance to the door, saw he'd never make it in time, and turned to face me. And still the energy gun in the ceiling fired again and again, targeting first me and then Edmund, doing neither of us any damage but destroying everything around us with its ricochets.

Fires had broken out all over the Old Curiosities Room. Restraints were broken, and ancient locks blew apart. Things woke up, shook off their shackles, and went staggering down the aisles, driven on by long-unsatisfied needs and hungers. The energy gun stopped firing at me and Edmund and concentrated on blasting the exhibits, one after another. Because as far as the room's security systems were concerned, the exhibits were what mattered. They were the prisoners, and the gun was the guard. It was putting down a jail-break. I grinned at Edmund behind my featureless mask. My death's-head grin. Edmund was mine, and I was damned if I would let anything get between him and me.

And that was when a pair of inhumanly strong arms closed around me from behind and held me close, while a soft, malignant voice murmured in my ear.

"Oh, Eddie, my joy, my love . . . You've come back to me. I always knew you would."

I froze. My heart missed a beat. I knew that voice. It was the voice of the Dead Drood, the mummified creature my family had given over into the Museum's keeping all those years ago. Because it insisted on living long after it should have admitted it was dead. The exhibit that tried to make me its own the last time I was here.

"Eddie. Darling. You've come home."

I looked down at the bandage-wrapped arms encircling me. And decided I didn't have time for this. I broke their hold with a surge from my golden arms, spun round, and hit the thing in the head with a spiked golden fist. The sheer strength of the blow smashed in one side of its bandaged face and almost ripped the mummy's head off its shoulders. It staggered backwards, crying out with angry thwarted feelings. I didn't know how it had put itself back together again after everything I did to it last time, but back then I'd only had Heart armour. The mummy cocked its ruined head to one side and extended its bandaged arms appealingly.

"Don't fight me, Eddie. You know we belong together. Just give in, be mine, and we can live forever . . ."

"I didn't believe you then," I said steadily, "and I don't believe you now. You're not alive. Just an unquiet spirit possessing a body held together by bandages. A Drood who didn't have the guts to lie down and get it over with. I'm nothing like you."

"But I can make you like me, darling."

"I'd rather die," I said.

"We always hurt the ones we love," said the Dead Drood.

I surged forward, caught the mummy by surprise, picked it up, and threw it at the ceiling-mounted energy gun with all my strength. It smashed into the gun with such force the whole thing exploded, blowing the mummy apart. Burning pieces rained down all over the room.

And I wondered how I'd ever let such a stupid thing get to me.

I turned back to see Edmund advance on Molly as she snatched things up from the tables and threw them at him. Some exploded, some tried to cling on to him, and some surrounded him with monstrous energies, but none of them could get past his armour. Finally Molly reached behind her and produced the Hand of Glory made from the severed hand of an angel. Bright blue flames shot up from its fingertips, and just like that Edmund slammed to a halt, held motionless by the Hand's power. For a moment I thought the fight was over, and then Edmund broke the Hand's influence with one sweep of his arm. The blue flames puffed out, and the Hand was just a hand. Edmund surged forward impossibly quickly, grabbed Molly by the throat with one golden hand, and lifted her off her feet. And then he turned his featureless face mask to look at me.

"That's close enough, Eddie! Keep your distance, or I'll kill her! Let me go, and you can have her back."

I stopped where I was. I had no choice. Edmund looked at the door, saw it was still too far away, shrugged, and reached through his armoured side with his free hand. He brought out the Merlin Glass and shook it out to door size. It stood on the air beside him and opened to show a familiar scene. The cold open steppes of Siberia.

"I didn't want to have to use the Glass," said Edmund. "Punching through the Museum's protections will take up energies I might need later. But you always have to make things difficult for me, don't you, Eddie? Why couldn't you just die like you were supposed to? Ah well. Destiny calls. And you know what? I think I'll kill Molly, anyway, just for laughs."

His hand clamped down on her throat. A horrid choking sound burst from her mouth. She grabbed desperately at his golden wrist with both her hands but couldn't break his grip. Her feet kicked helplessly, far above the floor. Edmund laughed, and Molly disappeared from his hand. She reappeared immediately, only a few feet away, because that was as far as the last of her magic could carry her. She sprawled on the floor, gasping desperately for breath, and Edmund went after her. But I was already running straight at him. I threw the object I'd picked up along the way, and Edmund looked up just in time to see the statue of Kali coming. He cried out in shock and horror and raised an arm to defend himself, and the statue shattered harmlessly against his armour. But by then I'd reached Molly and put myself between her and Edmund.

He turned away and jumped through the Merlin Glass, and it slammed shut after him. A moment later they were both gone, and with them the Immaculate Key.

I armoured down and helped Molly to her feet. A lot of the room was on fire, and an awful lot of awful things were running around loose, but I didn't care. Molly leaned on me for a moment, getting her breath back, and then pushed me away angrily.

"I am nobody's hostage!"

"When were you going to tell me you'd stolen the Hand of Glory?" I said.

She pouted. "A girl's entitled to a souvenir. I had this feeling it might come in handy."

"I'd already picked you up a little something," I said. "I should have given it to you right away, and then we might have avoided all this."

I handed her the Manx Medallion, and she looked at it wonderingly.

"When did you . . . How . . . ?"

"It's all yours," I said. "A repository of stored magics, packed full of supernatural vitamins. Just what you need to recharge your batteries."

She closed her hand around the wooden amulet, and immediately violent energies sprang up around her, crackling fiercely on the air. They sank down into her, and Molly put back her head and laughed raucously as power surged through her. I could feel its presence in the room, beating on the air like the wings of a giant bird. Molly put the cord around her neck and let the amulet dangle between her breasts.

"Now, that's more like it! I feel like myself again." She stopped and looked at me. "All this power, and I still can't do the only thing that matters to me. I can save myself, but I can't save you. I'm so sorry, Eddie."

"You can help me stop Edmund from raising the Unforgiven God with the Immaculate Key," I said.

"Siberia's a big place," said Molly.

"But I know something about Grendel Rex's tomb that Edmund doesn't," I said. "Which means we can get there first. Are you game, Molly? One last throw of the dice, with everything to play for?"

"My kind of game," said Molly. And then she scowled. "It would have to be Siberia, wouldn't it? Like Scotland wasn't cold enough."

CHAPTER SEVEN

The God in the Cellar

didn't bother putting out any of the fires in the Old Curiosities
Room, or cleaning up any of the mess we'd made. The room could
do that for itself. Molly and I went sprinting back through the Museum, ignoring alarms shrieking on all sides like outraged aunts.
Doors to other rooms slammed shut and locked themselves as we
passed, and a few slammed shut in our faces to bar our way. I armoured up just long enough to smash right through them. I really
wasn't in the mood to be messed with. The doors soon realised I wasn't
going to be stopped, or they recognised my Drood armour, because
they started opening on their own to hurry me and Molly on our way.
Presumably on the grounds I'd do less damage to the Museum that
way. The front door took its own time opening, making a point for
pride's sake, and then realised I wasn't slowing down and threw itself
wide open at the last moment. Which was, after all, as it should be.
Doors should know their place.

The second we were outside, the front door slammed shut behind
us with almost spiteful force. I didn't look back; I was too busy staring
at the dragon, already settled comfortably on the flag-stones and waiting for us. He smiled smugly, which, given the sheer number of teeth

involved, was something to see, while two thin plumes of smoke rose steadily from his nostrils.

"I hadn't even called you yet!" I said.

"But you were going to," said the dragon. "I knew you were going to need me before you did. It's a dragon thing."

"Do you know where we need to go?" said Molly. "Or do we have to draw you a map, with longitude and latitude and pointy arrows and things?"

"It's all aboard for Siberia!" said the dragon. His toothy grin widened just a little at the look on our faces. "You have already mentioned the tomb of the Unforgiven God, buried under the Siberian steppes. And since you emerged from the Museum not carrying Edmund's severed head by its hair, I am forced to the conclusion that he got away from you. Again. And that he is currently on his way to Siberia, courtesy of the Merlin Glass. I do pay attention when people talk, you know. It's a skill you pick up when you spend centuries as a severed head under a burial mound. So, we should hurry if we want to get to the tomb before Edmund."

I gave him my best hard stare. "No one likes a smart-arse dragon."

"I'm sorry," the dragon said humbly.

"No you're not," said Molly.

"Of course I'm not," said the dragon. "I was being diplomatic."

"Why does a thirty-foot-long dragon feel the need to be diplomatic?" I said.

"Because you're never too big for good manners," said the dragon. "Where exactly in Siberia would you like me to take you? Only it is rather large, you know."

"I said that!" said Molly.

"I know," said the dragon. "I heard you."

"It doesn't matter," I said. "Edmund hasn't got a hope in hell of beating us to Grendel Rex's tomb."

"Oh, come on!" said Molly. "The dragon may be fast, but the Merlin Glass is instantaneous! Grendel Rex could already be loose!"

"Trust me," I said. "If he was out, we'd know. The whole world would be shaking in its shoes and crying for its mother. No, Grendel Rex is secure enough, for the time being at least."

"I know that self-satisfied look," Molly said to the dragon. "It means he knows something we don't know, and is about to be unbearably smug about it."

"More importantly," I said, "I know something Edmund doesn't know. Siberia may be a bit on the large side, but we only need to visit one very small part of it. And not the part Edmund thinks."

"But he's got the book!" said Molly. "The official history, with all the details!"

I had to grin. "The official history of Grendel Rex, his rise and his fall, does indeed contain the exact coordinates for his tomb. But not the correct ones. Drood policy, just in case some well-meaning fool decided to try to bring Grendel Rex back for their own reasons. The correct coordinates are only ever known to the Matriarch and the Sarjeant-at-Arms. And Maggie gave me the correct location just before I left, given that this is a special-needs situation."

Molly clapped her hands together delightedly. "So, Edmund's gone to the wrong place!"

"He can't even see the right location from where he is," I said. "We will get there first, and then . . ."

"And then?" said Molly. "And then what? Come on, Eddie—that is really not a good place to pause. What are we going to do when we get there?"

"I think . . . I'm going to have to try talking to Gerard Drood again," I said slowly. "I was the first member of the family to speak kindly to him in centuries. Hopefully, that will still mean something. Maybe I can convince Gerard not to trust Edmund, on the grounds that he isn't really one of us."

"That's it?" said Molly. "That's your great plan? Being the voice of reason? You really think the Unforgiven God is going to go along with that?"

"The odds would seem to be against it," I admitted. "If you have a better idea, I am more than ready to listen."

I looked at her hopefully, but Molly just scowled and shook her head. "My plans usually involve subterfuge, sneakiness, and extreme violence, and I don't see any of them working here. Okay. The tomb is just the access point to the pocket dimension that makes up Grendel Rex's real prison. So couldn't we just destroy the tomb, make it impossible for him to come back? Blow it up or something?"

"I could always dig down to the tomb and breathe flames on it," said the dragon. "My breath could set an igloo on fire."

"Nice thought," I said. "But the tomb was designed to be unbreakable. To keep everyone else in the world out, as well as him in. You could set off a nuke right on top of the tomb and not even scratch it."

"Really?" said Molly. "Has anyone ever tried?"

"Not as far as I know," I said. "I'm sure I would have heard. But I have seen the specifications for the tomb. Supposedly, the sun could go nova and incinerate the earth and the tomb would still survive, floating alone in space."

"If it's that tough, what's the problem?" said the dragon.

"Edmund has the Immaculate Key," I said.

"Ah," said the dragon. "Then Edmund doesn't need to break into the tomb, because the Key can unlock it."

"Right," I said.

"How did he get the Key?" said the dragon.

"Don't ask," I said.

Molly glanced back at the Museum. "We should go back in and look for a Weapons Room."

"We don't have the time," I said.

"You said Edmund isn't anywhere near the tomb!" said Molly. "So what's the hurry?"

"You don't understand," I said. "I mean, I don't have the time. I'm pretty much covered in armour now, under my clothes. I'm so tired, so worn-down, the armour is all that's keeping me going."

Molly looked at me, and I could see she wanted to say so many things . . . But we both knew emotions would only get in the way of what we had to do. So she just nodded briefly, being strong for both of us. When she did speak she made sure her voice was perfectly calm and steady.

"Why haven't you put on your full armour?"

"Because once I'm forced to do that, I might never find the strength to take it off again," I said. "I want to see the world with my own eyes for as long as I can. Feel its breath on my face and the sun on my skin."

"Are you up for this, Eddie?" Molly said bluntly. "Because we're only going to get one chance to stop Edmund."

"There's enough left of me to do what needs doing, to get the job done," I said. "My mind is still clear, my will is still strong, and my armour can carry me the rest of the way. But afterwards . . . Get me home, Molly. Promise you'll take me back to Drood Hall, so my ashes can be scattered across the grounds. So I can rest close to my family. I never used to think that mattered to me, but, somewhat to my surprise, I find it does."

"Of course I promise," said Molly. "We all want to go home, in the end."

We hugged each other, holding on tightly. Both of us silent, so we wouldn't say anything to upset each other, eyes squeezed shut to hold back tears. Neither of us wanted to let go, for fear this would be the last time we'd get to hold each other, but in the end I did. Because it was kinder for me to do it. Molly quickly stepped away from me, and then hugged herself tightly, as though to keep herself from falling apart. I knew the feeling. I turned to the dragon.

"The Matriarch put the exact coordinates for the tomb in my head. Can you read them?"

"Not without help," said the dragon. "Human minds are such small places to get into. I don't want to push too hard in case I break something. I have to be invited in."

I armoured up my right hand and placed it on the dragon's wide brow.

I was standing in a prehistoric landscape. Huge volcanoes spouted fire, blasting dark, tarry lava and great clouds of drifting ashes across a crimson sky, under a white-hot sun. The land below me was one massive jungle, with trees and ferns as big as skyscrapers. The vegetation was a blaze of bright and vivid colours, ripe and pulsing with life. Huge creatures crashed back and forth between the massive trees, killing and eating and mating, shaking the jungle with the passion of their raised voices.

I was high up on a mountainside, under a towering wall of jagged grey stone, in front of a great, dark cave. The dragon emerged from the cave like a newborn from its egg to stand beside me. There shouldn't have been room for both of us on such a narrow ledge, but somehow we managed. I went back to looking out over the jungle. The air was hot and humid, heavy with rich and exhilarating scents.

"Is this where you come from?" I said.

"This is the world I was born into," said the dragon. "I'm a lot older than people realise."

"You're older than Humanity, aren't you?"

"I was young when the world was young," said the dragon. "Leave it at that."

I felt very small in this world where everything else was so big. Life here had been written on the grand scale and was overpowering in its sheer vitality.

"How can you stand to live in our world?" I said. "Having known this?"

"Well, for a start, you get a much better level of conversation," said the dragon. "And civilisation does have its comforts."

"But we're so . . . insignificant, compared to all this!"

"But you shine so brightly," said the dragon. "That is the glory of the short-lived. Life means so much more to you because you only have it for such a brief time. You'd be amazed how much of immortality consists of boredom and memories."

"Why have you stayed on for so long? When all the world you know is gone?"

"Humanity fascinates me."

"Because we make such easy prey?"

"Because you make such worthy adversaries," said the dragon. "And, sometimes, friends."

I looked at the dragon, and a great wave of affection swept through me, warm and non-judgemental. Just having him with me made me feel safe, like a small child sitting on Santa's lap. If Santa Claus was real. The dragon picked up that thought and laughed quietly.

"What makes you think he isn't? It's a much larger hidden world than you humans realise."

I stared out over the violent, primeval world below us. "Are you all that's left of this?"

"Sometimes I think one thing," said the dragon, "and sometimes I think another. We need to hurry this up, Eddie. You're dying."

"I know," I said.

"No," said the dragon. "I mean, right now. I can see into you so clearly, now we're linked. Edmund's poison has almost completed its work, despite everything your torc has done to hold it back. Your body is shutting down."

I felt like I'd been punched in the stomach. It took my breath away to hear my death announced so calmly and implacably. I took a deep breath, just to reassure myself I still could.

"You're sure?" I said.

"I can see death moving through you," said the dragon.

I nodded stiffly. "Then let's do what we have to, while we still can."

"Of course," said the dragon. "Siberia awaits. And if the Unforgiven God gives you a hard time, Eddie, I will show him why dragons are so much more to be feared than little self-made gods."

"Thank you," I said.

"You're welcome," said the dragon. "Now will you please give me the damn coordinates so we can get this show on the road? Remember: It's opening night, and you're going out there a Drood, but you've got to come back a star!"

I shook my head. "Old movies on afternoon television have a lot to answer for."

I concentrated on the exact coordinates for the tomb.

And just like that, I was back in the world I knew. I patted the dragon in thanks on his bony forehead, and armoured down my hand. Molly looked at me suspiciously. She could tell she'd missed out on something.

"Well? What was it like?"

"An education," I said solemnly.

"It's not fair!" said Molly. "Why don't I ever get to mind-meld with a dragon? I'm sure I'd make a much better subject. I've read all of Anne McCaffrey's books!"

"Perhaps later," the dragon said kindly. "Now, all aboard the Siberian Express! No stop-offs, no in-flight movie, and I don't want to hear any complaints about missing baggage."

I climbed up onto the dragon's back. It took me longer than the last time, because my coordination wasn't what it was, even with my armour to support me. I dug my feet in hard, clamping my hands onto the emerald-scaled hide. The dragon didn't react. Molly didn't say anything to hurry me, so I knew she'd noticed too. She waited until I'd settled myself in place on the dragon's spine and then climbed quickly up to sit behind me. She put her arms round my waist, almost possessively, as though defying the world to take me from her. She started to say something, and then stopped and looked back at the Museum.

"Eddie, did you think to lock the front door?"

"No need," I said. "The lock will have reset itself and disappeared again by now. The Museum looks after itself."

"What about all the exhibits we ever so slightly trashed, destroyed, or let loose?"

I shrugged. "Plenty more where they came from."

"Are we finished with the light conversation?" said the dragon. "I'd really like to get started while the world is still as it should be."

"Siberia," Molly said disgustedly. "Places that cold should be illegal."

"Ultima Thule was worse," I said.

Molly shuddered. "Don't remind me."

"Can we go?" the dragon said loudly.

"Go! Go!" I said. "Atomic batteries to power, turbines to speed, and don't spare the horses!"

"Up, up, and away!" said the dragon.

He launched himself into the air, shooting up into the lead-grey sky so rapidly it was all I could do to stay in place on his back. The ground plummeted away, and for a moment I thought I'd left my stomach behind as well. I gritted my teeth and closed my eyes, and when I felt steady enough to open them again we were back in the freezing cold of the upper atmosphere. And I was shuddering so violently, Molly had to tighten her hold about me. I felt the cold more now, despite my extra armour and the dragon's protections. As though my body was anticipating the cold of the grave. Molly pressed herself against my back, trying to share the warmth of her body with me. I patted her hands fondly but didn't say anything. Because I didn't trust my voice.

The Rainbow slammed down ahead of us, filling the sky with co-lours so rich and deep I felt like I'd never really seen them before. The vivid hues and shades crashed down in a never-ending thunder, a pri-mal sound that I heard with my heart and my soul as much as my ears. It wasn't just a rainbow. It was something ancient and archetypal, like the dragon. He flew straight into the Rainbow and the colours leapt forward to fill my eyes and my head. When I could see and think again, we were over Siberia.

We flew through a deep blue sky, soaring over desolate steppes far be-low. Nothing but snow and ice for mile upon endless mile. No trees, no vegetation, not a living thing anywhere. My family once considered this to be the end of the earth, and looking at it now I felt moved to agree. Molly made low sounds of distress behind me as the bitter cold sank in, and I made some sort of noise in spite of myself. The dragon snorted loudly, and smoke shot briefly out of his nostrils.

"Wimps. According to my internal calendar—and, yes, I do have one; all dragons do—this is spring. Which means the weather is merely . . . bracing."

He was trying to lighten the mood in his own way, and I appreci-ated the effort, but it didn't make me feel any warmer. My hands were shaking, the cold burned my lungs with every breath I took, and my teeth were chattering so hard I couldn't speak. I had no choice. I had to armour up completely. I subvocalised the activating Words, with a sense that this might be the last time I'd ever use them, and the golden strange matter leapt out and closed over me in a moment, insulating me from the cold and sealing me off from the world. But I didn't feel as strong and fast and sure as I was used to feeling in my full armour. Perhaps because it was still using some of its strength to fight the poi-son, or perhaps . . . I was just so far gone now, there was a limit to what even the armour could do for me.

Molly swore harshly and protected herself from the cold with a shimmering force shield. I couldn't feel it through my armour, but the dragon giggled unexpectedly.

"Tickles," he explained.

"Oh hush up, you big baby," said Molly.

I had a vague feeling you shouldn't talk to a dragon like that, but couldn't quite put it into words. I leaned out a little to get a better look at the wide-open steppes below. Sunlight gleamed brightly back from the featureless snow, like a great ocean frozen in place. A thought occurred to me: *This is what the end of the world will look like. When the sun is dying and heat is just a memory.*

"What are you looking for?" said Molly. "There's nothing here! Not a tree or a shrub or a wandering shaman . . . Not even a yeti. Do they have yetis here? It doesn't matter, because there isn't anything here for as far as I can See, and I can See pretty damned far! Oh, dear God it's cold . . ."

"Look on the bright side," I said. "At least there aren't any Siberian Death Wurms around here. You do remember them from our last visit to this region?"

"You had to remind me, didn't you?" Molly said grimly. "After I'd gone to so much trouble to wipe them from my memory. And stop changing the subject! What are you looking for, Eddie? Eddie . . . Eddie Drood! Don't you ignore me, or I will push you off the dragon's back and the two of us will make bets as to how high you'll bounce when you finally hit the ground!"

The dragon laughed softly. "You know, she probably would."

"I know," I said. "Molly, when I was here before, certain things happened. Which I don't feel like discussing. But I was expecting there to be signs, things left behind. And there aren't."

"This is to do with what happened at the abandoned Science City, isn't it?" said Molly.

"Yes," I said.

"Were things really that bad?"

"Yes."

"Then don't think about it," Molly said firmly. "Concentrate on the matter at hand. Honestly, Eddie, you come with more psychic trauma and emotional baggage than anyone I've ever met. And I've lived in the Nightside! Dragon, are we anywhere near Grendel Rex's tomb yet?"

"We're right above it," he said. "Though I'm not Seeing anything . . ."

"You wouldn't," I said. "Take us down."

The dragon pulled in his wings and dropped vertically, the ground rushing up to meet us. At the very last moment he snapped his wings out and we came to an abrupt halt, before settling onto the snow-covered ground as gently as a falling leaf. The dragon tucked his wings neatly into place, and looked thoughtfully about him.

"I suppose it has a certain scenic quality," he said. "But it's a bit basic, isn't it? If this place were any emptier, it wouldn't even be a place. Hmmm . . . you're right, Eddie: There is something here. I can't see it, but I can feel it. Something deep down, in the cellar of the world."

I got down from the dragon. It took me such a long time, because I was so tired and my grip was so weak, that Molly had to come down and help me. It was a sign of how weak I was that I let her—and a sign of how worried she was that she didn't say anything. We stood together eventually, the man in the golden armour and the witch in her shimmering force shield. There was no sign of Edmund anywhere, and I felt a small lift in my heart. He shouldn't have been here; in fact, there was no way he could have got here before us, but he'd beaten me so many times, I was glad to seize even this small advantage.

I reached out to the Matriarch through my torc to let the family know where we were and what the situation was . . . and found I couldn't. My voice just fell away into a great silence. I turned to Molly.

"I can't reach my family. Something is blocking me."

"Grendel Rex?" said Molly. "Or maybe something to do with the tomb?"

"I don't know," I said. "We're in unknown territory here."

Molly placed the fingertips of her left hand on the torc at my throat and concentrated. Trying to boost my signal with her magics. But after a moment she shook her head and took her hand away.

"We're cut off, Eddie. Something here doesn't want us talking to anyone."

"I think it's time for me to take to the sky again," said the dragon. "Fly around, get a feel for the territory, be your eye in the sky."

"Are you by any chance just a bit concerned about what might happen if a living god like Grendel Rex were to get out?" said Molly.

"I don't believe in gods," said the dragon. "And I should know; I've eaten a few."

He leapt up into the sky, and in a matter of moments he was just a speck in the distance. Molly looked around slowly and carefully, and then moved in close so she could murmur in my ear.

"Is there any chance Edmund could have found his way here and is hiding behind a glamour again?"

"You're just full of worrying ideas, aren't you? I can't See him, and I'm assuming you can't, but feel free to check things out."

Molly unleashed the same Reveal spell she'd used in the Museum. The air heaved and shimmered, and there was a sense of something brittle cracking and falling apart. Weird local phenomena manifested suddenly all around Grendel Rex's resting place. The sky became heavily overcast, crackling with wild aurora borealis. The ground stirred uneasily under our feet, as though something unimaginably huge had just turned over in its sleep. And the snow was suddenly a deep crimson, forming a great circle almost half a mile wide. The world's biggest bloodstain, and we were standing right in the middle of it.

"Tell me that's not really blood," said Molly.

"That's not really blood," I said. "Just a psychic imprint. A stain stamped on the world by what my family did here. Or possibly from Grendel Rex, dreaming about his many victims."

"Does that mean he's feeling guilty?" said Molly.

"More likely he's enjoying old times."

Molly glowered about her. "I've heard of X marks the spot, but this . . ."

"Wait a minute," I said. "There's something else. Look."

I pointed straight ahead, quietly pleased my golden hand didn't shake at all. Molly nodded slowly as she saw it too. A disturbance in the air, like a crack in reality or a channel etched into Space itself. It stabbed down out of the sky, right into the centre of the blood circle.

"What is that?" said Molly.

"A psychic scar," I said. "Carved into the atmosphere of the place. Showing Grendel Rex's fall."

"How far did he fall?" said Molly, looking up into the disturbed sky.

"All the way," I said. "Though of course he didn't fall; he was pushed. And then my family pushed him outside the world, imprisoning him in a place no one else could reach. So he could be forgotten by the world forever. Not because we were afraid of Gerard Drood, but because we were ashamed of him."

"And this is who you plan to sweet-talk?" said Molly.

"I'm rather going off that idea, to be honest," I said. "Still haven't come up with a better one, though."

I looked around me, taking my time. So did Molly. The empty steppes stared back at us, the Drood in his armour and the witch surrounded by her magics.

"I'm picking up on something," I said finally. "A feeling . . . that we're not supposed to be here. That nothing is supposed to be here. A really powerful aversion field, presumably put in place long ago to dissuade anyone from coming here. They wouldn't even know why; they'd just feel it in their gut. People, beasts, birds . . . not even wanting to look in this direction, for fear of what they might see."

"Why isn't it affecting us?" said Molly.

"Because you're the wild witch of the woods, and I'm a Drood. We're used to feeling unwanted and not giving a damn."

But the skin on my back was crawling under my armour, right between my shoulder blades. Standing in the middle of the world's biggest bloodstain felt very much like standing on a target.

"At least this time we quite definitely got here first," I said, trying for a light touch.

"I just had a thought," said Molly. "And not a pleasant one. What if Edmund doesn't find his way here? I mean, how can we ambush him if he doesn't turn up?"

"He'll be here," I said. "When we set loose all the local phenomena, we might as well have lit a beacon. Psychics all around the world will be shaking their heads and complaining about the noise. Edmund will See it, and the Merlin Glass will bring him straight here."

"And then we kill him," said Molly.

"That's the plan," I said.

I didn't mean to be short with her. I'd killed a great many people who needed killing in my time as a field agent. I really thought I'd killed enough; I didn't want to kill any more. But after everything I'd been put through, I didn't much care if I went to meet my maker with more blood on my hands, as long as I took Edmund down first. Not just for what he'd done to me, but for what he'd done to so many others.

Molly kicked moodily at the crimson snow. "What did happen here, exactly? What did your family do to Grendel Rex?"

"I don't know," I said. "There were no details in the official history. I always wondered if there was another, more complete version, but the Librarian said not."

"Who wrote the history?" said Molly

"Not surprisingly, no one felt like putting their name to it," I said.

"Why did you read the book in the first place, Eddie?"

"Because I always want to know things I'm not supposed to. And, besides, I was running the family at the time. It seemed something I should know."

"But you didn't know the proper coordinates for the tomb," said Molly. "The Matriarch had to tell you."

"It was a tricky situation," I said. "My grandmother, the old Matriarch, was still alive then. And I wasn't really talking to the old Sarjeant-at-Arms. I'm sure we would have gotten round to it if I'd stayed on as head."

"They didn't trust you!" said Molly. "That is so typical of the Droods."

"Trust is a hard thing to come by in my family," I said. "We all have so many secrets. I think my ancestors may have found it necessary to do things here that they were ashamed of afterwards."

"That would take some doing for Droods," said Molly.

"Yes," I said. "It would."

"Is it possible," Molly said carefully, "that your family might have allied themselves with certain . . . Powers, to get the job done? Someone or something they would normally have enough sense not to go anywhere near? I mean, after seeing Heaven and Hell's Droods, I have to wonder if there's anything your family would draw the line at."

I thought about that for a while before finally shaking my head. "I don't think so. This was a family affair. We wouldn't have wanted anyone else to know. That's why we went to such pains to clean up afterwards, and remove all mention of Grendel Rex from the history books. We couldn't afford for anyone to know just how close one Drood came to destroying all of Humanity. They'd never have trusted us again."

"They don't trust you now!" said Molly.

"All right," I said. "They would have trusted us even less. Whatever my family did here was justified, Molly. Grendel Rex really would have broken all Humanity to his will. In the end there would have been just him, living in billions of bodies at once. Thinking his thoughts, speaking with his voice, carrying out his wishes. He would have been . . . everyone."

"What did he plan to do then?" said Molly. "I mean, what was he going to do with all those bodies?"

"I'm not convinced he'd thought that far ahead," I said. "I can't help feeling it would have been a very lonely existence, with no one left to talk to but himself. But maybe that's what he wanted. To be left alone, with no one to tell him what to do. And that's what happened to him, anyway, locked up in his tomb, alone in the dark. Forever."

"He probably only did it to impress some girl," Molly said wisely. "You'd be surprised how often that turns out to be at the bottom of things."

"No," I said. Smiling, behind my mask. "I wouldn't be surprised at all."

"All right," Molly said briskly. "We're here. What are we going to do? I thought we'd have to fight Edmund to keep him from opening the tomb. Hot armour-on-armour action, and general destruction on a grand scale. But despite your psychic beacon, he still hasn't turned up yet."

"We need to do something to make it impossible for Edmund to release Gerard Drood from his tomb," I said.

"Okay," said Molly. "Such as?"

"I have a plan," I said. "Though you're probably not going to like it."

"Probably?"

"Almost certainly."

She smiled grimly. "There hasn't been much about today I have liked. Go on, hit me with it."

"I've gone back to thinking I need to talk to Gerard."

"Eddie! I thought we agreed that is a really bad idea!"

"You're right. It is. Unfortunately, I haven't been able to come up with anything else that might work. Edmund has the Immaculate Key, the one thing that could quite definitely open the tomb and release Gerard from his chains."

"Your family should have destroyed the Key long ago," said Molly. "Just to make sure that couldn't happen."

I shrugged. "You know my family. Never throw out anything you might need someday."

"And how many times has that come back to bite them on the arse?"

"Moving on . . . ," I said. "Edmund must believe he has something that will control Grendel Rex after the Key has released him. Something strong enough to protect him from the living god's power. Our only hope is to make it impossible for Edmund to get to Grendel Rex. And that means . . . talking to Gerard."

"You're really comfortable calling him Gerard?"

"That's his name," I said. "We need to remind him what it was like to be human, and part of a family. He must miss that, after so long on his own."

"Eddie, if he wasn't crazy before, the odds are centuries of being buried alive will have finished the job."

"I'm hoping it's the other way round," I said. "That all this time alone worked as shock treatment. Showing him the error of his ways."

"You always were a hopeless optimist. You're really planning to appeal to his better nature?"

"I'm going to appeal to his humanity," I said. "On the grounds that being a living god didn't work out too well for him."

"But what can you offer him in return for his cooperation?" said Molly. "A chance for early parole? A few millennia off for good behaviour?"

"I can offer him company," I said. "Someone to talk to. Look at the dragon. Baron Frankenstein beheaded the dragon to stop him destroying towns and killing people. Lots of people. But years of contemplation under a burial mound, and all the Droods who've been talking to him clearly made a difference. I'm hoping the same process will have the same effect on Gerard."

"You and your damned strays," said Molly.

"I need to persuade Gerard to stay where he is! To remain in his tomb, no matter what Edmund does or what he offers him. Such behaviour, a clear sign of sanity and repentance, would go a really long way to arguing for his release. He could come home again."

"That doesn't strike me as very likely, Eddie."

"I know! It's a long shot! But it seems to me that we did get on the last time we spoke."

"I'm still having trouble following what happened then," said Molly. "How were you able to awaken him from his long sleep in the first place?"

"I don't believe I did," I said. "I just reached out for help, and he answered. As though he'd been waiting. I'm increasingly convinced that reaching out to him was never my idea. I think he was already awake and influencing me."

"Okay, you are seriously creeping me out now," said Molly. "Could he still be influencing you? Is being here right now your idea or his?"

"Let's not panic ourselves," I said. "The very fact we're able to ask the question is a good sign. It could be that he just detected a Drood's presence, and wanted someone to talk to."

Molly didn't look at all convinced. "What did he say to you?"

I thought back, and Gerard's words sounded in my head as though I'd only just heard them.

"We can all be gods, or devils. We can shine like stars. We were never meant to stay human. We are just the chrysalis, from which something greater will emerge."

When I'd finished speaking, Molly and I looked at each other for a long moment.

"Yes, well," said Molly, "he doesn't sound at all crazy, does he?"

"Maybe he wants us all to be living gods, just like him," I said. "So he won't be lonely."

"Is there anything in what he did that makes him seem like the kind of living god who'd want to share his power?" said Molly.

"Good point," I said. "The last thing he said to me was: *Tell the family I'll be seeing them.*"

"Which doesn't sound at all ominous, threatening, or pants-wettingly scary," said Molly. "Come on, give it to me straight, Eddie. Just how bad would it be if Grendel Rex did break free from his tomb and he's just as crazy as he ever was?"

"The whole world, and everything in it, would be in danger," I said steadily. "He came really close to succeeding last time. Even carved his face into the surface of the Moon so he could look down on us in triumph forever. Of course, he would face a lot more opposition these days. From all kinds of subterranean groups and organisations, and individuals of mass destruction. Like you. But, then, there are some Powers and Dominations who might work with him, against Humanity."

"So at best we're hoping all these organisations and Powers would just cancel each other out?" said Molly.

"Pretty much," I said.

"The more you think things through, the more disturbed I feel," said Molly. "Try this one on for size: Is Grendel Rex likely to be more or less powerful, after centuries of being buried alive?"

"Nobody knows," I said. "Not least because we've never been able to figure out exactly what it was he did to make himself so powerful. He only had Heart armour back then. He shouldn't have been able to do any of the things he did."

"Why didn't the Heart do something to stop him?"

"Good question," I said. "The only answer that makes any sense is that Grendel Rex made himself more powerful than the Heart. Is there anything scarier than a self-made god who's pulled himself up by his own spiritual boot-straps?"

Molly turned away from me. I didn't need to see her face to know how upset she was. With anyone else I would have said *scared*, but Molly didn't do scared. She went straight to angry. She looked out over the vast open spaces of the Siberian tundra, and her hands closed into fists at her sides. She wanted someone to hit. She always felt better when a problem presented her with someone she could hit. She turned back to look at me, and her face was set in harsh, dangerous lines.

"What was the Immaculate Key doing in the Museum? Something as powerful as that?"

"My family put it there," I said. "Working on the *Hide in plain sight* principle. Just another old key, surrounded by junk; it should have been safe enough. Either Edmund knew about the Key from his world's Museum, or . . ."

"Or?"

"Or someone in my family told him it was there," I said slowly. "Someone who's been working with Edmund all along."

"You really think that's possible?" said Molly.

"With my family that's always possible. Damn. I really didn't need something else to worry about."

"Then don't," said Molly. "Stick with what matters. Go on, Eddie. Talk to your old family god or devil. See what he has to say for himself."

I stamped hard on the ground, by way of knocking. My golden foot sank deep into the crimson snow, muffling the sound, but it was the gesture that mattered.

"Gerard Drood!" I said loudly. "Old ancestor. This is Eddie Drood. You remember me. We need to talk."

And immediately I was answered. By a calm, assured voice that felt like it came from down below, from the deepest part of the frozen Earth . . . and yet it sounded like Gerard was standing right in front of me. Molly almost jumped out of her skin. She hadn't expected to be able to hear him too.

"Hello, Eddie," said Gerard Drood. "Welcome back. I've been expecting you."

Molly looked at me. "Only three sentences and already he's freaking me out. How could he be expecting us?"

"Because I arranged all of this," said Gerard. "Hello, Molly Metcalf. You are welcome here too. Try not to get in the way."

Molly glared at me. "He knows who I am. How does he know who I am?" She raised her voice. "How do you know who I am?"

"I foresaw all of this long ago, before the family imprisoned me," said Gerard. His voice was calm and even and very patient. "It's why I allowed them to put me away."

"Who?" I said. "Who put you away, exactly?"

"They called themselves the very-secret agents," said Gerard. "So secret I never even knew they existed. They watched and waited, until I weakened myself in a moment of sentiment, transforming the surface of the Moon. And then they struck. Using weapons and powers I had no idea existed, because the family never knew they existed. Sneaky, underhanded sons of bitches . . . Typical Drood agents, really. Do they still exist, these very-secret agents?"

"Not any more," I said.

"Good. I knew I couldn't beat them, not then, so I didn't even try to fight. I let them put me in the earth, so I could rest and gather my strength—and become more powerful than the family ever dreamed possible. To grow stronger as the family grew weaker."

Molly leaned in close so she could murmur in my ear. "Do you actually believe any of this?"

"Some of it rings true. As for the rest, maybe he believes it. Maybe he made himself believe it."

"You can't hide anything from me," said Gerard. "I'm listening to your thoughts, not your voices. Picking the modern words right out of your heads. Language has changed so much since my time, become larger and more evocative. I approve. Only living things change and grow, even if they have their roots in dead things. The Droods are the past, and I am the future. I know why you're here, Eddie."

"Bet you don't," I said.

He laughed suddenly. "How refreshing to have an element of surprise in my life again. I've missed conversation."

"I thought you might," I said. "That's why I'm here."

I was surprised at how calm and easy Gerard's manner was. Apparently centuries of being buried alive, wrapped in unbreakable chains, had done nothing to break his spirit. He was still talking as though he was in charge. I did my best to sound earnest and convincing. The rational voice in this conversation.

"You need to go back to sleep, Gerard. Your time is over. Everything you know is gone. You wouldn't even recognise the world as it is today."

"Then I'll just have to change it until I do," said Gerard. "That was always my intent, after all."

"I have to ask," said Molly. "What was your plan, exactly? Once you'd subjugated all of Humanity, and made everyone in the world think your thoughts . . . what then?"

"Why stop at Humanity?" said Gerard. "Why stop at the world? I wanted to remake the whole universe in my image."

"Is that why you carved your face into the Moon?" said Molly.

"A moment's weakness, for which I paid dearly. It wasn't even why I went to the Moon. The family left something there long ago. I just never got the chance to use it.

Eddie knows what I'm talking about, don't you, Eddie?"

"Moonbreaker," I said numbly. "You're talking about Moonbreaker. You really meant to use that?"

"It would have set me free. Set us all free."

"What's he talking about, Eddie?" said Molly.

"Not now."

"Eddie!"

"Not now! Gerard, what good would it do you to gain the world if you destroy it in the process?"

"Birds have to leave the nest if they're to learn how to fly," said Gerard. "I would have made a new world and a new heaven. Isn't that what gods are supposed to do?"

"You were never a god," I said. "Just a Drood with an upgrade. How did you do that, Gerard? How could that old Heart armour transform you so completely?"

"By my not thinking of it as armour. Such a limiting concept. I took it inside me, joined with it on every physical and spiritual level there is. It wasn't easy; the process nearly killed me. But then . . . I woke up. All the way up, and found myself a god."

"If you were a god, the family wouldn't have been able to stuff you in a tomb, wrap you in chains, and bury you all the way out here," I said.

"I allowed all of that to happen," Gerard said patiently. "Because what is Time to a god? All that matters is I've won. I used you, Eddie, to set in motion events that would inevitably lead to this moment. When I shall throw off my chains, walk out of my tomb, and be free again."

"With my help," said Edmund.

I spun around and there he was, some distance behind me, standing before a Door-sized Merlin Glass, smiling happily. He wasn't wearing his armour, but the cold didn't seem to bother him at all. Molly snarled something and started forward, but I stopped her with a sharp gesture.

"Going head-to-head with him hasn't gotten us anywhere, Molly. We need to be smarter this time."

"Finally, you're getting the hang of things," said Edmund. He looked around him. "So, this is the proper location for the tomb. Looks just as dreary as the other place. I should have known the book would be misleading; it's what I would have done. I was just considering what to do next when you set off a fireworks show just for me! And now . . . here I am. Hello, ancestor Gerard! I've come to set you free."

"Hello, Edmund," said Gerard. "Here you are, just as I foresaw.

Though not quite what I expected. I'm no ancestor of yours . . . because you're not from around here, are you?"

I could see Edmund was thrown by that, but he recovered quickly. "It doesn't matter where I'm from; what matters is what I've brought with me. The Immaculate Key! Just the thing to open a tomb that was never meant to be opened."

"I know," said Gerard. "That's why I created it. So it could do what I needed it to do." He laughed softly. "Don't look so surprised, Eddie. When you're a living god, Time is just another direction to look in."

"I won't let you do this," I said to Edmund.

He smiled happily. "You can't stop me, Eddie."

I charged forward, churning up the bloodstained snow as I headed straight for him, because there was nothing else left to do. And I had to do it now, while I still had the strength. Molly sent a lightning bolt crackling past me. Edmund armoured up, and the vicious energies shattered harmlessly against his golden chest. And while I was still ploughing through the deep snow, Edmund bent calmly forward and thrust the Immaculate Key into the ground. I think I cried out then; because for something like the Key, intent was everything.

I staggered to a halt, and Molly quickly caught up with me. And then we both grabbed hold of each other as the ground beneath us shook violently as something exploded deep underground. The ground cracked jaggedly and then tore itself apart, crimson snow collapsing into the widening gap. Molly and I clung on to each other to keep from falling, riding the ground as it rose and fell. The crack widened into a crevice, and up from out of the depths rose Grendel Rex's tomb. It hung unsupported on the air above the break in the earth, a brightly glowing golden coffin.

I should have known. What else could my family use to make Grendel Rex's prison, except their own armour? The very-secret agents of that time had sacrificed their torcs and their lives to do their duty.

Anything for the family.

And it had all been for nothing. Hairline cracks raced across the surface of the coffin, lengthening and branching as the ancient bindings grew weaker, until suddenly the tomb just disappeared. And Gerard Drood, Grendel Rex, the Unforgiven God himself, stood alone on the air, hovering effortlessly over the bottomless drop.

It was all I could do to stay on my feet. The last of my strength was running out, like the sand from a broken hour-glass. I'd left it too late. I felt sick and weak. I didn't even want to think about what state my body was in now underneath my armour. I slowly realised Molly was shouting at me. I forced the weakness back by sheer strength of will, and made myself concentrate on what was happening in front of me.

Gerard Drood was just a man, after all. An ordinary-looking man in a plain white robe, with an entirely unremarkable face. He still wore his chains, lengths of fiercely crackling energies wrapping around him in overlapping coils that blazed so brightly they hurt my eyes, even through my golden face mask. Knowing they would die when they gave up their torcs, the very-secret agents had given up their life energies to make the chains that would bind Grendel Rex. The only chains that could hope to hold a living god and outlast eternity. For a moment, I allowed myself to hope, and then the Immaculate Key jerked itself out of the ground and shot through the air to slap into the waiting hand of Grendel Rex. The Key sank into his hand and disappeared. Gerard flexed his arms, and the glowing chains shattered and blew away, dissipating into the freezing air.

I don't know whether I heard the last dying screams of the very-secret agents then or whether I just thought I did.

Gerard stepped lightly forward across the open air, as easily as walking on water, before finally stepping down onto the crimson snow. He looked around him, entranced by the light of a world he hadn't seen in a millennium. Edmund hurried forward to greet him, smiling easily, as though he met living gods every day. The Merlin Glass vanished from where it was and reappeared beside the two of them. Gerard barely gave it a glance. Through the open doorway I could clearly see the dusty grey surface of the Moon. Air rushed and whistled through the open Door, sucked in by the vacuum beyond.

I raised my voice, calling out desperately to Gerard. "Don't go with him! You can't trust him! *He murdered all the Droods in his world!*"

Gerard favoured me with his smile. "A man after my own heart."

Edmund gestured grandly for Gerard to go first, and the living god stepped calmly out of this world and onto the Moon. Edmund waved cheerfully to me, and followed Gerard through. The Door slammed shut and the Merlin Glass disappeared, while I just stood there, paralysed with shock. Molly grabbed me by my golden shoulders and shook me hard, shouting right into my face.

"Eddie! What are we going to do now? What can we do?"

"We go after him," I said. And she never knew how much it cost me to keep my voice calm and steady.

"How?"

"Dragon!" I yelled. "Where are you?"

He dropped out of the sky to land lightly right in front of us.

"Where have you been?" Molly said loudly.

"I was busy," said the dragon. "No need to brief me; I know what's happened. Pretty inevitable, really, all things considered. I know where they've gone, and, yes, I can take you there. Climb aboard."

This time, Molly had to shove and then half carry me up the side of the dragon and plant me on his back. My hands were numb inside my gloves, and my feet weren't much better. I barely had enough strength to settle into place on the dragon's spine. Which rather raised the question of what use I was going to be once we caught up with Edmund and Gerard. I pushed the thought aside. I would find the strength to do what needed doing, when I needed it. Because I was a Drood and that's what Droods do. Molly swung into position behind me and put her arms round my waist. As much to hold me up as anything else. I made myself sit up as straight as I could, for pride's sake.

"Eddie . . ."

"It's almost over, Molly," I said. "I can do this. One last chance to save the day. Business as usual."

"Tell me you've got a plan!"

"I've got a plan."

"Oh good," said Molly. "For a moment there, I was worried."

I laughed despite myself. "Droods are never more dangerous than when we're dying. Because that's when we'll try anything!"

"I feel so confident," said Molly.

"Dragon!" I said. "Follow that god!"

"To the Moon!" said the dragon. And he threw himself into the sky, heading straight for the waiting Rainbow.

CHAPTER EIGHT

Journey's End

"Where were you when we needed you?" I said to the dragon. "And don't just say busy."

"But I was!" protested the dragon.

"Doing what?" said Molly.

"I had to contact the Droods," the dragon said patiently. "I could tell they were trying to reach you, Eddie. It's a dragon thing. But something about the tomb was keeping them out. They really needed to talk to you about something that was urgent as well as important, so I had to fly outside the affected area. And that took some time."

"Why didn't you just jump there, through the Rainbow?" said Molly.

"Because you only use something like the Rainbow when it's really important," said the dragon. "It's a miracle, not a convenience. Anyway, once I'd crossed the boundary I was able to phone home. Your family were really impressed that I was able to talk to them directly." The dragon paused. "Actually, *impressed* isn't quite the right word. I think *shocked and appalled* would probably be more accurate. But they soon settled down and stopped hyperventilating, and the Matriarch gave me a message to pass on. She's had people reading through the

Drood Diaries. Quite a lot of them, given the sheer number of Diaries. First, they found Gerard's diary."

"You're kidding!" said Molly.

"No, I don't do that. It's not a dragon thing. This particular diary was written when Gerard was just another Drood. Before he went off the deep end, for a long swim in the Dramatically Disturbed Pool. Apparently he was part of a team of Droods sent to the Moon to install a very important device."

"Moonbreaker," I said.

"Yes!" said the dragon. "That was it. What's Moonbreaker, Eddie?"

"One of my family's oldest secrets," I said. "And a very unpleasant one. If Gerard was involved with that, it could explain why he ended up losing the plot so completely."

"There's more to the story," said the dragon. "Gerard was married to Elspeth, also part of the installation team. Something went wrong during their time on the Moon, and Elspeth was killed. Gerard was never the same after that."

"I told you!" said Molly. "I knew there'd be a love gone wrong at the bottom of all this."

"He lost his wife doing his duty to the family," I said. "Much becomes clear."

"It does?" said the dragon.

"He wanted to punish the family, and he wanted everyone else to be him, so he'd never have to be alone again."

"But instead he ended up condemned to spend centuries on his own," said Molly. "Buried alive in his tomb. Life can be cruel."

"Yes," I said. "It can."

I would have liked to spend some time just sitting and brooding on the unfairness and injustice of life, but Molly knew better than to let me feel sorry for myself.

"Hey, dragon," she said. "And second?"

"What?" said the dragon.

"You said, 'First, they found Gerard's diary.' Which rather implies there was a second thing they found."

"Oh! Yes!" said the dragon. "They also found Peter's diary. The Librarian got quite excited over that. It seems Peter was the last of the very-secret agents in the family, and they don't usually write Diaries."

"We know about Peter," I said. "We met him."

"You did?" said the dragon. "I swear, no one ever tells me anything. Anyway, he knew all about the Moonbreaker device. Where it is and how to activate it. And a whole bunch of other things that not even the Matriarch knew. Somewhat to her surprise. Peter only wrote all this down because he was the last of the very-secret agents, and didn't want the knowledge to die with him. The Matriarch said I was to pass all this information on to you, Eddie. So you can stop Gerard and Edmund from doing anything unfortunate with Moonbreaker."

"Do we need to link again?" I said.

"No, Eddie. We're always linked now."

I was still trying to figure out how I felt about that when a blast of information hit me in the brain like a steel peg being hammered into the ground. I cried out, and swayed heavily on the dragon's back. I would have fallen if Molly hadn't had her arms around me. She had to wrestle me back into place as I reeled under the impact. My thoughts scattered like a flight of birds after a shock and only slowly settled down again. My head ached fiercely, but now I knew all there was to know about Moonbreaker. I realised Molly was shouting at me.

"Eddie! Eddie! Are you all right?"

"Yes. I'm fine. And please stop shouting. I have a headache."

"You've got really grumpy since you started dying," said Molly. "Next time I'll let you fall."

"Are you all right, Eddie?" said the dragon. "I know it was a lot of information to assimilate."

"I'm fine!" I said. "But please stay out of my head. There's really only room in it for me."

"Gladly," said the dragon. "Don't you ever clean up in there?"

"Don't you think it's time you told me what Moonbreaker is, Eddie?" said Molly. Just a bit pointedly.

"Later," I said. "When I'm feeling stronger."

"Time to go," said the dragon. "The Moon awaits."

The Rainbow cascaded down before us. Tumbling endlessly out of nowhere, the blazing colours filled the sky until there was nothing else left, and the dragon flew straight into them. I could hear the true song of the Rainbow now, in my heart and in my soul. It wasn't just a doorway, like the Merlin Glass; the Rainbow was alive. An elemental thing, old as the universe. The dragon didn't summon the Rainbow; it came because it chose to.

Because we needed it.

This time, the transition wasn't instantaneous. There was a sense of falling forever, in a place that wasn't a place. I couldn't feel the dragon's spine beneath me or Molly's arms around my waist, and I wondered, *Is this what it will feel like to be dead?* And then we burst out the other side of the Rainbow and all the colours were gone, replaced by a shimmering silver-grey light as the dragon went soaring over the surface of the Moon.

I heard Molly gasp, and I would have too if I hadn't been so exhausted. I'd seen recordings of the *Apollo* landings on television, but I'd never seen the Moon for myself, up close and personal. The dusty surface stretched away like a solid grey sea. There were mountains like frozen crested waves and craters the size of cities, full of mysteries and concealing darkness. Anything might be lurking at the bottom of craters like those. And all of it unnaturally still and silent, like the ghost of the world. The dragon descended steadily, until the grey plains were so close it felt like I could reach down and touch them. I expected the beating of the dragon's wings to stir up great clouds of dust as we passed, but nothing moved. When I looked at the dragon's wings, I saw they weren't moving either. He was just gliding serenely over the lunar surface, with no effort at all.

"Enjoying the view?" said the dragon. "I thought you might appreciate the scenic route."

"It's amazing!" said Molly. "I've never been to the Moon. Been pretty much everywhere else, but . . . How far are we from where the eagle landed?"

I pointed off to the left. "Fifty, sixty miles. Which was actually a lot closer to Moonbreaker than my family was comfortable with, but it wasn't like we could say anything."

"If you're interested," said the dragon, "I can tell you that Gerard and Edmund are already on the Moon. Somewhere."

"Is this, by any chance, a dragon thing?" I said.

"Of course."

"But you don't know exactly where they are?" said Molly.

"No," said the dragon. "Must be a living god thing."

"I know where they're heading," I said. "The only place they could go to activate Moonbreaker. Under the surface, inside the Moon."

"What is there inside the Moon?" said Molly.

"You'd be surprised," I said.

"That's what I'm afraid of," Molly said darkly. "I mean, being here is cool, but the Moon doesn't strike me as a particularly hospitable place."

"Dragon," I said, "why didn't the Rainbow transport us directly to Moonbreaker?"

"Something to do with the nature of its location," said the dragon. "No use pressing me for details; it's not like I have long conversations with the Rainbow. I just know things."

"Then we'll have to get down to Moonbreaker the way my family did," I said. "All those years ago . . ."

"You know how to do that?" said Molly.

"I do now," I said. "It was part of the information package the dragon passed on. We need to find one particular crater."

"Already there," said the dragon. "We're almost on top of it."

"Hold everything!" Molly said sharply. "I have questions. Urgent and very practical questions. How are we still breathing? Why aren't we floating right off the dragon's back, due to the low gravity? Why aren't we dying from the subzero temperature and the vacuum? Answer the first question first, but don't skimp on the others."

"Relax," said the dragon. "You're protected from any and all local conditions as long as you're with me. Just part of the package when you fly Dragon Airways!"

A crater loomed up before us. It looked like one of the smaller impact sites, barely two or three hundred feet in diameter. I tried to visualise the size of the meteor that could have caused such damage, and then thought about what meteors that big would do to Earth if the atmosphere wasn't there to burn them up. The sheer number of craters made it clear that as far as the universe was concerned, the Moon was just one big target. The crater before us looked increasingly deep as we approached, its base concealed by dark shadows.

Molly leaned in close to put her mouth right next to my ear. "How are you feeling, Eddie?"

"Like there's less and less of me, all the time," I said. "I can't feel anything now inside my armour. I don't even want to think about what shape my body must be in if my armour has had to cut off all sensations. I probably don't look very pretty any more."

"But, then, what's going to happen when you have to take off your armour?" said Molly.

"I can't," I said. "If I armour down now, even for a moment, I'll die."

"You mean you're going to have to live in it forever?"

"No," I said. "Only until it can't keep me alive any longer. We're in the end game now, Molly. No way back, not for me. I've known that all along, but it's still hard to accept. I wish . . . I'd found the time to hold you in my arms and kiss you good-bye properly before I sealed myself up inside the armour. So many things I should have done while I still had time."

Molly couldn't bring herself to say anything. I saw her tighten her arms around my waist, but couldn't feel them. I was isolated from everything now, like a ghost haunting my own life.

"We'll be landing soon," I said. "And then we'll have to leave the dragon and his protections. My armour will support me, but what about you, Molly?"

"I am perfectly capable of looking after myself," Molly said immediately.

"Good to know," I said.

The dragon touched down on the lunar surface, just short of the crater. Dust rose in thick clouds all around us, before settling back again very slowly. I thought about how long it must have been since anything disturbed the dust in this still, silent world. The silence of the tomb, in a dead place.

"Why aren't you bothered by the lack of air?" I asked the dragon.

"Because to an unnatural creature such as myself, all natural conditions are equally irrelevant." The dragon peered around him with a certain sense of satisfaction, studying the various marks his landing had left on the Moon's dusty ground. "Just think! In years to come, when the astronauts finally return to the Moon, they will come here . . . and find dragon tracks in the dust."

"No they won't," I said firmly. "Because whatever happens, you are going to clean up all traces of our visit before you leave. Humanity isn't supposed to know about the likes of us and the things we do. For everyone's peace of mind. Do this for me, dragon. It's a Drood thing."

"Of course, Eddie," said the dragon. "Anything for the family."

Molly surrounded herself with a protective force field. I caught sight of it out of the corner of my mask and glanced back, over my shoulder. The field shimmered and sparkled, suggesting it had energy to spare, but it didn't seem very big.

"How much oxygen do you have inside there?" I said. "How far can you travel before it runs out?"

"The field generates its own air," said Molly. "Don't ask how; you know you never understand my explanations. And don't fuss!"

Her tone made it clear there was no point in pressing her. I swung one leg over the dragon's spine and started to climb down his side. Molly went to help me, the way she'd helped me climb up, but I stopped her with a gesture. I appreciated the offer, but I needed to do things for myself, while I still could. I worked my way down the dragon's side, slowly and carefully, watching where I put my hands and feet, because I had no feeling in them. I had to dig my feet in hard to make sure they wouldn't slip, but the dragon didn't say anything. I finally dropped down onto the Moon's surface, and dust puffed silently up. I peered around me, into the spectral light, taking in craters named after people who had never been here, and mountains no one ever climbed. A world that had grown old and tired, waiting for Man to come and visit.

Molly was right. Even after all the places we'd been, the Moon was special.

Molly clambered quickly down the dragon's side to join me. And then we allowed ourselves a moment to just stand there and admire the sheer spectacle of the scene. All of it bathed in an eerie silver-grey light that made everything seem like a half-remembered dream. Molly suddenly grabbed hold of my arm, and raised her voice excitedly.

"Eddie! I just realised! I'm the first woman to walk on the Moon!"

"Well," I said, "given that Elspeth Drood was part of the original installation team . . ."

Molly scowled and pushed my arm away. "You had to spoil my moment, didn't you?"

"Sorry. I suppose there's always the chance . . ."

"No. Too late. The moment's gone."

"You must have been the first woman to walk in far more exciting places than this, Molly."

"Of course I have! It's just, this is the Moon." And then she stopped and turned back to glare at the dragon. "Are you positive this is the right crater? I mean, there are an awful lot of them."

"This is where you need to be," said the dragon. "Trust me; I'm a dragon."

"This is the right place," I said. "Trust me; I'm a Drood."

Molly looked at me challengingly. "How can you be so sure?"

"Because my family provided me with the exact coordinates, and a map downloaded into my armour. I couldn't get lost if I tried." I studied the rising wall of the crater carefully. "We need to get moving. It's possible the Merlin Glass transported Edmund and Gerard straight to Moonbreaker. It's always been good at getting into places it shouldn't be able to."

"How could it do that, when the Rainbow couldn't?" said Molly.

"Because it's Merlin's Glass," I said. "A man famous for doing things no one else could."

"He wasn't infallible," said Molly. "As you'd know, if you'd met his last girlfriend. I've talked with him, remember, in the Nightside. Of course, that was after he was dead, and he'd slowed down a bit."

"Just more proof, if proof were needed, that he was far more powerful than one man should ever be," I said.

Molly scowled at the crater. "If Moonbreaker's buried underneath that crater, how are we supposed to get down to it? I didn't think to bring my digging equipment with me."

"There's a door at the bottom of the crater," I said

"Of course there is." Molly folded her arms stubbornly. "I am not taking one more step until I know exactly what I'm getting into. You've been keeping too many things from me, Eddie Drood, and this is where I draw my line in the sand. Or the dust. So, talk to me. What is Moonbreaker?"

"Something so appalling, most of my family couldn't be allowed to know about it," I said steadily. "So they could sleep at night. I only know because I used to run the family. I had to be told, in case I ever needed to authorize its use. There is a bomb inside the Moon. Powerful enough to blow the Moon apart and send its pieces crashing down onto Earth. Pieces big enough to destroy Earth and every living thing on it."

Molly stared at me. "Dear God . . . If the world knew about this, they'd tear your family apart!"

"I know," I said. "That's why we keep it to ourselves. And why most of my family can't be trusted with the knowledge. Someone might have an attack of conscience and give the game away."

"But why?" Molly said angrily. "Why would your family want to put such a thing here?"

"In case we ever need to destroy Earth," I said. "As a last resort, to take a conquering enemy with us. Or to provide a compassionate end for Humanity. One last act of mercy in an unbearable situation. Think, Molly: What if the Hungry Gods had won their war against us? Would you have wanted to go on living in the world they would have made? Endless horror and endless suffering? There had to be a way out, we decided. And it must be said, my family have always been very bad losers."

Molly shook her head slowly, trying to come to terms with my family's idea of forward planning. "How could you . . . ?"

"That's my family's job sometimes. To think the things no one else wants to think about. To do the things no one else is prepared to do or can be trusted to do. We are the defenders of Humanity . . . but when that's no longer possible, we are prepared to be Humanity's avengers."

"Why not place the bomb inside the earth?"

"Because that's the first place anyone would look," I said. "I wonder, were Gerard and Elspeth part of the planning team that came up with the Moonbreaker scenario? Were they made to think the unthinkable, and that's what started Gerard down his path? Is my family responsible for creating Grendel Rex?"

"Gerard made himself into the Unforgiven God," said Molly. "He chose to make himself more dangerous than Moonbreaker could ever be. Grendel Rex didn't want to just kill Humanity; he wanted to replace it."

"This is why he came to the Moon," I said. "Not to carve his features into the surface; he was here for Moonbreaker."

"So he did want to destroy Earth, after all?"

"No," I said. "No, you're right, that doesn't make sense. That was never what he wanted . . ."

"All right," said Molly. "Was there anything else Moonbreaker could do?"

"Not as far as I know," I said. "What did Grendel Rex want with Moonbreaker? And why waste time with such an act of vanity? If he hadn't exhausted his powers carving his face into the surface of the Moon, my family might never have been able to take him down."

"Could he really have set off Moonbreaker on his own?" said Molly.

"Oh yes," I said. "It was designed to be simple to operate in an emergency. So that even if only one of us was left, we could still do what was necessary to put Humanity out of its misery."

"But how did Edmund know about any of this?" said Molly. "He never ran his family."

"Who knows what information he had access to in the Other World?"

"But if he knew about Moonbreaker, why not use it to destroy his Earth?"

"Because he never meant to destroy all of Humanity," I said. "Just the Droods."

"Then why is he ready to destroy Earth now?"

I felt like shouting at her to stop asking me questions, but that was just the tiredness. Molly was right. I was missing something.

"Edmund isn't crazy," I said. "As such. He still needs somewhere to live. Unless he's had enough of our world and intends to move on to some other earth."

"He must have a plan," said Molly.

"Of course. Edmund always has a plan."

"Where is Moonbreaker, exactly?"

"In the City."

Molly looked at me. "City? What city?"

"Droods know lots of things," I said. "We are, after all, the keepers of the secret histories. I'm talking about the underground City of the Selenites. The original inhabitants of the lunar interior. A very old race."

"As old as Humanity?" said Molly.

"Older," I said. "All gone now, of course."

"Oh," said Molly. "Like when we visited the Martian Tombs?"

"Not really," I said. "Whoever or whatever lived on Mars disappeared millennia ago. The Selenites have only been gone a few centuries."

Molly looked at me suspiciously. "Did your family do something to them?"

"No," I said. "They did something to themselves."

"But they were here, when your family first installed the Moonbreaker device?"

"Oh yes."

"And the Selenites were fine with you people putting a bomb here?" said Molly. "Something big enough to blow the whole Moon right out from under them?"

"They understood the need for it," I said. "They were in charge of guarding Moonbreaker."

"So what changed a few hundred years ago?"

"It's complicated."

She gave me a hard look. "Simplify it!"

"Wait till we get to the City," I said. "Everything will be much clearer once we get to the City."

Molly sniffed loudly, in a way that made it plain the conversation wasn't over, just postponed.

"All right," she said. "Where is this underground City of the Selenites, and how do we get to it?"

"There's a door at the bottom of the crater."

"I don't know why I even ask you things," said Molly. "No, hold on. It's only just occurred to me, but . . . How are we able to talk to each other without radios or anything?"

"My torc allows me to contact your mind directly."

"You can read my thoughts?" said Molly.

"I wouldn't dare."

Molly smiled suddenly. "You do know that was the only acceptable answer?"

"Of course," I said.

I turned to the patiently waiting dragon. "I'm sorry, but you're going to have to stay on the surface. You can't follow where we have to go."

"Suits me," said the dragon. "Think I'll go for a nice fly around. Take in the sights, see if I can scare up a little action."

"On the Moon?" said Molly.

"You humans have such limited expectations," said the dragon. "I see all kinds of possibilities here."

"I still don't see how you can fly when there isn't any air," I said.

He looked at me crushingly. "Because I'm a dragon."

"Fair enough," I said. "Wait a few hours. If we're not back by then, call the Rainbow and return to Earth. Because we won't be coming back. Tell my family what's happened. Warn them of what might happen. Hopefully by now they'll have come up with some kind of backup plan."

"I will not leave the Moon until you return," said the dragon.

"You'll go," I said harshly. "Because the world must be saved."

"I'll go," said the dragon. "Good-bye, Eddie. Good-bye, Molly."

Dust went tumbling in all directions as the dragon launched himself up and away, and soared gracefully off over the cratered surface. Molly and I swept our arms back and forth, trying to clear the dust away so we could see what we were doing, but it took its own sweet time settling back. I expected some of it to cling to my armour, but the dust particles seemed almost determined to avoid me. I had to look down at the footprints I was leaving in the dust to reassure myself I was actually there.

I started forward, and found I had to shuffle slowly along to maintain contact with the surface. Trying to walk normally in the reduced gravity just sent me lurching in all directions. Molly suddenly took me by the hand and swung me around, and then moved me carefully through the familiar steps of an old-fashioned waltz. I was a little clumsy, because I couldn't feel my feet, but Molly always knows what I need to calm my soul in moments of crisis. We laughed quietly as we danced together in the Moonlight. Just because we could.

In the end, I broke away. Because sweet as this was, I didn't have the time.

I clambered up the outer wall of the crater. Watching where I put my hands and feet, because I had no feeling left in them. I was getting really tired of having to do that. Molly made a point of not trying to assist me, for which I was quietly grateful. It took a while to reach the summit, and then I clung on to the jagged rim with both hands as I looked down into the crater. The interior wall curved away before me, and the shadows at the base were very deep and very dark. Molly started to say something, but I preempted her by pulling myself up and over the rim and starting down the inner wall.

I danced down the sloping surface, my feet leaving little puffs of dust every time they made contact. I was almost vertical, relative to the grey wall, and I laughed out loud as I skipped and bounced along. Being set free from the drag of gravity was exhilarating. Molly quickly caught up with me, her laughter mingling with mine as we descended into the depths of the crater.

Light reflecting from my armour and Molly's protective shield finally revealed the base, filled with a thick layer of dust. Molly started to slow down, but I just jumped right into it, sinking all the way down to my chest before I stopped. A great grey cloud rose around me, and Molly dropped elegantly through it to stand lightly on the surface of the dust pool. I was already digging, throwing dust behind me like a dog searching for a bone. Molly gestured dramatically, and big puffs of dust were blasted right out of the crater.

It didn't take us long to uncover a great metal wheel some twelve feet in diameter. Solid steel, with a heavy rim and thick spokes. I grabbed hold of the rim with both hands, watching my golden fingers to make sure they closed properly. I had to throw all my armour's power against the wheel before the stubborn thing finally moved round an inch and then another, until eventually the wheel began turning in a series of small jerks. God alone knew how long it had been since the wheel was last used. I kept expecting to hear creaking noises, or the straining sounds of protesting machinery, but there was never any sound on the Moon. Everything happened in the same relentless silence. The only thing I could hear was my own increasingly ragged breathing. The wheel slammed to a halt, and I strained uselessly against it for a long moment before realising it had gone as far as it could. I pushed the wheel up, and the air lock attached to its underside rose too.

Dust spiralled down into the new opening, disappearing into the darkness like sand through an hour-glass. No air came rushing out, because there was no atmosphere in what lay below. Molly conjured up one of her glowing spheres, and it went bouncing happily down through the opening. The gentle green glow illuminated a steel tunnel, with a ladder bolted to the inner wall. The tunnel fell away farther than the light could reach, disappearing into darkness. Molly crowded in beside me and stared into the opening. She looked dubiously at the ladder and then at me.

"Is that thing going to be strong enough to support you and your armour?"

"The ladder was put there by Droods," I said. "With Droods in mind. I'm sure it's perfectly safe."

"Can I have that in writing?"

"I'll go first."

"Damned right you will."

I went down the ladder one step at a time, positioning my numb feet carefully. Molly came after, mindful not to hurry me. We descended for a long time, rung by rung. At the bottom of the steel shaft, the ladder just stopped. I let go, and slowly fell a dozen feet or more into a large cavern. Before me, a roughly hewn stone passageway dropped away into the Moon's interior. The glowing sphere was already some distance down the passage, bouncing up and down on the air, impatient to get going. Molly dropped slowly down out of the shaft to land gracefully beside me, and I started forward before she could begin asking questions again.

The curving walls and ceiling had been carved out of a dark grey stone, shot through with blue mineral veins. The floor was entirely free of dust. After a while, it suddenly became a stairway, each step a massive wedge of stone with a good two-foot drop between each one. The impact of each descent should have jarred me to my bones, but I didn't feel anything. The growing distance between my thoughts and my body was disquieting, but I wouldn't let it get to me. I just kept going, concentrating on the job at hand.

The stairs finally emerged from the long tunnel and stopped abruptly, at the very edge of a huge stone amphitheatre. Miles and miles across, it was filled to bursting with an intricate warren of intersecting stone galleries. Huge structures, wide streets, intercrossing passageways, and accumulations of stone hollows like an immense honeycomb, overwhelming in size and scale. The details and dimensions went far beyond any human sensibilities. The City stretched away in every direction, with no gaps or breaks, as though it was all one creation, conceived and carved as a single thing. The sheer interconnectedness of everything made me think of a hive. Efficiency, but no aesthetics. No comforts, nothing decorative; just pure, brutal function.

"This is it," I said to Molly. "The City of the Selenites."

"Ugly-looking place," said Molly. "Does it have a name?"

"I don't think they went in for human things like names," I said.

The City was utterly deserted, a shadowy gathering of random shapes and strange angles. There were structures that might have been storehouses or tombs. Or things built to serve purposes beyond human understanding. Circular holes in the walls might have been doors or windows. Narrow connecting corridors laced the buildings together in an intricate web. Studying the Selenite city was like looking at a Rorschach inkblot, imposing my own perceptions on what was before me and almost certainly putting inaccurate meanings on things.

"According to my armour, there's still no atmosphere," I said. "No heat either, just deep cold. Suggesting there's been no heat or life in this place for a really long time. This is a dead city."

"A city of the dead?" said Molly.

"No. The Selenites aren't dead. Just gone."

"What were they like, Eddie?"

"There isn't much in the files when it comes to the Selenites them-selves," I said. "Not even a suggestion as to what they might have been."

"Bigger than us, I'd say, given the sheer scale of everything," said Molly. "But something about all of this definitely says *insects* to me."

"I thought that," I said. "But this is all they left behind. No artefacts, no personal possessions, nothing to suggest what their civilisation might have involved."

"No photos?" said Molly. "No artist's impressions? Not even a writ-ten description?"

"Most references to Drood contact with the Selenites were re-moved from the family records long ago," I said.

"Well, that's not in any way suspicious," said Molly. "Why would your family do that?"

"Guilt, perhaps."

Molly looked around the deserted city. "They must have done something really bad here, if it could make even your family feel guilty."

"There's all kinds of guilt," I said.

"This isn't like that old film, is it?" said Molly. "You know, the one where Earth people bring the common cold to the Moon, and it wipes out the indigenous population because they don't have any resistance to it?"

"No," I said. "That isn't what happened."

Molly waited, and then made a short, disgusted sound as she realised that was all the answer she was going to get. And then she shrugged, and smiled suddenly.

"Still! Look at it. A whole alien city, so close to Earth, and I never knew. No one knew! It's not right to just leave it like this, Eddie. Your family should have told someone. There should be archaeologists working here, digging for facts and puzzling out the City's secrets. All right, maybe not mainstream archaeologists, but there are any number of specialised groups who'd be more than happy to take on the work. If someone else provided the transport."

"There's no hurry," I said. "The City's not going anywhere. There are no bodies, no atmosphere; nothing to disturb the peace or lend itself to decay. The City of the Selenites has stood for hundreds of years and will stand for hundreds more, untouched by Time or history. This is so big it should belong to everyone. Wait until Space exploration begins again, and when we finally return to the Moon, the City will be waiting. With all of its mysteries still intact and in place."

"Is this the only Selenite City?" said Molly.

"No, there are dozens of them scattered around under the surface. They all look much the same. No one in my family has visited them in ages. This is the one that matters."

"Couldn't there be just a few Selenites left somewhere? Hiding out and keeping their heads down?"

"No," I said. "They're all gone. The records are quite firm on that."

I accessed the map my family gave me, flashing up its details on the inside of my mask. A glowing line traced a path through the intersecting streets, pointing the way to Moonbreaker. I set off confidently, tiptoeing along in the low gravity, and Molly moved quickly into position at my side. The glowing sphere bobbed along on the air, shooting ahead and then waiting for us to catch up, like an impatient dog on a scent. Shadows jumped and danced, giving an illusion of life to the empty streets. Dark, cavernous holes in the giant buildings seemed to watch like empty eyes. I didn't look at them, in case something looked back. I knew we were alone in the City, but I didn't necessarily believe it.

The silence was getting on my nerves. I couldn't even hear my own footsteps on the stone floor. Some of the map's directions made no sense at all, but I followed them, anyway. There were no landmarks, nothing to help me judge the distance we'd covered, so all I could do was trust the map.

"Are you sure your map is up to date?" said Molly, following my thoughts as always.

"Nothing has changed in this city for centuries," I said.

Molly sniffed loudly. "It's all very impressive, in a deeply unsettling sort of way, but you can have too much of a good thing. I'm starting to feel like those archaeologists who uncovered the ancient Egyptian burial chambers in the Valley of the Kings, looking at the remains of a lost civilisation and trying to make sense of it."

"I can assure you," I said solemnly, "there are no mummies here."

"Might be cocoons," said Molly.

"Well, be careful where you tread."

We rounded a corner and found ourselves at the top of another stairway. A narrow stone spiral, falling away into the depths. We followed it down for some time until it suddenly turned and then opened out abruptly, into a circular chamber perhaps a hundred feet in diameter, with a ceiling only ten or twelve feet above us. The floor's polished stone shone so brightly its light filled the whole chamber and reflected back from the crystalline ceiling. Molly dismissed her glowing sphere. Dozens of open doorways stood side by side, with barely a gap between them, lining the perimeter. No Doors; just doorways. Filled with nothing but a kind of visual static that pushed the gaze away.

"Are those what I think they are?" Molly said quietly.

"Yes," I said. "Dimensional Doors. Already activated, and waiting to take us to all kinds of interesting places. Don't get too close, Molly. They're nothing like the Doors we're used to. Drop your guard and you could get sucked in."

Molly smiled. "Drop my guard. Right. That'll be the day."

"These are Selenite Doors," I said. "Leading to other worlds, other dimensions . . . other realities."

"But this is the right place?" said Molly. "We are where we're supposed to be, finally?"

"Definitely," I said. "This is where my family left Moonbreaker, and hoped they'd never have to come back for it."

"Then why aren't Gerard and Edmund here?" said Molly. "They had enough of a head start on us."

"This chamber has its own defences," I said. "Enough to deflect even the Merlin Glass. Edmund and Gerard are probably out in the City somewhere, making their way here. If Gerard still remembers the way, after all these years."

"Are you sure there isn't some hidden danger here that they know about but we don't?" said Molly. "They could just be waiting for us to trigger it so they can come in safely."

"Always possible," I said.

"Did your family leave any booby-traps? To protect Moonbreaker from unauthorized visitors?"

"Nothing about that in the files," I said. "But it does sound like the kind of thing my family would do."

"Terrific," said Molly.

"Watch where you step," I said.

We moved slowly round the chamber, peering into various open doorways. If we moved close enough the visual static would disappear, to show us what lay beyond. Strange alien landscapes, unknown worlds, and some places so strange, I wasn't even sure they qualified as places. The Selenites had opened doorways to locations human beings had no business even knowing about.

Through another doorway, a desert of shifting, shimmering sands, under a bottle-green sky and a sharp blue-white sun. Cities on the horizon, made up of shining lights. Huge stone shapes stumbled across the desert like a slow-motion avalanche, unknown forms on unknowable missions. The ground shuddered under their slow, relentless march, as though it was frightened.

This time a night world, with no moon and only a smattering of stars. Fires from a single huge volcanic pit illuminated a human city of steel and bronze, with turreted towers and barricaded buildings. Encircled by a thick defensive wall, because the city was surrounded and besieged by an army of hideous monsters. Waiting for some order to attack, or for the city's inhabitants to come out and fight. The hatred, the thwarted malignant rage of these terrible creatures, was an almost palpable presence in the night.

Huge stone hives clumped together on a desolate wasteland, under a purple sky pockmarked with dreary stars. Insects the size of men scuttled over the exterior of the hives, darting in and out of shadowed holes.

A metal plain glowed like burnished steel, across which homicidal machines threw themselves at one another in a never-ending war. With buzz-saws and grappling hooks, vicious weapons and pounding guns. Metal skin tore like paper, and silicon insides spilled out onto the metal plain. All of it under an unbearably harsh actinic glare.

Things got stranger as we moved from Door to Door. Mountains that sang, and skies that bled. A heaving sea of swirling colours, with great abstract shapes swimming in it under a psychedelic sky. A place of mists and shadows, giving brief glimpses of uncertain things, moving slowly but with sinister purpose. A place where nothing was ever solid or definite, whose inhabitants were constantly turning into something else, straining and twisting from one form to another. Uncertain shapes, always on the brink of becoming distinct and recognisable, but never able to hang on to the state for long. Flesh that ran like rivers. Bodies big as buildings. Dreams and nightmares and everything in between. Sights beyond human comprehension or sanity.

Some Doors showed glimpses of paradise, the kind of places you never dared believe could actually exist. Fairy-tale palaces with knights and unicorns and countryside like the scene of every jig-saw puzzle you ever loved as a child. Other Doors showed things too complex or too strange for the human mind to comprehend. Creatures that existed in more than three spatial dimensions, endlessly unfolding. Shapes without edges, creatures without boundaries, life without meaning.

And then there were Doors that opened onto vistas of Deep Space and all that it contained. A planet made of maggots. Stars that winked on and off like faulty light bulbs. A world that sneaked up on its moon and ate it. A staring, insane eye the size of a galaxy. By then I wasn't sure anything I was seeing was real; my mind was just interpreting and trying to make sense of what it was being presented with. I've seen more than my share of strange things, but this . . . I glanced at Molly, to see how she was coping. Her face was deathly pale, but she wouldn't look away from anything. She seemed fascinated and disturbed at the same time. We kept moving, until finally we returned to where we'd started. No wiser, and a lot less comfortable.

Now and again things would approach the doorways from the other side and look through. Living things, from worlds where life had taken very different paths. Bent and twisted creatures, all teeth and claws and malevolent intent. Tall and lofty beings, glowing with supernatural light. A wild shape made out of jagged sticks raised a single twiggy hand to tap thoughtfully on the other side of the Door, as though testing how strong the barrier was.

I was ready to turn my back on all of it, take a deep breath and grab my spiritual second wind, when I felt strangely drawn to one particular Door. I moved closer, peering curiously into a confused place of flaring lights. Dark shapes drifted towards the Door, but somehow never quite seemed to reach it. A sound issued from the Door, coming clearly to me through my armour. I lunged forward, and Molly grabbed me by the arm and hauled me back. I jerked my arm free and turned on her angrily.

"What is the matter with you? Can't you hear that? There's a baby screaming in there! We have to save it!"

"Listen to yourself," Molly said steadily. "There is no baby. It's just something pretending, to lure you in. No, Eddie, stay where you are! Stop and think! What would a human baby be doing in there? How could it even survive?"

I looked back at the Door, and the baby's screams grew louder and more desperate, but somehow less real. Like an impostor trying too hard. I turned my back on the Door and the crying cut off immediately. I shuddered as I realised how close I'd come to charging blindly through the Door. I moved back to the centre of the chamber, and Molly went with me. I swallowed hard and nodded quickly to her.

"I'm back," I said. "I'm not sure I could have got through the Door, anyway. My armour would probably have stopped me."

"Of course," said Molly. "I was just being cautious." She looked at the Doors surrounding us. "You know, some of those worlds are simply . . . incredible."

"That's why the Selenites created the Doors," I said. "As an escape from their dead world."

Molly grinned at me suddenly. "Of course! I get it now! This is what you meant when you said all the Selenites were gone. They didn't die; they left through the Doors!"

"Got it in one," I said. "Centuries sitting on top of Moonbreaker did nothing for their nerves, and they finally decided they'd had enough and wanted out. Drood Armourers and a whole army of lab assistants worked for years to help the Selenites build all of this; that much is in the family records. Though why the Selenites chose some of these destinations . . . I suppose they just wanted as wide a choice as possible."

"No accounting for alien taste," said Molly. "Do you know where they went in the end?"

"No," I said. "No one was here when they left. We respected the Selenites' privacy. Maybe . . . they went to all of them."

"Did any of the Selenites ever change their minds and come back?"

"No. But, then, why would they want to return to a dead world?"

Molly looked at some of the things pressing up against the other sides of the doorways. "I hope there are defences in place to keep those guys from coming through. They don't look like tourists to me."

"Relax," I said. "My family put some serious locks and protections on these Doors after the Selenites left."

"You sure about that?"

"You don't think we'd leave Moonbreaker here if it was at all vulnerable? The Selenites could come home, but no one else."

"Where is this appalling device?" said Molly. "I don't see it anywhere."

"Buried under the City," I said. "Miles down. This is simply where you access the controls."

"I don't see any controls either."

"They were designed to reveal themselves only to a Drood," I said patiently. "Like this."

I knelt down, placed one golden hand flat on the brightly shining floor, and said my name. And then I stepped back quickly, as one whole section of the centre floor disappeared and Moonbreaker's control column rose steadily up before me. When it finally came to a halt, it stood ten feet tall and almost half as wide. Crusted with silicon grafts like coral growths, studded with blinking lights, interspersed with all kinds of switches and levers.

"What the hell is that?" said Molly. "It looks more like a piece of modern art than a control column."

"Supposedly, the core mechanism was retrieved and repurposed from a crashed alien starship, and everything else was just . . . wrapped around it. I know it looks a bit crude to modern eyes, but given that this was cobbled together by my family back in the Eleventh Century, I don't think they did too badly."

"Do you know how to work it?" said Molly.

"I don't want to activate Moonbreaker," I said, "just secure the control column so Edmund and Gerard can't."

"Sorry, Eddie," Edmund said happily behind me. "But that's not how things are going to work out."

I spun round to see Edmund and Gerard standing before a Door-sized Merlin Glass on the other side of the chamber. Edmund smiled cheerfully at me. He wasn't wearing his armour but seemed entirely unaffected by his surroundings. Presumably the fake torc the Immortals made for him came with its own built-in protections. Gerard didn't seem bothered by the lack of air or pressure or gravity, but, then, he was a living god and presumably above such things.

I made myself concentrate on Edmund. Whatever kind of torc he had, it was no match for my strange-matter armour. I had to believe that. Whatever happened in this place, Edmund was going down. No more tricks. No more last-minute escapes. In this chamber full of Doors, deep beneath the surface of the Moon, his story and mine would finally come to an end.

"Hi guys," said Edmund. "Miss me?"

I didn't answer him, just placed myself between Edmund and Gerard and the control column. Molly was right there with me, scowling impartially at both of them. The Unforgiven God didn't look at her or me. His expression was cold, uninterested, his gaze strangely far away. Edmund struck a casual pose, leaning on Gerard as though the living god were just something useful that happened to be there.

"We had no trouble finding this place," he said. "Gerard spent a lot of time here, after all, helping to install Moonbreaker. We've just been waiting for you to catch up. Somewhat impatiently, I might add. We were beginning to think you were never going to get here. Isn't that right, Gerard?"

The living god said nothing. His expression didn't change. Edmund didn't even glance at him.

"Gerard has been very forthcoming. I could have called up the control column at any time and given Moonbreaker its long-awaited marching orders. But where would have been the fun in that?"

"Really?" I said. "How very strong-willed of you . . . Or could it be that you did call, and the column wouldn't respond to your fake torc? If you don't have real Drood armour, you're not really a Drood. Are you?"

"You can talk," said Edmund. "Lounging around in those newfangled strange-matter pyjamas."

"My family updated Moonbreaker when we took on the new armour," I said. "Because we think of everything. The control column will never take orders from that fake armour of yours."

"Possibly," said Edmund. "Good thing for me, then, that I've got Gerard. He helped design Moonbreaker, and apparently he put in a few backdoor commands that he never got around to telling his family about. Believe me, Eddie, I can set off the bomb anytime I want. But I had to wait, so you could watch me do it. I need you to see the look on my face as I destroy not just your family, but your whole world as well. I'd like to see the look on your face as you realise you've lost everything. But you can't drop your armour now, can you? Not after what my lovely poison has done to your poor, defenceless body. I've seen the end results on some of my victims. Bodies riddled with cancers, twisted and deformed by the poison's progress. Flesh rotting away from the bones . . . What's left of you inside that armour must be pretty high by now."

"You bastard," said Molly. And her voice was a cold and deadly thing.

"Hush, dear," said Edmund, not looking round. "Adults talking."

"Talk to me, you little turd," said Molly. "Why do you need to destroy the whole world?"

Edmund sighed and turned his charming smile on her. "You're expecting me to say for revenge, aren't you? That it's the only way I could be sure of wiping out Eddie's dismal little family. Really, Molly, do you honestly think I'm that petty? That limited in my vision? No, I've got something else in mind. The energies released by Moonbreaker's destruction of the earth will be enough to fill the Merlin Glass to capacity. Energies I can then use to transport me back to my own earth. And of course there's nothing like having your very own living god at your side, to make sure everyone will bend their knees and bow their heads. Oh, the fun I'm going to have . . . I mean, your earth is all very well, but there's no place like home, is there? So, blow up the Moon, return home in triumph, and kill off a whole family of Droods in the process! A plan with no drawbacks!"

"You don't need Moonbreaker to get you home," I said. "Look around you. You're surrounded by dimensional Doors. It shouldn't be too difficult to reprogram one to take you home."

"Dear Eddie, always the reasonable voice," said Edmund. "But, really, if all I wanted was to go home, I could have used Alpha Red Alpha and then slammed it shut behind me. I wanted to go home with enough power to put me in charge forever. For that I needed Grendel Rex. And besides, I want to destroy this earth. Just because it's yours. I want to make you suffer, Eddie. I need that like I need to breathe. For all the indignities and inconveniences you've brought into my life."

"You'd destroy the whole world and all the people on it just for spite?" I said.

"Of course!" said Edmund. "That's the difference between you and me right there, Eddie. You don't think big enough."

"I saw the statue of Kali in your Drood Hall," I said. "Saw the blood caked around her feet. You grew up in a culture of human sacrifice, didn't you?"

"Now, you say that like it's a bad thing," said Edmund. "But killing the unworthy was actually one of the few things about my family that I never had any problems with. I loved getting involved, and they were always happy to see someone with a real enthusiasm for the task . . . Right up until they discovered I'd been quietly sacrificing fellow members of the family to Kali. They reacted very badly to that, the hypocrites."

"No," Molly said bluntly. "I still don't get it."

Edmund looked at her patiently. "What don't you get, Molly?"

"Why you turned out the way you did," said Molly. "Why you're so different from Eddie. His family made him rogue and tried to kill him, but he still came back to take control and change them for the better."

"You want everything to be so simple, don't you?" said Edmund. "You want me to reveal some terrible secret, some private hurt or loss, to explain everything. But I am the way I am . . . because I've always been this way. And I love it! The family only ever held me back. They named me rogue and threw me out. But having to fly the nest early turned out to be the making of me. The sheer joy I felt when I discovered I didn't need them. And the satisfaction I took watching them all die because of me. The only real difference between your darling Eddie and me, dear Molly, is that I know how to have a good time!"

I looked past him at Gerard. "And you're prepared to let him do this, Grendel Rex? I thought you wanted to rule Earth when you returned? You can't rule it if Edmund destroys it, and it doesn't sound like he plans to share his toys once he gets back to his own world."

But Gerard didn't say anything. He just stood where he was, look-ing at nothing, and for the first time I realised how empty his eyes were.

"Gerard?" I said. "What's wrong with you?"

Edmund sniggered softly. Like a schoolboy who thinks he's gotten away with something and can't wait to show you how clever he's been.

"I'm afraid the Unforgiven God isn't home right now. He only an-swers to me. You do remember, I told you there was someone else in-side the Merlin Glass, imprisoned there by Merlin himself long ago? I found them waiting for me when I was forced to hide out inside your Glass. And they were ever so grateful for the company, after so many centuries in solitude. I made a deal with them, for the temporary loan of their power. To hide me from the Powers in this world, so I could operate as Dr DOA and put my plans in motion, and now to make sure Gerard only does what I tell him to do. In return, I will take the Glass and its prisoner back to my world, where it should prove much easier to help them escape."

"Why do you need to control Gerard now?" said Molly.

"Because Edmund thought he could use Gerard to control Moon-breaker," I said. "But even with Gerard's knowledge, he couldn't raise the control column. He needed me and my new armour to do that. By coming here, I've given him what he needs."

"You're so clever, Eddie," said Edmund. "Almost as clever as me."

"The only way you'll get to Moonbreaker's controls," I said steadily, "is over my dead body."

"Oh, dear sweet Eddie . . . I wouldn't have it any other way."

And then he stopped smiling as I laughed at him. "You've miscal-culated, Edmund. And I mean really screwed up. Thanks to you, I have nothing left to lose. And a man who knows he's dying can do anything."

For the first time, Edmund appeared uncertain. He looked at me and then at the control column. He tried his smile again, but his heart wasn't in it. So he just shrugged and turned to Gerard.

"Be a good little living god, Gerard, and strike down these unbe-lievers. Remove these inconveniences from my life. Kill them both, and make it bloody. And then bring me Eddie's torc, so we can get this show on the road."

Gerard stepped forward, his face entirely empty. My armour picked up the power gathering slowly around him, like the wrath of God manifesting in the world.

"Wake up, Gerard!" I said loudly. "You're a living god and a Drood! Fight back!"

But nothing moved in Gerard's face. I glanced at the Merlin Glass behind him. Who the hell had Merlin imprisoned in that thing with power enough to control Grendel Rex? I was still trying to decide what to do for the best when Molly stepped forward, putting herself be-tween me and Gerard. She raised her hands, and dark magics stained the air around her closed fists. Fierce and deadly energies from the primordial heart of the wild woods. Edmund sneered at her.

"Oh please. Even the infamous wild witch is no match for the power of the Unforgiven God."

"She can be if she has allies," said Molly.

She raised both hands above her head in the stance of summoning and spoke a Word of Power. A new tension, a new presence, formed in the chamber, and Molly grabbed hold of it with both hands and threw it at the nearest Door. Brilliant lights crackled and coruscated all over the Door, and then the visual static snapped off as all the locks and protections blew apart. The flaring lights then jumped from Door to Door, racing around the perimeter of the chamber, blowing locks apart like a string of firecrackers. And one by one . . . the Doors opened.

Strange creatures stepped through the opened doorways all around the chamber. Some tentatively, as though they couldn't believe their good fortune, while others burst through as though afraid the Doors might slam shut at any moment. Some strode, some lurched, and some were so big they had to bend right over to squeeze through the openings. Some of the new arrivals were almost human, and some were so monstrous their very presence threatened to break the underlying laws of our reality.

Edmund stared wildly around him, his face slack with shock and horror. "What have you done, you bitch? *What have you done?*"

"Evened the odds," said Molly.

A thing made out of sticks headed straight for the control column. It smelled of forest fires and the decaying materials from which all life springs. A flood of writhing tentacles burst through another doorway lined with unblinking eyes and barbed sucker mouths. They snapped forward to wrap themselves around Gerard, only to stop abruptly as he looked at them. More and more creatures emerged from the opened Doors: things with insect heads, machine heads, star-shaped heads— or no heads at all. Creatures lunged forward from all sides, with vicious snapping teeth, metal claws, and limbs like bludgeons. There were faces that shone like the sun, and others too awful to look at.

Soon the chamber was packed from wall to wall with enough monstrosities to overwhelm all of us, including a living god. But fortunately for us, they all took one look at each other and went mad with rage. Each launched itself at its nearest enemy, attacking with savage strength and terrible intensity. Blood sprayed across the chamber in a dozen different colours, splashing on the struggling crowd. Some fell to the floor, to hiss and steam as they ate into the glowing stone.

Molly and I stood back to back by the control column, ready to defend it and ourselves, but for the moment none of the creatures seemed interested in us.

"Gerard!" Edmund screamed, his back pressed up against the Merlin Glass. "Stop this! Send them all back!"

And just like that, every single creature stopped dead, frozen in place, brought to a standstill by the power of Grendel Rex's will. Creatures still emerging through open doorways were stopped and forced back by the sheer psychic pressure in the chamber. Slowly, one by one, the creatures turned away from their private war and headed back to their own Doors. Grendel Rex was sending them home, because we already had enough monsters in this chamber.

Molly looked at me. "Go on, Eddie. Get Edmund. Gerard won't stay distracted for long."

Some of the creatures were already fighting the compulsion of Gerard's augmented will. Molly moved quickly forward to guard his back. She hit the struggling creatures with blasts of her own magic, driving them on like a cattle prod. Slowly, the chamber began to empty.

And while the creatures were only concerned with their Doors, and Gerard was concerned only with the creatures, I went for Edmund. He armoured up at last to face me, golden armour closing over him in a moment. I saw my own reflection in his featureless golden mask, and I looked like death. Then the two of us slammed together, striking at each other with fists that could have shattered mountains, driven on by hate and rage without limit, and our armour took it. The impacts from our fists sounded like tolling bells, but neither my armour nor his cracked or dented. They'd grown accustomed to each other. We raged back and forth across the chamber, knocking creatures down and trampling them underfoot. And still the broken things crawled and heaved themselves towards their waiting Doors.

"Why don't you just die and get it over with?" said Edmund.

"Why don't you?" I said.

I grabbed hold of him, lifted him off his feet, and threw him the length of the chamber. He smashed through a line of shuffling creatures, slammed into a closed Door, rebounded, and hit the floor hard. And while he was struggling to get back onto his feet, I took a moment to see how Gerard and Molly were doing. Gerard's will was still driving the intruders back through their Doors. The thing made up of sticks broke free and went for Molly, twiggy hands reaching for her face. She gestured briefly and the creature blew apart, hundreds of sticks flying in all directions. The moment they hit the floor, they started humping back to the Door they came through.

Edmund charged straight at me, making sounds so full of rage they weren't even words. I held my ground. This was what I'd been waiting for: Edmund so mad he wouldn't see what I was planning until it was too late. I waited till the very last moment and then sidestepped neatly. Edmund staggered on, caught off balance, and I punched him in the side of the head so hard his knees buckled. I kicked his feet out from under him and he sprawled on the floor on his back. I dropped on top of him, kneeling astride his chest, holding him down. Edmund tried to throw me off and found he couldn't. With no leverage to help him, my weight held him in place where my strength alone might not have. He bucked and struggled, slamming vicious blows into my sides. I didn't feel them.

Edmund should have been stronger than me. He was fit and powerful, while I was dying. But he was fighting for himself, while I was fighting for my family and my world.

I locked my golden hands around his golden throat, took a savage hold, and bore down with everything I had. Remembering what I'd done to the Angelic Drood outside Drood Hall. Where my superior armour had briefly overwhelmed the old Heart-derived armour. I also remembered how my Merlin Glass had joined and melded with the Glass from Edmund's world. Two similar objects, becoming one. I grinned under my mask. I'd been thinking about how to take Edmund down for a long time.

I concentrated, and my hands passed through my armour and his until they fastened onto Edmund's bare neck. I made my armour return feeling to my hands, so I could feel Edmund's throat convulse and close under my grip. My hands hurt horribly, but it was worth it to feel the breath stop in Edmund's throat. He panicked, thrashing wildly underneath me, striking out hysterically with both fists. And then he grabbed my golden wrists with his golden hands and tried to break my hold. But I had come too far to be stopped now. I was ready to kill Edmund for all the things he'd done. I was ready to die, to keep Edmund from Moonbreaker.

Unless . . . my plan worked.

My armour was more powerful than Edmund's, which meant the torc Ethel gave me should be more powerful than the fake torc the Immortals made for Edmund. And if the Merlin Glass could join with another Merlin Glass . . . And if Edmund and I really were the same person, with two different minds . . . I laughed as it all came together, finally. One last plan to deal with everything.

It might not have worked anywhere else. But in this place, at this time, in a chamber saturated with unnatural energies from so many different worlds . . . I reached out through my torc and took control of Edmund's. And then I used both torcs to switch my consciousness with that of Edmund's, putting my mind in his body and trapping his mind in what used to be my body. I took my torc with me, snapping it around my new throat, and put the fake torc on Edmund's.

Suddenly I felt well and healthy, better than I had in ages. Sensations blasted through me, all the feelings I'd been cut off from, and it felt good, so good. I'd never felt so alive. Edmund cried out, shrieking in shock and horror, as everything I'd been enduring hit him all at once. His hands fell away from my throat as his whole body convulsed from the poison raging unchecked through his system. I put one hand on his chest and pushed, and he fell backwards onto the stone floor, thrashing violently. He tried to get up and couldn't.

"What have you done?" he screamed. *"What have you done to me?"*

I waited a moment. My throat was still sore from where I'd strangled it, and I wanted to be sure I could speak clearly. I wanted Edmund to understand me.

"You took my body away from me," I said finally. "So I've taken yours. Seems only fair. Justice and revenge, in one neat package."

Edmund tried to say something, but his voice fell apart into inco-
herent screams as the agonies of his new home raged through him. I'd
trapped him in a dying, decaying body with no way out. I turned my
back on him and looked round the chamber. The last of the creatures
disappeared back through their various Doors, which then closed and
locked themselves. Molly looked exhausted, but she still made herself
check that every Door was properly locked and sealed.

She finally finished and looked round, to see two golden armoured
figures. One standing tall and easy, the other thrashing in agony on
the floor. Her face hardened. She thought the Drood on the floor was
me. She raised one hand, and her gaze was a killing thing. I raised my
hand.

"It's all right, Molly! It's me."

"Prove it."

"Well, I could tell you where you're ticklish," I said. "Or name your
favourite Hawkwind album. But what would be the point? You know
it's me, Molly. You know."

She smiled and lowered her hand. "Yes, I do. But you sound fine.
What's happened?"

"I swapped minds with Edmund," I said. "And locked him up in
my old body. So now I'm alive and well, and he's dying. I do love a
happy ending, don't you?"

Molly laughed delightedly. "I knew you'd pull off some kind of
miracle cure at the very last moment! It's what you do."

Somehow, Edmund fought back his pain and called out to Gerard.

"I still command you, old god! Kill them! Kill them both!"

Molly and I moved quickly to stand side by side, facing Gerard.
Facing Grendel Rex, the Unforgiven God.

"Okay," said Molly. "How do we stop him?"

"I already used up every idea I had," I said. "Don't you have any ideas?"

"Ideas are your department. I just hit things. What are we going to
do, Eddie?"

"I'm thinking!"

"Think faster!"

Gerard looked at us, and then at the golden figure convulsing on the floor. A slow animation returned to his face and his eyes came alive again.

"No," he said to Edmund. "You don't command me. I am myself again."

Molly glanced at me. "Is that good?"

"Hard to tell," I said.

Edmund's golden head turned jerkily to face the Merlin Glass still standing on the other side of the chamber.

"Help me! You have to help me! Come out and take control of Grendel Rex!"

But whoever was in the Glass either didn't recognise Edmund in his new body or knew a lost cause when they saw one. Edmund rolled slowly onto his side and reached out a shaking golden hand to Moonbreaker's control console . . . but it was well out of his reach.

I nodded to Molly to keep an eye on Edmund and Gerard, while I moved quickly over to the Merlin Glass. Its Door stood a good head taller than me, but the mirror was just a mirror. All it showed me was my own reflection: a Drood in his armour. I considered the Glass thoughtfully. I had to know: Who could be in there, powerful enough to control Grendel Rex? I pressed the golden fingertips of one hand against the mirror and then extended a series of golden tendrils, the way I do when I want my armour to hack a computer. The tendrils tapped across the reflective surface, unable to find or force a way in, and then they were sucked suddenly forward into the Glass, diving into the mirror as though it was a bottomless pool. I was about to jerk my hand back when the tendrils came flying out again, as though they'd burned themselves. I backed quickly away from the Merlin Glass, the tendrils snapping back into my glove. Through my armoured mask I could see all the old locks in the Glass opening. All the protections put in place by Merlin Satanspawn himself were disappearing, one by one. And finally, after so many centuries of solitary confinement, the prisoner in the Merlin Glass stepped out into the light.

She was tall and stately and supernaturally beautiful, the kind of woman you dream of during really bad fevers. She smiled at me, sweet as cyanide, attractive and seductive as every impulse you just know is going to get you into trouble. She wore long, sweeping scarlet silks and a towering jewelled headdress to show off her tumbling flame-red hair. She smiled at me and at Molly, and Molly flinched.

"Oh shit," she said.

I looked at her. "It's never good when you say that. How bad is this?"

"You don't know who that is?"

"No. Should I?"

"How can you not know who that is?" said Molly, not taking her eyes off the newcomer for a moment.

"Well, pardon me for being a bit slow," I said. "But I was dying until just a moment ago. Who are we looking at?"

"All witches know her," said Molly. "All witches know Morgana La Fae."

"Oh shit," I said.

"Right," said Molly. "The only magic user ever to be the equal of Merlin Satanspawn. Half-sister to King Arthur, and mother to his son, Mordred. The destroyer of Camelot."

"The original woman of mystery," I said. "The power behind thrones . . . Heaven and Hell, wrapped up in one beautiful vision."

"She's dangerous, Eddie," said Molly.

"I know," I said.

I took a step forward to face Morgana, and her deep green eyes fixed me with a slow, thoughtful look that hit me with an almost physical impact.

"A Drood," she said, in a voice rich as poisoned honey. "I always knew there'd be a Drood waiting when I finally got out."

"We didn't imprison you," I said.

"You didn't do anything to free me either," said Morgana.

"We didn't know you were in there," I said.

"How did you get out of the Glass, after all this time?" said Molly.

"You made it possible, little witch," said Morgana. "Edmund wedged the Door open when he called on my power to subdue Gerard Drood. But then you broke the seals on all the Doors, letting loose all kinds of interesting energies for me to make use of."

"How are you still alive?" I said. "According to legend, Merlin killed you. For your part in Camelot's fall."

"Legends are just stories people tell to fill in the holes in history," said Morgana. "Only those of us who were there can tell you what really happened. Merlin did try to kill me for putting an end to all his fun and games, but ultimately he just couldn't do it. Not because he wasn't powerful enough, or because I fought him off, but because he decided . . . we were simply too alike. He said killing me would have been like killing himself. He always was a sentimental old fool. But he couldn't let me go, not after everything I'd done. So he fashioned the Glass to be a prison for me, as a punishment and a fail-safe. Just in case the Droods ever lost their way and needed someone to take them down."

"That's why Merlin gave the Glass to my family," I said. "He always had a plan within a plan . . . and he never did trust anyone."

"I could have told you that," said Molly.

"Why did you agree to help Edmund, Morgana?" I said.

"Because he said he could free me." Morgana looked dispassionately at the golden figure writhing on the floor. "You were never my ally, Edmund; just a means to an end. And now . . . I don't need you. I am free at last. And after all this time plotting my revenges, I think I'll start with you."

She gestured sharply, and Edmund was suddenly hanging helplessly on the air before her. For a moment I felt like I should intervene, or at least say something, but the moment passed. I didn't have any mercy left in me for Edmund or Dr DOA, who killed so many people just because he could. Morgana gestured again, and Edmund's armour disappeared. I made a sound, and so did Molly, as we saw what had become of my old body. What Edmund's poison had done to it.

He was just a horrid cancerous mass now, devastated and distorted by the poison raging unchecked through his system. He looked like he was made out of malignant growths, like sickness and death made solid. His flesh was scarlet and purple, glistening wetly and shot through with dark, bulging veins. Without the armour to hold it back, his body swelled up to more than human size, driven beyond human limitations by the sheer power of the poison. Rows of human eyes stared out of the pulpy mass that had once been my face. The body continued to grow in sudden jerks and convulsions as the cancers ran wild, multiplying beyond sense or reason, until what had been the thing's head slammed up against the crystal ceiling. New limbs burst out of the central mass, as though reaching out for help that would never come.

The fate Edmund had meant for me.

"Seems almost a shame to kill you," said Morgana. "You suffer so beautifully, Edmund. But I think I'd better. There's always the chance you might pull off some last-minute miracle save, like your counterpart."

"Go ahead," said Molly. "Put him out of everyone's misery."

"Hold it," I said. "I have a better idea."

Because I recognised the thing before me. I'd seen it once before long ago, and now I saw an opportunity for some real poetic justice, along with the final solution to a long-standing mystery. I told Morgana what I had in mind, and she laughed softly.

"Trust a Drood to find a measure of revenge in justice and duty. Very well, Eddie. A favour, for old time's sake. And because it amuses me."

She gestured dismissively at Edmund and sent him hurtling back through Time. To reappear back in Drood Hall at the moment I remembered all those years ago. When a hideous cancer monster had appeared out of nowhere in the Sanctity. We all thought it had come to attack the Heart, so we banded together and destroyed the thing. I remembered how it died, and I smiled. It seemed fitting that the man who'd killed one family of Droods should be killed by another. Justice and revenge, in one neat package.

Gerard Drood, Grendel Rex, the Unforgiven God, stepped forward. Morgana La Fae turned unhurriedly to face him, and the two old monsters looked each other over. Molly and I stood side by side, bracing ourselves. Two of the most dangerous people the world had ever known considered each other with great interest, and I had absolutely no idea how to stop them from doing anything they felt like. And then I glanced back at Moonbreaker's control column.

There was still one thing I could do.

"I know who you are," Gerard said to Morgana.

"I know you," said Morgana.

"We have so much in common," said Gerard.

"Two powers, imprisoned by the Droods," said Morgana. "For daring to dream bigger dreams than they could stand."

"Our ambitions always were too great for them," said Gerard.

They moved closer, standing face-to-face, staring into each other's eyes.

"And now your thoughts are so clear to me," said Morgana. "You were so alone for so long."

"Even before I was imprisoned," said Gerard. "And you . . . always looking for someone you could call your equal. And when you finally found him, he trapped you inside his Glass."

"Such a long journey for both of us," said Morgana. "To find who we've been looking for, for so very long."

"Journeys end in lovers meeting," said Gerard.

They stood staring into each other's eyes, smiling the same smile.

Molly looked at me, but I shook my head quickly. Something was happening between the Unforgiven God and the greatest witch of all time . . . and I didn't want it interrupted.

"What interest could either of us have now in an Earth neither of us would even recognise?" said Gerard.

"Why limit ourselves to the Past, when the Future seems so much more inviting?" said Morgana. "Consider all these Doors and the possibilities they offer."

Gerard laughed softly. "So many worlds and realities to explore."

"Together," said Morgana.

"Together, at last," said Gerard.

Morgana glanced at the Merlin Glass, and it opened to reveal a strange new world, full of a light so bright I couldn't look at it. Gerard and Morgana walked into the light, hand in hand. At the last moment, Gerard paused to look back at me.

"Just for the record," he said, "it was never my face I carved into the Moon's surface. It was Elspeth's."

They disappeared into the light and were gone. The Merlin Glass slammed shut behind them, and disappeared after them. It was suddenly very quiet in the great open chamber.

"How romantic," said Molly.

"As long as they keep going, yes," I said.

Molly whooped loudly. She punched the air and hugged me tightly. "You're alive! You're all right! You're not going to die!"

"Journey's end," I said. "Now, if you'll let me go for just a moment, I have one last duty to take care of."

I pushed Molly gently away from me so I could turn to face Moonbreaker's control column. And then I smashed it with one blow from my golden fist. It shattered into a thousand pieces, clattering quietly on the glowing floor.

"I can't reach the bomb," I said. "But at least now no one can activate it."

"The device is still there," Molly said carefully. "Deep inside the Moon."

"Yes," I said. "Because it's always possible that someday my family will need it. That Humanity might need its compassionate final mercy. I've just made sure no one can ever think of Moonbreaker as an easy option."

"Damn right," said Molly. "Because it was never a good idea."

"The mission is over," I said. "Finally. Let's go home."

"Because we have so much to catch up on," said Molly.

"Because we have so much to live for," I said.

CHAPTER NINE

Carpe Diem

opened the door to my cosy little cottage in the woods, and everything looked just as I'd left it. On what I'd thought would be just
another mission. It all looked wonderfully warm and inviting, my
home away from home. I hurried in, stamping the snow from my
shoes. It had been a long walk through the wintry forest, and I'd
enjoyed every moment of it. Bracing and invigorating, and a whole
bunch of other things I was sure were good for me. I was enjoying so
much now that I'd never expected to enjoy again.

It felt so good to be alive.

Molly and the robot dog, Scraps.2, hurried in after me. Molly shut
the door on the cold, while I turned on the clockwork radio. A cathe-
dral choir was singing Christmas carols, just as they had before I was
called away. I was struck suddenly by how much had happened in such
a short time. My whole life had been turned upside down and threatened with a premature end, but I'd put it all back together again,
through brute force and sheer tenacity. And yet the world had just
carried on, as though nothing important had happened.

That's life.

I took off my heavy coat and hung it on the coat-rack. Molly
handed me hers to hang up, and shook her head slowly.

"When I said I thought we were entitled to a vacation, I was thinking of somewhere a little more exciting."

"Haven't you had enough of that?" I said.

"You can never have too much excitement," said Molly.

She gestured at my fireplace, and the logs and coals burst into flame. Scraps.2 pushed between our legs and headed straight for the fire. He was wearing his *I'm just an ordinary dog, move along, nothing to see here* disguise again. He circled round several times, and dropped down heavily in front of the fire.

"Why do you do that?" I said.

"Centuries of instinct," growled Scraps.2.

"But you're artificial!"

"Speciesist."

"You know your family were getting ready to throw you a *Welcome home and glad you're not dead after all* party," said Molly.

"Can you think of a better reason not to be there? You can bet there'll be speeches and loyal toasts . . . and absolutely everyone will ask me how I feel!" I shuddered. "No, they're better off without us. I'd only get bored and say something I shouldn't, and you'd heckle."

"I like parties at the Hall!" said Molly.

"Only because they give you an excuse to get drunk, behave appallingly, and smash the place up."

"Exactly!" said Molly.

I sat down in my favourite chair, beside the fire. It was large and comfortable, and for the first time in what seemed a very long time, I felt like I could relax. Molly planted herself on my lap and put her arms around me.

"You know," I said, "that dinner I put in the oven, just before we left, is probably about ready by now."

"It can wait," said Molly. "I like it here. Very comfortable. Very cosy. Nothing to worry about. Nothing to do . . ."

And that, of course, was when the phone rang. We all looked at it. Even Scraps.2. It sounded very loud in the quiet.

"Tell them to go to hell," said Molly. "We've earned a little peace and quiet."

"My family knows that," I said. "They wouldn't be calling me now unless it was important."

"It's always important with your family!"

"I mean really important." I eased her off my lap, got to my feet, and picked up the old-fashioned Bakelite phone. "What?"

"Come home, Eddie," said the Matriarch. "All hell is breaking loose in the Nightside."

"Hell is always breaking loose in the Nightside," I said. "And, anyway, what can we do about it? We're banned from entering the Nightside by long-standing pacts and agreements."

"That's all over," said the Matriarch. "After what's just happened, we can't look away any longer. We're going into the Nightside and taking control. By force."

"You're talking about going to war," I said.

"Yes," said the Matriarch. "We have no choice. Come home, Eddie."

"Why?" I said. "What the hell happened that we have to go to war?"

"The Nightside has broken its boundaries," said the Matriarch. "It's expanding into the waking world. Either we stop it or the long night will cover everything there is."

The phone went dead. I put it down, and then turned to look at Molly and Scraps.2.

"Well," I said. "Guess where we're going."

Shaman Bond

and

John Taylor

Will Return in

NIGHT FALL